GOVERNED BY WHIMSY
THE ANTHOLOGY

MARKED BY STARS

FOLLOWED BY THUNDER

DRAGGED THROUGH HEDGEROWS

GOVERNED BY WHIMSY

TWINKLE PRESS

FORTHWRITES.COM

because there are stories within stories

A wolf without a pack and a boy in need of roots become founders. After a heavenly visitation, one young wolf turns his back on his pack and on the moon in order to tread a lonesome path. A blaze of stars. A brand of copper. A burden of trust. First of Dogs, he takes a new name, makes peace with group of weary humans, and helps to found the In-between. This is a tale of the Kindred. This is the lore of the Starmark clan.

TABLE OF CONTENTS

One sister, a pure light that beckons, the other, a fierce light that burns. Fira and her sister are chased out of another village. Fleeing on foot across the empty moors, they're caught by a storm that roars like the monsters ever in pursuit. But the wind changes and the thundering brings a stampede of defenders who carry them off to a secret place. Where mares dance and rabbits mine. Where the lost clans hid a lasting treasure. Where the girls' curse is considered a blessing.

TABLE OF CONTENTS

He had one job. Becoming a family pet wasn't it. For the sake of his people, Daroo-fen has lived among humans, working as a lawyer in a little mountain town. He's vowed to protect the surrounding woodlands, no matter the cost. But in the course of duty, he meets a man who needs help ... and a friend. Too long a loner, Daroo cannot keep away, but there's a fine line between getting close and getting too close. If the Cooper family finds out his secret, two worlds might brand the wolf a traitor.

TABLE OF CONTENTS

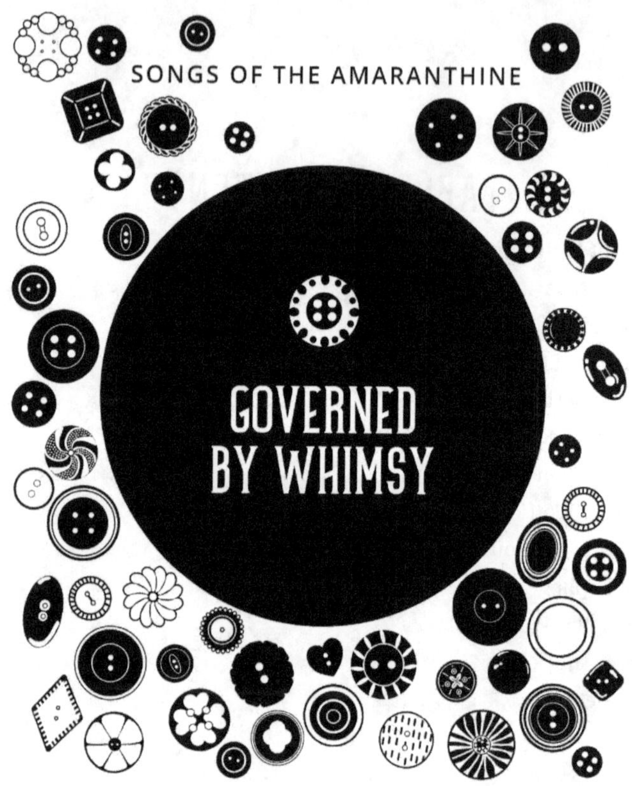

His whims drove off her predecessors. Her whimsy drives him to distraction. To Ambrose P. Merriman, a stage actor who's gained acclaim on three continents, reaver escorts are more trouble than they're worth. Easy-come, easy-go, he hardly bothers to learn their names anymore. But the director and producer of their theater troupe, who are already dancing on the fringes of acceptability, won't risk losing their independence by neglecting this duty to the In-between.

Reaver Greta Demerara comes with suspiciously excellent references, but by the time the Evernhold brothers realize she's carrying considerably more baggage than anyone bothered to mention, the train's already left the station. What's more, it's quickly apparent that Greta's no easier to deal with than their star. It's either a game of cat and canary or a courtship. And Ambrose would give almost anything for a look at the script.

TABLE OF CONTENTS

MARKED BY STARS

because your trust is precious to me

"You shine. Like Soriel of the Dawning,
like Auriel of the Golden Seed.
Like every tale of the Kindred,
the Broken, and the Blessed, you shine."

TSUMIKO AND THE ENSLAVED FOX

LOOR

oor-ket's head turned as a chorus of howls welcomed another caravan, sending their skittish Kith side-stepping into a snowbank. Red-caped Amaranthine quickly moved among the reindeer, patting and soothing their kindred, no doubt reminding them that the Highwind pack did not consider them prey.

Once a decade, a migration heralded this festival week. The Song Circle guaranteed peace to all who made the journey. Here in the depths of winter, the clans would fill the longest nights with light and life and laughter.

Representatives from every clan on the continent had been arriving for days, each bringing their share of peddlers, artisans, musicians, and storytellers. To *this* place. Grounds set apart since long ago, watched over by trees that were older than the oldest of them, kept safe by the Highwind wolves.

Staying well out of the way of the incoming droves, Loor-ket slouched against the base of one of the Song Circle's sentinel pines. In summer, this vast meadow was all soft grasses and shy flowers, but Loor liked it best in winter, when hushing snows turned the circle into an echo of the moon—round, pale, and serene.

Not that there would be any peace for a while.

Dozens of lanterns ringed the expanse, one for each family unit, be it den or warren, flock or herd. By the opening song, there would be hundreds.

One of Loor's aunts directed newcomers toward the patchwork of tents arrayed among the trees. Someone was cooking with a spice that made his mouth water. A cheer went up from the direction of the bear camp. A wrestling match, no doubt.

From a nearby brush pile—reserve fuel for one of the many upcoming bonfires—a youngster from one of the squirrel clans tumbled into the open, checking the stride of the wolf coming Loor's way.

The wolf—who had the advantage of being in his speaking form—scooped up the startled squirrel. No bigger than a wolf cub, the kit tucked neatly into the crook of the wolf's arm. But the youngster protested the cuddling. Sharp scolding and tail puffing ineffective, he transformed into a squirming boy with a thatch of red hair.

Too many other voices filled the meadow for Loor to catch any words—teasing on the wolf's part, grumbling on the squirrel's. With a tweak to the boy's pointed ear, the scamp was loose, running off to rejoin his friends. Pausing long enough to make sure the child found his way, the wolf resumed his slow trek toward Loor's vantage.

Like all Highwind wolves, he was tall and broad through the shoulders, with auburn hair and ghostly ice-gray eyes. But Beloordex hadn't yet attained the powerful musculature that would come with greater maturity. By right and by rite, he was counted as an adult, but he was still young.

They both were.

"You missed the ceremony." Beloor-dex slid down beside Loor and pressed close, matching his posture so they were hip-to-hip, knee-to-knee, ankle-to-ankle.

"No one noticed." Loor insinuated an arm around his brother's waist.

Beloor gently contradicted. "I did."

Loor offered his most disgruntled of grunts.

His brother's expression took on the added softness of sympathy.

Unbending a little, Loor kissed his twin's cheek.

Beloor-dex and Loor-ket were alike in every way except significance. Loor had missed his only chance to stand out by being born five minutes too late. Beloor was the Highwind pack's second tithe, born twentieth. His birthright set him apart from their whole family, including his younger twin. Which left Loor-ket lost in the middle of an ever-increasing pack.

At least he had Beloor. Their bond was enough. It had to be.

Loor sighed. "Well, what did they pick?"

"Elderbough and Moontide."

Two brothers just ahead them in the lengthy Highwind registry were establishing their own dens. They'd each earned the accompanying privileges—a mate, a name, a crest.

Loor let his chin drop to his chest. "They're good names. They have a nice ring to them."

"They'll sing well," agreed Beloor. "Next time, it will be your turn."

"No."

"Can't bear to leave me?"

Loor could hear the teasing in his brother's tone, but he answered seriously. "I'd never leave you alone."

His twin was too still, too silent.

"Bel?"

"There has been some ... talk."

Loor wanted to flee from this new tone in his brother's voice, but he tightened his hold.

"Nothing is *settled*," Beloor went on. "Father only thought to mention it to me earlier today. I hardly know what to think."

If not for the fragility in his brother's gaze, Loor might have exploded with impatience. Somehow, he confined himself to a ragged, "What's happened?"

"A ... a suitor."

He shook his head, not following. All their older brothers were settled, and none of their younger ones had reached the appropriate age. "A suitor," Loor echoed. "Who's a suitor?"

"Someone from the Ambervelte pack."

Loor knew the clan, of course. The Highwinds had ties to all the northern dens. An older sister had been courted by an Ambervelte, and her strength had been added to their pack. And there had been additional intermingling among his many nieces, nephews, and cousins.

Beloor said, "We played together as cubs."

Loor glanced at the Song Circle, as if the children and their games could give him some clue to the tentative hope creeping into his brother's expression. Although twinned births were far less common now—a cause for concerned debate during the last dozen festivals—Amaranthine were prolific. "*Everyone* plays here, no matter their clan."

"She remembered me."

A female? Loor could only shake his head.

Taking a deeper breath than needed for such a small voice, Beloor put the matter plainly. "I have a suitor. Terloo-soh Ambervelte says she will have me and no other."

Loor could hear the wonder in his brother's tone. A tenth child never pursued a mate or established a den of their own, for they served the whole pack. But once in a great while, one was chosen. A female because she was beautiful. A male because he was beloved.

He needed to say something. Anything. But the only sound that made its way past the constriction in Loor's heart and throat was a thin whine.

Loor-ket couldn't remember how his twin managed to get him away from the Song Circle. Had they walked together into the wood? Or had Bel carried him? Loor didn't recognize the clearing spread before them, a sheltered basin of pristine snow, filled with the serenity he craved ... and the solitude he feared.

Taking him by the hand, Bel led him along the edge to a place where the ground split. They dropped into the gully, springing from stone to stone as they followed its jagged course. Walls rose up on either side, and dark recesses began to appear. Bel turned, took both of Loor's hands and rose from the ground. A short flight. Halfway up the sheer rockface, a narrow ledge served as a threshold. Thick hangings draped the entrance to a cave.

"My den," Bel whispered.

"You had a den?" Loor's heart wrenched, for he'd thought they shared everything. He'd never wanted anything of his own.

"This territory belongs to the Highwind tributes, for hunting and for training." Beloor drew him deeper inside, to a mound of furs. "Only my mentor knows I have a den, for he bid me establish one. But even he does not know this place. I warded it myself."

"I can tell." Even though much of Bel's training was a mystery, he'd freely shared all he knew of sigilcraft. Loor's lessons may have come secondhand, but the weaving of power came easily. It was a useful little secret for someone who wanted to avoid notice. An ironic skill for someone who was already beneath it.

"No one will come. No one can hear." Beloor shed his fine tunic and stole Loor's before pulling back heavy furs and jostling him under. Sliding in beside him, he pulled his brother close. "It's only us."

Loor clung to his twin, who made soothing noises and stroked his hair. Treating him like a child. Reassurances flowed—touch and taste and tangling. Beloor accepted Loor's possessive posturing without complaint. Affection for aggression. Balm for bitterness. Love for love.

Hours passed, and Loor refused to loosen his hold. If he let go, Bel would leave him for another. Nothing should ever be allowed to come between them. Beloor was Loor's, and Loor was Beloor's. This was how it had always been. This is how it should always be.

Days may have passed. Beloor woke Loor from his doze with a nip and nuzzle.

Loor opened his eyes, his arms tightening reflexively.

"All right, brother. I do understand." Beloor's palm smoothed along Loor's spine, settling at the base of his tail. Intimate territory. "If you ask it, I will refuse her."

Here it was. All he'd ever wanted. Loor had won. At a word, Bel would be his and his alone. His twin would give up everything that had been denied him because he'd been born five minutes too soon.

Loor gasped for air. The words were so hard to say, but he pushed them out between sobs. "I will not ask it."

Bel cradled Loor, who howled and wept for the lonesome years he must endure. And when no more tears would come, his twin surprised him by falling apart. Loor comforted him in turn, giving as freely as he'd received.

On it went. Pressed together under the weight of ticklish furs, they whispered and wrestled, teased and tugged. All their growling and grappling was probably childish, but they'd soon be leaving childhood behind.

This was their goodbye.

DEX

When the twins finally emerged, colors whispered through a night sky, shifting currents that seemed to dance in time to the distant piping of flutes.

"Are you hungry?" Bel asked solicitously.

Loor smiled and shook his head. A meal wouldn't touch the hollow he needed to hide.

"We could hunt," his brother said.

He may as well have added, *one last time*. Finality hung in the air, dragging Loor back even as it propelled Beloor forward. Strange, to be able to tell that his twin's heart already beat for another. So he declined with all the grace he could muster. "Let's join the feast."

Bel flashed a grateful smile and moved away, toward the Song Circle. Loor followed with flagging steps as their pack's Kith mobbed Bel. The sentient wolves were in his care, and he belonged to them. Loor had never considered them rivals for his twin's affection, for they understood the strength of a brother-bond.

Loor had planned to pact with Bel. To share a lifetime, to live as one. He had thought to rescue his twin from solitude, only to be the one left behind.

He hung back further, watching the rest of the Highwind pack welcome Beloor-dex with tails in full swing and glasses high. Loor's own tail hung limp as he marked the Ambervelte she-wolf whose whole posture spoke of relief.

Bel only had eyes for her, and his expression was something Loor had never seen, would never inspire. He was hers now. Loor felt his existence dwindle. What do you become when the only one who ever saw you looked away?

Nobody noticed him leave. No one raised questions when he jogged away from the lights, the life, and the laughter. Loor trudged determinedly along a faint trail, too lost in his morose thoughts to care where it might lead. The whimper drew him up short.

A voice—childish, chiding—slipped into his mind and startled him. *"I won't let you take her! She's mine!"*

Loor had been about to tread upon two cubs huddled together

in the snow, a whelp and a weanling. These Kith were hardly visible in the snow, for the soft puff of their baby fur was pure white. "What are you doing way out here?"

The young male bared his teeth. *"Mine!"*

He didn't want to deal with cubs, but he couldn't very well leave them. Precious is the cub to their pack, and these two were obviously beyond boundaries.

"I'm not after your packmate. Is she a sister?" Loor reached for the whimpering ball of fuzz.

Jaws snapped at his hand.

"Easy now. She needs warming." He caught the baby's scruff, and his concern doubled. She was so small, she couldn't be weaned. "She should be with her mother. Let's bring her back together."

To his surprise, the older one took speaking form. "No!" he snarled. "Marnoo is *mine!*"

"She's also cold, hungry, and beyond help if *you* are her only defense," Loor said mildly. He loosened the bindings around his midriff and settled the baby against his skin. Closing his fur vest around her, he offered his free hand to the furious boy. "Peace, whelp. Would you have me ignore her needs?"

The boy scooted closer and grudgingly met his palm. "Moonkin Ambervelte."

Loor ran his thumb over the back of the boy's hand, which was covered in soft fur. "This is unusual. Are you manifesting it for warmth?"

"This is how I am."

"I've never seen someone with your features." Loor took the boy's chin, turning his face. "Where are your ears?"

A set of pointed ears slowly lifted above his snowy hair, angled in an attitude of embarrassment. Loor was tempted to unbundle the boy to see how much of his body retained the fur of his true form. He murmured, "Extraordinary."

"Me and Marnoo have the same mam, but different sires." The boy was blushing badly, for the implication wasn't flattering. He tugged at Loor's sleeve. "Because she's a dex."

Comprehension came with lashings of curiosity. "Our pack has no Kith-kin. This is a pleasure!"

Moon's eyes lost some of their wariness. "You know what I am?"

"My twin is a dex, so I know what it means better than most. Your mam must be strong if the Amberveltes asked her to improve the bloodlines of your Kith."

The boy's tail began a tentative sway. Was he really so surprised to be recognized and accepted? Perhaps the other children had teased him. Loor pulled the boy closer. "Help me warm Marnoo while we chat. Is her sire another Kith from your pack?"

"No." The boy leaned trustingly against his shoulder. "Marnoo's sire is mam's bondmate. Da's a dex, too, and he fosters all those born to his den."

Loor could see the sense in uniting two tributes. Both would understand their role and its needs. "So your sister was born in true form." It was an old custom, but not unheard of.

Moon nodded. "And she's mine. Da gave her to me."

"Are you a tenth child, then?"

"Halfway." His tone and smile were shy. "I'm my sire's tenth cub, but the Maker doesn't require a tenth from the Kith."

"But you'll foster Marnoo in the manner of tributes."

"Yes."

"Good lad." Loor mussed up Moon's hair and gave his ear a cautious scratch. "I should get you back. Your sister needs to suckle."

"A little longer? I came prepared."

The boy brought a bottle from an inner pocket. With careful deliberation, he soaked a twist of soft cloth in the warm liquid. A twitching nose poked into the open, for the hungry cub had caught the scent of her next meal. As Moon offered her the sop, Loor quickly cupped his hand under it, lest they lose a single drop.

Marnoo suckled greedily and growled when Moon took the cloth away to wet it. Loor chuckled. "Patience, little one."

The cub opened her eyes, which were the rich copper of a harvest moon. Nosing his palm, she licked it clean and whined for more.

"Here, Marnoo," her brother crooned. "I brought plenty."

Loor smiled at the boy's earnest devotion. He was a little young to foster a child, being a child himself, but Ambervelte decisions weren't Highwind business. So Loor struck a balance, addressing the boy as he would an equal while encouraging him to nestle in. Moon was doing his best. The least Loor could do was lend his support.

By and by, the bottle was emptied. Loor settled the sated cub against his belly and coaxed Moon closer. For a little while, they simply listened to Marnoo's wuffling snores. The peace of a den shared by three with none.

"Why are you out here alone?" Loor asked.

Moon's ears twitched. "Because I was lonely."

"Isn't it strange to go off by yourself if you're lonesome?"

The boy curled against him. "When everyone is happy except me, it's sadder than sad."

Loor found himself nodding. "Better to be happy with two than alone in the crowd."

"Yes. Just like that." Moon leaned up and kissed Loor's chin. "Tell me a story?"

"All the best storytellers will be at the Song Circle."

"A little longer?" wheedled the boy.

He gave in, telling the story of two brothers. One embraced the life of a dex, becoming the favorite of every Kith and respected by the Kindred. The other was his grumpy younger twin, whose only weapon was a needle and whose only friend was a Kith-kin.

"You sew?" asked Moon.

"Nothing so humble," drawled Loor. "I embroider."

"Do males embroider?"

Only the truth, and only a little. "There are so many cubs in my father's den, I'm quite sure my mother mistook me for one of her daughters. What can I say? I have a knack."

Moon giggled. He gently traced the fanciful stitching on Loor's festival tunic—white upon midnight blue. "Did you make this?"

"I did. Am I not grand in my finery?"

Furry fingers reached and rested upon Loor's cheek, and Moon's voice came into his mind. *"Do they tease you?"*

"Worse. They never noticed."

Moon's voice took a fragile note. *"They tease me."*

"Then you must be strong, like your mam and your da and your sire. Trust their voices first. And mine." Loor leaned into his touch. "You have a place and a purpose. Sing your song with all your might."

The boy sniffled and sighed. "Glad I listened, even though I had to walk so far."

"Hmm? What do you mean?"

"Almost didn't come," Moon mumbled sheepishly.

Loor's bafflement doubled. Had someone sent the poor boy into the woods on a fool's errand? He had half a mind to track down the prankster. "Who sent you here?"

"A star came down and showed the way."

What an imagination. "*You* are the one who should be telling stories."

Moon's smile had a dreamy quality. "Loor?"

"Hmm?"

"Am I really your only friend?"

"Without you and Marnoo, I'd be wretchedly alone." Loor kissed his forehead. "I'm glad our paths crossed, Moon-kin. You are my friend for life."

STAR

Loor carried the sleeping cubs back into livelier territory. An elder elk's voice rose and fell, adding drama to the old sagas, and a colony of songbirds warmed their voices with hot brews and honeyed ciders. Bears paced through the complex patterns of a walking dance, weaving their way around a newly bonded pair.

He didn't catch sight of any Highwinds, but then he was watching for the lighter browns and pure white pelts for which the Ambervelte pack was known. Passing a cluster of owls and gray squirrels, he caught a peevish thread about the Woodacre clan, who'd gone from bold to brazen after forming an alliance with wolves.

The cheek.

Loor saw no reason for the fuss, except perhaps jealousy. The cozy clans liked protectors, and there were none better than wolves. But the packs usually kept to themselves—unfettered and free.

Good for the Woodacres.

Cooperatives were becoming increasingly common, out of fear for rogues and for human raiding parties. Trackers now reported annually to the pack leaders about these newcomers—colonists, trappers, explorers. They felled trees and tilled fields far to the east. Most Amaranthine saw no cause for concern; humans were slow-moving and short-lived. So far, the consensus at each Song Circle remained the same—watch and see.

Amaranthine lived wherever their counterparts flourished, watching over the animals, akin yet apart. If territories and migration patterns changed to accommodate humanity, then their people would change with them.

Humans were far from this place. The Song Circle, at least, was safe.

Loor had no trouble finding the cubs' temporary den. A lean wolf clansman with the same copper eyes as Marnoo hurried his way, flicking through apologies and gratitude before gasping out a greeting. "He was only just missed. We were about to search."

"Da," murmured Moon, his tail giving a sleepy twitch. "I made a friend."

The Ambervelte male met Loor's gaze as he gathered the boy to his heart. "Is that so?"

"Moon-kin is a tribute to your den, and Marnoo is fortunate to have such a devoted protector."

Their da leaned close and pressed his cheek to Loor's, murmuring thanks and blessings. And as he carried the cubs homeward, Loor could hear the gentleness in his tone. "Why did you leave the tent?"

"A star came down," said Moon.

"You saw a falling star?"

"He didn't fall. He flew."

Loor shook his head and turned away, moving automatically toward the Highwind camp. Moon and Marnoo had needed him, and perhaps he'd needed them, too. If not for the cubs, he probably would have run and kept running, an aimless rogue, ill-prepared for life without a pack.

Like Moon, he'd left because he didn't want to be alone. What good could come of that?

"Much good."

Loor stopped and turned, trying to pinpoint the speaker. He didn't recognize the voice, nor were there any wolf Kith close by. "Who spoke, please?"

His question was ignored, but the voice returned, clarion-clear. *"I am waiting."*

Baffled, Loor asked, "Where?"

"Come, prepare for your journey."

Loor scented the air but found nothing unusual. Even so, he rushed toward the small tent he shared with Bel. The moment it came into view, he knew something was wrong. Light poured from every gap and seam as if the interior was aflame.

He reached for the flap with a trembling hand.

"Gather your things."

Gritting his teeth, Loor stepped inside, only to be blinded by the figure awaiting him. Squinting through his lashes, he tried to understand what he was seeing. Could this be the star Moon claimed to have seen?

"Who …?"

"I am Soriel. I stand in the presence of heaven's throne, and I speak for the One who made all things."

Not a star then. Loor sank to his knees as suspicion became certainty—*angel.*

Soriel blazed across his senses—too bright, too clean, too much. Like the hair-raising tales of humans with fury in their souls, this creature put Loor in fear of his life. He was suddenly attuned to his shortcomings, ashamed of his selfishness, aware of his own stench. Groveling wasn't enough. He wanted to bury himself like spoor. Face covered, tail tucked, he groaned.

Then hands were at his shoulders. "Lift your head, Loor-ket Highwind."

When he obeyed, the dazzle was gone, and he was kneeling face-to-face with an angel upon the furs that carpeted the tent. Wings rustled. Skin flashed. Eyes blazed. But Soriel's posture promised peace as he presented his palms.

Loor met them, wanting to see if he was real. "You know my name."

Soriel smiled. "And now you know mine. Is this not common ground?"

He could barely breathe, let alone argue, so Loor only shook his head.

"You accepted Moon-kin's personhood." That shining countenance leaned closer. "You did not hesitate to call him friend."

This was so confusing. Loor's voice caught and tripped over itself. "I don't understand."

The angel stood, hauling Loor up so that his feet no longer touched the ground. He dangled there, as limp as his tail, waiting to see what the angel intended. But Soriel simply set him on his feet, then bent to bestow a kiss upon his forehead.

"Fear not, son of the packs. I bring a message."

He was aghast. The Maker had a message for him?

Soriel studied his face and smiled. "Slave of the moon, lift your gaze to a place between. Shed your wildness to walk as men do, and in their midst, find a haven, forge a bond, found a future."

Loor's skin prickled, and a shiver ran down his spine. "How do I do all that?"

"Go to the place I will show you. Follow my star. It will go before you." Soriel sketched a scant tenth of the night's turning. "Gather what you will carry and walk away. Do not run or leap or fly. *Walk.*"

Finally, Loor dared to ask, "Why?"

"Because every step demands your trust, confirms your choice, requires your patience. That is your pace." Soriel lifted shining wings and pointed to the east. "There is your path."

PATH

Before Loor had run across the cubs, he'd already committed to a course, no matter the consequences. He'd run away. He'd live alone. Unwanted, unneeded, he'd obeyed the impulse to disappear, sure that no one would miss him, even while hoping his brother would suffer a little for his sake.

A petty vengeance.

A pitiful reason.

Yet Loor would have run and kept running, an aimless rogue harboring bitterness. Feeling betrayed, he'd been ready to betray. To go without a word. To cut the only one who'd ever cared. But Moon and Marnoo had gotten in the way, forced him to pause, and given him time to rethink his recklessness. With cubs to carry, it was easier to admit that pack was precious.

In returning them to the Song Circle, Loor had remembered what it meant to hear the old stories, to have a voice in the song, to belong.

They had changed his course, and he'd known he would stay.

Only to be sent away. And without a word to the brother who might believe the worst and blame himself.

Bereft of Kith or Kindred. Estranged to the moon to which all wolves sang. Stripped of ties and—he'd been stricken to discover— his tail. Loor did wish that this mark of the Maker's favor hadn't cost him his pride as a wolf.

Loor rummaged in the small chest he shared with his brother, lifting aside embroidered sashes, uncovering boyhood treasures. His sewing kit and hunting knife were already in the carry-sack at his feet, but Loor wanted desperately to reassure his twin.

Bel's carving tools were no help, nor his brother's stash of wood, stone, and bone. Loor set them aside, but more items found their way into his pack—a medicinal pouch of herbs and ointments, three bowstrings, and an ember cache. He hesitated for a moment over a half-forgotten length of loomed cloth that had been one of his earliest assignments. It was clumsily made, but it was *his*, and it might prove useful.

Near the bottom, he found matching keepsake cords from his and Bel's whelping feast. They were a Highwind tradition, knotted with pledges of protection from both parents and packmates. Loor broke the bands to steal the anchoring bead from each. With no time to braid anything new, he pulled the cord from his topknot. Auburn hair hung loose around his shoulders, framing his face, hiding his expression as he threaded the twin stones, holding them in place with knots of unity, loyalty, and journeying.

"Please understand," he whispered.

Pressing his lips to the refashioned cord, he set it atop Beloor's neat stack of sleeping furs and fussed with its arrangement for the scant minute that remained between obedience and rebellion. Then he ducked under the drape that blanketed the entrance to the only home he'd known for more than a century and strode into an uncertain future.

Loor pulled the hood of his travel cloak up around his ears and skirted the Song Circle. To avoid notice, he'd hidden his pack beneath its fur-lined folds, but he attracted neither interest nor concern as he knelt beside a flagging cookfire to tease a few embers into the warded carrier that he knotted to one ankle.

Perhaps Soriel had rendered him invisible.

The alternative left him sad, yet surly.

Even though he wanted to run, run, run from the sting of his own insignificance, he heeded the angel's command and walked through the pain. Every step a choice.

Along an eastbound trail, he strode past a flock of jugglers, festive in their feathered waistcoats. Past steaming basins of sweet cider and mulled wine. Past a double-ring of dancers, lithe and lovely as they threaded through a naming dance for the new daughter added to their cloister. Past high-stepping maidens in the mossy drape of the Daphollow herd.

His sense of loss was vexing. Could he lose something he'd never possessed?

On and on he walked until the circle's song was nothing but memory, and the only voices were in his head.

Beloor saying, "Can't bear to leave me?"

Moon-kin saying, "A star came down and showed the way."

And Soriel saying, "Walk away."

DEN

Loor marked the new star in the sky and knew it for his guide. The twinkling blaze never moved faster than he could follow, and when his steps lagged to a standstill, the star sank from the heights and settled into a nearby tree like a bird come to roost. Which brought to mind old tales about sky imps and star clans, but Loor couldn't test his theories without breaking his pace to give chase. All he could do was watch and wonder and walk on.

After the passing of many days, his progress slowed, for the way grew difficult. Trees banished his view of the sky, and he was forced to trudge up and down hills that would have been nothing if only he could take to the sky. Yet here he was, scrabbling over every rock and rise.

He bound his feet and resigned himself to long stretches of uncertainty.

From time to time, the trees thinned, and he glimpsed the distant shine of his star, which drew him onward, correcting his course through the long winter nights.

During brief hours of daylight, Loor hunted or slept. In the foothills of a mountain, he found a deep pool of dark water warmed by buried heat and stopped to bathe and rebind his bruised feet. In the process, he caught a glimpse of his reflection. He stilled, waiting for the ripples to settle and the surface to yield a startling truth.

Loor slowly lifted his hand to touch his forehead.

There, in its very center, gleamed a copper star.

The star stopped and stayed over a human village tucked into that same mountain's heights. On the third night, without any further sign of moving on, Loor had to concede that *this* was his destination, even though he couldn't fathom *why*.

Soriel didn't return with further instructions.

His star remained steadfast, confirming his arrival.

And so Loor began to explore the mountain valley and the mismatched pack of humanity that tended flocks and toiled in fields. This was his first encounter with people of this sort, and he kept his distance from their strange voices, labors, and smells.

One season passed into another, and the busyness of the humans left Loor even lonelier than before. They talked and laughed. They formed little packs and cared for young. They tamed animals and used them for meat and for milk and even for companionship. He was most curious about the tame canines that came to heel for hunters and herders alike.

Dogs.

While similar to wolves, their features varied in interesting ways. Some he found quite ugly, but there were beauties in their midst. They had no words, being dumb beasts, but their barks and body language reminded him of home and stoked a craving for the closeness of one's packmates.

Curiosity carried him closer to their strange dens, only to set off a chorus of warning barks. He admired their protective instincts but chafed at their exclusion. Which is what drove him to take his truest form.

On all fours, he was a little larger than a wolf. Nose to the ground, he savored the scents that were growing more familiar. The trapper and his sled dogs. The shepherd and his herders. The headman and his kennel of hunting dogs.

The latter drew him unerringly to the man's barn. Loor transformed long enough to let himself inside, then reverted to the form of a ruddy wolf with silver eyes. Only one dog had been closed in for the night, a bitch and her litter. He approached with care, and she seemed to understand that he was something other than a threat.

Instinct worked in his favor.

She recognized him as a protector, and after long weeks

alone, he was able to enjoy the scents and sounds of a proper den. Her pups tumbled around him, and she looked on with tail slowly wagging. Nightly, he returned, and always he found welcome.

And in finding this scrap of peace, he threw himself into his newfound role.

He let himself go, following instinct, abandoning words. This was his den, his territory, so he prowled the headman's borders, protecting his holdings. But Loor's peaceful days ended far too soon, for a dog's life was short.

When the bitch breathed her last, he roved the village, seeking a new den. What he found changed everything.

A farmer with vast herds on the high slopes north of the village had purchased a new bitch—a leggy hound with intelligence in her gaze. He kept her shut away because she was in heat, and Loor liked her looks and the privacy her owner had so thoughtfully provided.

There was a brief outcry when the farmer realized that his best hunting dog was pregnant, but no one in his household knew where to lay blame. Perhaps the pups would give some clue to their father's identity.

Unconcerned by the circulating speculations, Loor took to patrolling this farmer's boundaries. He protected the man's herd, his crops, and even warned off a dray of squirrel Kith. Before the week was out, he'd been spotted by more than one villager, and tales of a red wolf with ghostly eyes began to spread.

Loor watched over the bitch and waited, and this waiting was not the same as waiting on stars. For these were days he knew how to number, and their end would bring a new life into the world. This hound carried his cubs. No, she was no wolf. Her young would be pups. *His* pups.

NAME

The weight of *that* realization drove Loor into speaking form for the first time in years. He shuddered to think what might happen to pups if they bore any resemblance to the dreaded red wolf. Before their birth, he needed to find a better den for his pack.

Sitting cross-legged in the straw, he waited to see if the expectant mother would recognize him in speaking form. Loor extended a hand, and said, "Forgive me for not offering my pledge until now, dear one. I am with you and will keep you. Can you accept an ill-mannered mate?"

She licked his fingertips and scooted forward to lay her head upon his knee.

"You deserve a name." He gazed thoughtfully into her eyes, and at length, he said, "I'll call you Generous, since your gifts are good. I will treasure them."

The only answer he received was the wag of her tail.

"I'll find a good place," he promised.

That night, he searched the sky and found his star, burning faithfully over the village's center. He could not leave, and so he looked for a den within its boundaries. Up and down the beaten tracks, he considered his options, which were few. In the end, he chose a disused animal barn at the edge of a fallow field belonging to the headman. Snug against an embankment, it would be spared the worst of winter's winds, and it wasn't readily visible from any road. With careful warding, the village would soon forget it ever existed.

Generous only carried one pup, and she carried the little one well past the usual season for birthing. More waiting. At least now, Loor could fill the hours. He reinforced the shed, shoring up its foundations and digging into its dirt floor. Adding a fire pit took days, and he spent weeks filling the loft with fragrant branches and harvesting grasses for bedding.

Loor's first wards had been hastily drawn in the dirt, but he needed something that would withstand the curiosity of critters and the whims of weather. He couldn't pull anything complex out of midair, so he needed an anchor—wood, stone, paper. Crystals were ideal, but scarce. Inspiration struck, and he sifted through the meager contents of his pack, coming up with his neglected sewing kit.

Working sigils into fabric couldn't be any more complicated than stitching a crest. He was on his third attempt at anchoring wards into embroidery when Generous finally showed signs of delivering her pup.

His son.

Loor named him Path, because every step of his journey had brought him to this place. He spent hours curled around the pup, whose baby fuzz was decidedly red. "Will you favor your sire?" he crooned, tugging at one tiny drooping ear.

Path's answering whine was not a sound, but a thought.

Loor's hand shook, and his eyes misted. "Do you have a voice, Path?"

Within days, there was no doubt, for the pup's burbling and babbling was a constant in Loor's mind. He was a Kith-sire. He was no longer alone.

Embroidery proved an excellent medium for sigilcraft, especially when Loor twined his own hair with the threads. While not as potent as the illusions of the trickster clans, he was able to deflect notice and deter pests. As Path grew, Loor expanded his holdings to include the entire pasture. Room to romp and tussle and laze in the sun.

Generous bore him a second son, and Loor called the pup Soon, because he still chose to believe that Soriel's promise would find its fulfillment.

Her last pup, another male, he called Trio, because now there were three voices in Loor's head, and his loneliness was at a low ebb.

Was this part of the Maker's purpose, setting him apart from his pack in order to live as a dex? While Loor hadn't been born twentieth, he'd shared an equal place in his mother's twentieth pregnancy. Where the Highwind pack had quibbled and divided, perhaps the Maker was asserting a prior claim. It was a comforting thought.

This mountain, this village, this den—he knew they must be his, for his star never strayed. But even knowing he was in the right place, Loor grew restless. Ranging through the human community, he searched for a way to add to his pack.

Finding a young sled dog with eyes the color of a winter sky, he took her for his own. He called her Restless.

She gave birth to another Kith, a son he named Pace, to remind himself that the seasons were not his to direct. And before her brief life ended, she bore a second pup. This son he named Rile, because a piece of his soul howled against heaven.

Thus far, all his sons resembled their sire, with shaggy red-brown fur. The variances they inherited from their mothers. Generous' pups had drooping ears, and Path had inherited the lively brown eyes Loor had found so lovely. Restless' pups were stockier, with curling tails and blue eyes.

He took them on hunts, taught them the woodland trails, and showed them the heavenly star that blazed above their home. They ranged over the whole of the mountain, which he urged them to protect—both it and its human community. And the villagers added to their store of tales. His pack had become the Demon Dogs of Denholm.

A newcomer to the mountain brought a new breed of dogs. Loor quietly absconded with a pup, who quickly grew into a gentle-natured companion. Beauty had a lavish coat of golden hair, which he never tired of brushing, and in due course, he needed that same comb to keep his first daughter's red-gold fur in order.

She became Dawn, because this was a new beginning.

His Kith were the first Amaranthine dogs, and he took the name "First of Dogs." His children never learned the name Loor-ket Highwind, nor did he hand down any wolf lore. When he sang, it was of the descent of an angel and the rise of a star.

Though they had no crest, and their den was little more than a shed, they were a clan unto themselves. He took the name Starmark, and his children knew him as Glint.

BOY

"Why do you keep taking mates?"

Glint turned to face his eldest son. "What kind of question is that?"

"Your mate is barely cold, and your eye is already wandering over the village bitches. Does full blood run hotter than half? Or are you just a greedy rutter?"

There was a bitter edge to Path's voice, and Glint could feel the depths of his disdain. But he couldn't bring himself to be upset with his son. "Is that what you think of me?"

Path's tail tucked. *"Sometimes."*

He grabbed his son by his considerable ruff, hauling until the dog's bowed head butted into his breastbone, making it easier to lavish affection on his four-footed child. Path and his siblings were tall as moose and burly as bears, but little more than pups in the eyes of their sire.

"I take no pleasure in watching a mate's life wink out after so brief a bonding," said Glint. "Have you ever seen me handle a bitch in an unworthy manner?"

The answer came soft and earnest. *"Never."*

Glint had taken many mates over the decades, and most had borne him a pup or two. "Your mothers have each been dear to me." Glint searched for a way to explain his choices. "Their deaths do break my heart, but I've resolved to endure the losses. These bitches are both your heritage and our future."

Path grumbled, *"You want more pups."*

"Naturally."

"Why?"

"For your sake. For the sake of our pack." Glint asked, "Would you banish any of your younger brothers or sisters from this world? Would you deny Trio his newfound bond with Dawn? Would you turn down the chance at an equal match, should one of your half-sisters or future nieces welcome your pursuit?"

"I don't want a mate."

"Why not?"

"I have you." More softly, *"That's enough ... for me."*

"Path." Glint threaded his fingers through shaggy fur. "Please don't think I added to our pack because I found my firstborn lacking."

His son whined and nosed the shining star left behind by an angel's kiss.

Glint rested his forehead against Path's. "I came to this mountain alone, but your birth ended my solitude. Your steadfastness has been my support, and your happiness is my only wish."

"We are not the same." Path's voice turned stern. *"Stop asking me to find your version of happiness, when I have chosen my own."*

"When did my son learn wisdom?"

Taking the question literally, Path earnestly answered, *"A little at a time. Mostly on clear nights, when a soft wind blows from the east."*

Glint chuckled. "And why are *those* considered favorable conditions."

Path's tail wagged. *"They are the only times you can hear our star singing."*

Weeks passed before the winds took a favorable turn. Gentle gusts carried a piercingly sweet song Glint hadn't even realized he should be listening for. For two centuries and more, the star had kept its distance from him, but its lyric promised that hope was near. And drawing nearer.

Dawn's first litter arrived in springtime, two females—Hope and Help—and a scrappy male he called Romp.

Glint had wondered why the domesticated dogs he'd claimed only ever bore one pup at a time. Highwind Kith often had litters of three or four wolf cubs. Dawn's litter meant that their pack could transition from addition to multiplication.

If only he could bring in a few Kith from other packs. Would wolves willingly mingle with his sons? Or would that mean losing their distinction as dogs?

He was muddling through different approaches to the problem when the shed door opened with a violent *creak*. Since he and his children generally made use of a convenient gap in the back wall, those hinges hadn't budged in more than a century. And there on the threshold stood a human child.

Small and brown and barefoot, he had straight black hair hanging around his shoulders. His pants seemed to have been sewn from skins, but his shirt was the homespun typical of the humans in this village. But Glint guessed he wasn't one of the village brats. Any of them would have taken one look and run screaming. If not from him, then from Path, whose flank currently served as his backrest.

But this boy took a step forward, babbling in an unintelligible language.

Glint grunted. "You have a lot to say, but your language is strange. It's no use, boy. I can't respond in kind."

The boy pursed his lips in frustration, intelligence shining in black eyes. He came two steps further into the den and spoke again, slower. Tugging at his own ear, he gestured at Glint's. Pointed ears were one way in which humans could be distinguished from Amaranthine in speaking form.

To acknowledge their difference, Glint touched the tip of an ear. "Yes, boy. I'm different from you, and we both know it."

Again, the boy spoke, and this time, he enunciated each syllable. The word was strangely accented, but clear enough—Amaranthine.

"You know the word for me?" Glint chuckled and offered the *correct* pronunciation.

The boy muttered it under his breath a few times, practicing the syllables.

"What is he saying?" asked Path. *"What is that word?"*

"He knows what we are. This human child is somehow familiar with our race."

"We are Starmark."

"Starmark is our clan name. We are the first of the dog clans, but every creature has its Kindred, and all those clans together have one beginning, one Maker, one purpose, and one name. We are Amaranthine."

"Amaranthine," echoed the boy, his pronunciation correct.

Nodding, he tapped his chest. "Glint Starmark."

The boy shuffled closer, hands outstretched, tone questioning.

Glint gestured him forward. "It's your good fortune to be correct, but whoever taught you the form for greetings should be reprimanded for his accent."

The boy wriggled his toes and tried a different word.

"Peace," Glint said clearly. "Peace, little fool. My son and I mean you no harm."

Glint was rewarded with a gap-toothed grin, and the boy closed the distance with a skip in his step. Without a trace of concern for Glint's claws, he met palms.

"Brave little thing," remarked Glint.

"What do we call him?"

"Let's find out." Glint tapped his own shoulder and repeated his name. Then he tapped the boy's scrawny chest and arched his brows inquiringly.

The grin widened, and the boy mimicked Glint, tapping his own shoulder. "Waaseyaa." And without a trace of shyness, Waaseyaa reached up to touch Glint's thick hair.

He huffed and bowed his head, inviting the boy's curiosity.

Suddenly, fingers grazed his forehead.

Glint didn't move, but he lifted his gaze to find the boy's face inches from his. Excitement added a sparkle to his eyes, but his tone was entirely serious. "Glint Starmark," he said.

"Waaseyaa," he replied dutifully.

With a laugh, the boy threw his arms around Glint's neck and babbled nonsense, then kissed his cheek. The touch sent an unanticipated thrill through Glint's soul—dazzling in its brightness, fainter but familiar nonetheless.

Here was something he hadn't tasted in many long years. Not since an angel kissed his forehead.

PEACE

Path asked, *"Is this bad?"*

"It might be," Glint muttered. The boy had gone away, only to return leading a burly man with pale eyes, whose frizzled beard looked in need of a good brushing.

"I don't know his scent. Where did he come from?" Trio was understandably antsy with strangers so near his pups. *"How did he find us?"*

Soon asked, *"Did they break your wards?"*

"I'll check them later," promised Glint. "Calm your hackles. I think they're simply curious about us."

This new stranger was armed, but he never once reached for the weapons at his belt. And he listened more than he spoke. After Waaseyaa finished telling his side of a story that seemed unnecessarily long, the man nodded and turned to Glint with palms extended.

To Glint's surprise, the man addressed him in heavily-accented Amaranthine. "This village fears demon dogs."

Glint snorted. "My Kith and I aren't demons."

"I see. I know." The man grimaced apologetically. "This village is gone. Empty. This village is ours. We will stay."

Things had been quieter lately. But Glint's only thought had been for Dawn's litter. How much had he missed? He shook his head and firmly declared, "I'm staying."

With a sign for peace, the man said, "Good. Stay. Good. Welcome you. Welcome us?"

His Amaranthine was an old hinge, rusty from disuse. Glint chose simple words. "As long as you leave me and my pack in peace, you can do as you please."

The man gestured a helpless apology. His words were too few for much understanding.

Waaseyaa spoke again, waving between himself and Glint.

"Learn." The man indicated the boy and searched his vocabulary. "Learn. Speak. Teach?"

"You want me to teach the boy?" Glint considered Waaseyaa, whose hopeful gaze needed no translation. "He seems quick enough, and I can rid him of your wretched accent."

Another hesitant headshake.

Glint sighed and said, "Good. Teach Waaseyaa. Good. Peace."

Relief and happiness shifted into the humans' scents.

The man said, "Good. Glad. Grateful." With a wince, he added, "Too long ago Gerard learn. Mother-kin from enclave. Silverprong."

"That explains the accent." Glint chuckled and explained to his sons, "The deer clans speak with an adorable lisp."

"What's an enclave?" asked Path.

"I have no idea. Once the boy has the words, we can ask him." Glint stepped forward to cover the man's palms, carefully enunciating his name and going so far to introduce his Kith as well.

The man nodded to each in turn, then offered his own name. "Gerard Reaver."

Glint searched for and found the gap in his wards and reinforced his boundary, etching some additional sigils into the dirt for good measure. While he was at it, he watched to see what his new neighbors were doing. The air hung thick with strange smoke and the stringent odors of bruised herbs. He recognized salt and wax and the tang of ore, but there was a musk he'd never encountered.

Reaver's men were a strange bunch. On the surface, they behaved as the previous villagers had—herding and tilling and making improvements to houses and barns. But they also razed three houses in order to expand the village center, and weeks of back-breaking labor went into the construction of a low stone wall that encircled all the occupied homes.

Most unusual was the way their presence stirred him up. With the former villagers, once he'd grown accustomed to their scents and noises, he hadn't given them much thought. But these people appealed to him. "They make my blood rise," Glint murmured. An unsettling thought occurred to him. "They make me hungry."

To varying degrees, all of Reaver's men piqued his interest, but none more than Waaseyaa.

Path was the only one to voice similar inclinations. *"Would they taste good?"*

"I pledged peace," Glint reminded. "Would you make your father a liar?"

"I don't want to eat them. I want to understand why they steal into my thoughts." Path cocked his head to one side. *"Our boy is best. I want him near because I am gladder, lighter, stronger when he is near."*

Glint grunted, for Path's words echoed the feelings that had been growing in his own heart. "We used to guard the villagers. Now we must guard ourselves around them."

Path's tail beat the ground. *"Can we keep him?"*

"Waaseyaa?"

"He's the brightest. He's the best."

"We can't claim him without consent," said Glint. "But we have our own allure. He seems fascinated by our differences, our language, our customs."

"We should keep him."

Glint slipped his arm around Path's thick neck, leaning into his bulk. "While they live longer than a common dog, humans have short lives."

Path whined.

"I'll do my best to encourage his interest."

But wooing Waaseyaa was far from difficult. The boy was not only enamored of Glint and his pack, he was lonely. He lingered in their den after their lessons were done. Many evenings he stayed long after the humans' usual dinner hour, nestled between Path's forepaws, playing with Dawn's pups.

On such nights, Gerard came looking for him. "You should not impose!" he chided.

Glint hastily assured, "My den is brighter for his presence. He's welcome."

Conversation had grown easier with his eager young pupil. For every word Glint taught Waaseyaa, he was given its equivalent in exchange. Glint was learning Reaver's language, and the man offered gruff gratitude for the consideration.

"Can I stay?" wheedled Waaseyaa.

A dozen tails beat their bedding of summer hay in unanimous approval.

Gerard tugged at his beard, his gaze slanting thoughtfully to Glint. "You are willing?"

He signaled affirmative. "The boy may consider my den his home, and I will consider him a packmate."

"I cannot say which of you has more courage." Gerard tousled Waaseyaa's hair, then gave him a push in Glint's direction. "But I do know that we are honored."

That night, Waaseyaa clambered into the midst of the pack, and Glint allowed his children and grandchildren to vie for the boy's attention. However, once Waaseyaa's eyes grew heavy, Glint asserted his right. Remaining in speaking form for once, he waded into the mound of fur to pull the drowsing boy against his side.

Waaseyaa stirred and blinked up at him, then smiled and nestled in.

Glint rumbled approval.

Long into the night, he basked in the boy's trust and wondered if this is what it would have been like if his children could take speaking form. Did Beloor nestle with sons and daughters in this way? Would he be more shocked to learn that his tailless brother had founded a clan of dogs or that his pack now included a human boy?

CREST

Glint hadn't slept so deeply since the night he and Bel had smuggled star wine into their den to toast their attainment. Jaws closed over his hip, and Path's voice was a shout in his mind.

"Please, wake! Wake up! Why can't you hear me, Da?"

He grunted and reached for the offending muzzle. "Calm down. I'm awake."

Path whined.

"I'm awake," Glint repeated, though he felt loose and languid. He started to sit up, only to recall the boy currently using his shoulder for a pillow. Nothing else seemed out of place. In low tones, he asked, "What is it?"

"The star is singing."

Waaseyaa didn't notice when Glint eased from the pile to follow Path out into the night.

Urgency bade Glint to rush, but even now, years after the command was given, he couldn't bring himself to disobey. So he *walked* through the pasture, and he *walked* the narrow path that led to their property's high point. He resolutely checked his stride. Every step a choice.

And as he walked, he shed his strange stupor. The night was moon-bright and balmy, with a hint of distant rainstorms on the wind. Tonight's song carried well, and it lifted Glint's spirits. Here was a psalm of beginnings and of bonds, a tale of those between and of blessings. But a warning note shivered through every refrain, telling of a people touched by power and the dangers of their allure.

Glint stood his ground and listened until dawn took the sky, humming along until he was sure he would remember every word. Because if the song was right, then Reaver's people were a danger—not only to him, but to themselves. And Waaseyaa most of all.

"What are you doing?" Waaseyaa hung over Glint's shoulder. "Can I try?"

"You want to learn to sew?"

"I want to learn ... this." The boy's finger trailed along the edge of Glint's threadwork.

Glint had settled on a design for the Starmark crest, which included a sinking moon, half-hidden by the horizon. The ascending star matched the blaze on his forehead. But most important—and most time consuming—was the tracery of protective sigils around the border. Glint hoped to work the wards for a barrier directly into the cloth.

"Sigilcraft interests you?" he asked.

"A new word?"

"Two words in one—*sigil* and *craft*." Touching the circular design, Glint said, "This is a sigil. I am its crafter. I make them."

Waaseyaa continued to brush the edge, as if testing a boundary. "What is it for?"

"It will protect you. It will protect me." He held up his hand. "Like a wall."

The boy gasped. "You are a ward?"

"I am Glint."

"Our wards are not here yet, but when they come, they will bring the stone wall to life." He fumbled for a moment, then switched to his own language. "A barrier."

"*When they come*? Who is coming ... more like Reaver?"

"Many more. And Amaranthine." Waaseyaa's hands described circles in the air. "We cleared the center, and we're building the wall. The rest are coming, and they will share Wardenclave with us—Fullstash and Dimityblest and Duntuffet."

Glint recognized those clan names—squirrel, moth, and rabbit. "What is Wardenclave?"

"Two words in one." Waaseyaa leaned forward, eager to share this heretofore unmentioned bit of news. "*Ward* and *enclave*. We must build a barrier."

"What are you keeping out?"

Waaseyaa's eyes lost their shine. "Everywhere we go, they follow. We are hunted. We are prey." He hesitated, then quietly added, "They took my family."

Responding to the fear and sadness in Waaseyaa's scent, Glint set aside his needlework and tugged him onto his lap. "I didn't know there was anything that hunted humans."

"Amaranthine."

Glint was almost afraid to ask. "Why would Amaranthine hunt humans?"

"To eat." He looked up into Glint's face. "They want our souls."

With the warnings of his star reeling through his mind, he shook his head incredulously. "If Amaranthine predators are your enemies, why weren't you afraid of me?"

Waaseyaa hesitated.

Glint waited.

Finally, the boy admitted, "Because you only looked surprised."

"Anyone would be, when a strange child strolls past several decades worth of sigilcraft." He picked up his handiwork again and scrutinized the delicate balance of its seal. It should work. It would have to. "Give me your shirt."

With no real need for sleep but an abundant need for clarity, Glint took his stitching outside. Away from Waaseyaa, he was more himself, but having been with the boy, his stitches were more potent, and his sigils shimmered with strength he hadn't known he possessed.

Path's description from those earliest days was proving true and truer. Glint whispered, "Gladder. Lighter. Stronger."

By moonlight, he duplicated his crest, embroidering it directly onto Waaseyaa's shirt. It was as much a claim as it was a promise of protection. The boy was his now. A fosterling.

Mid-high saw the task finished, so Glint called the Kith into a circle, to bear witness to the boy's attainment. "Take your shirt back. Wear it well."

Waaseyaa quickly obeyed, pulling the cloth away from his skin to admire Glint's addition. "A sigil for me?"

"That's the mark of my clan, the Starmark crest. Wearing it means you belong to our den." He dropped to one knee and looked him in the eye. "We are your pack."

"What kind of pack?"

Glint grinned. "We are dogs."

"Den is like … *house*?"

"More than a house, not just a building." Glint offered him new words. "Home. Pack. *Mine*."

"I belong to Glint?"

"Do you have a family name? What is your clan called?"

The boy blinked. "Reaver found us and saved us and took us in. He shared his name and keeps us safe until the enclave is ready. I was his, but he gave me to you." Touching the crest on his shirt, he asked, "What should I be called?"

Glint considered birthnames of great importance, so he pressed. "How did your mother call you?"

"Waaseyaa means 'first light from the rising sun.'" He shook his head. "I was born among the trees, but I have no roots. I escaped. I ran. I wander."

Once he learned more words, Glint would talk to Gerard. To one made for dens, endless wandering sounded wretched. He wanted to know the bounds of his territory and to learn its every whiff and way. To protect it and to find pleasure in its peace. And to share it.

"You are a Reaver, then?" Glint asked. "Or would you like to be called Starmark."

"Both are good names," Waaseyaa said tentatively. "But I will have a new name when … when I keep my promise. I should wait."

The boy's scent twisted with secrets and fears, and Glint pulled him close. "You do not share my name, but you bear my crest, Waaseyaa the Wanderer. If you have made a promise, then you must keep it, and I will be your support."

He clung and mumbled, "I can still belong to Glint?"

"Never doubt that, boy."

Glint was pleased to see that his sigilcraft worked well enough. Waaseyaa's presence was snug as a nutmeat in its shell. The giddying soul no longer stoked his senses and stirred his appetite. Even better, he was well-hidden from the predators who might still be on the hunt. But with Waaseyaa muffled, it was possible to pick out other points of brightness throughout the village.

Reaver's men might be a raggle-taggle crew of mismatched humanity, but they gathered at the same circle. Those who worked on the wall, those who cleared the village center, those who minded the flocks, those who scavenged in forest and field—Glint could sense them all.

And that meant they were in danger.

PACT

When Swift, the white-muzzled bitch who'd borne him both a daughter and a son, succumbed to her years, Glint did not seek a new mate.

Path noticed.

"The boy demands too much attention." Glint wasn't sure why he felt the need to make excuses. "You have to admit he's as bad as Dawn's litter for getting into things."

He had only ever had to deal with one pup at a time, so three left them feeling rather overrun.

"You will devote yourself to him?" asked Path. *"Is he your new mate?"*

Glint settled back, needing to explain. "There are different kinds of mates, but all require our loyalty. I took your mothers as mates to sire Kith, and so I am not alone. Denmates share a home. Packmates share blood. Pactmates share a promise. And if I were to choose and pursue an Amaranthine female, a mate who was my equal in every way, we would be bondmates."

Path's ears pricked and dipped, ending in cockeyed confusion. *"When you take a village bitch, it is for breeding without bonding?"*

"Your mother was Generous, and while she remained at my side, I pursued no other. But because she was a creature without words, my promise could not be returned. While I'd never say that made her devotion to me less real, we were unequal."

"Is Waaseyaa your equal?"

Glint pondered that and finally decided, "We are not the same, but we both have words. I cannot imagine treating him as less than I am, nor would I be tempted to revere him as more than I am. So yes, he is my equal."

"And me?"

"Are we not reasoning together?" He reached up and tugged his son's ear. "We are equal."

"Even though I cannot speak as you do?"

"You have words, and I can hear them. When I speak, you understand me. We are not the same, but what two individuals are?" Glint grinned up at his eldest. "We share the bonds of blood and of home."

"Packmates. Denmates."

"Yes."

Path asked, *"Would you share a pact with me?"*

Glint stood and wrapped his arms around his son's thick ruff. "If you yearn for more, I will not refuse. What promise shall we make?"

"I have watched you with Waaseyaa. You want a son."

"I have you. I have your brothers and sisters."

"Promise me you will find your equal. Promise me that your next mate can return your promise and become your bondmate." Path softly added, *"You deserve a true son."*

Glint growled. "You *are* my son. I'm proud of all of my children."

Path's head drooped, his ears low, tail tucking.

"Why would the son who so jealously guards his place at my side ask me to pursue another?" Glint was both angry and ashamed that his attentions to Waaseyaa had hurt his son. Path had been with him the longest, knew him best. It made no sense, and he grumbled, "Me, take a bondmate? And this from the stubborn whelp who refuses one."

Path whimpered.

"I'm not angry." Glint held on tight and stroked his son's fur. "I *am* confused, though. Who put this nonsense in your head?"

"Your star."

"I hadn't realized it was singing again."

"The boy demands much of your attention."

Glint did not appreciate having his excuses turned against him. He grunted and growled, but only asked, "Well?"

Path hesitated a moment. *"Do you have a brother?"*

"I have many, but they are far from this place."

"But ... a best-loved brother?"

He didn't want to speak of the past, but neither could he deny it. "The star has been singing about me?"

Path nodded—a human quirk he'd learned from Waaseyaa.

Glint heaved a sigh. "My twin. I loved him better than any other person in this world. But he was chosen by another, and he liked her pursuit."

"Pursuit?"

"Like when Dawn came into her own and Soon and Rile noticed, but she showed her preference for Trio." He looked away. "I made the same promise to my brother that you made to me—to be his and no one else's. But a female who was his equal made an offer for him. He was her choice, and she became his choice."

Path was silent for a long time. *"Females choose?"*

Glint chuckled. "In a bond between equals, each chooses the other. But in Bel's case, the female chose first. It's hard to explain. He was a dex, so that's the way it had to be."

"Are you a dex?"

"I live as one."

Path's tail took on a sway. *"I understand. Now will you share my pact?"*

"In a pact of this nature, promises are usually exchanged." Inspiration hit. "How about this. You want me to take a bondmate so you can meet my 'true son.' In return, you must take a bondmate someday, so that I can meet your son."

"I do not want a mate."

"If you are going to ask the impossible of me, I should be able to ask as much of you."

"Why impossible?"

"Path, there are no Amaranthine dogs for me to pursue. I am the First of Dogs, and there are no others."

His son's eyes narrowed. *"You were born without a mother?"*

"My mother is a wolf."

One ear cocked. *"How does a wolf become a dog?"*

"By listening to stars." Glint's smile turned wry. "By walking away."

"What about your son?"

"Which son? I have many."

"The son born to your bondmate."

"What if it's a daughter?" Glint asked, just to be contrary.

"Would they be a Starmark?" asked Path. *"Would they be a dog?"*

He allowed himself to imagine such a future. "Yes. A dog."

Path nosed his father's forehead, then licked his cheek. *"Be my pactmate."*

"I don't want to make a promise I can't keep."

"It will be kept." His son's voice had a teasing lilt. *"Your star said the moon is tracking you, and its radiance will touch your face."*

"What's that supposed to mean?"

"You are chosen," Path said simply.

Glint didn't exactly doubt his son or the star. Both were his by the Maker's design. All he could do was wait and watch and wait some more. And work with Waaseyaa in the meantime. "Yes, Path. I accept your pledge and give mine in return—a son for a son. May they each be a tribute to the Starmark clan."

WARD

Before their short summer ended, a caravan arrived bringing more of Reaver's people to Wardenclave. Colonists. Men and women, outcasts and orphans, and if Pace's and Soon's excited descriptions were correct, a small group of Amaranthine.

"What kind?" asked Glint.

Soon sat back on his haunches. *"Not like us."*

Perhaps Glint shouldn't have been so grateful that no wolves had entered his territory. An interested female could have meant the swift fulfillment of his pact with Path.

As if lasting bonds were ever swift or easy.

Propping his hands on his hips, he glared up at the star dancing in the twilit sky. Rather than showing any sign of contrition over Glint's ever-lengthening wait, it blazed twice as bright as usual, as if celebrating the arrival of so many sparkling souls.

The newcomers were better warded and better armed, but if Glint could taste them on the wind, so could any determined tracker. He hoped the promised barrier wouldn't be long in rising.

Gerard strode forward with two other men and tried to initiate a proper introduction, but the darker of the two cut across his words to demand, "What have you done with the Twinned Child?"

Glint glanced at Gerard, trying to get a sense of what was happening.

"Waaseyaa," he explained. "He seems to be missing."

This was the first Glint had heard of Waaseyaa being a twin. "He has a sibling among you? I thought he was all alone." Inwardly, he ordered whoever among his Kith had the boy to bring him quickly.

"Coming!"

That was Trio, and Glint turned and smiled at the sight they made. Waaseyaa was riding on Trio's back, with three pups gamboling around his paws, doing their level best to trip up their father. Waaseyaa beamed as if he'd taught Trio a new trick.

"My pack is fond of the boy," said Glint in mild reproach. "We watch over him."

"You *warded* him?" interrupted the other man, a flaxen-haired fellow with a pointed beard and eyes the hue of a morning sky. "I have never heard of a ward so ... *personal*! But how is it anchored?"

Before Glint could explain, the other one thrust out his hands, gruffly giving his name as Brings the Wind. "Please, forgive me. When I thought him gone, I assumed the worst. His loss would devastate our plans for Wardenclave. But to have found a place among wolves!"

"Dogs," Glint firmly corrected.

"I have never encountered a dog clan." Hemet was not a tall man, but he wasn't lacking in enthusiasm. "You are a ward? We found a warded farm on the edge of town. It must be yours—the warding, not the farm. Or *are* you a farmer?"

As Gerard did his best to explain a pack's presence in the middle of their village, Glint contemplated the newcomers, automatically relating them to animals of his acquaintance. Hemet was sturdy as a wild pony and just as prone to prancing. He wheeled and exclaimed and complimented every aspect of their view.

Brings the Wind had the bearing of a falcon and was equally inscrutable.

Both piqued his interest, but not with Waaseyaa's command. Compared to them, his boy burned like a small sun, and Glint could find no clan comparison. His first impression lingered still. Waaseyaa was an angel, and his presence was becoming increasingly entwined with Glint's feelings of strength and hope and purpose. If Soriel's message had sent him here simply so he could meet

Waaseyaa, then his solitude and centuries were well spent.

Of the four Amaranthine who arrived with the caravan, the first to seek him out was from one of the moth clans. Linlu Dimityblest was lithe and soft-spoken, with short hair mottled in powdery shades of brown and cream. The irises of his large eyes were nearly the same color as his skin—cool as river clay and glossy with interest. "You are a wolf."

"I am a son of the packs," he conceded. "But anything made can be remade. I am a dog. The first of my clan."

"Do you know of enclaves?"

"Not by that name." Glint thought back to the discussions at his last few Song Circles. "Alliances between clans have always seemed wise to me, but the cooperatives I heard about formed to hide from human encroachment. You're building *with* them."

"Gerard is on a crusade, and we support his purposes."

"And what *are* those purposes?" Glint was glad for this chance of a more thorough explanation than limited vocabularies had previously allowed.

"The ancient groves are gone. The tree-kin are scattered. Our guide calls them a flock without a shepherd." Linlu's dainty hands fluttered. "We have gathered them up to give them safe haven. Wardenclave will be their home."

Glint eyed him with concern. "What safety can moths, rabbits, and squirrels offer?"

"Camouflage." Linlu reached out to catch Glint's sleeve. "But you are strong. Do you intend to remain with us here?"

"I'm here by the Maker's leading, but I'm not privy to His purposes. All I know for certain is that I cannot leave unless my star leads."

"Then we are similarly guided." Linlu lifted his face to the spark that could be seen faintly against the blue of the sky. "Gerard chose me because I am sensitive to Impressions."

Only children believed in lorefolk, the so-called lost clans. Glint might have been more skeptical of Linlu's claim if he hadn't been sent out by an angel and trudged across tundras in the wake of a star.

"They're twins, you know—those stars."

Glint had thought his star brighter. Perhaps it was, but only because it no longer danced alone.

Linlu said, "You are protecting the boy."

He grunted an affirmative.

"His soul is especially clear and sweet. The brightest I have seen in three generations." With a reverent tone, he added, "My people call those like Waaseyaa *beacons*. He pulls people like us toward him."

Again, Glint grunted.

"You are patient."

He frowned. "With the boy? He's a child."

"He's a tempting prospect. Those who pursue us haven't the patience to cultivate a community like ours and the communion it fosters." Linlu edged closer, his voice dropping. "Have you noticed a change within yourself since the boy entered your care?"

Glint inclined his head. "I have less difficulty forming sigils, and those I create are more effective."

"Your reserves will double and redouble, and in truest form, you will gain in both speed and stature." Linlu's hands flowed gracefully as he spoke. "Little by little, as you tend to such a child, they tend to you. Strength for protection. And greater protection due to increasing strength."

"An exchange of sorts," Glint mused.

"Mutually beneficial," he agreed. "However, some have no patience. Rather than nurture a potent soul, they snatch at strength, tearing and consuming. So many have been lost already. These humans are growing increasingly rare."

"So Gerard is collecting them to keep their kind from being hunted out of existence."

"Yes."

"Why bring them *here*?"

Linlu's laugh was a gentle vibration, like wind through leaves. "The Maker of one path can surely make another."

Glint remembered Linlu's mention of a guide and squinted into the sky. "I was visited by an angel called Soriel. Ever heard that name?"

"No." The moth clansman's expression softened. "Ours was Auriel."

Now *that* was a name Glint knew. "Auriel of the Golden Seed?"

"The very same." Linlu's hand drummed lightly over his heart. "I am glad to learn there is so much truth in the old tales. We may all be here to witness a dawning."

THREAT

Even though Glint had come from a different direction and without any intention of founding an enclave, Linlu Dimityblest included his name on the charter, and the other Amaranthine deferred to Glint as if he were their leader.

"You have more years," reasoned Bram Duntuffet, a fast-talking rabbit who excelled at foraging.

"And you have our support," added Colt Hannick Alpenglow, a healer whose cart was a rolling herbiary.

Glint's gaze lifted to the branch where the final Amaranthine member of Reaver's team lounged. Salali Fullstash pulled a floppy-brimmed hat low over his eyes. Based on the subtle strength Glint could sense lurking behind his lazy exterior, the squirrel clansman might have taken charge. In fact, he probably *had* over the course of their journey. But now that they'd arrived, Salali was only too happy to yield.

"Lead on, pooch." The gray-haired Amaranthine only smirked and waved off Glint's glare. "We'll call it 'divine right' and expect great things of you. No pressure."

Linlu's smile was far too pleased. "With your agreement, we will be unanimous."

Glint considered the moth, whose pen poised over the book he was already writing, a record of Wardenclave's founding. Maybe this was an honor. He should probably take it seriously. But it didn't feel like he was making history … just picking up everyone else's slack. Even so, he mustered a bit of dignity. "I am where I belong. The people of Wardenclave may count on the Starmark clan's protection."

With a flourish of his pen, Linlu intoned, "So it has been agreed. So let it be done."

The attack came without warning—torrents and tremors. A battering began overhead, testing the strength of Hemet's barrier. Something else was hitting low. Based on the noise of scrabbling and the shift and rattle of stones, Glint could only assume the wall itself was in danger. If their attackers pried away Hemet's sigil-bearing crystals, Wardenclave's defenses would fall.

"What are we looking at?" whispered Linlu, who blinked nearsightedly.

"Foxes," snapped Bram, who shifted a short club from hand to hand. "Same lot that picked up our scent two mountain ranges back."

"The wards?" asked Hannick.

"Holding," said Salali. "Barely."

Glint bit back a growl as Waaseyaa scrambled up the rise and barreled into his side. "I told you to stay with Path."

"I did. He came with me." The boy's gaze darted from wall to sky. "They found us again?"

Just then, Hemet took a stand midway between the center of town and the stone wall. With a chunk of crystal in each hand, he sent a wave of power outward. The initial crack set Glint's hairs on end, and an aftershock singed their tips.

"That smarts," muttered Bram.

Salali was already throwing up a defensive barrier. "Keep your whiskers on."

"What exactly did he do?" demanded Glint. He'd never seen a human capable of harnessing any portion of their soul. Admittedly, Reaver's people were fundamentally different—as different as his

Kith were from their mothers.

"Hemet can create barriers, but he's even better with attacks. The crystals amplify his intent into an act of violence." Salali flashed a wry smile. "Don't underestimate these humans."

"Neither them nor cornered rodents." Glint braced himself against the backlash of another outburst. "Hasn't anyone tried refining his attack? If the crystal is his anchor, why not use it as a focus as well. Less waste. More damage."

Bram shot him an assessing look. "Spoken like a tribute. Were you set apart for war?"

"I'm not sure *why* I was set apart."

Salali's hands flashed, pulling complex patterns seemingly out of nowhere. As their lines snapped into place and gained strength, he drawled, "Is this *really* the time for a chat about sigilcraft and destiny? Refine later. Survive now."

Glint scanned the wall, picking out the places where his own sigils held the line. "Waaseyaa, can you do things like that?"

The boy shook his head.

Bram said, "A shame, given his considerable resources."

"He doesn't respond to any of Hemet's crystals, either," said Salali, his voice tight. "Not to say there aren't other types we can tune, but remnants are a limited resource. We're hoping Bram will find more in these parts."

"Is this *really* the time for a chat about mountain lore and mining?" The rabbit's nose wrinkled and twitched. "Ward me, so I can get in there."

TEAM

Glint watched the humans rally and rush, using wave after wave of raw power to drive back the three foxes beyond their boundary. From his vantage, it wasn't hard to spot the weakness in their strategy. Hemet's attacks had a limited range, so all their opponents needed to do was pull back to a safe distance. Having determined the length of Wardenclave's tether, they dodged the brunt of every blast.

"He needs to get in closer," muttered Glint.

"True enough," conceded Salali. "But we cannot withstand Hemet's destructive force."

"Bram's doing well enough."

The squirrel offered a thin smile. "My warding only holds up for a little while—five, six blasts at best."

Glint's mind was reeling through ways to improve on their system. If Reaver's men and Amaranthine were to work in tandem, shielding might help, but focusing the attack would be better for everyone. It was an intriguing puzzle.

Pushing those thoughts aside for later, Glint said, "Those foxes are going to drag this out in order to wear Hemet down. We need him and his crystals up under their chins if we're going to wipe those grins from their faces."

"I'll do it!"

Glint turned, startled to find Trio pawing the grass. "Do what?"

"Let me carry the Reaver to the enemy." He barked for emphasis. *"It's my right. My pups are in danger."*

"As are mine," Glint gruffly reminded.

Trio's gaze didn't waver. *"Come with me."*

It wasn't a bad plan. With a resigned huff, he ordered, "Trio, carry Salali. Salali, be flashy. Create a distraction. Have Bram withdraw, and see if you can lure one of those pests into closer quarters. I'll carry Hemet."

"Simple enough. Ward yourself well." Then Salali was offering his palms to Trio, and they sprang away together.

"Waaseyaa, stay with Path. He'll protect you."

"With my life."

The boy knotted his fingers into Path's fur and whispered, "I promise."

Glint knew he could make use of the sigils already embroidered into his tunic. The wards would render him—and Hemet—hard to notice. Mindful of his promise to the Maker, he strolled into battle. Advancing at his ordained pace. Every step a choice.

Glint only looked back once, to make certain Waaseyaa was safe. He needn't have worried for the boy. Path had stayed back, as promised, but he also rallied his brothers to follow Glint's lead.

Rile now carried Brings the Wind. Pace and Soon also found partners from among Reaver's men. Young Edge had even charged in, presenting himself to Gerard.

Glint took the time to ignite several sigils and bolster his sons' defenses. He didn't like seeing his pack endangered, but the dogs were far more suited to war with foxes than the frighteningly vulnerable colonists.

"I'll carry you."

Hemet rounded on him, his face a mask of confusion.

Glint repeated, "I'll carry you. On my back. In truest form."

"Oh!" The man's grip on his crystals tightened. "Are you sure, Glint? I don't want to hurt you."

"Keep that thought foremost in your mind, and your soul won't consider mine a threat." He clapped the man's shoulder. "Don't worry, man. I've taken measures to protect myself and my dogs."

Hemet's gaze hardened. "Together, then!"

Transformation at close quarters left Glint and Hemet momentarily stunned, and for similar reasons. The man clearly hadn't expected to be facing such a large beast, and Glint hadn't expected to tower so far over the field. It took a moment to haul himself into tight enough control to maintain a size closer to that of his Kith, making it much easier for Hemet to climb aboard.

The proximity of the man's crystals and conjurations rattled Glint to the very core of his being. But Hemet's searing attacks never turned on his mount. A promising sign. Reaver's men could be taught.

Under the cover of Glint's sigils, they made their way beyond the quavering barrier, and as soon as they were close enough, Hemet's power came crashing down on the nearest fox. The lone male dropped, killed outright, and the other two recoiled and retreated.

The dogs of the Starmark pack howled in defiance.

Reaver's men raised their fists and roared victoriously.

Not a soul lost.

Glint lifted his nose to the twin stars dancing in the evening sky and sang out a promise. To the Maker and his angels, to Reaver and his Amaranthine allies, to Waaseyaa and his packmates. Wardenclave was his to guard, and by the Maker, *all* its people would be safe.

Back in the safety of his den, Glint reassured himself by checking and brushing each of his children. Now that the brief skirmish was over, his heart lurched, and his hands trembled. As proud as he was of his sons, Glint quailed before the belated realization that any of them could have been hurt.

Worse, that possibility remained if the vixens they'd driven off proved vindictive.

Perhaps he should offer to work with Hemet. And Bram seemed to be a scrapper. Maybe the rabbit could show his Kith how to defend themselves while they defended the mountain.

Not until he'd finished brushing the smallest pup did Glint turn his attention to Waaseyaa. The boy had definitely caught his mood and remained quiet, curled into a tight ball between Path's forepaws.

"I haven't forgotten you." Glint beckoned.

Waaseyaa crawled forward, wide-eyed and wilted.

Gathering him up, Glint teasingly went through the motions, checking for injuries and chuffing the boy under his chin. He even loosened Waaseyaa's braid in order to brush out his hair, just as he'd done for his own.

The boy made a small noise of protest.

"No?"

Waaseyaa flushed. "I'm too old for this."

"How old are you supposed to be?"

"Practically grown!"

"Oho?" Glint hid his smile. "Well, *I'm* not too old for this, and I can boast centuries."

"How many?"

He paused to ponder. It was harder to keep track without marking every Song Circle. Finally, he guessed, "Four, I think."

"Truly?"

Glint chuckled. "I will go on and on for ages innumerable, but you are young. Be young."

Waaseyaa's dark eyes slowly filled with tears, and he curled into Glint. "Promise?"

"What pledge do you need from me?"

"Go on and on?"

"Is that all?" Glint kissed the boy's forehead. "That's how I was made. I can share all your years, Waaseyaa. Gladly."

The boy burst into tears and didn't stop until he'd cried himself to sleep.

"I don't understand." Path's voice was taut with concern and confusion.

"Strong emotions can lead to tears," murmured Glint. "Consider them a compliment. He's found a safe place to let them fall."

"But I thought tears were a mark of sadness." Path snuffled lightly. *"This scent is different."*

"I know." Glint brushed hair away from Waaseyaa's forehead. He'd been close to a similarly complex scent once before—when Bel told him of his suitor. "These were tears of joy."

SEED

Glint watched Waaseyaa wake, let him wriggle free to attend to his morning needs, and welcomed him back to the warmth of the pack … all without a word. The boy crowded close, and Glint offered the smallest of hums to let him know he was listening.

With a sigh, Waaseyaa began, "I was born in a wood where trees still sang."

An old grove? Glint had never given much credence to the sagas of storytellers, but lore seemed to be springing to life all around him.

"I was born to be sent." Waaseyaa's voice was steady, sure. "I am part of the scattering."

Having himself been sent away from his home, Glint's hum held sympathy.

"I was …." Waaseyaa looked up, searching Glint's face as he revealed, "I was born with a seed in my hand."

Glint blinked. Is *this* what Brings the Wind had meant, calling Waaseyaa a twinned child? He quietly asked, "A golden seed?"

"Yes." The boy sat up and pulled at a cord around his neck. A small pouch hung from it, securely knotted. "I have a golden seed."

In the stories, such seeds were the blessing of Amaranthine trees. A child born holding one was meant to plant it and tend to their twin, and in exchange, they would share the tree's years.

Waaseyaa's tone wobbled. "My parents could not run when the foxes came. My aunts and uncles, my older sisters, my friends—they could not get away because they could not leave. We have always been tree-kin, and we share their roots."

No wonder he was rare. No wonder he had no rival. Glint tugged Waaseyaa back down, holding him gently, trying to give back a little of what he'd lost.

"I was afraid to plant it anywhere we've been since then." Waaseyaa looked away shyly. "Once I do, it will be forever. And that's a long time to be alone."

Glint understood then, and he knew what it meant for him. Even if his star were to move on, he would not follow. Not if it meant leaving Waaseyaa behind. "*All* your years, boy," he pledged anew. "Gladly."

Waaseyaa tried to keep from smiling and failed. He hid his face with both hands, only to giggle behind them. The whole pile woke to their father in a playful tussle with the boy whose happiness washed over their souls in heartening waves.

Near midday, voices approached the den, and Glint opened his door to Brings the Wind, who was arguing in hushed tones with Gerard. Even though he'd heard every word and knew their purpose, Glint held his peace.

"About yesterday." Brings the Wind's gaze sought and found Rile. "Your dog made a fine partner, and I do not see the harm in asking. What would you trade for one of them?"

Gerard was mumbling apologies, but Glint raised a hand.

"You've taken a liking to Rile?"

The man's eyes lit up. "I didn't know his name. A good name. Yes, Rile."

Glint turned to his son and asked, "And what do you think of this man?"

"Stubborn. Rash. Fearless." His jaw dropped in a doggish laugh. *"I like him."*

Brings the Wind had gone very still. "Why ask your animal for his opinion?"

"Rile is one of my Kith." Glint inclined his head toward Gerard. "As you've already been told, these dogs aren't merely intelligent. They are people."

"I thought it uncanny, the way he responded to my wishes during battle." Brings the Wind strode to Rile and flung his arms wide. "I am making a bad impression on the very one I want to impress. Will you forgive me?"

"See what I mean?" Rile was on the verge of laughter. *"He's not even afraid to admit he's a fool."*

Glint did appreciate honesty. And Rile's opinion mattered more than anyone else's on the matter. So he addressed himself to Brings the Wind. "He likes you."

Hope rekindled in the man's eyes, and he reached for Rile. "You do?"

"He certainly does, and if he wants to spend time with you, I won't stand in his way." Glint tried not to show how much the words cost. "Rile is an adult and free to choose. If you can make peace with him, you will gain a lifelong friend."

A few years passed, and Wardenclave's foundations took shape.

The encircling wall gained height and breadth, and the cleared space in the village center became a proper Song Circle. Colt Alpenglow sowed the wide meadow with fragrant grasses, and Bram helped him set saplings in a ring around its edge. Glint suspected that the original plan had been for Waaseyaa to plant his golden seed in the middle, but the boy's twin had taken root beside his den's door.

The Starmark pack expanded by several litters, and Kith had become something of a commodity. Glint chose not to discuss his role as parent to the first generation of Kith, who were now spending more of their time in various households throughout Wardenclave. Only Path remained a constant in the home den.

Children arrived in the village, some by birth, others because Gerard still searched for those touched by the power that set apart Reaver's people. Glint agreed with Linlu that the trait was hereditary, so he took an interest in bloodlines.

Glint was soon branded a matchmaker.

Not *entirely* fair, given his pragmatic streak. As far as he was concerned, the preservation of reavers—as he'd begun to call them—was served as much by propagation as by protection.

TIME

Waaseyaa surged through adolescence with a speed that unsettled Glint. After promising to be there for all his years, they seemed determined to slip away. His boy was a boy no longer. And his interests would soon lead him elsewhere. Not far, of course. But not *here*. With a pang of loneliness, Glint pulled Waaseyaa closer.

That earned him a grunt, and a sleep-husky voice asked, "What is it?"

"My pup has reached his attainment and will leave my den to make his own." He injected a piteous note into his complaint. "Is my loyalty not enough?"

A slim brown hand patted his. "You're a good friend, Glint, but you're not the one I've been courting."

"I cannot fault your preference for Hemet's daughter. Only your decision to take her elsewhere. You would have been welcome here."

Waaseyaa snorted. "That might have proven awkward."

"In what sense?"

The young man patiently pointed out, "There's only one bed."

"And I have always been willing to share it."

One eye opened. "Are you done teasing?"

Glint grumbled, "What kind of question is that?"

"A futile one. You *enjoy* teasing me."

"I will do so for as long as I can, if not longer." He rumbled his contentment. "I do not begrudge you your mate. Go to her. Be fruitful, multiply. May your progeny be many and bright."

"What about you?" asked Waaseyaa.

Not this again. "Have you been talking to Path?"

"You know I can't hear Kith voices."

Glint grinned. "A mercy, I assure you."

Waaseyaa pressed, "Couldn't we find you a mate? Bram and Linlu managed."

"That's entirely different. They were already promised before making their journey to Wardenclave." He mussed the young man's hair. "Secure your own happiness, for it has become mine."

When Waaseyaa became a father, he had barely achieved his second decade, which was typical of the other humans in the village. Wardenclave celebrated. Their beacon had a son. The future would be bright. All was as it should be.

A little more time passed, and Waaseyaa's wife gave him a second and a third child—both daughters—each a dazzling addition to the reaver community. However, with the arrival of a fourth child, Glint noticed a change. Or rather, a lack of change.

Waaseyaa remained a youth of twenty, while his wife grew worn by years of carrying and caring. People remarked, and her customary smiles grew strained. Affection faltered, and no more children were conceived. Glint tried to speak with her, but her hurt ran deep. Waaseyaa's joy faltered, and Glint found that sadness, too, could be shared.

In a few more years Waaseyaa was almost indistinguishable from his eldest son, and the rift became a chasm. Waaseyaa quietly moved back into Glint's den.

"You were raised among trees." Glint cradled the man who was no longer young, despite appearances. "Did you know this might happen?"

Waaseyaa nodded.

Glint swallowed further comment. His boy stank of heartbreak and regret. What use were should-haves and could-haves?

"I knew, but I loved her." He nestled closer. "I thought it would be enough."

He loosened Waaseyaa's hair as he used to, dragging his fingers through its length. His boy might not be growing any older, but his hair continued to grow. "Is this why you planted your seed beside my door instead of your own?"

"It was easier to be brave knowing that you would take me back." Waaseyaa hid his face and mumbled, "Did I betray her?"

"Have you been loyal to the one you chose?" Glint asked. Not because he needed to inquire, but because Waaseyaa needed reminding.

"I have!"

"You devoted yourself to her happiness and shared it?"

"I did." Emotions played across his face. "I still will."

Glint's heart ached for the boy. "You left for her sake."

"Yes." Waaseyaa's lips trembled. "It was the only thing she wanted. The only thing left to do."

Over the next few days, Glint told Waaseyaa about the dogs he'd taken to his heart over the years. Because they had each taught him the everyday truths he now lived by. Simple lessons. That he was not made to be alone. That lives are all the more precious for their brevity. That words have power, be they promises, songs, or names. That heartache was true love's twin. And that life and death and change were part of going on and on.

"Our children," Waaseyaa said, his smile coming more easily. "We have fine children."

"None finer," Glint agreed. "Next time you take a wife, you

must explain things carefully. She must know the consequences of wedding herself to tree-kin."

Waaseyaa looked stunned. "I *have* a wife, even if she doesn't want me. And I really don't think there can ever *be* a next time."

"Remain loyal," Glint agreed. "But by and by, you should take a new mate. If not for yourself, then for the sake of the village. Your children outshine those of every other reaver."

"I ... I can't." Eyes on the ground, he muttered, "Who would want such a husband?"

"You might be surprised." Glint took his chin, forcing Waaseyaa to lift his eyes. "You are strong and comely, and your children are the pride of Wardenclave. When the time comes, we'll have Linlu begin a registry so that the names of your wives will stand alongside yours for all time. You will live to see their strength and beauty passed on to future generations."

Waaseyaa spoke haltingly, pleadingly. "Even Sanne?"

Glint rumbled approvingly. "Honor her in your heart and in our history—Sanne, First of Wards."

MOON

Not many years later, in the midst of a restless winter's night, Glint paced Wardenclave's new perimeter, which encompassed a much wider swath of territory. Much of the Denholm range had effectually disappeared, thanks to an intricate combination of sigil-based illusions—anchored by crystals, powered by reavers. But Gerard's son and successor was a cautious man, and Glint was inherently protective of their home. Their guard never wavered.

As he walked through heavy woodland, casually checking each ward in passing, Glint met a reaver coming in the other direction—Brings the Wind's granddaughter astride Rile. He lifted his hand, and she reached down. Their fingertips brushed, the same shy greeting they'd exchanged since she was small.

"How goes the night watch?" he asked.

Summer Breeze peered back the way they'd come, her lips pursed. "There is a wolf."

"I wouldn't worry. They'll catch the scent of the Demon Dogs of Denholm and steer clear."

"But Rile has been restless," she persisted. "He doesn't like this one, and it's getting closer."

"Oh?" Glint took his son's muzzle in both hands. "That's unusual."

"That's no ordinary wolf," said Rile. *"He has a voice."*

"You don't like the sound of him?"

Rile hesitated. *"I don't know. Maybe they are lost. Or lost someone. It worries me."*

Glint turned his head in the direction Summer Breeze had indicated, senses straining.

"I don't know if it's a word or a name," said Rile. *"But it sounds like he's calling ... Loor-ket."*

He grunted in surprise.

"Father?"

Glint roughed up his son's fur and smiled at his rider. "Don't worry, Summer Breeze. I'll check on the wolf and see if it intends us any mischief."

He walked to the crest of one of Denholm's foothills, a hilltop meadow where they sometimes grazed their flocks and herds. The moon was new, which allowed the lesser lights to rule the long night. Half a lifetime ago, he'd walked away from his home, slowly chasing his choices across snowfields to this place. Would he need to answer for those choices now?

Glint folded his arms over his chest and set his jaw. He would stand by them.

Finally, a howl cut through the night. Glint hadn't realized how high his hopes had been until they came crashing down. It wasn't Bel. His brother hadn't come searching.

Why would he?

Glint couldn't begin to fathom who else might care enough to track a centuries-gone loner. But he filled his lungs and let loose with a shrill whistle.

The hunter wasn't even trying for stealth. At a crashing in the underbrush, Glint turned in time to see a wolf bound into the open, pale as moonlight, tail flagging eagerness and joy.

Not a member of the Highwind pack.

His mystification momentarily deepened when the wolf tumbled into transformation and kept running on legs no less roughened by fur. Those ears, that tail. In his final leap, the young male was reaching with clawed hands, but Glint didn't even try to defend himself, only braced himself for the oncoming collision.

The Kith-kin wasn't going for his throat.

Arms wrapped around his neck, and breathless laughter came with a husky chant. "Found you, found you, found you!"

"Moon-kin!" Glint returned the fierce hug, if a bit bemusedly.

"Why are you here?"

"To find you." Moon stepped back and grinned with fierce triumph. "I had to keep my promise."

The scruffy whelp was gone, replaced by a fine figure of an adult—well-muscled and bristling with confidence. Moon was more animal than most Amaranthine, but he was clearly at ease in his form.

Startled, but glad, Glint pulled him into another embrace, welcoming him as he would a friend or packmate, ally or son. "What a chase you must have had."

"You have no idea." Moon butted his head under Glint's chin, as if he were a pup again. "I've been searching for a long time."

He stroked the younger wolf's hair and scratched affectionately behind canine ears. "Why would you need a loner like me?"

"I promised Marnoo."

Glint shook his head. "How is your fosterling?"

"She's strong, and her will is stronger." Easing from Glint's embrace, the young wolf drew himself up to answer more formally. "I am Marnoo-vel Ambervelte's go-between. She will have you and no other."

He stared blankly at Moon. Finally, he held up two hands, describing the size of the wolf cub he'd rescued so many years ago. "Your half-sister."

Moon lifted a hand, indicating a height close to his own. "My half-sister."

Glint rubbed at his forehead. Cubs did grow, and the centuries were sufficient to have brought Moon and Marnoo to adulthood. But this made no sense. "I met you once and briefly. We shared stories in a snowbank until you fell asleep, and I carried you to your people. That's all."

"You made a lasting impression."

On a cub not even weaned? Glint was increasingly perplexed. "That was never my intent."

"Yet to Marnoo, you are the scent of stars, the voice of an angel, and the hope of all her somedays." Moon searched his face, utterly serious. "Are you bonded to another? Promised?"

"No, there is no one here. I am ... well, I'm not *alone*." Glint didn't know where to begin. "My situation is complicated."

"Complexities are not objections." Moon's eyes sparkled. "Tell on!"

Glint bluntly stated, "I have no tail."

"I noticed."

"I'm no longer a wolf." Chin lifting, Glint announced, "I'm a dog."

Moon waited for several beats, then asked, "Tamed and tailless? Is that all?"

"No. I have a clan ... allies ... responsibilities."

"A clan? Do you want to appoint a go-between as well?" His ears swiveled as a voice reached the both of them.

"I will speak for my father." Path strolled into the open, head high and proud. *"He is Glint Starmark, First of Dogs, Friend of Beacons, Founder of Wardenclave."*

Glint huffed at the stiff boast and gestured between them. "This is my eldest son Path. I have become a Kith-sire."

"I am Moon-kin Ambervelte." He hurried to Path. "My half-sister is full-blooded like your father, and he is her choice. Would the pack accept her pursuit?"

"Wholeheartedly." Path touched his nose to Moon's brow. *"The stars have been singing about you. I didn't realize the* chasing moon *would be a wolf."*

The Kith-kin's tail wagged. "Our coming was foretold?"

Our. Glint had thought Moon was alone. He cast about with his senses.

Moon went right on, "If I am the moon, then Marnoo is its radiance."

Why did those words sound familiar?

And ... someone was nearby. He could feel a close-kept presence, like a huntress on the prowl. But before he could decide what to do, Moon was standing before him, proffering a small cloth-wrapped parcel.

Glint gasped and took it with reverent desperation. Because it smelled like his twin.

COMB

"A betrothal gift," said Moon. "Prepared for Marnoo-vel by Beloor-dex Ambervelte with every blessing ... and a promise."

Glint slowly unfolded the rippling copper cloth, which concealed a comb—a traditional courting gift—decorated with delicate clusters of stars. His brother's own handiwork. An intensely personal gift.

Moon spoke gently. "If you wish it, he will come to stand by your side and bear witness to your bonding."

"Bel would come here?"

"He has promised it."

Glint's emotions were already a mess when Moon's and Path's gazes swung to the same spot. A white wolf stepped into the open. She'd been a pretty cub, but Glint never would have recognized the oncoming she-wolf as that whimpering fuzz ball. *Beautiful* fell short. Marnoo was exquisite—fine-figured, graceful, and direct. He couldn't look away from those astonishing copper eyes, even as she took speaking form.

"Hello," he offered a little breathlessly.

She prowled around him, looking him over, testing the air, taking her time.

Glint flushed, suddenly conscious that he wore his shabbiest breeches and scuffed boots. Having rolled out of bed to stalk the perimeter, he was unbrushed, unkempt, and probably smelled strongly of Waaseyaa.

But Marnoo paused to trail her finger along the ornate embroidery decorating his tunic. Approval shone in her gaze. "You are arrayed as finely as a lord at his bonding feast. And those you keep closest have covered you in the scents of peace, trust, and power."

He was utterly tongue-tied.

"That's good, right?" Path asked, *"Now what?"*

Marnoo's lips curved. "Glint Starmark, First of Dogs, Friend of Beacons, Founder of Wardenclave, has my journey been worthwhile? Or will you send me into solitude?"

Glint sort of figured that her options weren't quite so limited. Nor was she any more alone than he was. Moon was a solid presence, looking on with an indulgent expression. But Glint knew what she meant, so he said, "It's not good to be alone."

Path asked, *"How do we accept?"*

"An exchange," prompted Moon.

Marnoo eased into Glint's personal space, touched his cheek, then placed a staggeringly possessive kiss on his lips. "If you can tame me, I will take your name. If you claim me, our clan will increase in strength and beauty."

She was quite … charismatic. Glint felt a little cornered and entirely outmatched. But humbled by this latest gift from the Maker's hand. With the music of stars teasing at the far reaches of his senses, he tucked his brother's gift into his sash in order to reach for her hands.

Low and gruff, he said, "For a gift. May I give you a name?"

Her brows arched. "Choose well."

Glint pressed his lips to her forehead, lingering there, savoring the moment. Was this how it was for Bel, being chosen, having a choice? When Glint drew back, he was astonished to see a tiny silvery star marked her brow. Had it always been there?

No.

His heart swelled with awe and pride. His mark. His mate.

She tilted her chin invitingly, so he kissed her lips. Everything was happening so fast—finding, feeling, falling. But his blood sang a true note, and she whispered encouragement. So Glint Starmark faced his future and gave her a name. "Radiance."

TREE

Several decades had passed since Waaseyaa planted the golden seed beside Glint's front step. Neither of them had known quite what to expect. Under Waaseyaa's careful watch, the tree took to earth and sky, gaining height with surprising speed, then doubling and tripling its girth until they had to move the threshold.

Glint tried to salvage the den by removing one wall, but the antiquated structure teetered into a heap that was little better than kindling. Radiance eagerly suggested a few changes when they rebuilt, and Glint belatedly realized that his bondmate was a patient, uncomplaining soul. They'd been living in a crowded shed for far too long.

With an eye to the future, they designed a spacious home with two ways in. One faced the village, a public entrance to the clan home of one of Wardenclave's five Amaranthine founders. The second entrance remained private, with its threshold resettled at what Waaseyaa deemed a safe distance from his tree.

Here, Waaseyaa had a little home of his own, looking out over the same old pasture where Glint still romped with the new generations of Kith pups born to the pack. Both the pasture and the tree towering over it were still heavily warded against notice. Thanks to Salali's expertise, citizens of Wardenclave tended to forget that Waaseyaa's twin dominated the mountaintop.

Once they were sure of the variety, Linlu Dimityblest disappeared for several seasons, traveling to one of the secret communities where the remnants of ancient groves clung to life. Without ever saying where he'd been or how he'd managed it, the moth clansman returned with five children in tow. Each wearing a special pendant, each carrying a golden seed.

The Alpenglow clan prepared homes at a modest distance from the Starmark holdings—three hilltops over and downwind. The horse clan became companions and caretakers for the children, whose plantings were the beginnings of a new grove.

"Why not closer to Waaseyaa?" grumbled Glint. "Two of them are girls; one of them might have made a good bride."

Linlu nodded sympathetically. "Who knows how much havoc one tree may cause? *Especially* if Waaseyaa's twin manifests as a female. Better to watch and wait, lest we take an unwise step."

Glint paused and paled. "Do you mean to say that the stories about the fruit of an Amaranthine tree are true?"

"Quite ... efficacious," Linlu said mildly.

"And the pollen itself?" he asked, gazing warily up into the branches overshadowing his home.

"Intoxicating." With a soft smile and a suggestive hand gesture, he added, "Invigorating."

"How often does it bloom?"

"The interval is usually five years."

Glint cleared his throat. "Is *this* the reason more than half of the females in the village are carrying?"

"Your bondmate included." Linlu laughed softly. "Congratulations."

He wasn't entirely sure why he should be so embarrassed. Linlu's family saw such regular additions, they already boasted a tribute. "A baby boom can only benefit the community."

"Agreed. The reavers are no longer in danger of disappearing, and the tree-kin have found another safe haven." The moth's gaze lingered on the large tree. "We are making a difference."

That same autumn, the cry came.

"Glint! Glint, I need you!"

There were times when it was difficult for Glint to maintain his self-imposed pace, but he managed to keep to an admittedly brisk walk in answer to his boy's call. Bursting through his back door, he stumbled to a halt before Waaseyaa.

He sat amidst roots that rose in smooth swirls, tangling around Waaseyaa's customary spot as if creating a throne for him. And he was hugging a naked child with a headful of blossoms where his hair should be.

Waaseyaa's eager expression told Glint everything, but he still asked, "What have we here?"

"My brother woke up."

The child was a beauty, with skin like fine-grained wood and thick-lashed eyes with a decidedly seductive tilt. Outwardly, he couldn't have been older than six, but Glint could tell he'd be trouble once he grew into the saucy allure for which storybook trees were famed.

Glint crouched before the pair and reached out to gently touch the cascade of sunset orange petals.

The tree-child caught and kissed his hand.

"Affectionate," Glint remarked.

Waaseyaa's lips quirked. "Extremely."

Glint sat on the ground, held out both hands, and found himself with his arms around a fabled imp. Would wonders never cease? "Do you have a name, boy? Or must I guess?"

"Brother named me." With a flash of dimples and a flutter of lashes, he sweetly said, "I am Zisa."

"It means *orange*," Waaseyaa murmured.

"Welcome, Zisa. We've been waiting for you."

"I know." The child was suddenly nose-to-nose with Glint. "I know *everything*."

Glint rolled his eyes toward Waaseyaa. "Precocious."

"Endearingly."

Waaseyaa showed every sign of being smitten with his impish counterpart. That was good. He needed a distraction, and Zisa seemed the sort of boy to ... well, to demand too much attention. Glint decided that counted as a family resemblance.

"Here, I have kept my word." Glint couldn't help feeling relieved by the wild beat of Path's tail against the ground. Slouching into the Kith's bulk, he showed off his newborn son, swaddled in a blanket he'd embellished himself, its frippery and flourishes only partially disguising the protective sigils he'd worked into the soft cloth Radiance had loomed from several brushings of the Starmark clan. "I think there's a resemblance."

Thick auburn fuzz was already long enough to curl over ears that came to perfect points.

"*My brother.*" Path sounded awed.

"Yes. You and he are both firstborn." Glint looked up into Path's face. "You each bear a great responsibility to our pack."

"*Did you name him?*"

"Oh, indeed." Glint tickled the pup's cheek, encouraging him to open copper eyes.

The little one's nose twitched, his lips pursed, and without any additional warning, he opened his mouth and howled.

Path was snickering, and Glint chuckled as well.

"Did you call him Noisy?"

"Apt though your suggestion may be, it's too late. Radiance and I agreed. We've named him for the future. This is Harmonious."

THE END

FOLLOWED BY THUNDER

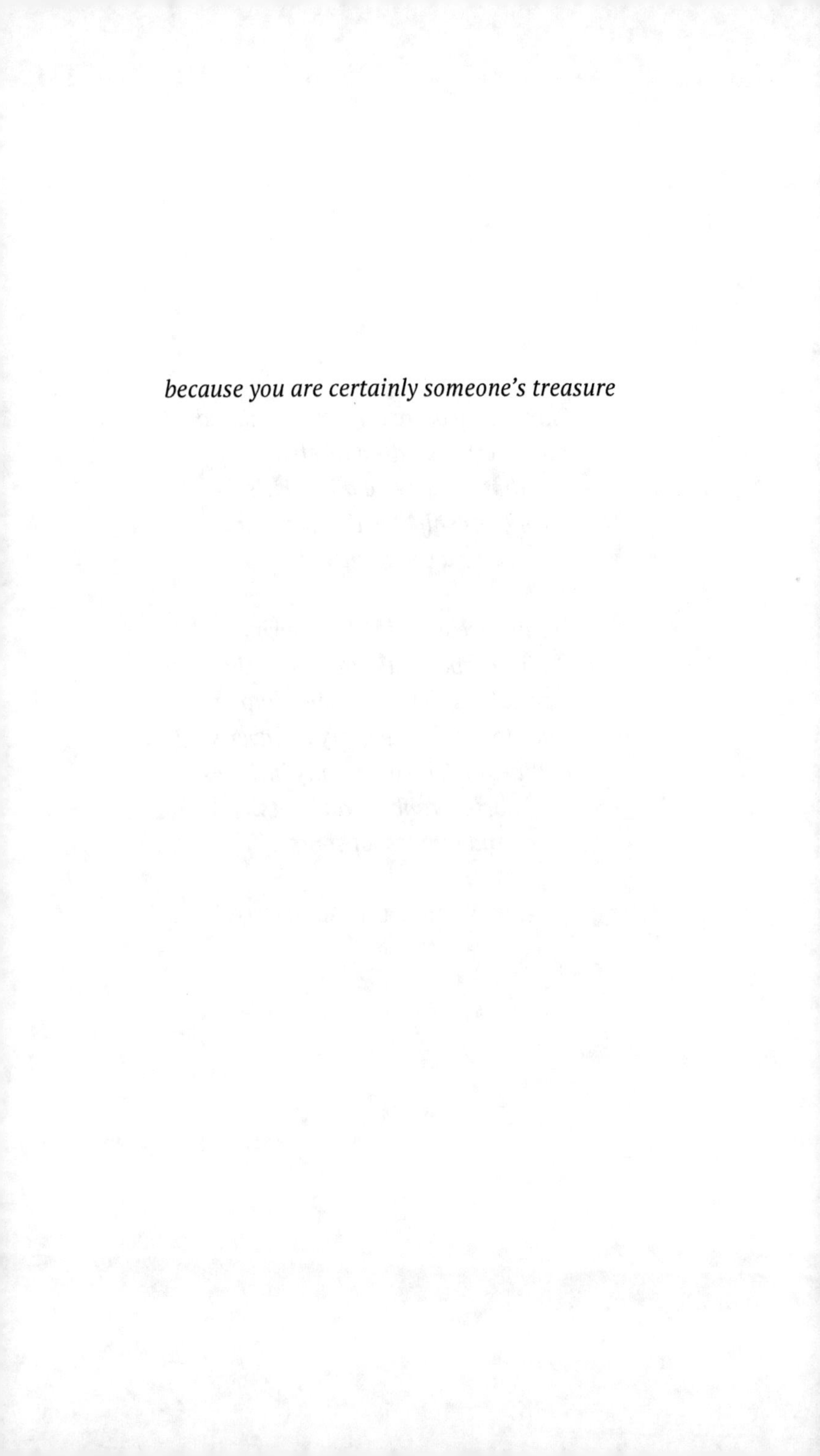

because you are certainly someone's treasure

*Tsumiko inspected the crest painted
on the crate's lid—a faceted flower
that looked like a jeweler's
workmanship. "Is this for a clan
or a cooperative?"*

*Michael set aside his crowbar.
"Glintrubble is a cooperative that
specializes in mining and shaping
the stones that amplify a reaver's
abilities. Their community includes
horses, rabbits, and bats.
And reavers, of course."*

TSUMIKO AND THE ENSLAVED FOX

CURSE BRINGERS

ira pulled her sister along, keeping her upright, urging her forward, praying she wouldn't look back. *Why* must they repay every kindness with a curse?

"Was it a dragon?" Lufu asked, her voice barely heard over the rain.

"It was."

"Is it gone?" Lufu's green eyes were too wide, her chin atremble.

"Let us hope so."

Clutching one hand over her heart, she said, "I am hoping hard."

Fira pushed impatiently at sodden hair and squinted at the sky, searching for bearings. The storm lashed on all sides, rain sheeting around them in pitiless torrents. Chilled to the bone, she was grateful, nonetheless. This endless drenching might be the *only* reason the monster hadn't seen them, smelled them, caught them.

"Is it my fault?" Lufu's voice quavered.

Fira stopped and pulled her younger sister into a fierce hug. At fifteen, Lufu was reckoned a woman grown, but her innocence made her seem more like a child. One in desperate need of protection … and reassurance. "*Not* your fault, Lufu," Fira said in her most commanding tone. "If anything, it was me. I stayed too long."

Lufu leaned into Fira's larger frame, confessing, "It was nice to stay. I liked them."

"And they liked you. But it is better for them if we move along." Assuming the dragon hadn't already taken out its frustration on the tidy farmstead. Fira had seen one of the milk cows carried off, and she feared for both the herd and its herders.

They'd been taken in by a soft-spoken farmer and his kind-hearted wife, whose reasons were plain enough—six strapping sons. Fira had firmly ignored the bashful looks and clumsy advances of the older boys. Still, the settled prosperity of their farm had tempted her to linger, and the second son had an admittedly nice smile. So when the missus kept finding little ways to delay the girls' departure, Fira had been fool enough to hope it would be different this time.

"Are Henry and Roger angry?" Lufu asked.

The littler boys had been all mischief and play, always begging for dares and boasting of heroic deeds. If Fira had wanted to shift blame, they were owed a share for hastening the disaster.

Fira asked, "How did they get your rock?"

"They asked to see it." Lufu ducked her head. "I only meant to show it."

"I know how they can be." She doubted the boys had planned to keep the chunk of crystal for themselves, but they'd run off with Lufu's lucky stone. It had always been with them. A link to a childhood that was more nightmare than memory. Their charm against the monsters.

Bad things happened when Lufu left it or lost it, so Fira made sure to stitch a hidden pocket into whatever rags they found to wear.

Lufu knew it was best kept secret. But the boys must have twitted her somehow—about her darker skin or her accent—or wheedled her into comparing treasures. And they'd snatched it. No sooner had Henry and Roger vanished behind the barn, the winds whipped up and the sky boiled black, and a dragon fell upon the farm like a blade of lightning.

Cows bawled.

Hens scattered.

Men shouted.

Fira had listened to Lufu's teary explanation and bolted after the boys, half-dragging her sister. She knew where the stone was, and she knew they must get it back. Even if Fira didn't know *why*, those two things had always been true.

That single stone was their parents' only legacy, a rough-hewn gem, clear as air, with winking facets and the tiniest kernel of yellow at its heart. Even at their coldest and hungriest, they never would have sold it. Some things were more precious than temporary comfort.

When Fira reclaimed it from the two quaking boys and bid them hide in the creek bottom, the sky had opened up, drowning the fields, covering their escape.

"How much further?" asked Lufu. "Will there be a house?"

With no answer to give, Fira kept silent.

"Fira?"

"I am here."

"Even a cave might be good."

She gave her sister's hand a squeeze. "If I spot one, we will stop."

But there was nothing to see but a gray and growling sky, hardscrabble rock, and an inhospitable expanse of scrub and shrubs that caught and tore at their heavy skirts.

A terrifying roar pierced the murk.

"Is it c-c-coming?" Lufu's teeth had begun to chatter.

Fira pointed to a small tumble of stones just visible through the spatter of raindrops, the first shelter she'd glimpsed. "There!"

Without another word, both girls picked up their skirts and ran.

THUNDERING HOOVES

The heap of boulders was farther than it seemed and bigger than it looked, but it made for a meager shelter. Huddling against bare stone was no kind of safety. Fira circled the haphazard monolith, but found no crack, no crevice, no burrow to hide them.

In the distance, the nightmare beast shrieked.

Lufu was sobbing now.

"The stone," Fira said. "Let me hold it."

Over the years, they'd realized that the stone liked Lufu better. It hid her from the beasts and soothed away bad dreams, so she curled around it to sleep. But when Fira held the crystal, it sparked and snarled like a cornered cat, all arched back and puffed tail and bared fangs. More than once, the monsters had recoiled as if stung and fled before the stone in Fira's hands.

She couldn't hide from them, but she could hurt them.

If only she could keep them from coming back.

A shrill roar came from closer quarters, and Fira whispered words of love, kissed Lufu's forehead, and took the crystal. It had to work. It would.

Lightning briefly blinded her, and thunder cracked directly overhead, but its rumble didn't fade. The noise kept building until it shook the very ground underfoot. Fira grabbed Lufu's hand. Something was coming. Something *big*.

"What is it?" her sister cried.

"I do not know! I cannot see!"

All of a sudden, the wind changed, whipping around them, pushing back the rain, clearing her view. Fira stood in the center of a whirlwind, frightened as much by the freakish weather as by the danger it revealed. A bronze dragon with red eyes and curling horns crouched upon the stony jumble, poised to spring.

Fira whirled, placing Lufu behind her. Raising the crystal between two hands, she shouted, "No!"

Fear and fury and frustration crackled in the usual way, but this time, it was as if her feelings were too much for the stone to contain. So they were flung outward, zinging like an arrow from the bow, striking the dragon with enough force to fling it backward over the rock.

Hands pulled at her arms.

Words buffeted her ears.

She shook her ringing head and let the stone drop from stinging fingers. There was blood. She was bleeding?

"Do you hear that?" Lufu's words finally filtered through. She was clinging to Fira, voice gaining the heights of hysteria. "What is it?"

Thunder.

And then horses broke into view, coming from behind. Massive animals, thick-bodied and triple Fira's height. They parted before the sisters, who clung to one another, shocked to find themselves amidst a stampede.

Rolling eyes. Pounding hooves.

Heavy feathering. Streaming manes.

Where had they all come from?

Lufu bent to rescue their stone from being trampled.

Without warning, a man tumbled out of nowhere, rolling to his feet before them. He was strangely dressed, big and broad, with gingered hair that was shaved up on both sides. The resulting mane exposed his ears, which were sharp as an elf's.

What manner of person was he?

"This is not a safe place." He extended a hand, saying, "Come with us."

Fira pushed Lufu out of sight, but there was nowhere to hide. They were an island in a river of horseflesh. All she could do was shake her head and glare.

The herd's stragglers passed by, and the stranger spoke again. "Can you ride?"

One of the horses had stopped—an imposing stallion with a golden coat and pale mane. He stamped an impatient hoof.

"He will let you ride." The man was easing closer, empty hands extended, gaze pleading for cooperation. "Let us get you out of here."

Fira's warning glare was wasted, for Lufu stepped forward.

"Here is a brave one," he murmured, and swung Lufu up onto the waiting horse's back. He turned back to Fira, eyebrow arched in silent challenge. As if calling her courage into question.

So she relented. But not without serious doubts. She could tell their stone buzzed with warnings. It was good that Lufu held the rock again. Let her quiet it. Let it calm her.

Then the man lifted Fira, and she quailed at his touch. He was different. He was other. He was one of them. But how was that possible? Her skirts distracted her, ending in an indecent tangle about her thighs. Fira tried to right them and slipped sideways.

He caught her by one stockinged ankle and urged, "Grip with your knees."

But how could she? People might remark upon her height—gawky, coltish, angular—but even *her* legs couldn't straddle a horse of this girth. Lufu was even worse off. Their mount shifted beneath them, and both girls squeaked in alarm.

"Never ridden?"

That much should have been obvious.

He made an odd sound deep in his chest and slapped the stallion's neck. "Apologies, brother."

The horse shook its mane, as if asserting an opinion, and then the man was seated snug against Fira's back. Wrapping one arm around both her and Lufu, he grabbed a fistful of mane and called, "Onward!"

A forward leap drove Fira into the strange man's chest. Far below, hooves pounded wet sod, and she lurched with the unfamiliar cadences of trot, canter, and gallop. She locked both her arms around Lufu, who was keening in the back of her throat.

"Hold the rock." Fira spoke into her sister's ear. "Keep it safe."

Lufu turned her face, pressing into Fira as the rain found them again, stinging now with the addition of speed.

When the noise vanished, Fira stiffened in surprise just as Lufu shrieked. The stallion still moved beneath them, muscles bunching, stride rolling, but the ground had vanished. All Fira could see below was the sheeting rain.

"What happened?" she demanded, voice taut.

The surrounding arm tightened, and the man spoke loud enough for both to hear. "We are flying, of course. And you are completely safe. I promise."

Flying. Since when did horses fly?

Fira twisted to look up into the face of the person who was either their rescuer or their captor. The elfin ears weren't the only thing wrong with him. From this proximity, she could see that his brown eyes were struck through with pupils like thorns. The same as every creature who'd ever overturned a village or farm to find them.

"Please, do not be afraid. Bavol and I are not any kind of threat." His face was smooth as a boy's, and its expression oddly hopeful. "Better us than the dragon."

She couldn't argue the point, but she didn't know his purposes. Were she and Lufu being carried off by fae creatures? For all she knew, they'd fallen in with some new breed of monster, one with a comelier face.

No armor. No weapons. That had to count for something. No leer. She'd learned to be wary of grasping, greedy men who were no better than monsters. But the deciding factor was far from heartening. No choice.

"Well met." He let go the stallion's mane and displayed a big hand. "I am called Ricker. May I know your names?"

Again, it was Lufu who acted first. Flashing a shy dimple, she settled her palm onto the big hand, which closed around hers. She said, "I am Lufu. This is Fira."

Fira would have liked to withhold her name, but Lufu had always been more generous, more trusting.

"Lufu," he repeated.

The gentling of Ricker's expression teased a sliver of Fira's trampled trust into the open, so when he offered his palm to her, she let her fingertips rest there and was rewarded with a grin.

"Fira," he said, sounding glad to know it.

"Where are you taking us?" she demanded.

"Home." Ricker pointed, even though there was nothing to see but swirling gray in every direction. "Our home is well-hidden. No dragon could ever find it."

"What about foxes?" asked Fira, for dragons weren't their only trouble. "Or cats. Or stoats. Or owls. Or bears."

Ricker's laugh reminded her of a horse's nicker. "You have had your share of trouble."

He said it as if he thought their troubles were over. Fira dared not believe it. They might elude the monsters for a little while, but they always returned. Always.

"No," said Ricker. "None of those. Glintrubble is home to rabbits and rock collectors. And horses, of course."

HORSE CLAN

Fira couldn't even begin to guess how far they'd traveled before their flying steed's hoofbeats returned. They landed on a patch of moor that looked the same as any other patch of moor, yet the stallion seemed to know that they'd arrived. He danced sideways, giving a small shake.

Ricker laughed his odd laugh. "Steady, and we will be off. We would not want the mares to get ideas."

The stallion held still long enough for Ricker to slide off and ferry the girls safely to the ground. Fira swayed in place, muscles quivering, bones aching, and chilled through. The rain had stopped, but she and Lufu were soaked and shivering.

What now? Would the man reveal himself to be a monster? Would she and Lufu meet their end in a landscape empty of hope or help?

But a very different revelation was in store, for Bavol the stallion reared back on his hind legs.

"We should give him some room," said Ricker, taking the sisters each by a shoulder.

Fira frowned at the touch, more from confusion than displeasure. That's when the horse they'd been riding vanished in a flurry of scattering light, which condensed into the form of a man. She stepped back fast, ramming into Ricker, who seemed to think she needed coddling. Part of her protested his sheltering arm, but a larger part noticed how much heat he radiated. And him in little more than shirtsleeves.

Bavol was similarly dressed in a loose shirt that hardly seemed warm enough for the weather. His pants were of fine cloth, which flowed with his movements, catching and clinging with every shift of his muscles. The horse-turned-man shared similar features to Ricker, but his hair was so fair, it neared white, and his eyes were a soft gray that made the narrowed pupil more obvious.

He was beautiful.

And now that Fira had some basis for comparison, she decided that Ricker looked and acted younger. Bavol's carriage and composure gave him an air of greater maturity.

With cordial solemnity, he presented his hands to her and Lufu, a more formal version of Ricker's earlier greeting. "I am Ricker's brother Bavol. You have entered the safety of our herd. Rest, assured of your welcome."

Quite the gentleman.

She and Lufu returned his touch, and he immediately frowned. "They are all but frozen!"

Ricker flinched. "How was I to warm them?"

With a gusty sigh, Bavol scooped up Lufu and strode off. "Bring her!" he called over his shoulder. "All will be lost if they sicken."

"You heard him," grumbled Ricker, reaching for Fira.

"I can walk."

"Bear with me a little longer," he murmured, acknowledging her protest while completely ignoring it. Pulling off his shirt, he wrapped it around her head and shoulder and hauled her into his arms. "The lead mare is a healer. Once you are safe in her care, I will leave you in peace."

Fira fixed her gaze on Bavol's broad back, not wanting to let Lufu out of her sight. "What kind of people are you?" she asked.

Ricker puffed out his chest and took a bragging tone. "We are the strength of the Thunderhoof clan, sons of the First Herd, sired by Dwennon."

She knew little of animal husbandry, but he almost made it sound like he was a horse. Were his people herdsmen, then? Or was he like his brother?

"Are you a stallion, too?" she asked.

Bavol glanced back. "He is a strong colt of the herd."

Ricker's cheeks pinkened, and he seemed disgruntled. "I have reached my attainment," he protested.

"Years do not make the stallion, little brother. The mares do."

His jaw worked, but Ricker dredged up a smile, albeit strained. "*For now,*" he said with pointed emphasis, "I am Colt Ricker Thunderhoof."

"Friendship begins with the exchange of names," said Bavol. "Two brothers, two sisters. It is a good balance."

Fira felt duty-bound to warn these brothers. "They say we are cursed."

"Who does?" asked Ricker.

"People." She lowered her voice. "All the farms, all the villages, everywhere we go, the monsters follow."

Ricker shook his head. "Where we are going, they cannot. I promise, Glintrubble is a good place."

"Why?"

His eyebrow lifted. "Why is it good?"

"Why take me and my sister there? We are not like you."

His gaze softened again, and his smile seemed more at home on his face. "You are not the first we found. You will be good company for Willum."

LEAD MARE

Fira woke to the murmur of voices—a man's and a woman's. No, that wasn't right. She'd fallen in with some gentler version of monsters, so the voices belonged to a stallion and a mare. Or a colt like Ricker. Which likely meant that *filly* was a possibility.

"... the dragon?" asked the female, sounding concerned.

"Beyond help." After a short pause, the male ventured, "Would you have given aid?"

"I *am* a healer."

Fira remembered a little, then. Glimpses of low stone buildings and rich hangings, of hot broth and warm beds. Bavol and Ricker had given her and Lufu to some women—mares—and left them to be stripped and dosed and bundled. Fira had been no match for the weariness that dragged her into darkness.

The male was speaking. "He was lost to baser instincts. His end was just and merciful."

Whose end? The dragon's? Was it dead, then?

"We shall mourn his passing."

A low noise—impatient, derisive.

The mare's voice again—challenging, chiding. "No matter what he became, he was once deemed *good* by the Maker. Every life is a treasure; every loss is a tragedy."

"Lead the mares as you will." His voice took on a more playful lilt. "She is awake."

"Go. You can ply her with charms and flirt with her innocence another time, once she is properly warned against you."

"Do you think so little of me?" he asked warmly.

With matching affection, she countered, "Do you think so much of yourself?"

"Mostly, I think of you."

Fira turned her head and blinked to focus on the pair framed by the open door. They reminded her of the sunrise, pale and shining, as they moved gracefully through some kind of walking dance. Circling. Touching. Twining.

The eyes that caught her looking were the same gray as Bavol's, and he lifted an eyebrow in the same manner as Ricker. Smirking at Fira, he bent to bestow another kiss upon the lady's smile, then swept away.

Fira scrunched down when the woman—mare—came to sit on the edge of the high bed. She had the appearance of a tall, stately woman, big-boned, yet balanced, all full figure and flowing hair. Her ears pointed, and her pupils were narrow slits within settings of topaz.

"I am Myla. How are you feeling, Fira?"

Cold. Achy. Crusty. But there were more important things. "Where is Lufu?"

Myla indicated the adjacent bed, similarly draped and buried in furs. Fira struggled to sit up.

The top of Lufu's head was just visible, pillowed between two others, each with a short ruffle of hair the color of porridge.

"I bedded her down with two Duntuffets," said Myla. "She woke earlier and took a little food and drink."

Fira scanned the unfamiliar surroundings. A long row of beds lined a room with stone walls and hay-strewn floors. The air smelled faintly of green things and woodfire and candlewax. Shutters kept out most of the gaining daylight, and herbs hung in bundles amidst the rafters overhead.

The mare's hand pressed against her forehead, and she repeated, "How are you feeling?"

"Where are we?"

She said, "A village of sorts, a small community of people who have similar needs and purposes. More specifically, you are in my quarters and in my keeping."

Wait. "Your keeping? Am I a slave then?"

Myla held up a hand. "My responsibility, *not* my property. You are under my care until you feel stronger, and you are under my protection for as long as you abide with the herd."

"Horses," she murmured.

"My bondmate is leader of the Thunderhoof clan. I am Bavol's mother."

"You cannot be," countered Fira. "You are too young."

A slow smile. A small shake of the head. "I am not human, child. My years are already many, and on they will multiply. In truth, I birthed seven other sons before Bavol, and I can boast twice as many daughters."

Fira didn't think she was lying, yet how could such things be true? "Are you magic?"

"*I* am not the one who works miracles. If there is a magician among us, he is called Willum." Myla reached for one of the cups on the small table beside the bed. "Drink."

The earthenware was heavy and warm, and Fira clutched it between bandaged fingers. The draught was bitter, but she was thirsty enough to swallow it all.

Myla took the cup and touched Fira's cheek. "How are you feeling?"

"Better." She didn't like to complain. Anything was better than what they'd survived.

The mare eyed her critically. "Still wracked, and no wonder. Cold has touched your bones, and fury has scattered your soul. I could continue to help you find your balance."

There was a question there, and it confused Fira.

"May I rejoin you?" Myla asked, indicating the wide bed.

Fira's gaze drifted to Lufu, snug between two bedmates. "You were with me before?"

"Through much of yesterday and all of last night."

"I do not remember."

Myla asked, "Are you still cold?"

She managed a small nod, which the mare took for acceptance. She plucked at the fastenings of a heavy, spring-green outer garment that clung alluringly to generous curves. Fira's fingers twitched to touch the cloth, which looked rich even without the fuss of ruffles or pleats. But there was dirt under her ragged nails, and she had need of a bath.

Clad in a plain white shift, the mare slipped into the bed and pulled closed its filmy drapery. "Come, now," she invited.

Fira balked, for her hair was matted, her skin clammy. But Myla ignored those things. Strong hands pulled and tucked and patted, bringing Fira into closer contact than she'd had with another woman since losing her mother. Barely-remembered comfort washed over her, stirring her emotions, loosening the tight hold under which she kept them.

The first sob caught her unready, and try as she might, Fira couldn't stop.

Myla crooned and kissed her hair, and Fira clung to her and cried. All the worries and fears, losses and injustices, doubts and devastations came rushing out, and the mare gathered them up, murmuring encouragement all the while.

In the aftermath, Myla looked into her eyes and stroked

her cheeks until they were flushed but dry. Drawing apart, she reached for something on a bedside table and presented her with a handkerchief.

Fira sat up to clear her muddled head and watched the mare pour a golden tea from a tiny pot warming over the flame of a squat candle. The cup Myla pressed into her hand was no bigger than an eggshell and just as delicate.

"Drink it down," ordered the mare.

This beverage was an improvement on the last. Sweet and thick, it coated her tongue and throat, hitting her belly with a burst of warmth. Fira stared dazedly into the empty cup and licked her lips. Had that been a tonic? It felt more like overheard tales about the burn of hard liquor.

"Is there more?" she found herself asking.

Myla laughed and drew her down. "Lovely stuff, huddlebud nectar."

"Lovely," Fira agreed through a pleasant haze. "Am I drunk?"

"Have you ever been drunk?"

"No."

The mare pulled her closer and kissed her cheek. "This is much nicer, love."

Fira liked that. She wasn't accustomed to endearments. And this bed was good. Had there ever been softer blankets? Everywhere was soft. Tugging one of the covers to her nose, she stared cross-eyed at the weave.

"Rabbit fur." Myla sounded amused. Were rabbits funny?

When Fira blinked, her eyelids took turns, as if they'd forgotten how to cooperate. "Are we truly safe?" she mumbled, struggling to focus on the beautiful mare.

"Yes, Fira, love." Myla kissed her nose, her lips. "You and your sister are safe."

She wanted desperately for it to be true, but did that make it so? Maybe it did, since this was a magical place. With handsome horses and funny rabbits. So Fira brought out the crumpled wreckage of her trust and offered it to Myla. "I will believe you."

"And I will watch over you," the mare promised.

Fira wanted this warmth, this safety, this place, but she also wanted to be clear. "I am not a child."

Myla seemed surprised by the suggestion. "You are not a child, slayer of dragons, wielder of stones, bringer of hope. I will take you to my heart as a sister of the herd."

Not a servant. Not a beggar. Not a bringer of curses.

"You might change your mind," Fira whispered.

"Rather, I will change yours."

The mare kneaded and stroked, repeating her assurances until they took on the lilt of a bard's song in Fira's mind. When Myla said she was fierce as a warrior and courageous in battle, it made a good story. When she praised Fira as a true sister for watching over her kin, she felt warm all over. When Myla called her a rare beauty, capable of leading any male into the dance, it almost sounded possible.

Fira sighed and snuggled and even smiled while the mare murmured to her about a brave boy with fiery hair who sang with the souls of stones and wrote his hopes upon the very winds.

MOUNTAIN LORE

When Fira next woke, Myla was gone from the bed, and its hangings were drawn apart. Sunlight angled through a different set of windows, and she could hear Lufu chatting away with someone.

"Well, twitch my nose!" exclaimed a merry voice. In a blink, a girl was standing beside Fira's bed, hands extended. "Rhoslyn Duntuffet. Up you come, my lovely. We're under strict orders from the Mare herself. Into the bath, for the sun won't tarry!"

This person could not possibly belong to the Thunderhoof herd, for she cut a dainty figure, all slim lines and scant curves. She wore a gay piecemeal tunic over heavy breeches, and her eyes were the color of toffee. They sparkled with good cheer.

"Never seen the like, have you?" Her arm slipped easily around Fira's waist. "The novelty will be gone in a lollop, but never forget … I was your first!"

"My first what?" Fira wondered where the girl got her strength. She was a staunch support.

"Your first rabbit, my lovely. There's a whole warren hereabouts." She tapped the floor with one foot. "Mostly beneath notice, if you catch my meaning."

Fira was half a head taller than Rhoslyn, which gave her an excellent view of the rabbit girl's hair. Never before had she seen such an unruly thatch, which looked to have been shorn with a bread knife. Nor could she find a word for the color, which seemed an even mix of gray and dun and cream.

"Fira!" called Lufu. "Come see what they gave me!"

Rhoslyn steadied her across the room to a curtained corner where a great trough of water steamed invitingly. Lufu perched on a stool while another girl carried on brushing her hair as it dried.

"Shake my tail, they're a match!" this second girl exclaimed. "Rhoswen Duntuffet—miner and occasional lady's maid. Come have your scrub."

Fira glanced between the two and had to smile, for this was the second time she'd seen an unruly thatch. "Are you sisters?"

"You can tell?" they asked in unison.

Lufu giggled. "They are twins. But look at my dress! Have you ever seen one so fine?"

"Never." The cut of the dress reminded Fira of Myla's earlier attire, for it draped and clung, making Lufu look years older than she had in her former rags. Moss green set off her eyes, which shone with understandable delight. Fira smiled and asked, "Where has my baby sister gone? For here sits a lady."

Caught up in admiring her Lufu's transformation, Fira hardly noticed when Rhoslyn bundled away her tattered underthings and chivvied her into the bath. She sank to her chin with a blissful sigh, soaking in the heat.

Lufu's attention returned to Rhoswen. "Do not leave off. I want more of the story."

"And you shall have it! Now, where was I?"

"You were telling about the Notches." Lufu looked to Fira and eagerly explained, "That is where we are—these mountains."

"We call them the Notches because there never was a more ragged, jagged set of peaks. It's as if an ancient beast stumbled onto the Moor and fell asleep upon the heather, only to forget to wake. Times turned, and he's only settled further into his bed." Rhoswen kept right on lifting and combing, adding luster to the length of Lufu's light brown hair.

"Truly?" asked Lufu.

"Well," hedged the rabbit girl. "It makes a fine bedtime story for wee tuffets, but there's not much truth to the tale. Otherwise, we'd be burrowing amidst old bones. But *that's* not what we find under those ragged, jagged peaks."

As Fira accepted a fat bar of soap from Rhoslyn, she smiled over how quickly Rhoswen re-caught Lufu's interest. The rabbit girl was a good storyteller.

"What *do* you find?" Lufu begged.

Instead of answering straightway, Rhoswen sidestepped into another story. "When Time was young and reckless, the old places teemed with the truth of our lore. Clans of earth and sea and sky lived in peace, and the trees led them into songs and dancing. Such were the days before the Amaranthine."

Lufu turned her head. "What is that?"

"That's *us*—me, my twin, the Mare, and all." Rhoswen dropped a kiss on Lufu's cheek. "And according to our lore, which is truer than the truest heart, the clans of earth found reason to hide, but they did not vanish without a trace. It was the Maker's wish that their legacy continue upon the earth."

"How could they know such a wish?"

"An angel told them." Rhoswen set aside her combs and brushes and began to weave Lufu's hair into a crown.

"Like Gabriel?"

"*Like* him, I daresay, for wasn't he a messenger? As were Soriel of the Dawning and Auriel of the Golden Seed. But *this* story belongs to Cadmiel of the Echoing Song. Many a miner shares his name, for it was he that threaded the earth with veins of gold and ribbons of silver."

"Treasure?" asked Lufu.

"Like no other," assured Rhoswen. "The clans of earth, every soul of them, in all their wisdom and wiliness, bequeathed a treasure. Precious metals and stones fit for polishing. Jewels and minerals and gems—they are all remnants of their lost clans. But most precious and most rare are the crystals that still echo with Cadmiel's song."

"Rocks sing?" Lufu asked, her hand pressed over the pocket where their own bequest rested.

"For those who can hear them," assured Rhoswen.

Rhoslyn winked at Fira and whispered, "For men like Willum."

DRAGON DANCE

Fira felt overly tall and entirely conspicuous, escorted as she was by two slender rabbits. They'd dressed her in some generous filly's cast-offs, tucking and tugging and pinning until the dress's dark green folds cooperated with her leaner figure.

"Where are we going?" asked Lufu, whose hair sparkled with borrowed jewels.

Rhoswen gave the eager girl a twirl. "To the Circle, for the mares will dance."

"Do rabbits dance?"

"Oh, we're a merry mess compared to the dignity of our sister mares. But it's a rare rabbit who won't beg for another turn around the Circle."

"We adore it," added Rhoslyn. "Who wouldn't?"

"But this first dance calls for quiet," warned Rhoswen. "Hush a bit."

Rhoslyn lowered her voice as they drew near the edge of a crowd. "Myla will do right by that dragon."

Music reached them first, a lone instrument in the lap of a Duntuffet male, who drew a long bow across strings, filling the air with a wistful melody. A ring of stones defined the edges of a slightly hollowed space covered in moss. Upon this springy carpet, five mares paced through a stately dance, each holding a bouquet of grasses, flowers, and leaves bound with trailing ribbons that shone like bronze.

They were the only ones in motion, but they weren't the only participants, for the hollow soon began to thrum. The stallions were humming in close harmony, deep and compelling.

Fira paled, for though she'd been praised as its slayer, she'd had a part in this grief. Her fear and fury had ended the life of one meant for endless days. Her eyes prickled, and she tipped her head back, trying to blink away her tears before they fell. Only to lock gazes with Ricker.

He stood amidst a group of children. One straddled his shoulders, more clung to his arms, his legs. Her rescuer looked for all the world like the village's favorite uncle. But concern crossed his face. He spoke a few words, tousled a few heads, and slipped free of his many admirers.

Within moments, he was at her back. Not touching, but close enough she could hear his humming. He took the tenor part. And then another stallion joined him, taking the lower notes. She glanced back, expecting to see Bavol beside his brother, but it was the stallion who'd been kissing Myla. She couldn't recall his name, but Ricker had bragged that he was son of the herd's leader.

Bavol may have inherited his sire's beauty, and Ricker had his stature and swagger. Father and son seemed bent on out-humming the other. So much for dignity.

When the dragon dance ended, Fira thought perhaps Ricker would introduce her to the lead stallion, but some silent understanding passed between them, and his father slipped away. Ricker explained, "He will greet you formally in his private glade. I will show you the way later."

"Thank you."

Ricker bent closer. "It is natural to cry. You do not need to hide your sadness."

"I feel two-faced." She gritted her teeth. "This is all my fault."

"Defending yourself was natural, as well." He slowly shook his head. "I was prepared to strike, as was Bavol, but we would have arrived too late to save you and Lufu. Is this not the better outcome?"

She couldn't deny that.

He nodded and straightened, and his attention strayed. Apparently forgetting all about her, he shouldered his way to the Circle's edge.

Rhoswen and Rhoslyn bunched her in. "Here come the mares," they hissed in excited unison.

The herd shed any trace of solemnity, for the Circle now hummed with whispers and giggles and murmurs.

Fira couldn't see past the barrier of broad male backs, but the rabbit sisters pulled her and Lufu around to a set of stairs leading to the top of overlooking terraces. Children perched here—sturdy Thunderhoofs and slimsy Duntuffets—all watching with interest as twenty or so mares took their places around the song circle.

"All the mares are wearing green." A dozen shades at least.

"Summer is the greening season," reasoned Rhoslyn. "They're dressed for Midsummer Month. See the garlands in their hair?"

Bright blooms had been twisted into showy wreaths, which graced the brows of every dancer. A pair of musicians struck the opening chords of a new tune—slow as the dirge, but far sweeter— and the mares wove together in an intricate pattern of swaying steps and flourishing turns.

Rhoslyn jostled her arm. "There she is! That's her."

At first, Fira couldn't tell which mare she meant.

"The fairest one, with eyes blue as violets," prompted Rhoswen.

Lufu murmured, "So pretty."

Fira thought that an understatement. The mare in question had a regal bearing, sun-gold skin, and a glossy tumble of wavy hair, light as cream. Her bare arms chimed with an array of tiny bangles, and a single gem had somehow been affixed to the center of her forehead.

"Synnis is an excellent filly, and this is the first time she's joined the dance," said Rhoslyn in gossipy tones. "Every colt and stallion would leap to her call."

Rhoswen added, "We're curious, since some say she'll accept nothing less than all."

"What does that mean?" asked Fira.

"She wants more than a coupling and a foal. Synnis is after a bondmate."

"Many are willing." Rhoslyn rolled her eyes significantly. "Some more than others."

Fira followed her line of sight and spotted a lovesick Ricker. "Will he ask her to wed?" she whispered.

Both rabbits shook their heads. "There's an order to things, isn't there?" said Rhoslyn. "This is the females' display. They'll consider any male, so every colt and stallion in the herd will be trying to distinguish themselves."

Rhoswen tapped off fingers. "Gifts, pledges, dares, races, strutting, jostling, capering, courting."

"Tournaments, mock battles, quests, bragging," said Rhoslyn. "Did we mention strutting?"

"Plenty of strutting," Rhoswen confirmed with a solemn wink.

Lufu asked, "The ladies of the herd want husbands?"

"They want *foals*," corrected Rhoswen. "They'll look over their options, and if a mare is suitably impressed by a colt or stallion, she'll lead him to a quiet place."

"What for?" asked Lufu.

Rhoslyn dimpled. "Coupling."

Fira could feel the blush creeping into her cheeks, but the sight of one of the dancers startled her. "Is that Myla?"

"Yes, yes."

The lead mare flowed gracefully through the movements, a secretive smile on her face.

Rhoswen giggled. "She's due."

"Definitely due," agreed her sister. "Who do you think she'd consider?"

Fira rocked back on her heels. "I thought she was married to Dwennon."

The sisters missed a beat, as if trying to understand what she was asking. With some delicacy, Rhoslyn indicated the Circle. "Midsummer is for breeding, not bonding."

"There's a difference?"

Rhoswen spoke kindly, but she was blunt. "Myla is Dwennon's bondmate, and while in speaking form, no other would dare touch her. But to strengthen the herd, she might choose another fine stallion and carry his foal."

Lufu was frowning. "Husbands and wives should be true to one another."

"So it is with humans," agreed Rhoswen. "Horses are true to the herd and look to its strength."

"Myla may well choose Dwennon. More than half of her children are his," said Rhoslyn. "But there aren't many mares of the herd who *haven't* chosen Dwennon at some point. He's the source of the clan's strength."

"I would not like that," said Fira. She couldn't imagine sharing her husband with other women. Not for any reason. "I would not like that *at all*."

"Nor would I," Lufu staunchly agreed.

The rabbits shrugged unapologetically. "To us, this is the way of things."

Fira wondered if rabbits had similar customs where courtship and coupling were concerned. But she wasn't about to ask.

"Mares answer to no one for their choices, but that doesn't keep anyone from questioning them." Rhoslyn's dimple was back. "Or from placing wagers."

"Our own dear mum is speculating hard about Myla," whispered Rhoswen, forcing Fira and Lufu to lean in to hear. "She thinks if Ricker is disappointed at Midsummer, she'll take him herself. Make a stallion of him."

Fira made a face. "Her own son?"

Two blinks, then quick headshakes. "Dwennon is Ricker's sire, but his dam was Gwynnis Alpenglow, a mare from another herd."

"But," she protested, trying to reconcile what had to be a vast age difference. "But she's Bavol's mother."

"Oh, *him*!" The sisters exchanged a giddy look. Rhoslyn said, "Bavol is an excellent stallion, in high demand."

"Though no mare who's had him has kept him," added Rhoswen.

"Not for lack of trying!"

Rhoswen tapped her nose. "Bavol must be biding his time, waiting for some lucky filly to gain sufficient years."

But Fira wasn't interested in Bavol's prospects. "Ricker is even younger than Bavol."

Again, the rabbit sisters faltered. Clearly, there was no issue here. Only interesting odds.

"Ricker *is* young," Rhoslyn allowed. "Still a colt, but his lines are excellent, his manners good, when he remembers to use them."

"He dotes on the foals," said Rhoswen. "Still a foal at heart, that one."

"Too bad about his coloring."

Fira searched for Ricker and quickly spotted him. In a sea of white and gold, his head stood out. His hair had been darker when storm-wet, but it had dried to a light, gingered brown. It was different.

"Ricker is nice," said Lufu.

"The softest heart and the surest strut." Rhoswen smiled

down on the crowd of milling males. "Ricker has the makings of a fine sire."

Rhoslyn indicated the lead mare. "She's willing. He's wanting. As the herds do say, that's a good balance."

ROCK COLLECTOR

The sun was well up before the mares ended their display, and the rabbits took over the Circle. Lufu clapped and Fira smiled as the Duntuffets proved that they were indeed a "merry mess." Quick-paced, toe-tapping piping kept the partners in a dizzy whirl. When Rhoswen coaxed Lufu into a circle of young girls to teach her the steps to a simple jig, Fira hung back to watch.

Myla found her, linking arms and leading her away. "Do you need refreshment?"

"No, thank you." Fira hardly knew what else to say to the mare, and the silence grew awkward.

Stopping in the shadows beneath an ancient camphor tree, Myla asked, "Has something happened? Was it Dwennon? He is a wretched tease, but a steady sire and a fine lead."

"No. I mean, I *did* see him, but I have not met him properly."

"What, then?"

Fira wasn't sure what sorts of questions might be impolite. The Duntuffet sisters spoke frankly, but she wasn't comfortable asking Myla about … intimate matters. So she shook her head and murmured, "Everything is so different here."

"Which is why you must meet Willum." The mare steered her along the path. "He is human. Like you."

Since it was fresh in her mind, she wondered what Myla meant by *like*. Awkwardly tall, tragically orphaned, unfashionably dark, repeatedly banished, hounded by monsters? Or was her humanity all that mattered? She knew from long experience that being human wasn't any guarantee of finding welcome, let alone friendship.

Fira had a lurking suspicion that the mare was about to put her on display. Her steps slowed.

Myla glanced down.

"Did you bring me here to be Willum's wife?"

The mare hesitated. "He is a good man. Unique. Vibrant. Dwennon and I would like to see his line established, and for that he needs a willing female."

Her jaw clenched. "And if I am unwilling?"

"Peace, sister. While I hope for his happiness, yours is of equal value." Myla's smile was slow, almost seductive. "If he pleases you, have him. If he does not, he is young. There is time. Other girls may yet be found."

Fira wasn't entirely mollified. In her experience, "good" men were usually ugly, and "unique" men indulged in strange habits or hobbies. What sort of man appealed to a horse-person?

Along a path where the homes seemed to have been heaped together and all the doors were rabbit-sized and brightly painted, they came to a low building.

"The primary entrance to the Warren is along here. Most of the Duntuffets are miners, and when they find anything interesting, they bring it here. To Willum." She rapped on the door and opened it, calling, "You are missing the dancing, dear boy. Did you forget your promise?"

Fira followed her into a long, crowded room that was surprisingly well-lit. She had rarely seen window glass, for it was unheard of in the out-of-the-way corners where she and Lufu usually hid. Yet four panes dominated the opposite wall, welcoming in light that was further scattered by a series of round mirrors and strange lamps. The nearest glowed with pale blue light.

Unique, indeed.

"Willum, the dance," repeated Myla. "Were you not eager to meet our newcomers?"

On the other side of a long table heaped with tools and clamps and glittering stones, a man paced with his back to them. He was muttering to himself as he tugged with both hands at his hair, which was a rampant shade of red.

Vibrant, indeed.

"Willum!"

He whirled, clearly startled to have guests. "Oh, Myla," he said. "Is something going on just now? Or yesterday? It started yesterday, and I cannot think what changed. I can hardly hear my own ... thoughts ...."

Having caught sight of Fira, Willum slowly lowered his hands.

He was perhaps a little older than she, but astonishment made him seem very young indeed. Willum's slender frame and sharp cheekbones made him look underfed, and a profusion of freckles livened up his pallor.

Willum grabbed the edge of his worktable as if needing it support.

Myla said, "Here is Fira. She arrived ..."

"...yesterday?" he asked sharply.

"Yes." With exaggerated patience, the mare said, "Did Bavol not tell you?"

"Bavol?" Willum had begun picking through the rocks on the table—blue, violet, lavender. "I thought it was the storm. A true wind will resonate, you know. Earth and sky have always been compatible, which is why crystals can reinforce a well-wrought sigil, provided the crafter takes the time to tune their soul … to …."

He lapsed into muttering.

A smile lurked on Myla's lips. Perhaps this was normal?

Willum came out from behind the table, a purple stone extended. "Excuse me, but would you hold this for a moment?"

On closer inspection, Fira learned that Willum's eyes were a brilliant green, his eyelashes were so pale as to be nearly invisible, and his jaw showed a faint line of stubble.

With a politeness that made him seem slightly less mad, he said, "Please. I think it must be you."

"Ricker thought so, too," said Myla. "She is like you."

He shuffled a half-step forward, suddenly shy. "Can you hear them, too?"

"Hear them?"

"The stones. Their songs have changed." He angled the purple crystal, which glittered with many facets. "It is *beautiful*. And I think they must be tuning themselves to you."

Fira felt oddly complimented. Should she tell him about their lucky stone? If she did, would he take it from her and Lufu?

"Please?" he repeated.

She lifted a hand, and he placed the crystal on her palm.

Nothing happened. Was something supposed to happen?

But when she looked up, Willum's whole expression bespoke awe. Fira glanced between him and Myla. "What?"

Willum's hands came up around hers, closing her fingers around the crystal. Eyes shut, he seemed to be listening, and whatever he heard clearly pleased him. He nodded and announced, "It *is* you."

Myla looked utterly smug.

Fira was beginning to be annoyed.

But then Willum laughed softly and sought her gaze. With a lopsided smile, he said, "Hullo."

ECHOING SONG

Myla abandoned her so that she and Willum could become better acquainted. Fira had no idea what to make of the man, who spent the better part of an hour placing different rocks in the palm of her hand to see what they would do.

If this was his idea of a display, she wasn't impressed. But she *was* amused, and the crystals were beautiful, and she was relieved that he seemed more interested in his work than in a wife.

Ricker found her there. "Dwennon will be waiting."

"Now?"

He shook his head and pulled up a stool. "Was I right, Willum?"

"Yes, but you would know that better than I." The redhead gently placed a fragment of pink crystal on Fira's outstretched hand. He held his breath for several moments, then exhaled to a smile. "I do know that the stones are responding. Quite favorably. You are wonderful!"

Fira was startled to realize that last bit was meant for her. She could feel the burn in her cheeks and shot a rebellious look at Ricker.

He only grinned and said, "This is a good outcome."

Maybe it could be.

To Willum, Ricker said, "You should teach her what you know. Take her for your apprentice."

Willum eagerly asked, "Would you like that?"

She asked, "What would I be learning?"

He seemed at a loss, but then he came to some sort of decision. "Watch."

Fira looked to Ricker, whose nod reinforced the command. And then Willum's hands began to move. It was like he was drawing in the air, quick and sure. With each flick of his fingers, he pulled light from nowhere, until a pattern shimmered in the air between them. All around the room, crystals began to glow. Their light pulsed like a shared heartbeat.

Choosing one of the smaller stones from the table, he used the tip of his finger to move it into the center of the glowing pattern. And the stone began to sing.

A sweet treble swelled like birdsong, throbbing with notes that caught Fira by surprise. They seemed to resonate with her bones, plucking at heartstrings, whispering to her soul. She saw the wind take the form of a woman, who danced with a winged man through a sky dazzled by lightning bolts.

The song ended when Willum banished the pattern and set aside the stone. "Did you hear?"

Words failed, but she offered a nod.

It occurred to Fira that *this* made for a fine display, and she was favorably impressed.

Ricker guided her to a place called the Vantage, which looked out over a wide valley filled with horses. They must have been the same ones who'd stampeded across the moor. Had it really only been two days ago?

Dwennon awaited, and Ricker left her alone with him.

She would rather he had stayed.

The leader of the Thunderhoof clan turned from the view and held out his hands. "Fira," he said warmly. "Do you have a family name? A house or clan?"

If she did, her father and mother had never taught it to her. She shook her head

He seemed dismayed on her behalf. "Your parents?" he prompted.

"Dead."

"Your kindred?"

"None."

The sound he made deep in his chest might have been displeasure.

Fira tried not to flinch away when he brushed his knuckles across her cheek. "I have not seen your coloring in the villages hereabouts."

Well she knew it. But given the circumstances, she supposed he deserved some explanation. "My mother was from a different land, somewhere far away. Her skin was even darker than mine." Fira's throat ached with sadness. "She was very beautiful."

"As are her daughters." And without so much as a by-your-leave, he kissed her.

She staggered back, unsettled by someone so free with his affections. "I do not think that was *at all* appropriate!"

His smile held no apology. "You will not accept the most basic of courtesies? I could take offense, you know."

"You are taking liberties!"

"No, I am not." Dwennon calmly said, "I am merely following the lead of my mare. You are Myla's, so you are mine."

"Wh-what?" He had to be teasing.

"Did she hold you?" he asked.

"Yes."

"Did she claim sisterhood?"

"She did."

"Did she kiss you?"

Fira's cheeks flamed, which was answer enough for the smirking stallion.

"Then I am free to hold, to kiss, and even to claim, *if* you were from one of our clans."

"I am not!"

"Correct." Dwennon took her by the shoulders and soothed, "You were never meant for me, little beauty. Rather, choose Willum. If you can lure him away from his precious stones, his line can be established. Bear him vigorous sons and proud daughters."

"Is that why you brought us here?" she asked moodily. "To become Willum's herd."

"Ask my sons for their reasons if you need them." Dwennon asked, "Do you dislike Willum?"

She grudgingly admitted, "No."

"That is as good a beginning as any." He smiled disarmingly. "If you decide you find our dappled boy comely, claim him and keep him all to yourself. You know, I have never been possessive, but the idea has a certain appeal. I have heard it called *romantic*."

Fira wondered if she was as big a mystery to him as he was to her.

Heaving a gusty sigh, Dwennon said, "I have come to terms with your resolve. I understand that you are in no danger of falling for my considerable charms. Had you four hooves and a frisky trot, I might try harder to curry favor. As it is, Myla's sisterhood ensures my brotherhood, my protection, and my teasing."

So he *was* toying with her!

"Do not be angry, Fira," he warned. "I am only welcoming you to the herd."

This time, he kissed her forehead.

When she stubbornly held his gaze, he seemed to take it for a dare and kissed her nose.

She got the distinct impression that Dwennon was used to getting exactly what he wanted.

"Brave little warrior, I find I like you." He touched her hair, her cheek. "Can you bear up under the weight of my most ardent affection?"

He was exasperating, but so nice about it.

Dwennon kissed her lips again, soft and light. "Good girl. With both willing, we have found a balance. I am proud to count you as kin. Welcome to the Thunderhoof herd."

Mercifully, that seemed to be the end of formalities.

Herd relationships and behavior confused her, though. "You are my brother?"

"In an honorary sense," he allowed.

"What does that make Bavol and Ricker?"

The smirk slid from Dwennon's face, and he looked away. His answer, when it came, was either straightforward or cryptic. Possibly both. "Rivals."

CADMIEL'S TUMP

A week passed, and then another. Midsummer loomed near, and Fira was adjusting to her new home. Not that she understood half of what was going on around her. Every day, she learned something that was both startling and obvious, if only in retrospect.

For instance, she learned that Bavol's mentor was his dam. Myla planned to announce his mastery of the healing arts at the next Song Circle, which was three years hence. Fira's own apprenticeship to Willum was baffling and beautiful by turns. Truly, he was a magician in the flesh, though he denied it assiduously.

She had seen him illuminate crystals with a whispered word, then send them spinning overhead until the workroom sparkled. And she'd watched him puzzle out dozens of patterns on paper, which he then etched into empty air, making invisible walls or nets or bubbles, and even a whirlwind.

But sitting and watching a man think grew dull.

And he wouldn't let her touch his precious piles.

Fira had grumbled that she'd be more useful to him if he let her take up a pick and join the rabbits down in the mines. Surely someone who could resonate with the remnants could locate more.

Willum found the notion intriguing, but in the meantime, she was at odd ends. So she walked out, quite certain the inattentive young man would never notice her absence.

Not long into her wandering, she crossed paths with Ricker, who had three youngsters in tow. Mindful of her latest discovery about Bavol, she asked, "Are you apprenticed to someone?"

Ricker seemed embarrassed. "I take a turn pulling ore carts, and I help patrol the boundaries."

"You do not … specialize?" So far, everyone she'd met had a role or task for which they were proud.

The tips of his ears had gone quite pink. "Today, these three are my specialty."

All three—two girls and a boy—perked up at their mention, beaming over their own importance.

She learned their names, met their palms, and when they raced ahead, she hung back, preferring to walk with Ricker. "Are they your nieces and nephews?"

"They are children of the herd who have found their speaking form," he replied cautiously. He didn't seem to understand the terms. Perhaps horses didn't have the same family names?

Fira attempted to clarify. "Are they the children of your older siblings?"

His bafflement turned to bemusement. "They are some of my younger siblings."

"I did not realize Myla had children so young."

"Myla is not their dam." Ricker was watching her face.

"Dwennon sired them on other mares. They are like me."

She had no idea how to respond.

Ricker spoke quietly. "You seem displeased."

"I am not *displeased*. I am confused." Fira's memories of the home she'd lost were few and precious. "My mother only loved my father, and my father only loved my mother."

"They were bondmates with no herd."

Fira didn't like how sad he sounded for their sake. "They had each other. They had me and Lufu. We were happy."

He hummed. "Some Amaranthine thrive upon such unions. Among the herds, mingling bloodlines is more common than exclusivity, perhaps because our numbers were once small. Or perhaps we are influenced by instincts related to the animals in our keeping."

"You behave like a horse because you are a horse?"

"Yet I am no mere beast."

She agreed. "You and your people are people."

Ricker ambled along at a pace she could match, quieter than she'd ever seen him. At length, he spoke again. "I may leave the herd."

Fira jerked to a stop. "Why?"

"Colts of my coloring are better favored in other clans. Dwennon is willing to send me away, to become another herd's strength." He didn't sound happy.

"Do you want to go?"

Ricker studied his feet. "I want to be chosen."

"You cannot have both?"

"A few days remain. I may yet distinguish myself." He looked tense, uneasy.

Fira rolled her eyes. "You attacked a dragon. You saved me and my sister."

He grimaced. "Bavol attacked a dragon. Bavol saved you and Lufu."

She snorted. "Do the mares know we rode him home?"

Ricker chuckled. That was better.

They reached their destination, a perfectly round green mound with a ring of upright stones surrounding its base. The youngsters clambered all over them, skipping from one to the next with impressive agility.

"What is this place?" Fira asked.

"Cadmiel's Tump."

"Really?" She couldn't hide her surprise. "Because every other place I have been has a plain, boring name—the Circle, the Warren, the Notches, the Vantage."

He was grinning again. "The Wide, the Wallow, the Patch."

Fira nodded wisely. "Dull as a sunless day."

"We are close to the sea. Would a look liven up your afternoon?"

"Nicely."

Ricker rallied his little troupe, and they strolled on. As promised, they didn't have far to go, and the view was fine, for they stood atop steep cliffs.

"And what do you call this place?" Fira asked.

"We call it what it is." There was a teasing note to his statement, followed—rather predictably—by a challenge. "Can you guess?"

Fira searched her mind for the most boring label. "The Cliffs."

Ricker gave a low, nickering laugh. "No."

"The Edge."

He rolled his eyes. Clearly mocking her.

"The Shore."

His pitying look assured her that she was falling far short of the horse standard.

She said, "I cannot guess. Tell me, then."

"We call it the Leap."

"That is ominous. Casting yourself from a cliff of this height would mean certain death. A quick end to a sad life."

Ricker's eyes widened. "Have you wished for death?"

"I have run from it often enough, and I have never been tempted to stop." He still seemed unsettled, so Fira said, "No, Ricker. I cannot die. Lufu needs me."

His gaze darted to the children, and she thought his glance was guilty. Did he consider leaving the herd a kind of death?

But he shook back his mane of hair, arched a cocky brow, and beckoned with both hands. "Not that kind of leap. Come, I will show you."

She held her ground. He was up to something.

Ricker came and took her hand, drawing her toward the sheer drop.

Fira immediately dug in her heels.

He ignored her warning glare, eyes bright with merriment, coaxing all the while. "There is no danger here. Not while you are with me."

"I am *not* afraid, but neither am I a fool."

"You do not trust your friend and savior?"

"I thought that was Bavol," she challenged.

Ricker wasn't put off. "*I* saw you first—bright as stars, ablaze with power, beautiful in battle."

She was so startled by his description, she left herself open. He had both wrists now, and he pulled her along as he backed toward the edge.

"Ricker, I do not want to fall."

"I will not let you," he said gently, earnestly. "Please, trust me, Fira."

And suddenly, it wasn't a game anymore. He wanted to display, if for no one else than her and his younger siblings. So she said, "Yes."

He instantly stepped closer to her, away from the edge, and he was drawing her arms around his waist. "This is a game for little ones," he said happily. "Nothing bad can happen if we make this leap together."

Having promised to trust him, there was no going back.

Ricker said, "Step on my feet."

She was pressed against him now. His steps backward became her steps forward, and she clutched at his shirt, inadvertently yanking his hair.

"Look at me," he ordered.

So she did, even though her face probably betrayed her fear.

His eyes softened as he took another step. "You are so brave, Fira. I wish I had your courage."

"I do not feel brave." She hated the tremor in her voice.

"Trust takes courage."

"Then you are doubly daring," she countered. "To tease a woman who can slay dragons."

Ricker grew solemn. "I never thought of that."

Fira bit her lip to keep from laughing.

"Look down," he urged.

She did. And shrieked. Then pounded his shoulder and pulled his hair for good measure.

He hugged her close. "You should trust me more, little faith."

They hung suspended between sea and sky.

"What are you standing on?" she gasped.

"Is it still standing if my feet are not on the ground?" he asked innocently.

"What is this?"

"Flying." He patted her head. "Did you forget how we arrived? Bavol flew."

Fira craned her neck, looking up, down, around. "You can fly."

"Yes."

"How?" She demanded. "Why?"

Ricker puffed out his cheeks. "May as well ask me how I dream or why I crave apples out of season. It is simply the way I am."

"Do *not* drop me."

"Do not let go."

She firmed her grip, and he laughed softly and swayed through the steps of a walking dance. With her feet upon his, the dance was shared. He hummed little snatches of melody, and she slowly relaxed.

"Do you want to go back?" he offered.

"Stay a little longer," she begged.

It was the right thing to say.

Ricker added a twirl to his steps, and her skirt flared out. He moved her hands to his shoulders, slipped his own to her waist. She felt safe, and he looked so happy. Moving through their childish dance with a far-off look in his eyes.

Fira decided to say what was on her mind. "I do not want you to leave."

"I do not want to go."

She found herself repeating, "Stay a little longer."

He lifted her effortlessly by her waist, bringing them eye to eye. "I cannot go," he said, testing the words. "Fira needs me."

Had he been hoping someone would ask?

Fira patted his head and sternly said, "Do not go."

Ricker glibly countered, "Do not let go."

WINGED PREDATOR

Fira was with Lufu and the Duntuffet sisters when the first faint whisper of trouble reached her. She lifted her crystal-illumined lantern and touched the rough-hewn wall of the mine shaft, unsettled by the warning note that rang with her soul. The sensation reminded her a little of Willum's ward stones, the ones that kept Glintrubble hidden. Only this was discordant and less distinct, like the fading echo of a cry in the night.

She turned to check on Lufu, but her sister was listening to Rhoswen, whose enthusiasm for mining was contagious.

Half a moment later, Rhoslyn interrupted with a sharp, "Twitch my whiskers."

Her twin turned, and the Duntuffet sisters' heads tilted to matching angles of attentiveness.

Into the sudden silence, Lufu whispered, "Is something happening?"

Rhoslyn stared at the stone ceiling as if she could see straight through. "Predator."

"Armed," added Rhoswen.

Both miners hefted picks and quick-trotted back the way they'd come.

Fira chased after them, calling, "How can you tell?"

"Good ears, dear. Come along, now! You're wanted."

Dread spiked through Fira's heart. It was happening again. Their curse had not ended. This was their fault, just as it had always been. Would Dwennon cast them out, now that he realized how much trouble she and Lufu could bring to his home?

They clambered out of a narrow passage and into the Duntuffet sisters' root cellar. It seemed that every rabbit in Glintrubble had a private shaft or two under their home. Fira lengthened her stride, following Rhoslyn and Rhoswen out their cottage's front door.

In the open, Lufu gasped and ducked. She needn't have, for the dark shape was higher than the treetops, but Fira could understand the impulse.

The creature wobbled through another turn, wings flapping erratically.

"What *is* that?" asked Lufu, who clung tightly to Rhoslyn's arm.

"A bat," answered the rabbit.

"In daytime?"

Fira couldn't help smiling. "Is *that* what worries you, sister? I would have thought its *size* more concerning." It was monstrous—easily as big as the Duntuffet sisters' cozy house, with a wingspan that brought dragons to mind.

"We get all kinds here," said Rhoswen. "His posture is peaceful, though the rhythms are faltering. An injury?"

Rhoslyn tutted. "I smell blood. Has Myla been called for?"

"There is Bavol."

Rhoswen pointed to two figures standing in midair, arms outflung in peace or welcome. Fira recognized the other as Ricker. The brothers kept gesturing to the bat, who only spiraled away.

"Fira!" Dwennon strode up and cheerily decreed, "Come, little warrior. We may have need of your skill. Willum!"

"Here, sir." The young man hastened over, poking through a small collection of crystals in his hand. "This one might do."

He placed a small blue stone in her hand.

"Or this one," he mumbled, considering a wine-colored crystal half its size. "But not both at once. That *would* be unfortunate."

Fira shook her head, protesting, "These are your stones."

Willum added a second blue stone to her hand and closed her fingers around them. "Use them," he said, more focused than she'd ever seen him. "Protect your herd and your home."

"Is the bat attacking?"

Dwennon seemed surprised. "The Kindred of the Thunderhoof clan are known to be healers. They need our help."

More confused than before, Fira asked, "Why do you need me?"

Willum jumped in to explain. "While I lower the barrier to give them entrance, something else could slip inside. Be ready."

She started when Bavol and Ricker dropped to the ground in front of their father. Ricker spared her a smile, but the mood was serious.

"We have tried everything, but he keeps warning us off," said Bavol.

"Match him, courtesy for courtesy," said Dwennon. "Take truest form. Let him see the make of you. It may put him more at ease."

Ricker's gaze strayed to the circling bat. "He is carrying someone. He seems worried for them."

Dwennon snapped, "Willum, open the way."

He did so with a *crack* that resounded like a thunderclap through Fira's soul.

Bavol muttered an oath and launched upward, calling, "Ricker, he is falling!"

Willum's hands flew, sketching intricate patterns in the air and sending them spinning upward in quick succession. They were his gossamer nets, not strong enough to stop the bat from plunging, but each caught and held for a heartbeat or two—slowing his descent, giving the others time.

"Almost there," Dwennon murmured, his hand on Willum's shoulder.

Fira had missed the transformation. As a horse, Ricker had the same powerful build as his brother and matched him stride-for-stride. Where Bavol's coat was golden, Ricker's was burnished to a warmer gloss, like blushing apricots.

As Willum's fragile support trembled, Bavol and Ricker positioned themselves underneath, so when it snapped, the bat landed in a huddle across both their broad backs. They descended at a walk into the Circle.

Willum was at work again, and Dwennon seemed to be helping. As the invisible walls reformed, the power they wielded made Fira's hair stand on end. Belatedly, she recalled that she was meant to be watching for danger. She glanced guiltily around, but immediately felt better. The Duntuffet clan ringed the clearing, facing outward, picks and shovels casually propped on shoulders. The rabbits had keener senses than she, and they looked ready for anything.

In the center of the Circle, Bavol and Ricker took speaking form, as did the bat. The man—male—staggered to his feet, clumsily drew a blade, and bared fangs. In a language Fira didn't know, he flung sharp words that felt like a warning.

Bavol and Ricker both backed up and knelt a few paces away, faces averted.

Dwennon stepped forward, arms open, speaking words that seemed to match the bat's language.

"He is hurt," Fira whispered.

As the bat wheeled, it was possible to see torn cloth and dark blood where something had scored his back. She didn't like seeing his weapon flashing so near Ricker and Bavol, and without thinking, she started forward.

Immediately, the bat was pointing to her and talking fast.

Dwennon answered soothingly, then changed back to the language Fira could understand. "She is called Fira. Come forward, little beauty. He will not allow another male to touch his bondmate."

Bavol and Ricker both beckoned. What else could she do? She hastily pushed Willum's crystals into his hands, whispering, "Are bats safe?"

The redhead gave her arm a squeeze. "They are now."

Which wasn't what she'd meant at all. But maybe that was the best possible sign. No one was expecting trouble. They were focused on helping the bat and his bondmate. So she crossed to where Ricker and Bavol knelt and mirrored their offered palms. "May I help?"

The injured Amaranthine was pallid, with shoulder-length black hair, angular sideburns, and flaring eyebrows. He gestured for her to approach, bringing an alarming detail to her attention. His fingers were tipped by long, claw-like nails.

"Fee-rah," he tried, rolling the *r* in her name. Then he indicated his bondmate. "Glinna."

Taking that next step was a little like stepping off the Leap. She murmured, "Glinna."

He reached for her with those terrible claws, but they didn't slash or gouge. His touch was light, a pleading caress she'd seen the foals use with Ricker. Fira's heart hammered as she looked into the blackest eyes she'd ever seen. She was afraid of him, but he was afraid for his bondmate.

"Let me carry Glinna," she offered, working up a shaky smile.

He said something more, heavily accented but distinguishable. It sounded like *tender*.

Fira wasn't sure what he meant. Did he want her to treat his lady gently?

"Yes, we will tend to her," promised Bavol. He added further assurances in another language.

Ricker added, "The lead mare is nearby. She is a healer."

Bavol quietly urged, "Take her, Fira. He is at the end of his strength."

She worried she wouldn't be strong enough, but Glinna hardly weighed anything. If her husband—bondmate—was anything to go by, her pallor was normal. The lady also had black hair, though hers was coming loose from a pinned-up style. Finely-molded features, delicate brows, and the pointed ears that made Amaranthine look as though they'd stepped out of myths.

"You will be fine," Fira promised, taking a backward step toward Myla's.

Glinna's bondmate quickly reached after her, as if reluctant to lose touch. But then he wobbled and sank to his knees. Bavol was immediately at his side, lending support, mindful of the ragged wounds on his back.

Something tugged at her hair, and annoyance warred with amusement at finding Ricker looming over her in horse form.

"Yes, you are a sight to behold," she said blandly. "Every hand of you, quite handsome."

He lipped her hair again and whickered softly.

Bavol said, "Walk beside us, so Trisk does not lose sight of his mate."

"Good idea," she murmured.

"Ricker's idea," clarified Bavol as he helped Trisk to mount and sat behind to steady him.

Fira smiled into the familiar brown eye regarding her through thick lashes. She was not surprised by Ricker's consideration. Only surprised that the mares placed more value on the color of his coat. If her arms weren't so full, she would have liked to trail her fingers along the proud arch of his neck.

They didn't get very far before Fira spied Myla striding their way. With barely a glance for Glinna, she addressed herself to Trisk, speaking in the same strange language Dwennon had used.

Fira whispered, "What words are those?"

Ricker shook his mane, but of course he couldn't answer.

When Myla came to relieve Fira of her burden, she was kind enough to explain. "We call it Old Amaranthine. It is the language of lore and the lyric of lullabies. Even clans that normally use other languages and dialects know the oldest words."

"Will I need to learn it?" Fira adjusted her grip on Glinna to make the transfer easier.

Myla did not answer. Indeed, Myla did not move. "What is this?"

"He called her Glinna. She has been like this the whole time, but I suppose she must be a bat." What else could she offer that Trisk had not?

"She is pregnant."

"Yes." The dark folds of Glinna's dress could not hide her condition. If Fira had to guess, the lady was midway through the months needed to deliver a healthy child. No wonder Trisk was so protective.

The lead mare looked utterly baffled. "I do not understand."

Fira couldn't see any reason to fuss. She nodded pointedly toward the healer's quarters. "We should get her to a bed."

When Fira resumed walking, Ricker matched her pace. She glanced up to make sure Trisk could see, but he looked without really seeing. He must be exhausted and in a great deal of pain.

In the spacious recovery room, which Bavol and Ricker courteously did not enter, the mares pulled together two beds, and Myla supported Trisk onto the first. He all but collapsed, but stubbornly kept watch as Fira lowered Glinna beside him. Myla shooed out the mares before assuring herself—and Trisk—

that his lady was comfortable.

When his eyes next closed, they did not reopen.

"Will he be all right?" Fira asked.

Myla hummed, but her gaze was still pinned on the female.

Fira couldn't understand the mare's consternation. "Does she have a dangerous fever or something?"

"She is pregnant."

Another possibility came to her. There must have been a fight, and Trisk had fallen, albeit slowly, from a great height. And there had been a barrier. What if Willum's magic had harmed the child in the same way she'd harmed that dragon? Fira asked, "Is something amiss with her baby?"

Myla opened and closed her mouth, then leaned down to whisper, "I have never seen this. Never heard of it happening. Never imagined it possible."

Fira was growing frustrated. "What is wrong?"

"She is pregnant." But this time, Myla clarified. "She is carrying a child while in speaking form."

SLEEPING BEAUTY

That night, when Myla pulled Fira and Lufu close for sleep, she asked several embarrassing questions about human coupling. Fira couldn't really protest. Lufu was old enough to learn such things. But she shyly pointed out. "I have no experience. You should ask Glinna when she wakes."

"How long will she sleep?" asked Lufu, who was clearly interested in learning more.

"The Kindred do not need to retire every night, but we need rest. After weeks without, we can sleep for days." With a nod toward the nearby bed where Trisk and Glinna slept, Myla explained, "There was nothing wrong with his lady. Once sleeping, we are difficult to rouse. A day or two more, and she will wake on her own."

Lufu begged, "Can I be here when you ask about babies?"

Myla hesitated, so Fira answered, "Yes. We have no mother to tell us, so it would be wise to learn alongside the mares. But ... Myla, I do know a little about birthing. I was old enough to remember when Lufu was born."

"Did you assist?"

"The midwife would not let me look, for she said there was too much mess, but I would not leave my mother." Fira reached for Lufu's hand and gave it a squeeze. "I held her hand the whole time, so I heard the midwife telling her what to do. And I was the first to hold you."

"Was I tiny?"

"Only this big!" Fira held up both hands, measuring the distance.

Myla made a small sound.

Lufu rolled into the mare's side and placed a hand on her stomach. "Rhoswen says you want to be a mother again. Are you going to have a baby?"

"What an idea," murmured the mare, who put an end to their talk by singing to them, soft and low, of talking trees and whispering winds and the lullabies of stars.

On the morning of Midsummer's Eve, Fira was taking her turn at Glinna's bedside when their sleeping beauty finally stirred, opening eyes the rich red of blackberry juice.

Myla plied her with teas and sent Fira and Lufu for trays of food.

"Is she going to ask about babies while we are gone?" Lufu asked with a pout.

"Maybe about the kinds of things a married woman already knows," Fira replied delicately. "Private things."

Lufu suddenly asked, "If you marry Willum, do you think Ricker will go find me a husband?"

"Are you anxious to marry?"

"I want to marry a *man*, not a rabbit or a horse."

Fira was having a hard time taking her sister seriously. "Perhaps *you* should marry Willum, then."

"You saw him first."

Which sounded oddly familiar. And entirely beside the point.

They returned with two large trays and found Glinna propped up on pillows, her long hair freshly brushed and coiled, and her clawed hands plucking at the bedclothes. The food roused her interest. Although she picked at a salad, she tore gratefully into a grilled fish and hummed with delight over a thick custard.

When Glinna finished, she addressed Fira. "Myla tells me you came to my rescue."

"Everyone did," she answered, not realizing at first. "You speak our language!"

"I was born nearby but traveled a great distance before finding a male to my liking. His homeland and clan make their circle far to the east."

Fira asked, "How was he hurt?"

"We had the misfortune of coming too close to a dragon's nest."

"An Amaranthine dragon?"

"Not from a clan. Rather, a common beast." Glinna hugged herself. "They can still be found in remote places. This female had young to protect, and while I understand her instinct, Trisk did what was necessary."

"Glinna!" Trisk fairly flew through the door and slammed against the side of the bed, clambering up so he could gather her close.

She laughed and caressed his face, and her words relaxed him.

Trisk kissed her soundly, and Fira quickly looked away, only to find Lufu watching with rapt interest. She tapped her sister's nose and whispered, "We should give them some privacy."

Lufu gave in with grace, only saying, "They are beautiful together."

Fira had to agree. And judging by the pensive, yearning look on Myla's face, the lead mare was of a similar mind.

Since the mares' dance earlier that month, Fira had steered clear of the male horses, who jostled and strutted and flexed whenever there was a mare in view—which was *always*. Their displays didn't interest her, but it was hard to ignore the thunder of hooves as they raced through the valley below Glintrubble. Or the tumult caused by a stray remark that sent them into the sky to see who could fly the highest.

Fira had been captivated by the galloping whirlwind, even if she thought their stunts mostly silly. What did these dares prove?

The mares looked on with placid smiles, but Fira began to

notice signs that they, too, were establishing ranks.

Myla had explained that the females were vying for the order in which they would make their choices. "They cannot *all* have their way. Each mare's turn will come, and when it does, she takes the best choice that remains to her."

"What if the stallion she wanted has already been taken?"

"She can wait and see if another season favors her, or she might wait until after his midsummer obligation ends." Myla's brows had knit. "Some stallions sire two or three late foals."

Fira ranged out into the clear morning, only to find Glintrubble—and its citizens—transformed. The males of the horse clans wore fresh tunics with bright sashes, and every one of them had done something to their hair. Loops and knots. Ribbons and braids. Ferns and flowers.

Anticipation fizzed through the air, so palpable, she could feel its reverberation. The longer she spent in this place, the more strongly she felt the echo of its stones, the thrum of its people. They were glad, and she borrowed some of their joy.

But where was Ricker? Normally, the different color of his hair made him easy to spot, but with everyone crowned in festive blooms, he didn't stand out.

Nearly an hour of searching led Fira to the mine entrance, where Ricker slouched against a stone wall, half-hidden by an ore cart. She said, "There is supposed to be no work today."

Ricker didn't look up. "That would explain why everyone else is late."

She propped her hands on her hips and surveyed his attire. His tunic was as fine as anyone's and his sash was so vivid, it had to be new. But he hadn't taken any pains with his hair. "Why have you neglected your mane?"

"We do not array ourselves. The fillies adorn us ... for luck."

Fira crouched in front of him. "And how are they supposed to find you, hidden away back here?"

Ricker refused to meet her gaze.

Had he tried mingling with the other colts and not been given the tokens he longed for? She'd seen how generous the fillies were with their courtesies. This was a festival day, and no one had been left out of the fun. But Ricker had probably been hoping for favors from one filly in particular.

"Maybe all those silly fillies need is a little encouragement. If a colt has one admirer, he is suddenly worth considering." Fira reached for his hair, but he leaned away, gaze uncertain. She said, "I may not be a daughter of the herd, but I am counted as a sister. And I know how to braid. What flowers should I fetch?"

Ricker flicked her a grateful look and mumbled through a list of flowers with traditional meanings.

She patted his head and jogged to the Circle, where rabbits were distributing cut flowers to all comers. There, she found the two little girls who'd accompanied Ricker to the Leap. These daughters of Dwennon were very young, but weren't they fillies of the herd?

Tapping their shoulders, she bent to whisper, "Which flowers shall we bring to Ricker?"

Delighted gasps. Jumbled explanations. Abundant help.

By the time they trekked up the mountain path, trailing flower petals and ribbon streamers, Fira was accompanied by five little girls and a cherubic little boy who insisted he loved Ricker better than any girl ever. So Fira toted him along and placed him in an astonished Ricker's arms.

He laughed.

He relaxed.

He teased.

He tickled.

And the children divided his hair and plaited each section, changing his gingery mane into a rainbow riot and lifting his mood to the moon. Ricker caught her hand and reeled her in. "They left you my forelock."

"I am honored."

"The honor is mine," he returned quietly. "Thank you, Fira."

She braided a section so it would lie alongside his face, adding little clusters of orange flowers, which complemented his coloring. "When do the mares begin choosing?" she asked.

"When the drums start." He glanced at the sun and swallowed. "Soon."

The fillies declared him splendid, and he kissed them all. The little colt, who now sported a few flowers of his own, offered a shy peck.

Ricker placed a soft kiss on Fira's forehead and mumbled, "Wish me luck."

Fira couldn't pat his head, so she patted his cheek instead. "You deserve every happiness."

PASSED OVER

The children herded her toward the Circle, promising her that the best fun was to be had with the rabbits.

"What about the mares and their choosing?" she asked, trying to catch a glimpse of the smaller, partially secluded meadow where most of the Thunderhoof herd were gathered. She could see Dwennon and Bavol on the edge of the Circle, speaking in low tones with Trisk. The stallions had their attention entirely fixed on him, to the exclusion of the dozen or more mares undoubtedly responsible for the lavish state of their hair.

"The mares are boooring," assured one filly.

Another said, "They take all night."

One of the older girls explained, "It is like a slow dance that never begins. Once a mare chooses a partner, they leave."

"Rabbit dances are much more fun!"

Lufu arrived then, her hair once more a glory of gemstones. The Duntuffet sisters waved for Fira to join them, but she felt she should stay with the fillies until ... well, she wasn't sure. "How long before we find out who chose whom?" she asked.

To her surprise, Willum answered. "Rabbits are excellent eavesdroppers, but they also enjoy silly rumors. They will spread the most outlandish tales all night, but at dawn, the mares will return with their stallions to parade through the Circle."

"How long have you lived here?"

"I was born here," Willum said distractedly. "Fira ... who is that?"

She followed his gaze. "Lufu, my sister."

"Why have I never met your sister?"

Fira's protective instincts riled at his tone. "Perhaps because you rarely leave your workshop."

"The resemblance is uncanny." He looked at her, then back at Lufu. "Is she a crystal adept like you?"

"Is that what I am?"

"Well," he hedged. "That is what *I* call people like us. There may be other names in other places."

The *us* was nice. As was the implication that her curse was more of a talent.

"Fira." Willum had stepped closer, his eyes searching. "Is she?"

Drums began to beat. "Is she what?"

With more patience than she deserved, Willum repeated, "Do the remnants respond to your sister?"

"She has her own way with stones." Fira grudgingly admitted, "Ours likes her better."

Willum's eyes narrowed slightly, as if listening for something despite the low pulse of drumbeats and the merry piping of the rabbit minstrels. "Fira," he said slowly. "There is a crystal."

"Yes, I know."

He actually looked hurt. "Why are you hiding it from me?"

"We hide it from everyone. Our parents left it for us. It has helped us survive."

Nodding slowly, he asked, "Do you know what is rarest of all the colors?"

"Pink?" she ventured. Willum was very particular about his pink stones, most of which were quite small.

"Pink is the second rarest form."

Fira's pulse rushed, but she forced herself to ask, "What is the rarest?"

"Clear. Colorless. Like cloudless ice, yet not empty. They always harbor a fleck, a grain, a narrow seam of color, as if all the power has narrowed and focused." Willum calmly said, "I have two, and they are small. Hardly bigger than a pea. Yet they are the most potent crystals in my care."

She knew what he was asking, and she nodded. "Yellow," she whispered. "The tiniest droplet of yellow."

"And ... how large?"

Fira's hands shakily framed the familiar shape. "It is ours, Willum. It is all we have."

Willum's own hands were shaking when he tugged at hers and pleaded, "May I meet your stone?"

"Lufu has it."

She watched him go. From across the Circle, she saw him introduce himself, gesticulating in his enthusiasm. Fira saw Lufu—sweet, trusting Lufu—simply unfasten the pouch at her waist and bring out the crystal.

Even from here, Fira could hear its voice.

The moment her sister dropped the stone into Willum's hand, a bow screeched across strings, and the drumming faltered. Every head turned to the place where Willum and Lufu stood. Fira thought at first that he must be doing something to the stone, but he peered around. A murmur had begun—eager, excited.

From across the Circle, Willum's gaze locked with Fira's, and his mouth formed an 'o.' Then he hollered, "Sorry! Sorry! A moment, please!"

Quickly, he returned the stone to Lufu's hand and drew one of his glowing figures in the air, then gently pushed it toward Lufu until his finger rested against her chest. A ward. Why did Lufu have to be warded?

The ripple of whispers finally washed past Fira where she stood. One word repeating over and again—*beacon*.

Fira couldn't have explained *why* she was hiding behind Ricker's ore cart. Maybe for the same reason she understood how he sometimes felt. It wasn't easy having a sibling who was all the things that other people admired.

Lufu was beautiful, Lufu was desirable, Lufu was powerful. Willum was enthralled, though it wasn't clear to Fira if he was more interested in her sister or her stone. Dwennon was ecstatic, shouting something about an anchor before getting the drummers back to the task at hand. Even Trisk was all worked up, only this time he wanted Lufu to do something *tender* for Glinna.

So once she was sure Lufu was safely tucked between Rhoswen and Rhoslyn, Fira slipped outside alone, away from the festival lights and music, here to this hushed place to sort out her frazzled feelings.

All of a sudden, something pounded against the ore cart with a resounding *boom*. She yelped in fear, ears ringing, pulse racing. Peering cautiously around its edge, she met the startled gaze of Ricker, who was cradling a battered fist.

"Ricker?"

He cringed and sank to his knees. "Ow."

Fira had never seen violence from Ricker, but she wasn't frightened of him. More like frightened for him. His eyes were over-bright, and she knew, knew, knew what must have happened.

Crawling to his side, she asked, "Synnis chose another?"

He curled in on himself.

Fira tentatively said, "She had many choices. The herd is strong."

"I know!" he spat. Reining himself in, he quietly repeated, "I *know*. But did she have to choose Bavol?"

Hopes dashed.

Pride trampled.

Hurt plain.

She flung her arms around his neck and pulled his head to her shoulder. There was nothing that could be said, nothing that would help.

Hot tears dripped onto her neck as Ricker's shoulders shook.

It hardly seemed fair. Ricker might be young and impatient, and he played the fool to please the youngsters. But why should he be left to tend the young sired by other stallions when he would obviously be the very best of fathers?

A sob broke free.

She stole the flowers from his hair, tossing them aside. She teased out knots and unwound ribbon. Her fingers found each braid and loosened them until she was able to stroke through the length of his hair unhindered.

The weeping slowed, and he switched shoulders, probably to find a dry patch. He also grabbed hold of her, and Fira could tell he was trying to pull himself together. So she kept right on stroking his hair.

Finally, he snuffled wetly and nuzzled her neck, brushing his lips over damp skin. "Sorry, Fira. I am a mess, and you have been kind. Kinder than any mare I know."

And his hand cupped her cheek, and his smile was achingly sad. And then he touched his lips to hers in the gentlest of kisses.

She understood his intent—returning courtesy for kindness. This was simply the way of the herd, a show of acceptance and gratitude. But this wasn't the way it had been with Myla or Dwennon. Even after he pulled back, gently lifting her aside so he could stand and stagger off, Ricker's kiss lingered with her, like an echo that sang with her soul.

And it was both wonderful and utterly wretched, for all at once, she knew exactly how he felt. To love someone who could not, would not, did not love you back.

His tragedy had become hers as well.

TEND HER

Fira was growing accustomed to Myla's caresses and cuddling, but it was an honest relief when Glinna turned out to be more restrained. While less outwardly affectionate, she was more talkative. Fira was grateful for her stories of different places and other clans, for they often included details that helped her interpret Amaranthine behavior.

She found herself wishing she could be Glinna's apprentice instead of Willum's. The ward's approach to learning was imprecise.

Try it and see.

Give this a go.

I wonder what will happen.

Glinna held to a different style—listen and learn. She shared from a wealth of knowledge gained over a startling span of years.

Why had no one thought to mention that Amaranthine could live for centuries? Their history was rich and diverse, and their lore held Fira captive, especially when Glinna's tales echoed the songs of stones.

Today, Willum had become the pupil, for Trisk and Glinna had come to visit his workshop. The bondmates sat with arms touching, and Fira spent several minutes trying to put a name to the way their presence was so … *there*. Was it because she was surrounded by crystals? Could they echo and amplify a person?

Trisk met her gaze and offered a small nod.

Fira tried the greeting in his language that Glinna had taught her.

He flashed a pleased smile, made dangerous by fangs.

"There are others like you," Glinna was saying. "Those with beautiful souls."

Willum leaned forward. "Crystal adepts?"

Glinna inclined her head. "Ward," she said, nodding to him, then Fira. "Battler."

Trisk pointed to the door. "Beacon."

"Come in, Lufu!" Willum urged. "I have been meaning to introduce you to some of my crystals!"

Fira gestured for Lufu to join her on the bench against the wall, and Willum rolled a few crystals to her even as he said, "Please, continue, Lady Brunwinger."

"Lady?" whispered Lufu.

Trisk leaned forward and tapped his chest. "*My* lady."

Glinna laughed lightly. "No need to stand upon formalities. Every house in every clan among the bats may claim a lord and lady. Rarer by far are those like you. In quiet places where clans have banded together, we foster your precious lives."

"How?" Willum asked. "What do you mean by *foster*?"

"You were rescued by this herd."

He nodded. "Essentially. Dwennon rescued my mother, and I was born here. I am considered kin."

Glinna lifted a finger. "In Trisk's homeland, tree-kin dwell in the valleys surrounding a remote monastery. The good men look to the vineyards, and their wine cellars rest safely in the caves where bats thrive."

Willum looked between Trisk and Glinna. "Do you have to hide?"

"Wards and illusions," she replied. "The Brunwingers are allied to a clan of foxes, who passed along the secret of the sharing of souls. They call it *tending*."

Fira stole a look at Trisk. Had *that* been what he was asking when she thought he was saying *tender*? "Is it for healing?"

Glinna made a circular motion with one hand. "Healing, strengthening, understanding, trust. It is as much for peace as for power. We gain what is given, and in return, we guard you from those who would steal both soul and life."

Willum planted both hands on the table and leaned forward. "I would like a demonstration!"

Trisk and Glinna exchanged a glance.

A brow arched. A shoulder lifted.

"Lufu is brightest," Glinna said slowly. "But it is good that you warded her. She will need to learn restraint."

"Here, Fira." Willum placed a small pink crystal on her hand. "This one has a sweet song, and its protective properties may be beneficial."

"Why me?"

"Because you resonate well with ..."

Fira didn't let him finish. "*You* should do it, Willum."

His jaw dropped. Clearly, he was so keen on observing the phenomenon, it never occurred to him to participate.

She pointed out, "You have the most experience, the most control. You would probably understand what is happening better than either of us."

Lufu nodded. "If you learn how, you can teach us."

"I *am* curious." Willum offered his hands to the Brunwingers. "Will I do?"

Trisk murmured something to his bondmate, and Glinna moved to the other side of the table, joining Fira and Lufu. Then he turned sideways on the bench and drew Willum down to face him.

Glinna said, "Trisk is strong, bold. Find him quickly, trust him completely. All will be well."

Fira would have liked more detailed instructions, but Willum offered his hands to Trisk. "Touching?"

Trisk looked entirely pleased and said something more, his deep voice slipping into a lilting rhythm.

"His pain will lessen, and his injuries will heal more quickly," Glinna translated. "Thank you for your trust."

With a bit of tugging, Trisk encouraged Willum to come closer, guiding the young ward's hands to his shoulders. The Amaranthine was taller than the redhead, so he had to bend in order to rest their foreheads together. A clawed hand lifted to touch a freckled cheek, and Trisk murmured again.

"Close your eyes and find him," Glinna said into the breathless hush. "He awaits."

At first, nothing happened. Willum's face wore the same expression as when he was listening for a crystal's song. But then his breath caught, and his grip on Trisk's shoulders tightened. But just as quickly, he relaxed into a delighted chuckle. "Oh," he murmured. "I could get used to this."

"What's it like?" asked Lufu.

Willum's face was completely serene. "If stones hold the echo, Trisk is the song."

Glinna repeated the words so her bondmate could understand. With a little grumble, Trisk kissed Willum's forehead and pulled him into an embrace.

From where she sat, Fira could see that both were smiling ... and that Willum's lashes were wet.

SPARE FEELINGS

Fira was surprised at herself. Of all the things she'd needed to adjust to at Glintrubble, the most difficult was losing track of Lufu. All their lives, her little sister had hardly been out of reach, let alone out of sight. But this was a safe place. Lufu accepted her newfound freedom without a backward glance.

Running off.

Meeting people.

Making friends.

Growing apart.

Certainly, Lufu needed her independence, but Fira was still accustomed to watching over her. If not for her lucky stone and its familiar pull, she wouldn't have had any inkling what Lufu did to occupy her time. Or which paths she chose. Or whose workshop she frequented.

They still shared a bed in the mares' quarters, often with Myla's arms around them both, as if they were the lead mare's own daughters. But tonight, Fira and Lufu had the long, hushed room to themselves.

Whether it was because Lufu's lucky stone was picking up on her mood or simply because Fira knew her sister so well, she asked, "Is something on your mind?"

"Not at all," Lufu murmured.

Fira turned toward her sister and plucked at her nightdress. "So secretive."

Lufu pouted and wriggled closer. "Do not mind me."

"If *I* do not mind you, who will?" She wished she could sound as wise as Glinna, because this might be a touchy subject. "You have been dreamy-eyed and distracted, lately. Like a woman in love."

"Wh-what a thing to say," she mumbled, hiding her face.

Truly, she wore her heart on her sleeve.

Fira hid her smile and asked, "Did you know that Ricker had hoped to be chosen by Synnis?"

"Everyone knew." Lufu seemed grateful for the change of subject.

"Even Bavol?" Fira asked.

"He and Ricker seem very close," Lufu said slowly. "I cannot imagine he did not know."

Fira hummed her agreement. "Do you think Bavol should have denied Synnis in order to spare his brother's feelings?"

"I would have."

And there it was. Lufu was too generous for her own good.

Fira gently asked, "Why do you suppose Bavol accepted Synnis, even though he knew it would hurt Ricker?"

Eventually, Lufu answered, "He must have loved Synnis, too."

"I am glad Bavol was brave enough to be honest with himself and gave Synnis his pledge. Mutual love may be rarer than the pink crystals Willum loves so well. And many times more precious."

At the mention of Willum's name, Lufu sniffled.

"My sweet sister," she sighed. "Did you think I would not notice your efforts to spare my feelings?"

Lufu clung and mumbled apologies.

"Nonsense." Fira held on tight and said, "I do not love him, Lufu."

"May *I*, then?"

"As if any could stop you." She kissed her sister's hair and whispered, "You will surely be his treasure."

CRYSTAL ADEPT

Fira's mind wandered away from the crystal she was supposed to illuminate, drifting in a wistful, wishful direction.

"That!" Willum's stool overturned as he scrambled to reach her side. "That! That! That!"

She snapped upright, nearly dropping the stone.

He clapped his hands around hers, eyes wide. "*Gently* with this one, Fira. We have never seen its like and may never again."

"Sorry." Fira grumbled, "You startled me."

The pale blue crystal was quite large and normally served as one of Glintrubble's ward stones. He'd borrowed it from the boundary in order to help her grasp the basics of barrier formation.

"You had it for a moment," said Willum. "What were you thinking about just then?"

"Nothing." She could feel her cheeks warming. Pushing the stone toward the center of the table, she asked, "Why do I have to do this, anyhow? I thought Lufu is the one you want for an anchor. The stones like her, and she makes them happy. Train her."

Willum knelt by her chair. "Lufu is brilliant, and we need her strength. The whole cooperative's safety may one day depend on her. But I need you, too."

Fira wasn't in the mood to make this easy on him. She silently held his gaze, daring him to convince her.

He pulled at his ever-wild hair with both hands, then waved them around. "Lufu *is* power, which is lovely and good. But you can unlock that power. Shape it. Use it."

"Like when the dragon attacked."

Willum nodded. "Lufu attracts trouble, but she also lends strength to her defenders—Thunderhoofs and Duntuffets. And Trisk. Have you seen him with his swords?"

"No."

"Dwennon wants him to join the cooperative. Adding a predatory clan would give us an edge, especially now."

"Because Lufu and I are endangering you."

Willum poked her shoulder. "You and Lufu are also the best incentive the Brunwingers have to stay."

"A good outcome?" she asked softly.

His expression shifted, then slowly closed. "Will you tell me what you were thinking about just now ... or rather, *whom*?"

Fira averted her gaze.

"I do not think it was me."

She snorted.

"That may be for the best. Less complicated." Again, he poked her shoulder. His gaze was open and artless. "We are beginning with barriers because they are simplest. I can teach you how to befriend the wind later. Stones before sigils."

"I cannot imagine."

"One thing at a time, my dear apprentice." Willum bit his lip and lowered his voice. "May I tell you something that terrifies me?"

Fira nodded.

"The stones—they like you better than me."

Her laugh ended in a pitiful sob. What was wrong with her?

Willum gave her shoulder a tentative pat. "Enough. I decree a change of pace."

She dabbed at her eyes while he rummaged through one shelf, then another.

"Aha!" He hurried back and showed her a clear green crystal. It had been shaped into a rough column no wider than her finger. Polished smooth and pierced through, it had been threaded onto two long, narrow strips of leather.

"The rabbits favor armbands," he explained, wrapping the ties twice around her wrist to create a bracelet. "This should do nicely. Green, like your and Lufu's eyes. I am giving it to you."

"To keep?"

Willum nodded. "Hear its song. Learn its voice. Sense its mood. I have found this color useful for amplification. Indeed, the ward stones that are farthest from the Circle are encircled by green stones. With you and Lufu helping, we may be able to extend the boundaries."

"Who taught you how to use crystals?"

"The stones themselves." He peered around the room. "But the sigils for drawing out and applying their strengths—for that, I needed mentors. My first was a squirrel who was acquainted with the Duntuffets. When I showed promise, Dwennon arranged for an expert."

"A fox?" she guessed. Glinna had mentioned foxes.

"Their reputation is impressive, but no. Few understand the ways of the wind better than those who revere it." With a sad smile, he revealed, "Most of what I know about sigilcraft was taught to me by a dragon."

She ventured, "Was he … safe?"

Willum laughed. "He was whimsical and outrageous and learned and kind. If I can be half as good a teacher as he was, you will excel."

"I am willing to try."

He touched the stone at her wrist. "Your first assignment is child's play. You can ask the foals to help."

PLAYING HOUSE

Fira's best helpers were the same foals who had festooned Ricker, so it didn't come as any surprise when—after the passage of a few days—he came to investigate.

"I have been hearing the most outlandish things." Ricker loomed over her in a mockery of accusation. "The foals have been saying that your games are more fun than mine."

"Do you want to play?" she offered.

"I feel it is my duty." He scanned the group of giggling foals. "If I am lacking, I am willing to learn. Where are we bound?"

"Cadmiel's Tump?" Fira suggested. Her memories of their last visit were good.

With a sweep of his arm, Ricker said, "Let us away!"

While they walked, Fira explained Willum's assignment, which mostly involved hiding and searching, though also tracking movement.

She was interrupted when six gangly foals bolted past, tails high, manes bristling.

"Two feet are slower than four hooves." Ricker's brows lifted. "Want a ride?"

Fira pointed out, "I could never climb up."

"That was not a *no*." Ricker hoisted her onto his back, promising, "Easy. Just grab hold."

He transformed under her, scaring her half to death and thrilling her to her toes.

"Wonderful," she whispered.

Ricker shook his mane, and she grabbed hold with both hands. He took one step, then another—cautious, concerned.

"This is no faster than walking on two feet," she teased.

His ears swiveled back. She could feel him coil, and then he sprang. But there was no jarring thud. No drum of hooves. No bone-rattling cadence to shake her from her seat. Only the ripple of muscles—powerful, confident.

Fira yanked and clung as he gained speed, but she felt safe.

"You promised not to let me fall," she growled, though there was laughter under her warning.

A low whicker felt like amusement.

They weren't very high, merely skimming over the grasses, and they soon overtook the foals. The young ones capered and kicked and neighed. Cadmiel's Tump neared, and Ricker took the final length in a high-stepping trot, all strut and show.

The foals arrived just behind, back on two feet and giggling through their protests.

"No fair!"

"We cannot fly yet!"

"Give us a lesson?"

"Can we go to the Leap?"

"Later," said Ricker. "We are helping Fira with her training first."

The oldest filly, whose fair hair rippled as if recently released from braids, slyly asked, "Why did you give Fira a ride?"

Ricker hesitated a moment too long before casually answering, "She needed one."

Suspicious, Fira asked, "Did it mean something for Ricker to give me a ride?"

The fillies talked over one another, blurting out all the reasons they thought his gesture was enviable. Any of them would have gladly traded places with her, and for simpler reasons than she expected.

"Trading rides means you like each other both ways."

"Hoof and heel, you belong together."

"Ricker likes everyone, but he likes you extra more!"

So it was a show of acceptance and preference, the sort shared by close friends. Fira wished she could return the compliment in kind. In confiding tones, she told the foals, "That is well and good, since Ricker is my favorite."

"Mine, too! And mine!" chorused the youngsters in complete unanimity.

Ricker waved off the resounding praise, but he was grinning when he recalled them to the task at hand. Simple games quickly escalated, for he invited greater challenges.

"Can you see him?" asked Fira.

Two of the fillies pointed, and she thought she could make out a speck. It had been their idea to test both her limits and his. Like mares putting the stallions of the herd through their paces, they'd ordered Ricker aloft. Perhaps this was another children's game. Colts and fillies playing at herd, just as she and Lufu had played at house.

"Your eyes are better than mine," Fira confessed.

"But can you hear your stone's song?" asked the little colt.

Fira closed her eyes and searched her mind for some sign of the green crystal. "Yes, it is there."

"Ricker let you ride." It was the oldest of her filly friends. "And at midsummer, he saved you his forelock."

"Is that special?"

She nodded, eyes wide with the enormity of her revelation.

Fira wished she could grant his courtesies the same significance, but she knew Ricker had only been playing at herd, practicing for when it would hold meaning for a mare. So Fira shook her head. "There are so many horse customs. And I suppose there are just as many for the rabbits?"

"More!"

"And we shall all be learning bat customs, now that Trisk and Glinna have come." She stretched out in the sun-warmed grass, letting her eyes drift shut. "If they stay."

The foals arranged themselves around her, her filly informant claiming the closest quarters. "You should give him more tasks."

So much for distracting the girl.

Fira played along. "What sorts of things would *you* have him do?"

Their eager suggestions made one thing abundantly clear. They wanted nothing more than Ricker's time and attention. Games and adventures with their favorite brother.

GREEN STONE

Fira thought she knew the stone Willum had given her. She could orient herself to its presence—finding it, following it. But as she lay on the hillside, chasing the remnant's presence high into the sky, something new happened.

Perhaps it was her focus.

Perhaps it was Ricker's presence.

Perhaps it was a trick of the wind.

For as the green stone spiraled higher, it spun into a song. The melody pierced her soul and pulled her in, until it was all Fira could see and hear. It carried her off, filling her mind like a dream. She saw a fiery bird tangling with a winged dragon, twisting and twining over a churning sea. Only they were not fighting. Buffeted by a storm, they struggled to carry something precious between them. Or … was it someone?

"Fira?"

She opened her eyes to find Ricker bent close.

"Did you fall asleep?"

Had she?

He touched her cheek. "You were crying."

Fira gave a small shake of her head. "This stone has a beautiful song."

Ricker's expression cleared. "Could you follow it?"

"I knew where you were the whole time." She sat up, and he sat beside her. Fira asked the foals, "Is he not the best at this game?"

Adulation and agreement rose up on all sides, and Fira pushed onto her knees so she could better reach Ricker's hair. He didn't exactly shy away, but his expression was full of questions. However, he was also used to letting others have their way, so he sat docile while she divided his forelock into sections and began to weave.

"The stone," she directed, holding out a hand.

Ricker surrendered it, but asked, "Fira?"

She threaded and knotted and wove some more, twining the stone's leather ties through the braid so that the crystal rested secure. "I *like* knowing where you are."

"But this is yours." Color was creeping into Ricker's cheeks.

Fira glanced at the fillies and ventured, "Have I done something I should not?"

"No, no. Hardly that." Ricker touched the slender stone at his temple and asked his siblings, "Am I grand?"

The chorus of compliments quickly changed to pleas.

"Will you have more stones?"

"Can I wear one, too?"

"I want Fira to know where *I* am!"

She laughed and shrugged. "You could ask Willum, I suppose. Better yet, ask Rhoswen and Rhoslyn. They may know where to find more."

And like stallions spurred by a mare's whim, they scrambled up and away, eager to complete the task she'd set. Leaving her alone with Ricker.

Fira asked, "Have I embarrassed you? I can undo the ties."

But when she reached for the end knot, Ricker's hand caught hers. "I was only surprised, Fira. Since you do not know our customs, you would not know the significance of such a gift. This suggests that there is a promise between us."

"You promised me not to leave the herd."

"So I did. Yes, that is so." He stood and helped her to her feet, and they strolled a ways toward the village before he broke his distracted silence. "Myla chose Dwennon."

"They *are* bondmates."

"Yes, but I hear she warned the mares that she would permit no late foals."

Fira wasn't really surprised. "Does Dwennon mind?"

"No. He has been talking to Trisk."

"I think Myla wants a baby," Fira murmured.

Ricker's gaze had turned inward. "Dwennon and Bavol say that the herd is strong. It is time to build the clan."

The bats' arrival was stirring some interesting changes at Glintrubble. Fira wondered if Ricker was unhappy with the direction things were taking. "What do *you* think of Trisk and Glinna?"

"Their devotion is ... attractive." He blew out a gusty breath.

"And daunting. How can I secure a bondmate when I cannot even attract enough interest to stand stud? *Oh*. Forgive my crassness." His flush reached the tips of his ears.

"Did you know Glinna traveled a long way before she found Trisk?"

He hummed an unhappy affirmative. "I do not want to go. Indeed, you have my pledge to stay."

"What if we went together?" she asked lightly.

Ricker's expression gentled. "You are so brave, Fira."

Far from it. But she was brave enough to say, "You deserve every happiness."

His smile trembled at the edges. "I thought Synnis was perfect for me because I wanted the same thing."

"More than a foal."

Ricker made a soft noise in the back of his throat.

Fira said, "In human communities, men do the choosing. It is the women who wait and wonder if they will be chosen and cherished. Too many are traded like chattel."

"How backward."

She smiled at his obvious confusion. "When it comes to a love match, the only difference is in who speaks first."

"Here, you can choose for yourself. You can have Willum."

Fira scowled. "Having no choice is *not* a choice."

"Is it … because of his coloring?"

"*No*. My heart is not won or lost by something so trivial." Fira was still angry with the mares for slighting Ricker. "Willum knows I do not want him. Indeed, he seemed relieved to learn it. I daresay he will make a better brother than bridegroom."

"Lufu?"

"*Of course*, Lufu." Fira didn't mean for so much sharpness to steal into her tone. "Lufu the beacon. Lufu the beauty. Lufu the blushing bride."

Ricker came to an abrupt stop. "Maybe Bavol and I can search for other prospects ...?" he offered uncertainly.

"A waste of time." Fira folded her arms over her chest. "Human men like docile, doting, dainty wives."

He blinked. "You are not ... large."

"Compared to mares. But my stature is considered a misfortune. I am ungainly, cumbersome. You know, I have even been described as coltish."

He snorted his way into a whinnying laugh and swooped her into his arms. Swinging her around, he glibly asked, "Did you know Glinna traveled a long way before she found Trisk?"

She favored him with a sour look. "That comforts me even less than it did you."

Ricker slowed to a stop and gathered her much more gently. "At least you *tried*."

Fira hugged him back and whispered, "Hoof and heel, you are my favorite."

"Fira the battler. Fira the bold. Fira the coltish human." His lips grazed her cheek, and he spoke close to her ear. "You deserve every happiness."

HEAVY POCKETS

Over the next few days, all the young fillies and colts of Fira's acquaintance—and a handful of newcomers—came to her with their pockets filled with pebbles. Seated on the front step of Willum's workshop, she patiently inspected their findings.

"I am sorry," she said over and again. "Not every stone has a song. These are pretty, but they will not work."

Somehow, all the comings and goings caught Willum's notice. He came to the door and surveyed the gathered children. "What is this? I thought I was the only rock collector in Glintrubble."

The foals were only too happy for a second opinion.

Their excited explanations jumped over one another's, but the gist was clear. Fira was afraid Willum would be annoyed over the potential squandering of precious crystals, but he drummed his fingers on his thigh, then nodded.

"A moment, please!" He disappeared inside, only to return a moment later, pointing and muttering to himself as he counted heads. "Right. *Two* moments. Do not wander off!"

When he ducked inside again, the children traded grins.

To Fira's delight, Willum returned with a fistful of green crystals. None was bigger than her thumbnail, but each sang with a sweet note.

Sitting beside her on the step, he ordered, "Line up, you lot."

"Is this all right?" Fira asked softly.

"Ingenious!" He let the entire collection rattle into her cupped hands. "Your plan will work best if the stone's song suits the soul. With your aptitude, you should be able to coax the remnant into close harmony. Or even unison. That would be ideal."

Willum guided her through the first few, then sat back and watched her match the youngsters with their own special stone. When the last was sent running to the rabbits for help setting their crystal into a pendant or armband, the redhead bumped shoulders with her.

"Where is the stone I gave to you?"

Fira fumbled for an explanation and came up empty.

"I can tell where it is." He watched her face with a little half smile. "A short stroll would give me the answer, but I would rather hear it from you. Although … I can guess."

"If you tease me, I will hide every speck of pink in your trove."

"Ah." Willum gave her a sidelong look. "I would not tease, Fira. Not about the song of your soul."

"Hush," she growled.

Willum surprised her again, wrapping his arm around her shoulders, keeping his thoughts to himself, lending her his handkerchief.

PUSHING BOUNDARIES

By the next full moon, many of the mares seemed to vanish from Glintrubble. Fira finally asked about their absence.

Myla explained, "Those who danced at midsummer are now carrying. They will remain in truest form until the birth of their foals."

"*You* danced at midsummer, and you are here."

The lead mare folded her hands over her midriff and smiled softly.

"Will there be a baby?" Fira whispered.

"That is the shape of our hope." She gestured toward the din coming from the forest beyond the Circle. "Dwennon wishes to speak with you, love."

"About?" she asked warily.

The lead mare's brows arched. "Serious matters, for once. Regarding the safety of our herd and home. Trisk returned at sunrise from stretching his wings. He found signs of dragons."

Fira strode briskly toward the new worksite.

Dwennon had been rallying the stallions to gather wood and stone for beams and hearths. The Thunderhoof clan would divide and multiply, with three sons establishing their own houses. They would be formalized at the Song Circle three years hence—Blazelock, Dawnracer, and Canterbelle.

Up until now, all the houses in Glintrubble had been home to rabbits. The horses were less inclined to build. When they needed rest, they reverted to truest form and dozed in the wide valley beneath the Vantage, safe under the lead stallion's watchful eye.

But things were changing, little by little.

The first house would belong to Dwennon and Myla, and the second would suit the needs of Trisk and Glinna. Plans were in the works for personal quarters for each branch family; however, Glintrubble's boundaries would need to expand to make room for them.

That was the reason Fira knew so much about their plans.

She and Willum were expected to push the boundaries outward, adding new wards with what crystals they had available. Fira had pored over the maps, tuned countless crystals, and walked the proposed perimeter at least a dozen times. With Willum grumbling all the while about the need for a fresh supply of green, two more blue, and—if Cadmiel himself would be so kind—the added blessing of a sizable pink.

Needless to say, the miners were motivated.

"Here she is. Come, little warrior." Dwennon beckoned for her to join a gathering of bucks and stallions. "Willum tells me that you are the one I need most right now."

Fira fidgeted under the weight of so many gazes. "Because there are dragons?"

"No. Well, *yes*. But ... no." Dwennon sank to his knees before her, hands offered in urgent supplication. "I need you because one of my sons—a strong colt of the herd—is a reckless fool."

RECKLESS FOOL

Fira knew, but that made it no easier to ask. "Ricker?"

"We are the only ones who know." Dwennon's gaze slanted toward the mares' quarters. "I did not wish to worry the mares."

She harbored the uncharitable opinion that the mares wouldn't have offered anything more than polite dismay, but Ricker's absence would most certainly cast the foals into turmoil. For their sake—and his—Fira held her responses in check. But her thoughts were abuzz.

" ...before anyone noticed."

Dwennon was on his feet again. Someone had been speaking. Had it been Willum? She'd missed every word. Shaking her head, she stammered, "Wh-what?"

Bavol pushed forward, holding her shoulders, filling her view. "Trisk circled around to check on the area where he was attacked. No signs remained of the wild dragon, but he wanted to be sure her nest had grown cold."

"Do you mean ... eggs?"

Gently, patiently, Bavol went over everything again. "He discovered three surviving hatchlings, still small, but growing fast and sure to become a threat to the herd once their hunting range increases. Dwennon wants them removed. Trisk proposes elimination. By the time a message was composed and a messenger sent to the nearest heights, Ricker was already gone."

Dwennon's voice tightened on the verge of breaking. "He took one of Trisk's swords."

"Ricker knows how to use a sword?" Fira asked, trying to picture it.

"No."

"Then why would he try?" Fira couldn't make sense of the risk. "To impress the mares?"

Bavol spoke soothingly, like the healer he was. As if she were injured as well as afraid. "My brother rarely proceeds with so much forethought. Ricker is impulsive, acting upon his feelings. And ... he has paid little heed to the mares since midsummer."

A greater motive occurred to her. "Are the foals at risk?"

Expression softening, Bavol said, "He *is* protective of them. And of all the herd."

"Always has been." Dwennon reached for her hand. "But I would wager that his reasons are entirely coltish."

Fira had to ask, "What does that mean?"

"He wants to be chosen."

She already knew that.

Bavol sighed. "On some level, this *is* a display."

"I wonder if Ricker even realizes?" Dwennon leaned close and lowered his voice. "He is trying to impress a dragon-slayer."

ALL SPEED

Fira reached for the song of the green stone still woven into Ricker's forelock. Her gaze swung to the northwest, and everyone in the group oriented on the direction as if she were a compass.

"Thank you, little warrior," Dwennon murmured. Then he raised his voice. "Where is Trisk?"

Bavol said, "With Willum, gaining strength for the fight to come."

The lead stallion let loose a piercing whistle. Moments later, Trisk and Willum emerged from the woods, strides matched as they hastened to join the rest.

Fira had to admit she was curious about tending. Outwardly, the two did little more than hold hands, yet Willum always emerged from their sessions with starry eyes and a smile that lingered for hours.

It was a little easier to understand what Trisk gained from tending, for the air around him hummed with vitality, as if he had more power than he knew how to contain. In an intriguing clash of impressions, Fira felt sure that Trisk was becoming both more dangerous ... and more dedicated to Willum's safety. Which was very good for all of Glintrubble.

Alliance. Cooperation. Trust. Was this to be her future as well?

"How many do you suggest for the rescue party?" Dwennon asked Trisk.

The bat clansman's gaze lingered on each face, and he spoke with grim formality. However, he used the old language, and Fira understood nothing.

Inclining his head, Dwennon offered a clipped translation.

"Trisk will reclaim his blade and become Ricker's defense. Bavol, get to your brother's side. He may need a healer."

"I am going, too!" Fira exclaimed.

Dwennon nodded at Willum, who gently placed Lufu's lucky stone on Fira's palm.

She stared at it blankly for several moments. "But ... my sister cannot be without this. You said it yourself. Lufu is a beacon."

"I tuned a set of amethysts to Lufu's song. She is well and truly warded." Willum closed Fira's fingers over the crystal. "Bring him back."

"I must." She tucked the stone in the pouch at her hip. "That is the *only* outcome."

When she turned back to Bavol and Trisk, signaling her readiness, both balked. Worse, they backed up a step. Did they think she'd harm them? Fira didn't catch their mumbles, but Dwennon snorted ... and explained. Trisk, who would allow no other male to touch Glinna, was loath to hold another female. And guided by these same scruples, Bavol did not wish to give Synnis reason to doubt the singularity of his ardor.

"What do you suggest?" she asked sharply, frustrated even though she admired their newfound convictions.

"*Leaving.* Now," snapped Dwennon. "Hold tight, Fira."

Dwennon swept her up and swung her onto his back, much as Ricker had done. So she wasn't surprised when he transformed under her. But she *was* surprised. The sire of the First Herd, taking a rider. Fira knew enough now to understand the honor she was being afforded.

He sprang, and she quickly tangled her hands in his mane,

which rippled in a pale cascade right to the ground. Or would have, if he hadn't left it far below.

Leaning low over his shoulder, Fira asked, "Can you hear me, or should I guide you with my hands?"

Belatedly, she remembered that Dwennon had no voice to answer. And hers would not last if she was shouting against the roar of the wind. So she resorted to a series of tugs and pats, only raising her voice when the green stone's song changed.

"I think he is fighting," she relayed, heart pounding.

Dwennon increased his pace, but Fira was very afraid it wouldn't be enough.

"I think he is injured."

Her mount flattened his ears and rolled an eye at her, and she felt his urgency. Wrapping hanks of hair around her fists, she cried, "Onward!"

In one burst, the stallion showed his true strength. Rather than riding a horse, Fira felt as if she was astride a bolt of lightning. Thunder boomed in their wake. And it was too much for her.

Her heart squeezed, and she could not find her next breath. Dazed and deafened, she lost her hold on consciousness. But then the bolt struck, and there were arms to catch her. Strong hands pried at her fingers, and a mouth slanted over hers, pushing air into her lungs.

Fira gasped and coughed and pushed weakly at Dwennon's shoulder.

"Breathe, little warrior," he ordered.

Bavol was there, berating his father even as he claimed Fira, all traces of hesitation gone as he cupped her face, searched her eyes, and bade her to take deep breaths. He was in healer mode, and he did not relinquish his hold until he was sure Fira was steady on her feet.

"No wonder we could not find him," Dwennon remarked, ignoring his son's remonstrations. "This is a long ride from the place Trisk marked."

Fira spun on her heel, only swaying a little at the scene before her. Ricker had barricaded himself in a rough-hewn gully, thickly overhung by trees. None could have spotted him from above, nor the trio of fanged lizards trying to prise him from his paltry shelter.

Lean bodies. Curving claws. Twisting horns.

Ricker's eyes were wide and wild, and bloody scratches scored his face and arms.

Trisk was a blur of shadow, knocking two of the dragonlings sideways before joining the colt in his niche. He held out a hand. Ricker surrendered the sword and sank to the ground, head bowed as the bat clansman proved his predatory superiority.

With ruthless efficiency, Trisk engaged two of the dragons at once.

They hissed and keened and snapped their jaws.

One fell under his wicked blade, and one fell back. But where was the third? Fira shuffled forward, searching for some sign of wine-colored scales.

Dwennon's hand was at her elbow. "Can you stand?"

What a thing to ask.

Not only could Fira stand, she found that she could run.

WARRIOR MAIDEN

Fumbling in her pouch for the heirloom stone, Fira set her feet and framed the clear crystal between her fingers. She found its song, tuned it to the strength of her need, and narrowed her eyes at the dragon slinking over the rocks above and behind Ricker's hiding place.

"Trisk, get down!" bellowed Dwennon.

The bat clansman left his sword quivering in the heart of his remaining opponent. One glance Fira's way, and Trisk dove for Ricker, tumbling him to the side, rolling him out of range. In that moment, she smiled. She appreciated Trisk's intent, but the move was unnecessary. Her power could never harm Ricker.

Fira released the cry of her soul with a furious shout. She wouldn't let the monsters of this world harm the ones she loved. Not when she had the power to stop them.

Her resolve tore through a single moment, lengthening it, distilling it. With the same precision with which Trisk wielded his blade—and to much the same effect—Fira unleashed the blessing she'd once considered a curse.

The beast ceased to be a threat, for it had ceased to be. Its body lay empty, its song ended.

Willum stepped in front of her—lowering her arms, cradling her hands, coaxing the crystal from her grasp. She focused on his freckled face and began to tremble, shaken by what she'd done, by what could have happened.

He pocketed the precious stone and busied himself running light fingertips over her palms, checking each finger. "All here, and no burns." Pride shining in his eyes, Willum said, "My apprentice has improved."

She blinked several times, trying to quell an unexpected threat of tears.

Dwennon stepped up behind her, his hands settling on her shoulders. "Well done, Fira. This is a far better outcome than I could have wrought alone."

"Ricker?"

With a low, nickering laugh, the lead stallion gave her a gentle push in the right direction.

Bavol knelt with his brother, hands seeking and finding each rip and scratch, muttering all the while. At first, Fira thought scolding was simply part of Bavol's bedside manner, but as she came even with them, she caught a few phrases, then her own name. Bavol touched the green stone in Ricker's forelock, and Fira realized he must be explaining how help had come in time.

Ricker saw her coming, and his lips parted ... but no words passed them.

Bavol turned and beckoned her closer. "He was wanting; you were willing. A good balance."

The wording threw her off. It was the same phrasing used regarding the suitability of stallions. Surely, Bavol only meant the search. Or maybe the rescue?

Ricker looked as tongue-tied as she felt.

"Scold him thoroughly and make him mind." With all his customary solemnity, Bavol pressed a bottle and cloth into her hand. "Cleanse the wounds quickly, in case the hatchlings boasted a poison touch."

He withdrew to help Trisk and Dwennon, leaving her alone with his brother.

Ricker lowered his gaze, shoulders bowed.

Was he truly expecting criticism? She was sure Bavol had only been teasing about the scolding.

Kneeling before him, she set aside the medicine and reached for his chin. His gaze jumped to hers, and she moved slowly, mindful of all the little injuries she was supposed to be tending. But this came first. Kissing his forehead, Fira poured all her admiration into a handful of words. "Ricker, you are so brave."

BUCKING TRADITION

Arms wound around Fira, pulling her tight against Ricker's chest, and he pressed his face to her heart, which warmed along with her cheeks.

"I do not feel brave. I was so afraid."

"Me, too." She touched the stone woven into his hair. "If not for this, I would have been useless."

His upward glance held disbelief. "You are brilliant in battle, ablaze with fierce light. You captivate remnants and cull dragons. You are the farthest thing from useless."

Fira wasn't used to being heaped with so much praise. "Fierce, am I? Should you really be holding onto something so dangerous?"

Ricker's expression turned pensive. "I am not sure."

"You may consider the matter while I treat your injuries." With insistent pokes, she freed herself and began daubing Bavol's sharp-smelling concoction on Ricker's face. "The tunic is spoiled. Off."

He complied with a grunt, and more lacerations came to light. Across his chest, along his forearms, a deeper gouge in his thigh. Bavol would need to check that one. But there were no cuts on Ricker's back. He had not turned from his fight.

"You are so kind," he murmured.

"So you say."

"Because it is true."

Fira knew that they were dancing around something important. "I think you are mistaken, good colt, if you think I am here out of the kindness of my heart. Just as you are mistaken if you think me enormously brave. You stole all my courage with this stunt. Next time you decide to vanquish a dragon, at least take me with you."

"Next time?" He seemed flustered by the suggestion.

"Because of the crystal my parents left for Lufu and me, I have always had a dragon-slaying weapon close to hand. But carrying a weapon is not the same as knowing how to use it. I could hurt the monsters, but not without hurting myself." She set aside the near-empty bottle and studied her hands. "This time was different because of Willum. Having a mentor made a difference."

Ricker was listening, but she could tell he wasn't getting it.

"If you want to use your strength to protect the herd, do that," urged Fira. "Ask Trisk, since you admire his swordsmanship. Maybe he would be willing to take a reckless apprentice under his wing."

Understanding dawned, and Ricker gathered her hands between his. "You ...! Fira, you ...!"

She smiled, glad to see a return of his usual enthusiasm.

But a moment later, his smile faded, and he mumbled something, too soft to hear.

"What was that?"

Ricker blushed. "I wish *you* would lead me to a quiet place."

She knew what that meant. He was inviting her to choose him. Dwennon had hinted. Bavol had provided an opening. But did

Ricker really mean it? A minute ago, he'd been unsure. Yet his open expression suggested he was serious.

Fira hoped so. "You are very mixed up, Colt Ricker Thunderhoof. If I am not mistaken, *you* have led *me* to a quite place."

The others—and the bodies of all three dragons—were gone.

Ricker's face registered shock, then chagrin. Even though they were alone, his next words came in a small voice. "If a colt of the herds were to find a human female admirable, which customs would they follow? Because the colt only knows how to bide until he is chosen, yet the woman is accustomed to the arranging of males."

"You would choose me?" she asked.

"If the choice were mine."

"What if it was?"

The hint of a smile appeared. "Then I would lead my lady to a quiet place. And if she followed, I would give my pledge."

"What sort of pledge?" asked Fira. "I would not want to share you with half the herd."

He snorted. "The mares do not want me."

"That could change."

"I will not." His lips pressed softly to hers. "Do you want my pledge, Fira?"

Her heart danced, her soul sang, and her words failed, so she kissed him back. Long and lasting, as any pledge should be. Deepening like devotion. Affecting in its affection.

Fira lost track of all else, until a teasing voice said, "Now, son. Do not be so hasty."

Ricker hastily ended the kiss and blinked up at Dwennon.

"Let her go, son," commanded the lead stallion.

The arms around Fira only tightened. Ricker said, "Fira is my choice."

Dwennon's gaze tracked to the side, bringing Bavol's and Trisk's presence to Fira's attention. She didn't realize she was glaring until they failed to hide their widening smiles.

That was a good sign … probably.

"There is a proper order to things," said Dwennon patiently.

Fira blurted, "I wanted this."

The lead stallion's lips twitched. "Mares—and maidens—answer to no one for their choices, though some may question your tastes."

"I love Ricker."

Dwennon's expression softened. "I have no objections to your obvious ardor. Forge a bond, and I will bless it. But as I said, there is a proper order to things."

Trisk spoke up. Although it was more of an aside. And in the old language.

Bavol arched his brows at Ricker, whose flush deepened.

"What?" Fira demanded.

Both males suddenly found some other portion of the landscape fascinating.

With obvious enjoyment, Dwennon said, "Trisk merely raised a concern on your behalf. A meadow may do for a mare, and a field for a filly, but when it comes to a bride, a bed is best." To Ricker, he repeated, "Let her go, son. *For now.* Until the herd can gather, and the drums beat. Allow the clan to rejoice over you."

Fira thought it best to make her intentions plain. "I want nothing less than everything. Ricker has promised me his pledge. He will be my bondmate."

Dwennon quirked a challenging brow at his son.

Ricker stolidly affirmed, "I will have no other."

"So be it." The lead stallion offered the same pronouncement. "Forge your bond, and I will bless it."

SOUL'S ANCHOR

As it happened, there were certain traditions that accompanied the taking of a bondmate. Especially when one of the partners hailed from a different circle. Compensation. In a sense, Fira would rob the Thunderhoof herd of a fine colt, since she would not permit another mare to lead him away.

Gifts would normally be expected, but Dwennon was not requiring any. Provided Fira stayed at Glintrubble, continuing her apprenticeship with Willum, serving the community as a battler.

But Fira had no intention of skimping. Ricker was worthy of the finest she could offer. And she had all kinds of help in securing a suitable prize.

Rhoswen and Rhoslyn had talked her way into a dozen private corners of the Duntuffet warren, assuring aunts, uncles, siblings, and cousins that Fira's way with stones could lead to valuable discoveries. Which she had done, again and again. But Fira knew that she could do better, because she kept catching a remnant of a song—faint at first. Locating its source in the rabbit clan's tangled warren had taken days. Yet here it was, humming with anticipation, just out of reach.

"Are we close?" asked one of the fillies, her nose smudged with soil.

Fira smiled. "Yes, we are."

"Where?" asked another of her young friends.

"Which wall? That one?"

"Are you sure?"

"Show me!" exclaimed the littlest colt, who wielded a battered trowel. "I can dig!"

Their voices rang in the close quarters of the mine shaft.

Fira pressed her hand to chisel-scarred stone. "We are very close. Mister Duntuffet, you had better take over."

"It's Cadmiel, my lovely, but Cadge for short. No cause for mistering among friends." The rabbit clansman eased his way through the crowd of young helpers. "I'll have it free in a trifling, but only if you'll take it for your own."

"Oh, but Cadge ... I do not think you should give this stone away, sight unseen. We are in your mine, and the stone is especially fine."

He laughed and shook his head. "This passage hasn't lost so much as a chipping in seven centuries. What you've found you'll keep. For it was lost without you."

The foals rearranged themselves, craning their necks to see.

Fira coaxed a little more light from the crystal in her lantern and lifted it higher.

Cadge patiently prepared the stone wall for the sharp blow that laid bare its long-kept secret. Sitting back on his heels, he shook his head and reverently muttered, "Twitch my whiskers."

On the appointed day, at the appointed hour, Fira strode into the Circle with Willum close on her heels. Every male of the Thunderhoof clan formed the inner ring, with the mares arrayed in a second rank, higher up the gentle slope. Even the Duntuffets had set aside their work for the day, crowding with the children along the terraces.

Dwennon spoke into the hush. "You brought something?"

"A gift." Fira gestured.

Willum stepped forward, both arms wrapped around a linen-swathed bundle as if cradling his firstborn child—proud, protective, and still slightly dazed.

"The finest of gifts," said Fira. "Something rare and precious, which will be a blessing to all of us."

"While I required nothing, I am intrigued by your dedication to our traditions. Show us what you offer to the Thunderhoof herd and to all of Glintrubble."

She helped Willum loosen the folds of cloth, which fell away to a chorus of gasps and whistles. The pink crystal dwarfed any of the others in Willum's collection.

Dwennon strode forward for a closer inspection. "By your expressions, may I assume this is a remnant?"

"Yes, and more." Willum's voice trembled with excitement. "Dwennon, this can become our anchor, one that will endure. The herd, our home—Fira has seen to everyone's future."

Myla spoke up from her place. "For such a lavish gift, a lady might expect a double boon."

Murmurs of agreement rippled through the gathering, and Dwennon raised a hand for silence. "You have heard the Mare. A double boon. What do you wish from us, Fira?"

"Two things?" She stole a look in Ricker's direction.

"Name them," urged Dwennon.

"One house. One colt."

Dwennon's eyebrows arched. "You want us to build you a house?"

"No. I want a house to be established. Willum's house."

Ricker's eyes widened, then creased with ill-concealed amusement. He leaned over to whisper something in Bavol's ear, and his brother actually dimpled.

Willum looked uncertain. "Fira ...?"

"Your house. I will see it established. What name will you take?" More softly, she asked, "What name will you share with my sister?"

He managed a quiet, "Oh. I had not really ... ah."

"Will you deny the song of your soul?" she challenged.

Hugging the pink crystal to his chest, he offered a sheepish smile and a small shake of his head.

Meanwhile, the Duntuffets were weary of waiting for Willum to come up with a name. Cheerful suggestions came from all sides.

"Rockpicker!"

"Flamehair!"

"Stoneheart!"

"Dapplecheeks!"

Willum laughed along with the rest, then scanned until he spotted the one he wanted. "Lord Brunwinger?"

Trisk strode forward, quick as ever to the side of any who needed him.

"What was the name you gave to my aptitude?"

The bat clansman rested his fingertips over Willum's heart and spoke the word as if handing down a verdict. "Ward."

Willum looked to Dwennon like a child hoping for his father's approval.

The lead stallion inclined his head and lifted his voice. "Willum Ward. His house shall be established here in Glintrubble. Long may his line continue."

Once the cheers faded, Dwennon said, "A house for Willum, and a colt for yourself. My sons are the strength of the Thunderhoof clan. Which of them pleases you?"

She held out her hand, and Ricker separated from the herd, unhurried in his confidence. He joined Fira in the Circle, then guided her to its center.

All that remained was for him to give his pledge, plain and simple, for all to hear. But Ricker was Ricker. "You do not want a new house, a new name?" he asked.

"I will take your name."

"Fira Thunderhoof?" he asked.

"No. As much as I respect the herd that has taken me in, I want you and *only* you." She had wanted to surprise him, hoped he would approve. "Once your pledge is mine, I will be Fira Ricker."

Her declaration plunged the circle into silence, but then the drumming began. Feet upon the earth, stamping out their slow beat. Fira wasn't sure if they were showing their approval or egging Ricker on. But she *was* certain that Bavol had started it.

Ricker glanced around, found his grin, and laughed. Heedless of any dignity the occasion may have called for, he swept her off her feet and twirled her around, then pulled her close so they were almost nose-to-nose. "Fira, do you know? *You* are my every happiness."

She touched the green stone woven safely into his forelock. "Then do not let go."

"Will you hear my pledge?"

"I doubt *any* could hear it."

A warren's worth of Duntuffets were adding their encouragement to the herd's, with claps and chants, whoops and whistles.

Ricker pressed his cheek to hers. "My pledge is for you and *only* you."

"Onward," she challenged.

He gave a low whicker, and his smile brushed her temple. And so amidst the giddy clamor, beneath the herd's notice, Ricker recklessly promised, "Forever onward, I am your colt."

Fira accepted his pledge with an earnest kiss and answered in kind. "Hoof and heel, we belong together."

THE END

DRAGGED THROUGH HEDGEROWS

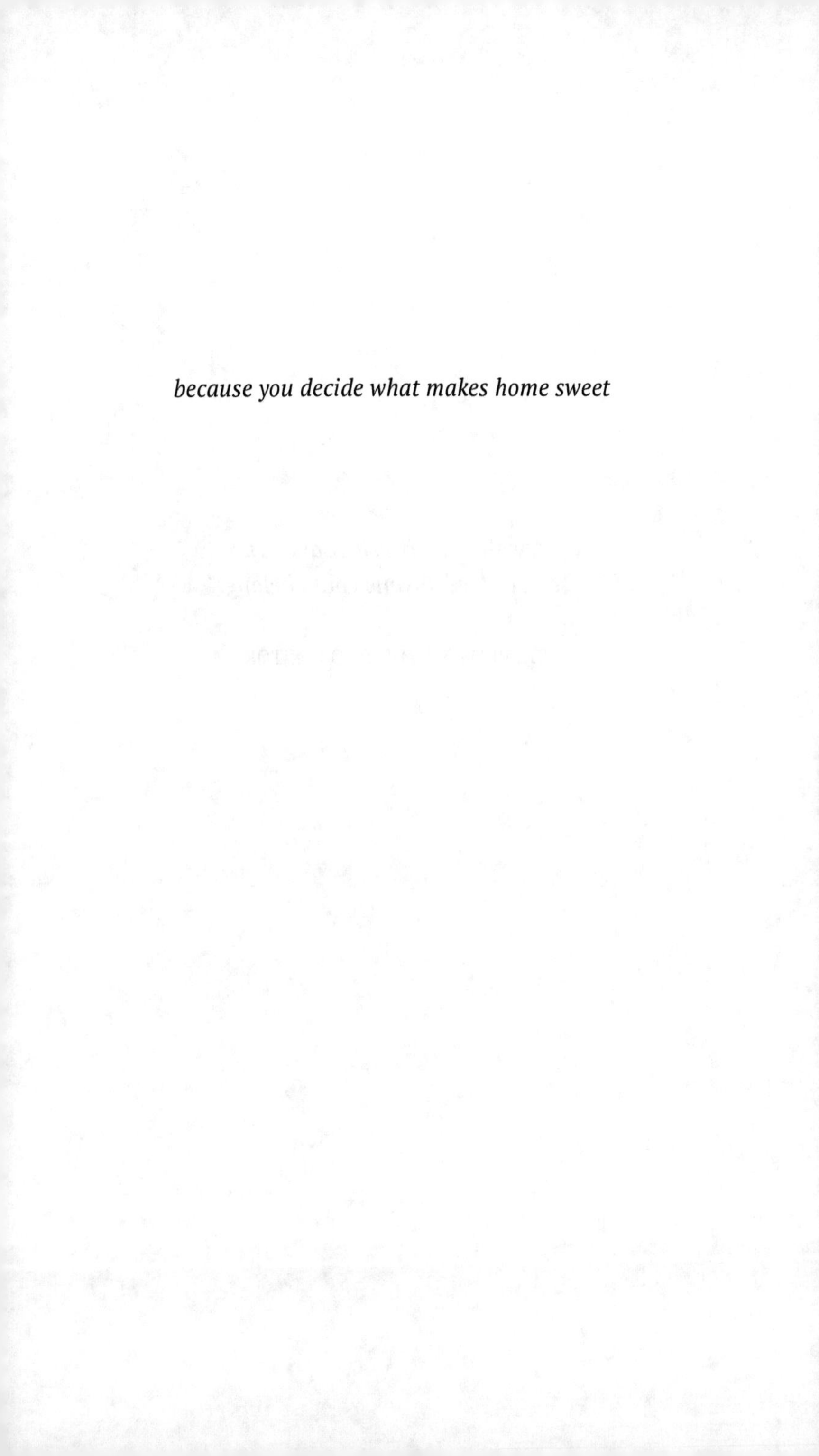

because you decide what makes home sweet

*"A wolf's heart is just about the
safest place anyone could belong."*

TAMIKO AND THE TWO JANITORS

WORN OUT WELCOME

aroo-fen rarely deviated from the little routines that reinforced the impression he needed to make. He jogged every morning, so that whenever people remarked on his build, someone could be counted on to say, "Oh, you know Drew. He works out."

He rented a bungalow two blocks from his office, where he kept regular hours, so that everyone would know he was as honest and upstanding as they come. And he shopped at the corner market every other day—except Sundays—so that the women of Pine Hall would see that he could take care of himself. Otherwise, they tended to show up at his door with casseroles and broad hints about nice, eligible girls who could help him settle down.

He bought Girl Scout cookies and yearbook ads. He attended town meetings and adopted a two-mile stretch of highway. He donated to the food shelf and returned his library books on time.

Nobody knew him well, but most folks would vouch for him. He was both a pillar of the community and an island unto himself. Not an easy balance to maintain, but Daroo-fen had considerable practice.

One thing he definitely did *not* do was make house calls.

So it was with well-concealed uneasiness that he walked the four blocks to End Street, where neat hedgerows defined the property lines of a section of modest homes. Because too many letters had gone unanswered. And the only phone number on file seemed to have been disconnected.

Turning up the walk of the last house before the dead end, Daroo-fen trod gingerly over pastel graffiti that continued right up the porch steps and across much of the front of the house. Powder pink letters warned all comers that **COOP LIVES HERE**.

The young culprit—a boy by the whiff of him—had passable handwriting.

Daroo-fen pressed the doorbell, then retreated off the stoop. It was a simple trick that served to diminish the inevitable height difference. He was widely recognized as the tallest citizen of Pine Hall, but he didn't like to loom in doorways.

Feet thudded on stairs, and the front door swung wide, revealing a boy-child clad in nothing but too-small pajama pants printed with a montage of superhero icons. He had spiky blond hair, wide-set blue eyes, and a smattering of freckles across the bridge of a pert nose. Bandages decorated both elbows, and another clung precariously to the underside of his chin.

Having each sized the other up, the boy asked, "Are you a stranger?"

"Yes."

The door slammed shut.

Daroo-fen sighed, reclimbed the steps, and rang the doorbell again.

From the other side of the door, the boy hollered, "Dad! It's a stranger!"

This time, the door was opened by an adult. The man was young, slight, and in need of a haircut, for loose brown curls all but obscured his eyes. His feet were bare, his pajama pants striped, and his arms occupied by a baby and her bottle. "Hi. Sorry. He's not supposed to open the door for strangers."

"Mr. Cooper?"

"Yes." He adjusted his hold on the baby and began to sway. "Well, maybe. I'm Charles Cooper. My father recently passed away. He was David Cooper."

"I knew your father. I'm sorry for your loss."

Charles accepted that with a cautious nod. "Who are you?"

"The name's Drew Hunter. I'm a lawyer here in town. You *should* have received a letter from our offices—Woodruff, Thackeray, and Hunter."

It was actually more like five letters. Daroo-fen had finally given up on hearing back.

"If you wrote any time in the last six weeks, it's probably in here." Charles bumped his foot against an oversized, overstuffed cardboard box with bold green letters that promised round-the-clock, leak-proof protection. He shook his head. "We just moved. Things are a mess. I haven't gotten around to sorting mail yet. Sorry."

The man's scent wasn't terribly promising—a pall of grief and a haze of stress. But under it all shone a glimmer of something Daroo-fen hadn't encountered in many years. The words were out of his mouth before he could give them proper consideration. "Do you need help?"

Charles was already shaking his head. "We're fine. We're great."

The smile might have worked to warn off the usual sort of polite inquiries, but Charles had a wolf at the door. Daroo said, "I could pitch in with the paperwork. It's what I do."

"No need. We're fine," insisted Charles, as if trying to convince himself. "Besides, I can't afford a lawyer."

Daroo-fen sifted through the mixed messages he was receiving—words and worries and weariness. "Think of it as an exchange. I'd be willing to help you if you'd be willing to hear me out."

Charles shook his head. "Are you trying to sell me something?"

"I'm a lawyer, Mr. Cooper, not a salesman." Daroo-fen pushed. "I have no other appointments today. Let me locate the documents my office sent. And if you like, I can create a checklist of the things you'll need to do in order to settle your father's affairs."

The man didn't so much give in as give up. "Sure. I guess. Come in."

LIFE IN BOXES

"Sorry for the mess." Charles was usually more on top of things, but the move had discombobulated everything. "We haven't been here long. A little over a week. We're packing and unpacking and ... sorry."

"You don't need to apologize, Mr. Cooper. This is a difficult time."

He had no idea. Edging past a wide-open suitcase with clothes spilling over its sides, he led the way into the dining room. The big walnut table was probably the best place for the lawyer to set up, but that's where Charles had unloaded everything. Was it sad that all his worldly possessions fit on a dining room table? They hadn't even needed a truck. Just a rental van that had rattled half-empty across three state lines.

He'd been reduced to two suitcases, three cardboard boxes, and a clumsy heap of baby stuff—seats and stroller, playpen and playthings. Charles was still too numb to be homesick for the pristine little Cape Cod that had been his whole world. All he really knew for sure was how glad he was that Ally hadn't argued when he said he'd take the kids. And how much it terrified him that she'd suddenly change her mind.

"Mr. Cooper?"

"Kitchen table, maybe," he suggested, pushing aside a laundry basket with one foot. It slid easily on wood floors that were dusty enough to show footprints. Dad had been letting things go for a while. Charles had wanted to come back sooner. Might always regret putting it off too long.

With one hand, he stacked cereal bowls and carried them to the sink. Snagging a dishcloth, he mumbled another apology, only to stagger to a full stop.

The lawyer stood just inside the kitchen door, the heaping box of mail casually balanced on one arm.

Charles was used to looking up at people. He'd matched his father's height at fourteen and never surpassed it. Five-two in his hiking boots, if he rounded up. He suddenly remembered how peevish Ally had been over having to wear flats for their wedding. And all the little tricks the photographer had used to make him look taller and her less pregnant.

This guy was well over six feet, a dominating presence. The

house seemed to shrink around him, and a part of Charles was shrinking as well. He'd always felt awkward around professionals.

"Mr. Cooper?"

"Is this okay?" Charles gave the table a quick swipe, then rubbed self-consciously at a sticky patch that was probably an ice cream dribble from the night before.

"Yes." Mr. Hunter set the box on a chair, shed his suit coat, unbuttoned his cuffs, and began to methodically roll up his sleeves.

Charles caught the change in sound that meant Rose's bottle was empty, set it aside, and lifted her to his shoulder. All the while, he kept an eye on the stranger he'd let in. Mr. Hunter's manner was stiff, his expression stern. His complexion was brown enough to suggest some degree of native ancestry. It was hard to guess his age. Probably Ally's age or older, since law school had to take at least as long as medical school.

Rose burped softly, and he kissed her downy hair. She was ready for her morning nap, but he hesitated to lay her in the playpen crowded into the corner. It was right next to the table. Maybe he didn't want to bother the lawyer, but maybe he wanted to be sure his baby girl was safe.

Was it rude to doubt the intentions of someone being neighborly?

Suddenly, the kitchen door rattled with a series of quick raps, then squeaked open. "Charlie! Oh, golly, just look at that precious baby girl!"

It was Mrs. Lundgren from next door, covered casserole in hand. She shouldered her way inside, as sure of her welcome as she'd ever been. A longtime neighbor. Mom's best friend.

"You hardly seem old enough to be a father, but *look* at you. All grown and getting along with two young'uns. I suppose Ally isn't here because of work?"

Charles' gut clenched.

Mr. Hunter spoke up. "Good morning, Cybil. Is that your famous cheesy potatoes?"

"Oh, Drew! How did you guess?" Mrs. Lungren's smile widened. "It shows good sense for Charlie here to hire a professional. Know your limits, that's what I say. Now, Drew, you be sure to thank your partners for their generous contribution to the bandstand fund. Isn't it exciting? There'll be a big groundbreaking ceremony and a band and one of those trailers that sells corndogs."

"I'll relay your kind words to Misters Woodruff and Thackeray." The lawyer had a handful of envelopes, most of which were probably junk mail, yet he managed to cradle them importantly. "Please, excuse us. Mr. Cooper and I have much to discuss."

"Say no more. I was only popping by on my way to bridge." Mrs. Lundgren bustled across the room, eyes roving all the while. Nosy in her concern. "Let me put this in your fridge. Oh, *dear*. Not much to speak of. Do you need help with the shopping, Charlie?"

"No, ma'am. We're fine. We're great."

The woman shook her head and smiled, then pinched his cheek on her way out, like he was six instead of twenty-six. "Send my love to Ally," she called as she hustled away.

Charles stared after her, unseeing. He'd gone away and grown up, but coming home meant losing any gains he'd made. Everyone still treated him like Dave and Linda's little boy.

"Mr. Cooper?"

"*Charles*," he quietly corrected. "Please, call me Charles."

Mr. Hunter was already seated at the table, a linoleum-topped square no wider than his shoulders. He looked like an adult shoehorned into a classroom desk designed for middle schoolers.

"Are you sure that's going to work?"

"Not a problem," the man assured. "Do you have a paper shredder?"

"I don't think so."

"I'll bring one next time."

Charles looked between the lawyer and the box. "Next time …?" he ventured.

"These things take time." He glanced up from the sheaf of paperwork. The look was steady and searching. "Unless I would be imposing."

"Let me think about it."

Mr. Hunter inclined his head and returned his attention to sorting. His movements were unhurried, yet unceasing. Confident. Decisive.

Charles hated that something so basic was so far outside his experience. Ally had always handled the finances. All he'd had to do was stick to his budget for diapers and groceries. Even a high school dropout who *knew his limits* could handle that much.

Suddenly, it occurred to Charles that his son was being far too quiet. "Cole …?"

The lawyer didn't look up, but he spoke up. "In the back, I believe."

Just then, the distinctive squeak of the hose being turned on came through the wall, and Charles quick-stepped to the kitchen door, which let out onto the driveway. Hurrying around the house, he found his son knee-deep in a bucket, standing under the hose, which he'd looped through the upper branches of a dwarf apricot tree so that it dangled down.

"Outdoor shower!" Cole explained brightly, though his teeth were clenched and his lips were turning blue. "Neat, right?"

Hardly. Cole wasn't neat. Or tidy. Ever. Charles simply asked, "What happened?"

"You know them bags in the shed with no labels?"

Pausing to turn off the hose—one-handed, since he was still carrying Rose—he gave his son's spiky blond hair a cursory inspection. "Cement mix. Let's apply soap before you turn into a statue."

Cole's eyes widened in fascination. "Really?"

Charles dredged up a smile. "Don't think so, but better safe than sorry."

Leaving the dripping hose and brimming bucket, he followed Cole's wet footprints to the first-floor bathroom, which doubled as a utility room—washer, dryer, water heater—and boasted the house's lone bathtub. His childhood home was old and odd and inconvenient. Unless you counted Cole's new rigging, they didn't have a shower.

Back home—the one he'd shared with Ally—Charles had worked out all the boundaries necessary for safety and sanity. Cole was mostly obedient, but only if his parents had established a specific rule. And closed the loopholes. Far beyond those familiar boundaries, Cole was creating whole new forms of havoc. Nothing bad. Sometimes funny. Often messy. And exhausting for someone whose whole life was already a mess.

Charles settled his baby girl in a laundry basket of clean towels. Three-months old and low in the percentiles, she fit with room to spare and without complaint. A good baby. Daddy's girl.

While Charles oversaw Cole's first bath of the day—there were usually two or three, depending on mayhem levels—the boy asked nonstop questions.

How come Grandpa kept cement? Did you just add water? Could they really make a statue?

With his arms draped on the edge of the tub, Charles explained about anchors and trellises and posts and rebar and his father's never-ending projects, which amounted to a hobby of sorts.

Once his son was sufficiently clean, Charles said, "Hey, Cole?"

"Yeah, Dad?"

"I love you."

His boy smiled. "I know."

"No more messing with cement until we pick a project we can do together."

"You know how to make cement?"

"My dad taught me, and I'll teach you." Charles firmly established a new boundary. "And no further exploration of the contents of the shed without me. Understood?"

"Yep."

"Try again," Charles said mildly.

Cole grinned in his no-hard-feelings way. "Yessir."

SEE YOU SATURDAY

Charles had half-forgotten the lawyer, who had several neat piles arranged on the table.

Fanning an assortment of envelopes bearing the familiar logos of local utilities, Mr. Hunter asked, "May I open these?"

"Go ahead." Charles cringed inwardly. "Are we in trouble?"

"Not really. There are extenuating circumstances," murmured Mr. Hunter as he scanned statements. "Have you dealt with the bank yet?"

"No."

The lawyer touched a stack of envelopes bearing the local bank's name. "Would you like me to act on your behalf?"

Charles wavered. He probably needed the help more than he wanted it. But should he be trusting a stranger with Dad's finances? Then again, Mrs. Lundgren had approved, and in Pine Hall, that was as good a reference as any.

"Officially?" he ventured, since he had an inkling that lawyers looked expensive because they were expensive.

Mr. Hunter gave him a whisper of a smile. "Unofficially. As part of our exchange."

"But isn't this a lot of work?"

"Nothing too onerous. There is more patience than effort involved." He shrugged those broad shoulders as if he had patience to spare.

Charles struggled against himself. Having spent his entire adult life with someone else in charge, it was far too tempting to simply hand over the reins. He fell back on his earlier answer. "Let me think about it."

And once again, Mr. Hunter nodded his acceptance.

Cole jogged into the room in clean shorts and a faded tee. Before he could assail the lawyer, Charles tapped the boy's head. "Rose is ready for her naptime story."

"Can I go get her?"

"Of course. We'll change her diaper, then get her settled." As Cole backtracked, Charles cast a sidelong look at the lawyer, whose attention followed Cole. Defensively, Charles said, "I trust him with Rose."

Mr. Hunter held his gaze for a long moment. "I can think of no higher compliment."

Hardly the reaction he was used to. Most people—including Ally—tried to rescue Rose from her big brother. Charles found their concern laughable. Cole was utterly awed by Rose and treated her like his own special treasure. Or possibly a pet. A much-loved, carefully guarded pet.

Cole came into the room, cradling his sister, and walked right up to the lawyer. "This is Rose. She's ours."

Mr. Hunter gravely said, "How do you do, Rose?"

"She does good," Cole proudly reported.

"And you are?"

"I'm Cole Pfeiffer-Cooper, but everyone calls me Coop."

Charles tried not to smile. "Cole, you're the only one."

"Only 'cause Rose can't talk yet. And you keep forgetting." The boy addressed himself to the lawyer again. "You gotta call me Coop."

Mr. Hunter considered the siblings. "May I ask why you have chosen a new name for yourself?"

"Because." And since that didn't seem to satisfy their guest, the boy staunchly added, "I'm with Dad."

Charles studied the floor. As much as he didn't want Cole taking sides with him against his mother, he appreciated the sentiment. He'd stood up for Cole so many times. Was it any wonder his son now stood up for him?

They changed Rose's diaper, and Charles no longer hesitated over tucking his daughter into the playpen. In part because Cole stood—or rather sat—guard over the baby, reading to her from a book of fables. The boy immersed himself in the story, adding funny voices and little asides for Rose's benefit.

Charles almost wished Cole's old teachers could see him like this. He could focus. He could learn. Pulling him from the confines of a classroom had been the right decision. There was nothing wrong with Cole, but school had been all wrong for him. So school would happen at home. They'd learn together.

Again, he half-forgot the lawyer, who was surprisingly unobtrusive for all his bulk. Charles washed dishes, wiped surfaces, and ran to the basement to start a washer load. Which may have been a mistake, since it gave Cole an opening.

When Charles returned, his son was at the lawyer's side. "What's that?"

"Utility bills."

Cole's brow furrowed. "What's *that*?"

Charles would have intervened, but the lawyer casually raised a hand, as if warning him off. Mr. Hunter asked, "Do you really want to know?"

"I really do."

"Pull up a chair."

So while Charles shifted boxes and bundled old newspapers, he listened in while Drew Hunter unraveled the mysteries of wattage and water pipes, power grids and phone lines. If he'd had the wherewithal, Charles would have hired the man then and there. As back-up. Cole and Rose weren't a burden, but he sometimes felt outnumbered.

Less than an hour later, Mr. Hunter demonstrated the practical application of binder clips and left Cole to secure each stack.

Following the lawyer to the door, Charles asked, "Are you from here?"

"Close. I was born one town over, as the eagle flies." He pointed toward the back of the house.

"On the other side of Pine Mountain?" When Mr. Hunter simply nodded, he asked, "How long have you been in Pine Hall?"

"Ever since college."

"Oh. I guess I was gone by then."

Again, the lawyer nodded. And again, he'd composed himself to listen. Charles had been trying to teach Cole the importance of eye contact. It was hard to get a kid as active as his son to settle down long enough to listen. Usually. Mr. Hunter was notable for being an exception.

"I grew up here," Charles offered lamely. That much had to be obvious, but he was suddenly reluctant to part ways.

"This is a good place to raise a family."

Charles hoped so. He had nowhere else to go. "I owe you a meeting?"

"Next time." The lawyer extended a hand. "Saturday."

The inflection offered an out. Charles could refuse, but he didn't want to.

He met and matched the firm grip, sealing the deal. "Saturday."

RUNNING ON EMPTY

Before Saturday rolled around, Charles was determined to be more prepared for Mr. Hunter's help. And that meant clearing space on the dining room table. It didn't take long, but it didn't really help. Moving a mess wasn't the same as putting things away. And his things didn't belong anywhere in this house.

Could he change that?

Over cornflakes, he asked Cole, "Have you ever seen an empty room before?"

"Don't think so. Except maybe … the gym at school's big and empty."

Charles nodded thoughtfully. "I guess people make rooms to fill them. Let's empty one."

"Which one?"

"The den." He jerked a thumb toward the house's back corner, where a bonus room had been collecting clutter for years. "We'll empty it and clean it top to bottom."

"How come?"

That was hard to explain. But it was also really simple. "I want to start over. Make it mine by deciding how to fill it. You know?"

Cole took such a big bite of cereal, milk dribbled down his chin as he chewed. He was thinking hard and fast, and Charles guessed the direction his thoughts were taking. He wasn't surprised by the boy's enthusiasm or by his question.

"Can I do that, too?"

Charles took a huge bite of cereal and pretended to deliberate. But Cole was as good as his dad at guessing. He was already grinning by the time Charles agreed. "Help me clear the den, and I'll help you clear your bedroom."

The house wasn't large, but it had always been plenty of space for three people. Downstairs, there was a front room, which Mom had called the sitting room. Across from that was the dining room, which led into the kitchen at the back. The kitchen had a pantry and a door leading to the basement. Somewhere along the way, an addition had been built, giving the house a three-season porch—where Charles had spent many a summer night in his sleeping bag—and the den.

"What's a den for?" asked Cole, who'd propped his fists on his hips the same as Charles.

"Like a family room. We used to watch television in here." After Mother had passed away, his father had encroached on the space. He'd moved in a potting bench, and gardening tools leaned against the far wall.

The room was boxy, with wood paneling on the walls and a door that led into Dad's little wilderness. Charles crossed the room—blazing a trail of footprints across dusty floorboards—to prop it open. "Have you seen this part yet?"

Cole came to look. His reaction would have made his grandfather smile.

"Dad, is this for real?" Goggling dramatically, Cole softly added, "Is it magic?"

"Maybe a little. At least, I always thought so." With a little wave of his hand, Charles suggested, "See where it goes, then come on back to help me."

The kid bolted.

Charles followed him out the door and stood barefoot on mossy flagstones, letting himself remember a time when this was his favorite place in the whole world. Maybe it still was.

David Cooper had worked all his life at the local hardware store and lumberyard. A professional handyman, a fixer of broken things, a contented putterer. Dad hadn't expected to raise anything more than trellises when Mother surprised him with a son. Both had been well into their forties. Delighted and doting.

He missed them.

So much.

Cole appeared at the bend in the long green tunnel that curved away from the house and into a labyrinth of covered paths. Dad had built arches, pergolas, and trellises galore, for he loved climbing vines. Especially flowering varieties.

"It's like a maze!" Cole reported.

"Did you get lost?"

"Only a little."

All the while they worked, Charles listened to Cole's raptures about sundials and benches and birdhouses and chimes.

"Did you find the bridges?"

"Where?" Cole demanded.

"Over the creek."

"There's a creek?" His son's expression was tragic. "Why didn't you *say* so?"

"I guess because I wanted to *show* you."

"Can we go?"

"One thing at a time," Charles said firmly. "Today, we're emptying rooms. Remember?"

Cole was clearly torn. "Tomorrow?"

"I have to go to the bank tomorrow. And we need groceries."

"The day after?"

That would be Saturday. "Maybe. Mr. Hunter's coming that morning to help with Grandpa's papers. I don't know how long it will take."

Cole pondered that, then offered what he obviously thought was the perfect solution. "We'll bring him along."

NO JOB EXPERIENCE

Daroo-fen knew all the reasons why he needed to cultivate a relationship with Charles Cooper, but those weren't foremost in his mind as he took the turning onto End Street on Saturday morning. Mr. Cooper had no appreciable rank, but there were certainly reavers somewhere in his pedigree. The man's inheritance was small—hardly a pittance—but Daroo couldn't deny its appeal.

He should have kept his distance—for both their sakes—but that brought Daroo-fen back around to all those reasons why he needed to gain Charles' trust. Those reasons made it easy to justify prolonging the association. Drew Hunter was being neighborly. And Charles' *other* legacy was of interest to the cooperative.

This was business. Plain and simple. A bit of shine wouldn't matter one way or the other.

Daroo-fen made his way past long hedgerows of holly, a paper shredder braced against one shoulder, his satchel in the other hand. Even before he reached the Cooper's residence, he was picking up the scents of oil soap and window cleaner.

Cole knelt on the front porch, busy with bucket and brush, scrubbing away his chalk artistry. However, when he spied Daroo-fen, he jumped to his feet and barred the way. "I'm inviting you," the boy said, all insistence and confidence. "So come with us later. It'll be a reward for doing a good job with Grandpa's papers."

"You want me to accompany you somewhere?"

"There's a creek, and Dad's gonna take us to see." Cole magnanimously added, "You can carry Rose."

Daroo-fen had little doubt that most businessmen in Pine Hall— even the most forbearing of souls—wouldn't have appreciated being volunteered to play attendant to a babe-in-arms. But he was touched. "Thank you for inviting me, Coop."

The boy grinned and turned to holler through the open door. "Dad! Your friend's here!"

Charles hurried forward, beckoning him inside. "Mr. Hunter. Sorry. You know how it is with kids. If you're not a stranger, you're a friend."

He murmured polite assurances, all the while wondering at this young man's apologetic quirk.

Quite a few things had changed over the past few days. The front room was clogged with assorted furniture, lamps, piles of seed catalogs, bric-a-brac, and leaning picture frames. Rose was out of sight, but somewhere nearby. He could smell diaper ointment, baby formula, and bananas. And ... was that tea? Something herbal with anise.

"We made room for you." Charles waved broadly at the dining room, which had been cleared of boxes and carefully cleaned. "Is this okay?"

"More than adequate. Thank you."

Today, he gained the necessary permission to go through David

Cooper's files, which amounted to a two-drawer filing cabinet and a fire-proof strongbox. Daroo-fen uncovered a host of personal information about Charles—birth certificate, health checks, report cards, school photos, certificates of achievement, newspaper clippings. All the milestones of Charles' boyhood, which hinted at a wealth of paternal pride.

An only son.

Loved, yet left behind.

Daroo-fen swallowed hard and moved on to the items he was supposed to be more interested in. Legacies involving deeded land.

All the while he worked, he was still very much aware of Charles' presence somewhere in the back quarter of the house. Whatever he was doing, it involved a stepladder and furniture wax, which was outmoded in this decade. Then again, times changed slowly in Pine Hall, and Charles' parents had been old-fashioned, even by local standards. He certainly wouldn't complain. The wax had a pleasant scent, vastly preferable to the harshness of modern cleaners.

Charles was in a better mood today. Lighter. Perhaps even brighter. Unclouded, at least. Daroo-fen's focus shifted both inward and outward as he tightened his focus on that slip of starlight that touched Charles' soul.

It was easy to imagine that his great-great-great-grandsire or marm had been some enclave's cosset. The generations had diminished the strength with which he shone, but quality bred true. It reminded Daroo of the distant echo of wolfsong, carrying across many miles, still pure and sweet, but forcing the listener to prick his ears and hold his breath.

More than once, Daroo was embarrassed to realize that his hands had fallen still, his breathing caught, his focus pulled tight. Charles was a reminder of what he'd given up. And Daroo-fen couldn't afford to dwell on feelings best left buried.

He cornered Charles in the kitchen, where Rose slept peacefully, despite the mechanical whirr of the paper shredder in the next room, where Cole was cheerfully feeding it a stack of junk mail.

"May I ask a personal question?" Daroo watched sadness steal into the young man's expression and mourned the dimming of his soul. But there were details he needed to know.

"Go ahead," said Charles.

"Are you planning to stay?"

"I was hoping to, yeah. I've got nowhere else to be." He fidgeted. "Is that a problem?"

"Not at all. I simply need to know which direction to take, which documents we'll need to file." Daroo-fen asked, "Are you currently employed."

Charles' jaw tightened, but he answered calmly. "I'm a homemaker, Mr. Hunter."

"And your spouse?"

"Seems like I'm no longer a husband." A deep breath. Another. "Ally's always had plans. I'm not part of them anymore."

"I see." Daroo hated uncovering this pain. "You have separated from her."

Anger. Fear. "No, sir. She separated from me."

"Will she be providing support for her children?"

"I honestly don't know." Charles' gaze strayed to the playpen in the corner, to the daughter he so clearly loved. "When I told Ally I needed to come here to take care of things, she told me not to come back."

"She is divorcing you?"

"Yeah."

"May I look at whatever papers she sends?"

His lips trembled, then firmed. "I'd be grateful."

"Charles." Daroo-fen waited for the man to lift his gaze. "This is a *good* place to raise a family."

The young man's eyes watered.

"Dad!"

Charles bit his knuckle and blinked hard, desperate to hide the hurt. Perhaps he hadn't yet told Cole? So Daroo placed himself between father and son, hiding Charles' distress. "Yes, Coop?"

"Did you talk to Dad? Are you coming with us?"

"Certainly."

"Did he tell you Grandpa's back yard is magic?"

Daroo-fen supposed that was true, in its way. "Your father and I were unable to discuss the plan in any detail. Perhaps you should tell me more?"

A hand touched Daroo's back. From his hiding place, Charles said, "Why don't you show Mr. Hunter what we've done to the den. You can take him out back, but wait for me. I'll need a few minutes to get Rose ready."

"Okay!" Cole charged out, calling, "This way!"

"Coming," assured Daroo-fen, though he turned to face

Charles first.

"Sorry," he whispered. "You don't really have to …."

"Drew." He gently grasped the man's shoulder. "Since we're friends, you really should call me Drew."

BIG BACK YARD

"We'll need a rake and a broom and a blanket. And a bucket and towels. Diaper bag, too."

Cole ran to the shed, hand hovering over the handle. "There's rakes and brooms in here."

"I'll get those," said Charles. "Can you bring two towels and one of the big blankets from inside?"

"Got it!"

His son was off like a shot, leaving Charles with Drew. "We're going a ways into the woods. Almost a mile. Would you rather carry equipment or …?"

Drew smiled faintly. "Let me free your hands so you can run with your son."

"You … have kids?" Charles ventured. He knew almost nothing about his new friend.

"I live alone."

Charles pocketed a small set of shears and reached for the canteen, which he filled at the spigot. Familiar routines, half-forgotten over the years. He eyed his companion. "You seem okay with her."

"Yes." Rose looked tiny in the lawyer's big hands. She gurgled. Drew's gaze softened in a way that reassured Charles. He murmured, "I come from a big family."

Cole came barreling back, and Charles found his old pack, which still hung from its peg. Like Dad had kept it ready. In case he ever came home and wanted another ramble. It hurt and it helped, both at the same time.

"Charles?" He dragged his attention to Drew, who inclined his head toward the distant bulk of Pine Mountain. "Are you aware how far this property extends?"

"Pretty far." He had to smile. "Dad used to joke about having the biggest back yard in the neighborhood. Why?"

But Cole was bouncing from one foot to the other, canteen sloshing against his hip. "Which way, Dad? I want to see the creek!"

"Do you know what wisteria looks like?"

"Show me!"

So Charles shouldered the pack and led the way along the same paths he'd walked with his father. To the seam between tame and wild. Where Dad had built sturdy supports for rampant plants, encouraging them to take over and taking pleasure in the resulting thicket.

The footpaths were still there, well-trod but no wider than deer tracks. He knew where each led—to berry brambles, to stands of fern, to a half-wild cluster of apple trees that stood beside one of four ponds. But every time Cole paused at a turning, Charles pointed them deeper into the forest, toward the creek that had always been his.

Drew had been following at an unhurried pace, and Charles paused to let him catch up. "How are you two doing?"

"We seem to have reached an accord," Drew said mildly. "This is familiar territory for you."

"My mother used to accuse me of living out here—all summer, every day after school. I was always wandering and exploring and thinking and listening." He paused, gaze lifting to the soft sighing of the tree branches overhead. He quoted his father. "A kid needs room to run a little wild, you know?"

"How far have you explored?"

"Dad set a few boundaries. Today, I'll show them to Cole." Charles gestured vaguely. "The safe zone is about a mile square, but Dad and I would sometimes hike farther."

"*Are* you aware how far your land extends?" Drew asked again.

"Not really." Maybe he'd have learned more if he hadn't left. Taking responsibility had taken him away from all this. "Did you find something in Dad's papers?"

"One thousand four hundred acres."

"What?"

Drew didn't repeat himself. With a bland expression, he asked, "Did you hear a splash?"

SLIPPERY WHEN WET

When they crested the next rise, Daroo was no more surprised than Charles at the sight of a sodden Coop, knee-deep in the promised creek. A wolf's ears were keen, as was this father's grasp on the inevitable. Why else were there towels in his pack?

It also became clear why he'd shouldered a rake and broom before making the trek. Not far from the creekbank, across a simple footbridge, waited a bench with a mossy stone for a stool, comfortably arranged beside what looked like a cabinet on stilts.

Charles dropped his backpack on the ground and set straight to work sweeping the bench clear of old leaves and spiderwebs. He did the same for the cabinet, which Coop circled squishily and knocked against.

"What's this for?"

"Take a guess," suggested his father.

"A birdhouse?"

"Nope."

"A beehive?"

"Nope." Charles' smile had the wistful tilt of nostalgia. "Grandpa built it for me. It's a library."

"In the *woods*?" Coop exclaimed.

"Why not? He planned gardens and planted vines for himself. The bridges and bench and bookshelf were for me. My dad thought it was important for boys to have hobbies, and ... this was mine."

"Can I open it?" asked Coop.

"It's not locked." His tone gave permission.

Inside the cupboard were three shelves, kept safe from the elements despite the intervening years. There were perhaps two dozen books, most slim. Hardly enough to fill the space. However, Daroo spotted other odds and ends. Fishing line and hooks, an enamel mug and a flashlight, a whetstone and hatchet, twine and a matchbox.

"You liked to read?" Coop poked through a pile of stones—agates by the look of them—and flipped open a compass.

"I liked the woods." His father's expression turned wistful. "I used to want to live out here, all by myself."

"Why didn't you?" asked the boy.

Charles smiled a little. "Maybe I got lonesome?"

"Not anymore." Coop patted his dad's arm. "We should try again."

Ruffling the boy's hair, Charles said, "I love you."

"I know."

With fresh lightness within, the man scanned the vicinity and stepped briskly to a low wall of greenery. He pulled and pruned the clamber of vines, revealing a length of plastic pipe suspended between two sturdy posts. Its purpose was made immediately obvious.

"Get out of those clothes."

Cole did as he was told and was back in the creek, quick as a wink. "It's freezing!" he reported gleefully.

"Spring fed," said Charles. "I'll show you where the water's safe to drink."

"This isn't?" The kid had already slurped down three handfuls.

His father snorted. "You'll survive. But better safe than sorry."

After hanging Cole's clothes to dry, Charles draped his own shirt over the post, shed his boots and socks, and joined his son in the creek.

The boy was all questions. Quite normal in Daroo-fen's experience.

Charles was all answers. Or better questions. A good combination.

Left to his own devices, Daroo availed himself of the bench. It was more suited to someone of Charles' stature, but the craftsmanship was solid. It offered no complaint when he settled himself ... and the diminutive Rose. Newborn, she probably would have made a scant handful. Elbows on knees, he cradled her on his forearms, which put them face-to-face. She seemed to favor her sire, with dark curls and blue eyes. Which suggested that Cole's fair hair was a Pfeiffer trait.

Thinking back, Daroo realized that there had been no photographs of Charles with his wife—not in the files, not on display. He understood that many children left home and lost touch. But he'd noticed something that prevented him from dismissing the signs … and the trail they suggested.

Despite David Cooper's diligent accumulation of his son's many milestones, there had been no report of grades for his twelfth year, nor had he posed for any kind of senior picture. No playbills or team photos. No highlights or hints of graduation day. It was as if Charles Cooper's life had ended at seventeen. And in scandal.

If his math was right, that made Cole eight years old.

Charles had left these woods to become a father.

"You have doubled his blessings, little flower," Daroo-fen murmured, nuzzling her cheek and letting her grab his nose. He hummed an ancient lullaby and told her things she probably already knew—that she was safe, that she was loved, and that she was where she'd always belonged.

"Everything okay? Sorry to leave you stranded." Charles picked his way from the creek, tender feet lending a limp to his gait.

"We're fine, as you can see." Daroo ignored the apology, though he wished he could banish them from Charles' lips. "Your son is learning woods lore from you, and I've handed down several trade secrets to your daughter. Their futures are bright."

"It might be a little early to enroll her in law school."

"Just a bit," he conceded. Not that his secrets had much to do with law.

Charles toweled his legs, spread the blanket, and opened the diaper bag. "I should have realized we'd stay and play. The only food I brought is a bottle for Rose and a granola bar to tide over Cole. Are you okay?"

"Never better." He watched Charles mix and shake. "We'll all have a good appetite for dinner."

"You're welcome to join us," Charles cautiously offered.

Daroo knew he really should say no. "Sounds like a plan."

Prep done, Charles beckoned for the baby, and Daroo surrendered her with more reluctance than was admissible. To distract himself, he perused the bookshelf. There wasn't much in the way of fiction. A few titles about boys surviving in the wild by foraging and hunting and fishing, getting by on little more than ingenuity and a healthy respect for nature. Most of the books were guides to birds, trees, and edible plants.

Daroo flipped through a boy scout manual, then pulled a slim volume on campfire cookery. Holding it up for Charles to see, he asked, "You have a firepit?"

"Not here. Too dangerous," said Charles. "There's a gully over that way that's nearly all stone. Dad and I built a fireplace in it. Much safer."

"A library *and* a kitchen."

"When I was younger, I had rooms all over the place. This is the only one that's furnished. The rest were just sort of ... up to the imagination." Charles shook his head. "I was going to be self-sufficient and independent. Now I need a lawyer to open my mail."

"You strike me as a capable man." Daroo found a recipe for rabbit stew that had his mouth watering. Showing Charles the page, he said, "Next time, we'll come better prepared."

Daroo-fen was in a bit of a quandary.

He'd been tasked with the safety and care of Rose, but she had little use for him. Not with her father curled protectively around her while she slept. Charles probably hadn't meant to doze off, as well. Daroo suspected the man wasn't sleeping properly.

A pity, given the human sleep requirement. But a greater problem had arisen. Coop was gone and still going. Charles may have wanted to give his son freedom, but he'd also wanted to give him safe boundaries. Daroo-fen knew the dangers of the former without the latter.

Setting aside his book and his boots, he strolled away, feet barely making a sound on the carpet of past seasons' leaves and needles. With a backward glance to make certain he was lost to view, Daroo-fen dropped to all fours and loped away.

BOY MEETS WOLF

How long had it been since he'd taken truest form?

Too long, given how hard his heart was pounding, how fast his blood was racing. Daroo-fen leapt easily over a fallen log and dodged around a rocky outcropping, getting a feel for being back on four feet. This was good and right, as natural as breathing, and true as the note of the howl already building in his heart. Not that he could let it loose. Not that he could stay for long.

No one could know.

That would be disastrous.

He would only make certain the boy was safe. Then back to business as usual.

Following Coop's trail along sun-dappled paths was no trouble whatsoever. He was a straightforward boy—no subterfuge, no doubling back, straight on without any doubt and without second thoughts. It probably never occurred to him how worried his father would be if he knew how far he'd wandered. Not that this part of the woods was particularly dangerous. But a parent—even one in need of some time apart—found no peace in absence.

Even when it was necessary.

Paying more heed to old times and lone ways than the trail to which he'd put his nose, Daroo-fen sprang lightly over a bramble and sat down hard. He'd found Coop.

The boy was on his knees. For the flicker of a moment, Daroo-fen panicked. The scent of blood was faint, but it was there. He thrust his nose into the boy's chest, his face, his hand, urgently seeking injuries.

But the streaks of red were nothing more than the juice of wild blackberries. And his fair skin bore faint scratches because of the thorns. And ... he was afraid. For good reason. Daroo-fen had all the appearance of a large, hungry predator, and Coop was a lone, shivering boy.

Bad combination.

Worse if word spread. The last thing these woods needed was a wolf hunt.

Daroo-fen backed up and lowered himself to his belly, giving a tentative wag of his tail. *Come on, Coop. I'm not the Big Bad Wolf.* He added a soft whine.

Coop slowly reached out, hand flat. He'd probably been taught to do so when being introduced to neighborhood dogs. Not exactly a good idea in the wild, but Daroo-fen wasn't about to complain. He sniffed trembling fingers and licked Coop's palm.

"You look like a wolf. Are you a wolf?"

I plead the fifth. And to prove how very un-wolfish he was, Daroo-fen rolled onto his back and let his tongue loll.

"I've never seen a real wolf before. Not up close." The boy scooted closer. "Do you live in our woods?"

Once upon a time. Fingers appeared before his muzzle again, and he proved again that he would not bite. Which was apparently permission to pet. And not any kind of cautious, conservative stroking of fur. Coop was more of a big-handfuls rougher and belly-rub scruffer.

It was undignified.

And he did everything he could to egg the boy on.

He allowed himself five minutes of bliss, then five more. But Charles might wake at any time, and Daroo-fen had no desire to add to his worries. Which meant coming up with an out. Or at least calling in his lawyer.

Wriggling free, he pretended to hear someone coming. He pricked his ears toward the creek. *Work with me here, Coop.*

The boy scrambled to his feet and followed his gaze. "What's up?" he whispered. "Is your family calling you home?"

Daroo-fen's heart clenched, but he seized the fiction.

With a parting lick, he bounded away, but not far. He changed back into speaking form, and with the inherent speed of his kind, he circled around to walk into view from the forecast direction. "There you are," Drew Hunter called. "Done swimming?"

The boy waved broadly. "I found berries!"

"Are they edible?"

Coop rubbed at his stomach. "What happens if they're not?"

This kid.

All the way back to Charles' woodland book nook, Daroo-fen offered salient points about hidden dangers and harmful plants. The boy's attention seemed to be everywhere at once, but he was quick on the uptake, asking questions, finding samples.

But he kept looking back over his shoulder.

And he never once mentioned the wolf.

THE EMPTY DOGHOUSE

Now that the den was cleared out, Charles was reluctant to clutter it up. It was a little barren, and the emptiness echoed slightly, but that sort of fit how he was feeling. He wasn't going to hide from his losses, so this was one way to face them.

Keeping it simple, he dragged the full-sized mattress from his parents' room and made a bed for himself on the floor. It was more comfortable than a couch. And it was big enough for those times when a bad dream or a fussing baby meant sharing.

He moved Rose's playpen into the corner, so she'd have a

quieter place to nap.

And it was enough. For now. But it was also the beginning, because having a project was keeping him sane. Charles went through closets and cupboards. He sorted through cabinets and drawers. Little by little, he began emptying the rest of the house, paring away the excess and unnecessary.

Cole was a big help.

Each item they brought out was given a minute's consideration. Sometimes there was a story. Sometimes it was a mystery. This became a kind of farewell ritual, for once done, they'd place the thing with respectful firmness into one of the boxes by the front door. And at the end of each afternoon, before closing time, they'd roll a wagonful to the donation center in town.

"We could bring a truck over," offered the pastor whose church ran the thrift store. "Load it all up at once, save you all these trips."

"No, thank you. I'm going through things a little at a time. There's no hurry."

"Fair enough. We can't complain when you've been so generous." The man's tone gentled. "If you ever need to talk ...?"

"Thanks, sir, but it's okay. We're fine. We're great."

It was shockingly easy to lie, and he was thoroughly ashamed of himself.

Day after day, Charles got rid of a lot. But he kept things, too.

Things with good memories still attached. Things they could use. They found fishing tackle and camping gear, lanterns and tools, scrap lumber and the old hammock that had once hung in one of his forest rooms.

"Dad! Look what I found!"

Charles followed the sound of Cole's voice to the back of the shed, where a tarp had been thrown over a large doghouse up on cinderblocks. Dad must have decided against getting another dog. His health had failed after Mom's death.

"It's a doghouse, right?"

"Yes."

"You had a dog?"

"Your grandpa always kept a dog, all through the years. The one I remember was Sheba. She was a German Shepherd, and she went everywhere with me. Slept in my room, too. Grandpa called her my second mother and my best friend, all wrapped into one."

Cole clambered inside the doghouse and poked his head out. "How come we never got one?"

"Your mother vetoed the idea." More than once.

"Too bad." His son's face was solemn. "Dogs are pretty great, huh?"

"I've always thought so." Charles waited for the inevitable plea for a puppy.

To his surprise, Cole only nodded to himself and repeated, "Dogs are pretty great."

"I've been thinking," said Cole, who was always contemplative over his cornflakes. "We should probably live wild *now*, before Rose is old enough to improve our manners."

Charles smiled over his choice in words. Probably borrowed from some book. "All right. What did you have in mind?"

"No shirt. No shoes. No homework."

It was June. Cole had missed a few months of school, but maybe this was another case of extenuating circumstances. Why not run wild? Wasn't that the whole point of summer?

"I suppose we could toughen up our feet for a while, but they won't let us into the library without shoes."

"I'll read your books in the woods."

Charles was liking this idea more than he probably should have. "They won't let us into the grocery store, either."

"There's a farmer's market every Tuesday and Friday."

"You've given this a lot of thought." He hated to put a damper on things, but they couldn't get everything they needed at a vegetable stand. "What about diapers and formula for Rose?"

Cole pondered that, then offered what he obviously considered the perfect solution. "Easy. We'll send our lawyer."

BE MY GOPHER

Daroo-fen knew something had changed the moment he turned in at the last house on End Street. Charles and Coop sat waiting for him on their front step—both shirtless, both barefoot, both watching his approach with grim resolve.

"I feel overdressed."

"That's okay," said Coop. "We need your shirt and shoes."

Charles jostled the boy with his elbow, who grinned and jostled him back. Shaking the hair out of his eyes, Charles said, "Would you be willing to run a small errand for us?"

The level of excitement buzzing between father and son had Daroo curious. "How may I be of service?"

Coop snickered.

His father grinned sheepishly. "We've decided to embrace a slightly different lifestyle for the summer. We're in the process of toughening up our feet."

"We're going to see how long we can go barefoot!" Cole interjected helpfully.

Charles extended a slip of paper and a couple of folded bills. "Could you stop in at the hardware store?"

Daroo-fen took and scanned the list. "Fishing line?"

"The hooks and tackle I found were good, but the line kept snapping. It'd gone brittle."

"I see." He pocketed the funds. "I will range into civilization on your behalf, since you're clearly determined to leave it behind."

Charles' smile was easy. "Come to the wild side. We have trout."

"I'll return shortly ... and prepared."

Daroo-fen strolled back the way he'd come, mentally tallying up a few things he'd like to bring along for a day in the woods, when the slap of bare feet stopped him in his tracks. Coop ran up, and Daroo assumed Charles had thought of something else to add to the list. But the boy offered him a crumpled twenty-dollar bill.

"This is mine. Birthday money from Grandma Pfeiffer." Coop's earlier determination hadn't faded. "I need a thing from the store. Will you get it for me?"

"Does your father know?"

"No. I want to surprise him."

"What kind of surprise are we talking about here?"

"Promise not to tell?"

"I can't promise that, Coop. Reason with me, and I'll keep your secret if it's safe to do so."

The boy bunched up his mouth, then rolled his eyes heavenward in obvious exasperation. Daroo couldn't help wondering if he was witnessing one of Ally's mannerisms ... and if it was too late to train it out of the boy.

"I need a dog collar. And a leash."

"You don't have a dog."

"I'm getting one," explained Coop. "I already found him, but I need to catch him."

An uneasy feeling crept up Daroo-fen's spine. "You found a stray?"

"Nope. He's a wolf."

This kid.

Very carefully, he asked, "Are you aware that wolves are wild?"

"Not this one." Coop sounded utterly convinced. "I'm going to catch him and give him to Dad."

"What for?"

"Father's Day," the boy answered with exaggerated patience. As if he were used to getting the third degree.

Daroo-fen figured the boy was in for a world of disappointment. But he had to ask, "Why would your father want a wolf?"

"Mom wouldn't let him have a dog."

"But ... you can't keep a wolf. They're meant to be free."

"This one's different. And so's Dad. We're wild, too." The inescapable reasoning of a child. "I think maybe he's like Dad. He got lonesome."

Daroo-fen feared that he was about to do something very foolish. In fact, he already had, for the crumpled bill was in his hand. As he pocketed it, he said, "I hope you'll treat him kindly."

"Sure we will." Coop's smile was sunny. "He's going to be part of our family."

WHITE COLLAR WOLF

The next day, Drew Hunter changed his answering machine message, stopped his mail, and posted a notice in the window of his office door. He was on vacation. Apologies for any inconvenience. Not that there would be any. Other than the occasional legal question, which Daroo-fen always responded to with a referral, the offices of Woodruff, Thackeray, and Hunter did little actual business. Not with humans.

But appearances must be maintained. This was a long game, and his role was essential.

He waited for dark before moving a few personal items to the woods. It had been years since he'd visited his old den, but the wardstones were still in place. And behind barriers, a sigil-crusted wall hummed contentedly. All their secrets were safe. And that was worth any sacrifice.

Even though it was hard.

Perhaps that's why he was taking this tiny risk. He'd spent decades pretending to be human—dressing the part, docking his tail, and walking the same patch as dogs. But underneath all his civility, some crumpled, bottled shred of his former life howled against necessities.

Why should he wear sensible shoes and keep office hours? If Charles and Coop could bare their chests and give up shoes and roam the woods for a summer, couldn't he? It would have to be a secret, but his whole life was built around them. What was one more?

If he could pass himself off as a human, he could pass himself off as a pet.

Daroo-fen almost talked himself out of his scheme a dozen different times before Coop finally picked his way through the woods to the bramble, equipped with nothing but a creaky length of weathered rope.

He immediately felt bad. The boy was barefoot and footsore, with grass-stained kneecaps and a bruised elbow. But his eyes were bright with a delight that put a sway into Daroo-fen's tail.

"I *knew* you'd be here."

Dropping the rope, he offered his hands. Daroo obligingly set his paw on them, giving their greeting a bit of polish. Coop laughed and called him smart. Then sat right down and explained his whole plan. Which Daroo-fen had already heard, and which any other wolf wouldn't have understood. But he rested his chin on folded paws and heard him out.

Once that formality was over, Daroo crept forward on his belly, then rolled invitingly onto his back. He wanted contact. Had been craving it since the last time. As soon as Coop was close enough, he snared the boy with his front paws and pulled him down.

Coop's surprise turned into a grin. "I *knew* you'd like my idea."

As much as he admired the boy's boundless confidence, he was more interested in another belly rub. And it had been forever since someone had scratched his ears. The kid pulled through, and Daroo-fen rewarded him by licking his nose.

"D'ya like that?" Coop asked.

Silly question. All four paws in the air, he drummed the ground with his tail. He was making a spectacle of himself, and he didn't care. Because such simple pleasures were never meant to feel foreign.

Not that a wolf didn't have his pride. When the rope came into play, Daroo couldn't bring himself to meekly submit to the harness. But neither did he discourage the boy. He'd sit still while Coop approached, then leap back—head low, paws spread, tail wagging encouragement.

This was more than a game of chase. Coop would value his catch more if he worked for it.

"Come on, wolfy-wolf-wolf," the boy coaxed. "I'm going to give you to Dad."

Daroo-fen danced out of range and *wuff*ed softly.

"We'll give you a good home, and you can still run all you want, since this is our back yard. And you gotta be good to Rose, since she's only a baby. But especially be good to Dad. You can be his, and then he won't be alone, and then maybe he won't cry so much."

The game lost its appeal.

Coop slipped the noose of rope over Daroo-fen's head. Awe suffused the boy's face. "I did it," he whispered. "Well, maybe it was both of us."

True enough. Although it was difficult to say which of them was the culprit and which the accomplice.

HAPPY FATHER'S DAY

Charles had grown accustomed to rude awakenings. They were one of Cole's favorite ways to express affection. So when a certain Sunday dawned, he wasn't especially surprised to find himself on the receiving end of a belly flop.

"Happy Father's Day!"

"Your special day," Charles mumbled, eyes shut.

That seemed to throw Cole for a loop. "Nuh-uh," he finally said. "Father's Day is for dads, and *you're* the dad."

"But who *made* me a dad?" he asked.

His son wriggled closer. "Me?"

"Yep. You." Charles hugged him tight. "I love you."

"I know." And more shyly, "I got you something."

He sniffed unobtrusively, to see if anything was burning. "Not breakfast in bed?"

"Nope. But you can have it in bed."

Charles peeled back the lid of one eye and squinted at his son. "I think I need a better clue."

Cole's smile was one of supreme satisfaction. Scooting to the edge of the mattress, he picked up and handed over the end of an old, frayed rope.

Mystified, he asked, "What's this?"

"Pull." The boy was bouncing with excitement.

So Charles gave the rope a tug. Which set something in motion. Something that tapped lightly against wood floors, the same way Sheba's claws had when they were due for trimming. But it wasn't a dog at the end of the rope.

An enormous wolf filled the doorway, all soft tans and medium browns. Since Charles' bed was low to the ground, he could see his creamy underbelly. And what big eyes he had. And what big teeth he had.

With a panicked glance toward Rose, Charles scrambled onto hands and knees. "Come up here by me," he ordered Cole.

But the boy misunderstood. Patting the mattress encouragingly, he said, "Come on, boy. Come up by us!"

The wolf sat where he was, watching Charles with an eerie intelligence. Like *he* hadn't misunderstood.

"Don't be shy *now*." And before Charles could stop him, Cole darted to the wolf and flung his arms around its neck. "This is your big moment!"

Charles was half out of bed, driven by the need to protect his son, but the wolf didn't seem to mind Cole's rough affections.

"You always wanted your own dog, but a wolf is better, don't you think? He's wild like us. But friendly, too."

The wolf blinked placidly.

"Where did you find him?" Charles asked weakly.

"In our woods. Me and him had a talk, and we both think he's perfect for you."

"Is that so?"

The wolf's tail gave two small thumps that settled the matter.

Charles sagged back onto the mattress and cautiously admitted, "He's beautiful."

"You like him?"

"Yes. Thank you, Cole." He patted the rumpled bedding and, in an entirely different tone, said, "Come up here by me."

This time, the wolf obeyed, walking over until he loomed over Charles.

"Does he have a name?"

"Nope. He's yours, so you should get to pick."

Charles offered his fingertips for canine perusal. "What will you answer to, you big, beautiful beast?"

"*Beast* is good," said Cole. "Oh! I almost forgot!"

The boy ran out. Meanwhile, the wolf lowered himself to the floor, his muzzle resting on Charles' knee, his gaze fixed beseechingly on his new master's face. The eyes were as tan as his fur, with subtle depth caused by fanning lines and flecks of dark and light. But the pupils were strange. Unusually narrow.

Cole returned with the rest of his gift—a collar and a leash. "Mr. Hunter ran an errand for me, too. He didn't tell on me, did he?"

"He never said a word." Charles scratched the wolf behind his ear. "It's a good surprise."

They spent much of the morning cleaning up the doghouse and moving it to its old spot on the back porch. That afternoon, they made lists and tried to figure out what to feed a wolf. Charles added dog food to the shopping list they were saving up for Drew, but it was a long way to Saturday. Beast dined on scrambled eggs and half of one of Mrs. Lundgren's casseroles.

That night, Cole pushed a folded blanket inside the doghouse and tried to lure the wolf inside. Charles wasn't convinced Beast would fit. Dad had loved big dogs, so the house was spacious, but this wolf was on a whole different scale.

Even so, Cole was determined.

He climbed inside to demonstrate how comfortable it was. And Beast listened with incredible patience while Cole explained all about doghouses and people houses and bedtime and the solemn duties of watchdogs through the ages.

Which apparently went double for wolves.

To Charles' amazement, the wolf actually inserted himself through the door of the newly dubbed *wolf*house, turned his body around, and settled with muzzle on paws. It was almost as if he'd understood Cole's words. Or at least his earnestness.

Charles couldn't understand why Beast was alone. He was intelligent, obedient, and housebroken. Patient with children. Even careful of babies. That suggested he'd belonged to a family. Was he lost? Surely not abandoned. Could they really keep someone else's pet? Maybe he should ask Drew's advice.

He was relying rather heavily on his Saturday friend.

Maybe he shouldn't.

Dependence had always made him feel like a burden. Now, it was a bad habit. One he wasn't sure how to shake. Ally had thrust independence on him because she wanted her own. Right now, independence was a frighteningly lonesome prospect.

Drew had called him a capable man. Was he capable of this?

DEN SWEET DEN

When Charles came downstairs after tucking in his son, Beast had abandoned the doghouse. He sat on the other side of the screen door, as if done with his performance and ready for something more sensible.

He held the door wide, and Beast accepted the invitation. Hunkering down before the animal, Charles gently took hold of the thick fur on either side of Beast's face, staring into eyes that were more feline than canine. "I don't blame you for not wanting to live out of a box. Want a spot with me in the den?"

The wolf's ears pricked, and he looked toward the correct door.

"You'll have to be quiet. We're sharing with Rose, so no growling or howling. Okay?"

Beast whined and wagged his tail.

"Good deal."

By the time Charles reached his room, the wolf had already claimed more than his fair share of the mattress. He dimmed the nightlight and changed in the dark, then lowered himself to the edge of his bed. "Hey, you," he muttered. "I know I don't take up much space, but this is *my* bed."

It took some shoving and shifting before Charles judged he'd claimed sufficient territory. Sighing, he reached for Beast and found an ear to fondle. The wolf pressed closer, resting his chin on Charles' chest, which made it easy for him to bury both hands in thick fur. He worked his way up to the back of Beast's ears, which he gave a good scratching.

This brought back memories.

Good ones. Better ones.

Father's Day had always been awkward. People acted weird about it, like he shouldn't be praised or honored for getting Ally pregnant. Like the whole thing was a mistake that was best forgotten. Like becoming a teen father meant he wasn't a good one.

"I'm not sure why it's always been my fault," he whispered.

Beast's ears pricked.

"Ally got exactly what she wanted." She'd bragged about it afterward—finishing school, finding a job, buying the house. He'd been the next phase in a long-range plan. "I was thrilled, and then I was scared, and then I was married."

Beast licked his ear, and Charles wrapped his arm around the wolf.

"My parents insisted I take responsibility, but all the decisions were made around me." He stared at the ceiling. "But I was fine with it. Why not? Everything was set. Ally would work, and I'd stay home with our baby."

Funny, how it helped to say these things out loud. Ally had her version of events, and he'd never set the record straight. You didn't contradict Ally. You didn't bite the hand that fed you.

He took a shaky breath. "I wanted more kids. She didn't. When she found out she was pregnant again, I was in the doghouse."

Beast whined.

"She did keep the baby." Charles didn't think she really would have gotten rid of Rose, but she'd used the threat to hurt him. "But I never made it off the couch."

The wolf made an odd grumbling sound and roused himself enough to drape more fully over Charles. Out of the doghouse and into the wolf's den.

"Are you trying to smother me?" he complained.

Beast huffed in his ear but didn't budge.

And Charles went along with it. Because it was so much better than being alone. Dogs—and apparently wolves—were such good listeners. They knew when they were needed.

"Know something?" he asked. Even though Beast couldn't answer. "It's a secret."

The wolf's nose snuffled against his hair, his ear, his neck.

Charles grabbed hold and tipped his chin toward the ceiling, blinking hard. He had to tell someone even more than he needed to hide the truth. And Cole had given him a confidante. So he whispered three words in the dark. "I'm. So. Scared."

COMING TO HEEL

Daroo-fen had never been someone's comfort before.

In years long past, he'd stood out as the strong one, the sure one, rightborn successor of the seven-score moons and valorous succor of the meek. Others had been his comfort, and he had been their confidence. How strange to have his role reversed.

To be part of a family without leading it. To listen and be mute, without a voice in decisions. To be held without holding, without an equal share in any embrace.

It was unsettling. But far from unpleasant.

Over the first few days, Daroo-fen learned several things about the household. That Charles was much the same when alone as he was when Drew Hunter dropped by. No front, no false face. That the Coopers had nothing resembling a schedule. Charles was less interested in the time than in the tasks he and Coop shared. Only Rose kept regular hours—napping and needing attention by turns.

He'd also underestimated Charles.

The man might cry himself to sleep every night, but he seized each day and put it to use. Giving proof to an old adage—night's prey could rule the day. And anyone could see that Charles had been basking in the sun. His shoulders burned, then bronzed, and gold threaded into his hair. He had to take a scrub brush to his feet every night, for he stubbornly went without shoes. And now there was grease under his nails. He'd taken apart a tiller, spreading its parts across a sheet of plywood

Coop sat by his side, eager to learn the lore handed down from one generation to the next. Scuffed and stained and freckled and fearless. Carefree because his father took all the cares upon himself. Yet canny enough to see the need for canine companionship.

So Daroo-fen watched like a dog. And waited his turn.

It had come every night. It would come again.

A lone wolf knew better than anyone that fear and courage ran together, rivals in a race with an uncertain course.

"Maybe it tastes bad?" Cole was looking more than a little concerned. "Do you think that's it?"

Charles checked his steps on his way to the clothesline, shifting a laundry basket so he could see. "Did he try any?"

"Nope. Maybe it smells bad?"

Abandoning the load of towels, Charles joined his son on the back porch where Beast was snubbing his first proper meal. The ever-helpful Mrs. Lundgren had sent her husband to the feed store on their behalf, where he'd secured fifty pounds of the best kibble money could buy. However, the food bowl of name brand dogfood might as well not exist for all the attention their wolf paid it.

"It's the same kind my dad always bought," said Charles. "I think it's supposed to provide Beast a balanced diet. It's good for him."

Cole picked up some kibble and sniffed. "Like broccoli for dogs?"

Charles followed suit and grimaced. "Closer to liver."

"Maybe wolves won't eat dogfood because they're wolves. Not dogs."

Beast's tail thumped the porch, as if he liked the excuse much better than the mysterious brown nuggets they expected him to eat.

"Dare you," said Cole, who held a single nugget to his mouth.

Charles smirked. "Double dare you."

Cole waited for him to select his own chunk of kibble. Together, they popped them into their mouths and crunched down. Beast's head had come up, and his nose was working overtime while awaiting their verdict.

"Ugh," said Cole.

"Double ugh. Split a bottle of root beer with me?"

While his son ran to the fridge for their chaser, Charles reached for Beast, roughing up his fur. "Sorry, boy. I shouldn't have bought such a big bag."

Beast delicately plucked a piece from the bowl and sat back, crunching contemplatively.

Cole returned with bottle and an opener shaped like an electric guitar. "Did he try it?" he asked eagerly.

Charles hummed. "I don't think he's impressed."

But the wolf kept eating.

"I'll keep sneaking him food under the table," promised Cole.

With eyebrows up, Charles said, "I thought *I* was the only one feeding Beast on the sly."

Cole snickered and passed him the root beer.

They kept Beast company while he worked his way through his portion, unhurried and unceasing. It reminded Charles a little of Drew sorting junk mail. He couldn't wait to introduce the two of them.

After some negotiations, he and Cole decided to put a little food in Beast's dish every day. And to feed him any wolf-friendly parts of their dinner. Since he was part of the family.

Beast finished the dogfood, but Charles was almost positive he did it to be polite.

"How many days?" asked Coop.

"Check the calendar," said Charles, in a tone that meant he knew but wasn't telling.

Daroo-fen pricked his ears. Did they have plans?

"Is this today?" Coop pointed to a square.

Was it Thursday already?

"Yes, that's today."

"Two more days?" the boy whined, as if that was too long to wait.

Charles smiled sympathetically. "It'll be Saturday soon."

Understanding took its time arriving, but Daroo-fen was sure as phases. They meant him. They were looking forward to Saturday, which would bring Drew Hunter to their door. They were counting on it. And him.

If he was going to keep his standing appointment, then Beast needed to establish his right to roam. Quickly. Which led Daroo-fen to one irrefutable conclusion. Although he wanted nothing more than to stay, it was time to run away.

RUN AWAY HOME

He timed his first vanishing act for later that morning. While Cole was reading a naptime story to Rose, Charles retreated into the den, where he knelt at the foot of his bed, folding a pile of tiny clothes that belonged to Rose.

Perfect.

With a whispery *wuff*, Daroo-fen gained the glance he needed. And the double-take that followed.

He was clumsier than he would have liked, but paws were limiting. Still, he was more than capable of turning a doorknob. On the second try, he opened the door leading onto the tunnel of greenery and the garden beyond.

"Aren't you clever," Charles said.

Daroo-fen trotted over, tail waving. He accepted Charles' praise and licked his cheek and chin, all the while willing the man to understand. *I can open and close doors. I can come and go as I please.*

He ran to the door, then bounded back, washing Charles' face again.

"Yes, I'm impressed. And covered in drool." He grabbed him

by the ruff, just the way Beast liked, and looked him in the eyes. "You're something else, you know?"

Yes, something else. Something other. And you need to trust me. He licked Charles' chin. *Trust me to come back.*

This time, he ran out the door and kept running.

He heard Charles call after him, softly, so as not to interrupt naptime. But Daroo-fen's ears were keen enough to catch the note of worry.

Daroo-fen ran faster, sure his resolve would crumble otherwise.

Hours took their time passing, and Daroo-fen lost patience with them. Surely this was enough. He ran all the way home and skidded to a halt under a trellis before properly registering the scents that hung in the air—smoke, soot, coal, and charring meat.

He loped closer. Were they grilling? Was Coop ... fanning?

"Dad! Dad! It worked!" exclaimed the boy. He dropped the clumsily pleated newspaper and ran to Daroo-fen. "I *knew* you'd come back!"

Coop babbled on about emergencies and good excuses and big plans. That's when Daroo realized that Charles and Coop were both wearing shoes.

"Smells good, doesn't it?" the boy asked, pleased and proud. "It's all the best stuff. Plus, Dad bought popsicles and ice cream sandwiches. But those aren't for you. Don't be sad though. You can have meat."

Daroo-fen's mouth was already watering. Had they really bought steaks and sausages to tempt him home? And had they really donned shirts and shoes in order to do so?

Charles came over then and knelt to look in his eyes.

To Daroo's utter mortification, the man's were threatening tears. He didn't scold or ask questions. Only muttered a gruff welcome.

Daroo bumped Charles onto his rump and bowled him over to bathe his face. That way, Coop would think his dad was only crying because he was laughing so hard.

That evening, Daroo decided that the Coopers' ploy might actually work. He'd snapped up every tender morsel they'd offered over dinnertime, and he now weighed too much to waddle away. All he wanted to do was sleep, but he couldn't allow himself to drop off. This was neither the time nor place for a long sleep. Or the kinds of dreams the moon sent.

By the time Charles retreated into his den for sleep, Daroo-fen was having trouble remembering why leaving had seemed like such a good idea in the first place. It was probably just as well that Charles reminded him.

"I think Drew will like you."

Daroo-fen bounded onto the bed ahead of Charles and sprawled expansively.

"He seemed comfortable in the woods. And you're very woodsy." Charles shoved and shimmied his way into his usual place. "You're gone for half a day, and you forget how to share?"

Rolling onto his back, he whined an apology.

Charles flung an arm around Daroo and mumbled, "I shouldn't have worried."

But he had. And regret made the wolf question his methods. If he was going to be a true comfort, he needed to help Charles find his confidence. How else could he have a share in it?

In the dark hours before dawn, Daroo's light doze was interrupted by a whimper. Charles was prone to nightmares. A jostling paw. A snort in his ear. The man woke enough to whisper his name and reach for him. He stifled a sob, and Daroo groaned in sympathy.

If only there were something he could do.

How could he comfort without words?

He wanted Charles to feel safe, to find solace. But Daroo's thoughts and feelings weren't going to reach him. Not in this form. Unless ....

Cautiously, Daroo-fen pushed against Charles, not with his body—though the young man still clung close—but with the person he was. As if the force of his will could settle over the shivering light of the man's soul, as warm a weight as furs in winter.

All his thoughts were bent on comfort. Could his presence have a calming effect? *I'm here. You're not alone. I didn't abandon you. Here I am. Right here.*

It was as clumsy as paws on a doorknob, but it seemed to help. Charles relaxed, and his breathing slowed. He fell into a deep sleep, and his grip slackened enough for Daroo to ease away.

Because small noises were coming from the playpen. And Charles *needed* sleep.

So Daroo-fen took speaking form in order to lift Rose, his tail swaying as he carried her into the kitchen. He readied a bottle and offered it with the little rumbles one reserved for cubs. She waved a hand at him, and he lowered his face, letting her pull at his nose.

She gurgled.

He hummed.

She took the bottle.

He took a seat.

A slanting moonbeam offered enough light to betray several of his truths, but Daroo-fen knew his secret was safe even as he revealed it. Rose regarded him with solemn eyes as she suckled. "Our secret, little flower," he rumbled.

When he smiled, she stopped eating long enough to smile milkily back.

FIVE WHITE ENVELOPES

When Drew Hunter arrived at the Cooper residence via the front door, Charles was a mess of mixed feelings. Offering his hand, Daroo-fen asked, "Is something amiss?"

"What? No. Sorry. We're fine. Except ... there was a delivery just now. Registered mail." His fingers were cold, and he held onto Drew a few beats too long. "I think I need a lawyer."

"Show me."

Two things waited on the dining room table—one fat packet

from an out-of-state lawyer and five white envelopes from Woodruff, Thackeray, and Hunter. Daroo-fen hadn't realized they might be having *that* particular conversation today.

Indicating the former, he asked, "May I?"

"Please." Charles mumbled, "I'll be in the kitchen."

Daroo-fen wasn't a divorce lawyer, but he'd made a couple of calls to old classmates in the wake of Charles' initial admission. Those—and several hours' reading—had informed him enough to understand the language in the papers Ally had served.

They riled him. And they left him heartsick.

What would they do to Charles?

He replaced everything in the envelope and went to find Charles. The man was at the kitchen sink, hands submerged in suds, unseeing eyes fixed on something beyond the backyard.

"Charles?"

"Sorry. Ready?" He dried his hands, scooped up Rose, and joined him in the dining room.

Daroo-fen asked, "Where's Coop?"

"Out back, getting things ready for a wander through the woods. You're invited." With a tight little smile, he promised, "We're better provisioned this time. Steak sandwiches."

"I would enjoy that." Daroo indicated the two items on their agenda and asked, "Where do you want to start?"

Charles' gaze flicked to the letters from his office. "Do all of those say the same thing?"

Only the topmost envelope had been slit. "They do."

His expression clouded. "Drew, am I rich?"

"Not especially. Unless you liquidate your assets through

land sales."

"So the reason you're here is because you want the land."

Daroo-fen sighed. "I do represent a group that is interested in procuring—and preserving—the property you've inherited."

"So you want the land."

"Yes."

Charles looked away, but not quickly enough to hide his disappointment. "Can it wait a while?"

Catching the leading tone, Daroo-fen asked, "Why?"

"To keep you around."

Daroo wasn't sure which part of that statement buoyed him more. The half-joking admission that his friendship was welcome. Or the implicit willingness to consider a sale.

"I'm here because I want to be." Daroo bluntly added, "I enjoy spending time with you and your family."

Charles' gaze softened. "We look forward to Saturdays."

"Me, too."

That seemed to satisfy Charles, for he changed the subject. "I wish I could show you the newest member of the family, but he ran off earlier. He's ours, but I think he still belongs to the woods, too."

Daroo inclined his head. "Coop confided his plans in me. You have a new pet?"

"He's more than a pet," Charles quickly countered. "You'd understand if you met him."

"A wolf needs its pack. He's probably grateful to have found a place in yours."

Charles' grin was boyish. "I hope that's it. Because I can't afford to keep feeding him steak."

Daroo coaxed the story out of him, then wheedled Rose out of his arms. And for a while, they chatted as if the fat envelope on the table didn't matter. Because Coop galloped through, and Charles chased him into the bathtub. And then the boy was full of news about the amazing Beast. After that, there were diapers to change, formula to mix, and sandwiches to pack.

Coop was reading to Rose before Daroo was able to guide Charles back into the dining room. He rested his finger on the envelopes from his office. "I am concerned that this will cause problems with this." He placed his hand on Ally's paperwork. "You didn't know about the acreage?"

"No."

"Is it safe to assume your wife doesn't know?"

"My parents didn't like her much. I can't see them volunteering information."

Daroo-fen asked, "Do you want my advice?"

"Please." Charles' voice was rough with pain, and sadness steeped his scent.

"Do nothing with the offer from my offices. Keep it a secret." He flicked his fingers at the divorce papers. "Give her everything she wants."

Charles' jaw tightened. "Except the kids."

Daroo shook his head. "She's granting you full custody."

The man winced.

He thought he understood the wounded expression. He sighed and lowered his voice. "Your worth does not depend on her estimation of it."

"She doesn't want any of us."

Daroo-fen resisted the instinct to reach for the man. For now, comfort would have to come in the form of words. "She will keep everything she values, and she has given you everything you value. The concession suggests that she knows you are a good parent."

"But she ...." Charles blinked hard. "She still doesn't want any of us. She doesn't want *me*."

"Yes."

"I vowed it," he whispered. "I promised to love her forever."

Daroo understood vows. And he thought he understood Charles. Slowly, he settled his hand on the man's shoulder. "You love her."

"I do." He laughed weakly at his own words and hid his eyes.

Nothing he could say would change matters, so Daroo-fen settled on a firm tug that pulled Charles into a one-armed hug. It was awkward, but not excessively so. Charles only needed a few moments to pull himself together. When he stepped back, it was with whispered thanks.

Daroo-fen said, "While I cannot fathom her reasons for abandoning you to your own resources, I *can* protect those resources. Trust me, and all will be well."

"Okay." Charles drew himself up to his full height and looked him in the eye. "I'll trust you."

DUTY AND DELIGHT

For the next several days, Charles determinedly cleared everything out of his parents' bedroom. It was one of only three upstairs rooms—theirs, his old one, and a large cedar closet for storage. By rights, he should have laid claim to the master bedroom, but in the end, he decided to keep to the den.

"Let's fix up the big room for Rose," he suggested over cornflakes. "For when she outgrows the playpen."

Cole considered this and asked, "Not right away, though. Right?"

"I'll keep her in with me for a while yet." Charles didn't like the idea of putting his daughter's bed so far from his own. "I'm just planning ahead."

"Because we're staying." Cole wasn't really asking.

"Yes." Charles poked at his cereal. "We'll stay."

"Okay," his son agreed, as if the matter was both simple and settled. "Is Mr. Hunter coming over?"

"Is it Saturday?"

Cole grinned. "Can I wait on the front step?"

"If you can wait for me, I'll wait with you."

Galvanized by their new goals, father and son shoveled cornflakes like it was a contest.

"You're looking especially scruffy," remarked Daroo-fen, who was trying not to look too eager. Or too winded. He'd gone out the back during breakfast, proceeding to and from his woodland den at speed. Because Mr. Hunter couldn't pull off neat-and-pressed after a week on four feet. A bath in the creek and a raid of his stores had left him presentable. And almost late.

Charles and Coop were waiting on their front step.

Once more, he marveled at how the Cooper males were both different in appearance and alike in expression. Daroo ruffled his fingers through the boy's fine hair. All the former spikiness had drooped under its own weight, leaving him with layers of sun-bleached blond.

"Good morning, Coop," he murmured.

"What's that?" the boy countered, pointing at the last-minute addition to Drew's ensemble.

Ignoring the question for the moment, Daroo-fen surprised Charles by giving him the same welcoming tousle. "Good morning, Charles," he said, using the same inflection. "Your rampant thatch, at least, bodes well for Rose."

Cole snickered. "Dad's got pretty hair?"

"I stand by my *scruffy* verdict as just and equitable."

Charles batted his hand away, but he was smiling. "We're scruffy, but clean. We scrub every night."

"Something that *also* bodes well for Rose. Is the young lady awake?" Daroo-fen touched the length of cloth he'd draped over his shoulder. "I found this among my things and brought it for her."

"What is it?" Coop asked again.

"It would be easier to demonstrate than explain." He hesitated. "Unless you have an errand for me?"

"Maybe later." Charles waved him in, and Coop held the door. Both radiated happiness.

"This is new." Daroo-fen had to feign ignorance, but his interest was real enough. He'd been curious about the new addition to the front room, since Charles had put so much effort into its procurement.

"New for us." The young man looked embarrassed. "I mean, it's a used couch. But it's in good shape, and it's big enough."

The couch was a ponderous thing, upholstered in turtle green, long, deep, and stalwart, able to bear up under the entire Cooper clan, plus one wolf. Or plus one friend. And for the first time Daroo-fen realized that it wasn't simply big enough. It was long enough. Had Charles wanted a guest bed?

In the longstanding tradition of ancestors unknown, he was offering hospitality as if it were his duty and his delight.

"Do you like baseball?" Charles nodded toward the television he'd set up opposite the couch.

"I have no objections to the sport."

"If you wanted to watch a game with us, there's room."

Daroo-fen offered a willing smile. "When's the next game?"

"There's one this afternoon. I was planning to do a little yardwork, then fire up the grill. Burgers, maybe?"

"Sounds like a plan."

"Dad! I can't find Beast!" Coop hurtled into the room and used the couch as a landing pad. "He's not in the yard. I checked *all* the places."

"He'll be back," Charles said mildly.

Coop bounced to his feet and hurried to Daroo. "Can you show us now?"

"With Rose's cooperation."

The swaddling had been at the very bottom of Daroo-fen's stores, and even through long years of disuse, it retained the faint scents of the wolves whose brushings had gone into its looming. With a careful series of twists, folds, and knots, he created a sling for Rose that freed his hands and tucked her safely over his heart.

Charles and Coop watched with matching expressions of fascination.

"I'm guessing you didn't learn that at law school," Charles said, checking for and finding his daughter's smile.

"She likes it," Coop reported enviously. "Where did you learn to do that?"

"Where does anyone learn anything worth knowing?" posed Daroo-fen.

With a quick glance at his father, the boy answered with confidence. "Home."

Charles' plans for the day kept Daroo-fen firmly on the sidelines, either because the man didn't want to put a guest to work ... or because he'd figured out how much Daroo enjoyed cuddling Rose. So the wolf did little more than steady the ladder from time to time, while Charles clambered up and down.

Vines grew along all sides of the house, sometimes on trellises, but just as often finding purchase on sections of brick and stonework. The only problem was, they also grew across windows. Charles was clearing the windowpanes in order to let in more sunlight.

"What about those?" Daroo-fen asked, indicating the set of windows belonging to the den.

"I'm leaving those." Charles sheepishly explained, "I like the greening light and the way everything dapples. It's almost like being in the woods."

This man.

Daroo-fen had resigned himself to a life as well-ordered

as the tidy hedgerows that lined every neighborhood in Pine Hall. But Charles had dragged him past the prickly frontages and into the half-wild garden he'd inherited. Where twining and tangling were encouraged and supported. And appreciated.

This was an in-between place, tended by a distant offshoot of the reaver lines. Rare and hidden and his to protect. Because he was their watchdog. Because he'd made himself at home in Charles' den. And because he wasn't ready to leave.

He doubted he could.

And he couldn't bring himself to mind.

Daroo-fen retreated to a bench under an arbor that offered him and Rose some shade. She dozed, and he hummed to guide her into deeper sleep. But he soon had company. Coop startled him by grabbing his face. The boy knelt beside him on the bench, smelling of grass clippings and bruised leaves ... and an excitement that put extra shine in his eyes.

"Is it time for me to go to the store?" Daroo inquired softly.

"Hang on a sec," the boy ordered.

Daroo tried to turn his head, to see where Charles was, to avoid this boy-child's clear gaze. But Coop held him there. And Daroo-fen let him.

Finally, Coop nodded and said, "You and Beast *really* need to meet."

An impossibility. But he was curious why the notion was suddenly so urgent. "Why is that?"

Coop searched his face a little bit longer, then shrugged. "Because you have the same eyes."

DANGERS OF INTOXICATION

It had been a good day—burgers and baseball and tucking in tuckered out kids. Drew had stayed late, lingering over bottles of root beer on the back porch, talking about random stuff. He'd been reluctant to go, so Charles had offered the couch.

Next time, he'd promised. Did Drew do that on purpose? He never left without promising to return.

Charles sat alone on the back porch, watching fireflies wander through the back garden. The scent of rain made the summer night soft, and heat lightning flickered through distant clouds. He should check the downspouts.

As he made sure everything was battened down for a storm, he paused every so often to listen. He wasn't exactly worried about Beast, but he'd rest easier if the wolf came home. Actually, he was pretty sure he wouldn't be able to sleep without him.

Maybe he should grab a flashlight, walk a little ways into the wood?

But Charles couldn't do it. He wouldn't leave the kids alone.

A shadowy form swung into view, and as Charles stood, it seemed to pick up speed at the sight of him. He was probably grinning like a fool, but he was too happy to pretend he wasn't glad to see the big, beautiful beast.

The wolf bounced around him, tail wagging. Then Beast planted his forepaws on Charles' shoulders and licked his forehead.

"Welcome back. I saved you a burger. Are you hungry?"

Dropping to all fours, Beast trotted to the kitchen door and waited for Charles to let him in.

While Beast ate, Charles tidied the kitchen.

While Charles bathed, Beast heard about the day.

And by the time they soft-footed it into the den, the storm had reached Pine Hall. Rain drummed on the roof and lashed at the windows. Charles opened the door and let in a breath of drenched night air—heavy, earthy, and invigorating.

"Listen to that," he murmured, for the rainfall was like an old song, half-forgotten to time, but still capable of tugging at his heartstrings. He used the doorstop to prop the door open an inch or two, checked to make sure Rose was covered, then navigated toward the bed.

Beast already owned the mattress, forcing Charles to reclaim and defend his territory. But he didn't mind at all. This was how it had always been with Beast. This is how he hoped it would stay. It was embarrassing how much he needed Beast to be here for him. Then again, it was better to be needy and clingy and selfish and lame with one's wolf than with one's lawyer.

"I love you," he whispered.

As he had once before, Beast resituated, draping himself over Charles. Holding him down, holding him together.

The weight and his weariness conspired with the storm, and Charles was soon drifting in a calm place that only found him when he was with his wolf. Dark and wild, like the woods at night, it was easier to forget his sadness and fears here.

Here was the rest he craved. Here was steadiness and safety.

Here, the loneliness vanished, because here, he wasn't alone.

Daroo-fen was getting better at comforting Charles. He may have fumbled at first, but he'd always been patient and methodical. It was why the pack had singled him out. Why they'd agreed he was right and ripe for the challenge he'd undertaken.

By degrees, he'd figured out that Charles responded best when he was in an in-between place—no longer awake, not truly asleep. Here, he was more receptive. Here, Daroo-fen was able to lend him a little of the strength he barely touched, the wildness that was going to waste.

These were euphemisms, of course. Word games to soothe a guilty conscience.

Comforting. Supporting. Nurturing. They amounted to a breach of trust, for such intimacies weren't meant to be stolen. True, it was all backwards. He was on the wrong side of the equation. But it was still tending.

He rationalized his way around his appalling lack of manners like a lawyer building his case. Several facts cast his actions in a more favorable light.

That the packs' truce was with reavers, and Charles wasn't one. Technically. That Daroo-fen only gave, never took. So there was no chance of harm. Probably. He wasn't sure if Charles ran the same risk as Amaranthine when it came to the give and take of souls. Addiction.

And Daroo-fen strongly suspected that on some level, Charles was aware of his efforts ... and welcomed them. For he resisted the pull of sleep, prolonging this connection Daroo had forged.

It had been a good day, and he was tired. Maybe that's why he gave in to the pull of Charles' presence. Dipping down. Lapping lightly. Finding bliss.

He shouldn't have. Really, really shouldn't have.

And he *definitely* shouldn't have allowed the intoxication to carry him into sleep.

CAN WE PRETEND

Charles woke to a deep growl that resonated through his chest and set his hair on end. An animal crouched over him, except it was a man, too. But people couldn't make such paralyzing sounds.

Very slowly, Charles raised his hands toward its chest, thinking to push it away before the thing realized it had a ready meal cowering under its very nose. He needed to get clear, fend it off, find the kids. He couldn't have been more shocked when the thing spoke.

"I will *not* abandon him! This one is *mine*, and I have become his. Any may know it, even the Moon herself and all her maidens."

A strange vow, slurred by sleep and roughened by the growl that wasn't letting up.

Charles' trembled in the dark. The nightlight outlined a hulking form. His heart jammed into overdrive as the thing snuffled at his neck. Would it tear out his throat?

Harsh breathing gave way to a huff and a grumble. Then a hushing and shushing that did little to reassure Charles. He tried to wriggle free, but its limbs framed him, penning him in, pinning him down.

He had to try.

His hand met bare skin, and he pushed.

The growling ceased as the thing's head snapped up, and they were face-to-face. An instant later, its forehead dropped to his chest, and a muffled voice asked, "Can we pretend this didn't happen?"

"Drew?"

"Yes," he sighed. "It's me."

Charles whispered, "Let me go?"

To his relief, Drew backed off, all the way to the far wall. But he had full range of the room. Charles scrambled to put himself between Drew and Rose.

"*Charles*," he said in injured tones.

There was something wrong with Drew's silhouette. Even though the light was low and the night was far from over, Charles could tell that the hair was wrong, the clothes were wrong, and the … the tail was *very* wrong. Should he turn on the light?

As if reading his mind, Drew suggested, "The kitchen? We shouldn't wake Rose."

Unable to turn around, Charles backed toward the door. Drew followed, which was unnerving, even though it was the point. He slapped the switch for the kitchen light, blinding himself, berating himself for his stupidity. But Drew didn't take advantage.

"Charles, I would never intentionally hurt you or the children."

"So this is unintentional?" he asked, voice tight.

"Yes." Drew eased into the light. "I am in a great deal of trouble, letting you see me like this."

Like always, he loomed large. But Drew Hunter had lost his professional polish. Not that he was any less intimidating. Charles' back hit the counter, and he gripped it with both hands, holding himself up. Moving slowly, Drew took a seat at the kitchen table and placed his hands on the surface.

He was sort of the same—skin tone, hair color, facial features, muscles for days. But now he had a man bun and a fur vest and claws. And yeah, he hadn't imagined the tail.

"You're what, a werewolf?" he asked.

Drew actually looked offended. "Nothing of the sort."

"But you're not … normal."

"I could debate that into the dust, but I'll grant you this—I am not human."

Charles was distracted then. Because Drew's pleading eyes were strange, with narrow pupils. And with the fur and the tail and his missing wolf, his mind made a disconcerting leap. "Beast?"

"Yes."

"Nooo," he moaned, not wanting it to be true. His knees had gone all wobbly, and his breath was coming in gasps. Charles sank to the floor before he could fall, and then Beast was there, large as life. But Drew was gone. Because Drew was Beast.

And even though it was stupid, he reached for his wolf, needing him to at least be real.

Beast came and sat with him, and when Charles wrapped his arms around him, he huffed in his ear, the same as always. But it wasn't the same, and it never would be again. And the loss cut deep, and Charles was crying.

His wolf whined, and that felt like an apology.

And then there were arms and a voice in his ear, and he was being carried. Which triggered a fresh wave of panic. But Drew cut him short with three words. "Rose is waking."

Charles begged, "Let me go to her."

But they were already there. Drew set him down beside the playpen, then stepped away. He crossed to the propped door and opened it wide. He leaned against the doorframe, gazing out into the night, tail switching and puffing by turns. Like he was as upset as Charles.

Putting on a brave face for his little girl, Charles changed her diaper, but he couldn't bear releasing her. Not in this uncertain atmosphere. So he sank wearily onto his own bed, pulling his sheet and blanket around him. A pitiful shield.

"Will you go away if I ask you to?" he asked.

Drew watched him from the doorway. "Would you keep my secret if I did?"

Was that a threat? Charles couldn't tell. "What happens if we pretend this didn't happen?"

"We stay friends."

Charles tried to imagine it, only to realize what that meant. And what he'd done.

He'd told Beast *everything*. How he'd been gutted. How much it galled him. Every confession and crying session came back to him, flocked by shame and humiliation. But there was so much stupid stuff, too.

"I made you eat *dogfood*."

"A minor indignity, I assure you."

"We've been ... I mean ... every night."

Drew's gaze was steady. "Thank you for that. I was lonesome."

Charles got the idea that Drew was willing to pretend if he

would. That he didn't want to lose what they'd been finding, little by little. However, Charles didn't think he could live with lies again. He didn't want them in his home. But he'd wanted Beast, and he'd wanted Drew. That was the truth. And that was the only place to start.

"What are you?"

Drew's gaze dropped. "A lawyer by trade."

"Who are you?"

A soft look. "Your friend."

"Why won't you tell me?" Charles was frustrated. "Tell me what I want to know."

Drew started toward him, hesitated, then knelt a short distance from the bed. "You need to know that I will never abandon you. And that I will always respect your wishes. If you ask me to leave, I will go. If you never want to see me again, you won't."

Charles shook his head.

"If you want me to stay, I will. In any guise." He placed one large hand over his heart. "All that you need, I will be."

Rose reached out then, waving one small hand toward Drew and making a funny little crooning noise. For the first time, it occurred to Charles that Drew's tuneless little lullabies sounded a whole lot like wolfsong.

"Who are you really?"

He crept closer, looking a whole lot like Beast when he was begging at the table. Offering both hands, palm up, he said, "My name is Daroo-fen Clearsong."

Charles found himself in an empty moment, and for once, he would get to choose how to fill it. Knowing was simple. He *knew* what it was like to want to stay and be told to go. And he *knew* he could never do that to a friend like Drew, to a wolf like Beast, or even to this uncanny version of them.

So he awkwardly patted the mattress. "Come on, then. Come up here by us."

COMING TO TERMS

Charles scooted to the very edge of the mattress. Maybe it was a healthy instinct, but he was horrified to find himself here again. Put in his place. How many times had Ally banished him to the fringes of comfort—warning him off, forbidding his touch, shunning every advance until desire shriveled? This place was no place. A precursor to either the couch or floor.

The mattress shifted.

By the time Charles realized that Beast had left the bed, the wolf had circled it and was doing his whole looming routine again. "What?" he whispered, clutching his blanket to his chest.

Beast huffed and herded him—all poking muzzle and butting head—to the very center of the mattress. Then trotted back around to his side, hopped back up, and settled in his usual way, with his chin resting on Charles chest.

He slowly wrapped his arms around the wolf and tentatively scratched behind one ear. "Is this weird for you?"

With a low huff, Beast licked his cheek.

Charles hated to ask, needed to know. "Did you just kiss me?"

The wolf yawned.

He should have left the nightlight on after tucking Rose back in. Then at least he could look Beast in the eyes and know if Drew was laughing at him from somewhere behind them. It was mindboggling to learn there was a person wrapped up in the animal who'd been his bedmate for days.

"I'm going to pretend this isn't weird."

Beast whined.

Charles kept remembering things he never would have done if he'd known. "I told you so many things. If you're also a lawyer, does that whole confidentiality thing kick in?"

The mattress shifted again, and Drew—who was actually Daroo—was suddenly right there, practically sharing his pillow. "Charles, if you want to talk, I must be in this form."

Misery swamped him. Regret and loss. How could he pretend nothing had changed? This changed everything.

"You're making me feel like a bad dream."

"Sorry. But you've got to admit, this is ...."

"Weird?" There was a smile in his voice.

Charles grumbled, "*So* weird."

"But not frightening?"

"No." He felt small and self-conscious and several kinds of embarrassed, but the initial panic was long gone.

Daroo tousled his hair, just the way Drew had ... was it only yesterday? It brought Charles' attention around to all the ways they were too close for comfort. He edged back. To his relief, Daroo let him.

"How's this going to work?" asked Charles.

"In what sense?"

"You can't just ... *stay* here."

Daroo finally said, "If that is what you want."

"Wait. What?" Charles didn't care for that stark tone. "Did you *want* to? Stay, I mean?"

"Only if I'm welcome."

"Well, yeah. But I mean ...." The questions piled up and spilled out. "Don't you have a place? What about your job? How much do we tell the kids? Where would we put you?"

Daroo scooped an arm under Charles' shoulders and rolled into him, laughing softly. "So I *am* welcome."

"Well ... yeah," Charles repeated weakly. "Isn't this a little close?"

"Same as always." He pulled the blankets higher. "Pack style."

Charles muttered, "I'm not a wolf. You have to know this is ...."

"Hospitable," cut in Daroo. "I'm honored that you would set aside your considerable discomfiture in order to meet with me here in the manner of my people."

"Are you doing a lawyer thing? What do they call it, leading the witness?"

"I'm providing context." More quietly, Daroo added, "I *do* want to stay."

Charles tried not to squirm. "Like *this*?"

"Like pack." He sighed a small, "Please?"

It was the verbal equivalent of puppy dog eyes, and Charles was defenseless against such pleading. In part because he'd been reduced to it more than once. It was an awful, wretched thing, having something withheld.

Making an effort to relax, Charles asked, "Which is the real you?"

"They're all me." Daroo shifted his hold so that one hand cradled the back of Charles' head. "Are you a father or a son, a friend or a neighbor, a homemaker or a man?"

He was all those things and more, but none of those things were all of who he was. "Okay. I get it."

Daroo nodded. Or nuzzled. It was kind of hard to tell them apart at this range.

Charles could hear the soft patter of rain. Always nice. But he doubted it was responsible for the familiar sensation that ebbed through him, deep and dark as the woods at night. "Why is it better when you're here?"

"You felt that?"

He grunted, and his fingers found purchase in the shaggy fur of Daroo's vest. "Can't hardly sleep without Beast anymore."

"There are reasons. It's a long story, but I'm not at liberty to share it."

Charles murmured, "I'll keep your secret."

"I made a promise."

That he could understand. "Vows shouldn't get broken."

"Charles, can you trust me?"

That was kind of a dumb question. He was smiling when he slurred, "Lemme think 'bout it."

Daroo's voice was low in his ear. "This is me. I'm able to get close because of a certain ... compatibility of souls."

He cracked an eye, not that it did any good. Everything was shadow. "You calling me your soulmate?"

"Nothing so romantic," he said blandly.

Okay, that was good. Because that would put this at a whole different level of weird. Sleeping with an honest-to-God trinity was enough of a stretch for tonight. He was both ratcheted up and totally relaxed. Like he was happy right where he was, but also in a highly charged state of anticipation for whatever might come next.

Daroo said, "I only mean that I find similar contentment in your presence."

"Uh-huh." Charles threw an arm around his wolf. "Lucky us."

And the dark of the woods was all around him, closer than ever, heady with wildness, anchored by trust. He was lost in its vastness, but he wasn't at all lonesome because he wasn't alone. Now, he knew why.

WHAT ARE YOU?

Charles woke to the strange sensation of fingers sifting through his hair. Not Cole's usual pell-mell way to start the day. But then he remembered and stirred. It was strange, seeing Beast's slit-pupiled eyes set into Drew Hunter's face. Had they always been that color? He'd honestly never noticed.

"Remember me?" Daroo asked. He sat on the floor beside Charles' mattress.

Charles grunted. He wasn't likely to forget. His friend's gaze was as soft as his smile was sharp. Were those fangs? Other details came into focus in the morning light dappling the den. He wasn't sure which looked stranger, the pointed ears or the long hair.

"Somebody wants her daddy."

He guiltily scrambled to sit up and reached for her. The hands that lowered Rose into his arms were clawed.

"I'll bring a bottle."

When Daroo strolled away, it was with much swishing of tail. Was he wagging it for the usual reasons canines did, or was he showing off a little? "Which do you think?"

Rose wriggled in ecstasy over having gained his attention.

Kissing the top of her head, he whispered, "I think so, too."

Daroo handed off a bottle at the same time Charles heard Cole coming downstairs in a series of two-footed thuds. The bathroom door half-closed while the boy answered nature's call. Charles murmured, "We probably shouldn't let him see ...."

But Daroo had been replaced by Beast, whose tail still swayed.

Because it's what he would have done, Charles reached for the wolf's ear, fondling and scratching. It was only a little weird. With a wry headshake, he admitted, "This might take some getting used to."

Beast licked his chin.

Charles pushed aside his muzzle.

Rose chortled happily.

Beast licked her, too.

Then Cole was charging in and flung himself at an open section of mattress, bouncing his way over to greet his baby sister. He chattered and coaxed and cooed. Although it was more accurate to say he *coop*ed. The boy was determined that his nickname would be her first word. Beast was tackled next, and the wolf obligingly rolled onto his back.

"You're a glutton for belly rubs," Charles accused.

Beast waved his paws in the air and cheerfully sneezed.

Little things changed, but they felt like a big deal to Charles.

Drew Hunter stopped waiting for Saturdays to drop by. He'd bring groceries or pick up pizzas. They'd fish in the creek or work in the yard. Or just lounge on the sofa watching baseball or movies. A couple of nights, he stayed over—officially—camping with them on the screen porch. Otherwise, Mr. Hunter would bid farewell at the front door, only to turn up later as Beast at the back.

All the switching certainly livened up Charles' days.

"What are you doing?" Charles asked.

Daroo's tail puffed, but he didn't stop his stealthy removal of the screen from one of the side windows. "Expanding my options."

"You'll let in flies."

Secreting the screen behind the china cupboard that stood empty against the dining room wall, Daroo whisked briefly into the pantry, where an old mesh flyswatter hung from its nail. Presenting it to Charles across his palms, he solemnly said, "You take the first watch."

That whole day, Daroo messed with Cole, making the kid believe that both the lawyer and the wolf were in the house at the same time.

In a door, out a window.

Up the stairs, into the kitchen.

Through the front door, down a garden path.

Charles was almost getting used to having Drew or Beast rush past, often diving headlong out a window with little more than the flutter of one of Mom's old lace curtains. Moving faster than humanly possible. Leading Cole on a merry chase.

It was a silly game, firmly grounded in affection. And Charles had no part in it, except to watch and smile and let it continue. And to prop open the door to the den. And to lower the top panes in the windows of the master suite upstairs. To let in some fresh air while he worked, of course.

He was halfway through disassembling the antique bedstead from which he'd stolen his mattress when Drew swung through and landed in a crouch on the rug. "What are you, anyhow? A mutant?"

"No."

"Bitten by a radioactive wolf?"

Drew's lips twitched. "No."

Charles went right back to unscrewing slats. "You and your familiar had a transporter accident."

"No." Drew paused to touch Rose's hair. She was fast asleep, despite the ruckus.

"Intergalactic castaway." Charles popped the next board loose and moved to stand it in the corner. "Emissary from another world."

With a soft huff, Drew shook his head.

"Part of an undiscovered ancient civilization." He'd been planning to make reference to Atlantis, but something in Drew's eyes hauled him short.

Drew softly said, "You watch too many movies."

Charles was kind of glad to know that while Daroo was good at secrets, he was terrible at lies. Looking away, he said, "I don't need to know. Doesn't matter, really. But since my world's falling apart, I distract myself by wondering about yours."

Drew seized his hands, enfolding them in his much larger ones. "Your world isn't falling apart," he said firmly. "You're holding it together for all of us."

He leaned down and whispered one word. Then he kissed Charles' brow, held a finger to his lips, changed into a wolf, and charged out the door, tail flagging.

Rubbing distractedly at his forehead, Charles echoed, "Alpha?"

HALF A BOTTLE

Charles tucked in Rose for the night—done in, but far from done. Taking a deep breath, he surveyed the besmeared kitchen and went into their bathroom-utility room combo to see if that's still where his parents kept the box of spare rags. "You two all right?" he asked.

"Dad! Dad! Look what Beast can do!"

The wolf sat on his haunches, balancing a rubber duck on his muzzle.

"I'm sure he's very proud," Charles said by way of acknowledgment. "Wash your hair."

"I did."

"You missed a spot." He gestured toward the left-hand side, where chocolate sauce still darkened Cole's hair. "While you do that, I'll do the kitchen."

"Sorry, Dad."

Charles grabbed a bucket and shrugged. "Accidents happen. We'll be more careful next time."

Fifteen minutes later, the footprints, pawprints, and skid marks were gone without a trace. Proof that Cole's little mishap hadn't *really* been a disaster to begin with. So why fuss?

He went to check on Cole again and stopped in the doorway. "How in the world did you get him in there with you?"

"He jumped."

Beast sat in the tub, head and ears drooping while Cole worked his thick coat into a lather. The boy had easily used half the bottle of baby shampoo. Charles covered his smile with his hand. Then added a second in order to hold back his laughter.

The wolf narrowed his eyes, then simply turned his head away.

Cole's thin arms barely reached around Beast's sodden bulk, but he kept up an enthusiastic—if disorganized—effort to spread suds everywhere.

Okay. Intervention time.

Charles came to kneel beside the tub. "You know, this *isn't* dog shampoo."

Cole hesitated. "Does that matter?"

"I think so. Let's get him rinsed."

It took the better part of an hour to slosh and spray all the soap out of Beast's fur. Naturally, this meant the entire vicinity was now sloshed, sprayed, and soapy. But they used several towels to fluff Beast dry, and then Charles ushered Cole to his room. It was now well past bedtime, so the boy offered no resistance. A weary grin. A whisper of love. A mumbled goodnight.

One last mess.

When he returned to the scene of the bath, the door closed behind him, and the lock made an ominous click. Daroo gave him no chance to react before lifting him right off his feet and lowering him—clothes and all—into a tub filled with soap scum, shed fur, and tepid water.

"Hey!"

Daroo poured a basin of water over his head.

"What are you doing?" he gasped.

"Returning favors." A slow drizzle became a big dose of baby shampoo in Daroo's hand. "You were amused."

He only had one defense for that. "It was *funny*. How did you even get into the tub?"

"You don't question how I can enter through upper-story windows, but *this* mystifies you?"

Charles couldn't tell if he was teasing. "Are you angry with Cole?"

"For his abundant and sometimes misguided shows of affection?" Daroo slathered the excess of shampoo over Charles' head. "Not in the least."

"Can I at least have fresh water?"

Daroo fished around for the chain and pulled the plug.

"Are you angry with *me*?" Charles took over the washing of his own hair.

"Not at all." With an approving nod, Daroo busied himself around the room, changing over the laundry load and beginning to wipe up the mess caused by Beast's impromptu bath. Meanwhile, Charles pulled a wad of wolf's fur out of the drain, opened the tap, and shimmied out of wet denim and cotton.

"Can you quick check on the kids?"

"They're both asleep."

"How can you tell?" The door was shut. The dryer was running.

Daroo sat back on his heels, head cocked to one side. "I have excellent hearing."

Charles didn't doubt it. And he wondered what else his friend could do. He ventured to ask, "Is the world you come from wonderful?"

"You seem to think so." He resumed his methodical mopping up. "I was telling the truth when I said I'm from the area. I grew up in these woods, as well."

He almost said that he wished they'd been friends sooner, but Charles couldn't bring himself to want things changed. It would almost be like wishing away parts of his past. Maybe even the choices that had given him Cole and Rose.

"Charles?"

He started. While he'd been lost in thought, Daroo had moved to the edge of the tub, draping his arms along the side the same way he did when watching over Cole's baths.

"Sorry. I was just thinking."

"You often do."

"I'm glad you're here." And because that came off sounding sappy, he gruffly added, "You're a decent watchdog."

"Watch*wolf*," Daroo said in tones of mild reproach. Then dumped a fresh basin of water over Charles.

It took considerable dousing to rid his hair of all that shampoo. Charles didn't protest, but he thought Daroo was enjoying the process a little too much. Like the connection they always wandered into at bedtime was still in force. Assuring him that Daroo was in a good mood.

Since they were alone in a locked room, Charles thought it was safe to ask. "Are there more like you?"

"Yes."

"Am I allowed to know *anything*?"

Daroo inclined his head. "I can tell you a little. Personal things. Things not bound by my vows."

"That makes you sound like a monk."

His gaze turned inward. "Not a bad analogy. Such is the life of a lone wolf."

Charles caught a tendril of something aching and empty.

"Ask anything. I'll answer if I can."

After a moment's thought, Charles shrugged. "What should I ask?"

Daroo chuckled. "Ask about my name."

"Which one?"

"My true name. For while I have borrowed many over the years, I've always been and always will be Daroo-fen Clearsong."

And then he did the strangest thing. Lifting his chin toward the ceiling, he crooned a series of soft notes. It was eerie, but also beautiful.

"Was that some kind of language?" he whispered.

"Wolvish does not translate exactly. My name is at its best when it is sung. It means, 'pooling moonlight,' for my home den overlooks a spring fed pool." Daroo spoke soft and slow, like he was reciting something he'd memorized long ago. "I was born at the headwater of your creek."

Charles grabbed the tub's rim. "You know where it is?"

"Can any forget the path home?"

"Dad and I hiked upstream more than once, searching for the spring. But there are so many splits and gullies and thickets."

"The wellspring and the way are hidden."

"No wonder." He thought back to expeditions past. "We couldn't find what we were looking for, but it never felt like we'd wasted our time. You know?"

Daroo gave one of his lawyerly nods, then announced, "Tonight,

I will tell you a song."

"Don't you usually *sing* songs?"

"Are you conversant in wolvish?" He offered Charles the last clean towel.

"Nope. I can't even pronounce your true name."

"Then I will tell you an old story, one that is usually sung by young wolves in pursuit of the moon and her maidens."

Charles wrapped himself in the towel and fished in a laundry basket for a clean pair of pajama pants. "Chasing moon maidens, huh? What happens if they catch one?"

Daroo smirked and sauntered out, tail flashing.

With a strong suspicion that this song wasn't intended for little ears, Charles took a moment to cool his face with a splash of water. That shiver of anticipation was back, dancing under his skin. The kind that came with telling secrets and taking dares.

In a way, friendship with Daroo-fen was turning out to be like all those expeditions into the woods, searching for a hidden water source. Only this time, he'd had no idea what he was supposed to be looking for. But despite that, or maybe *because* of it, Charles had finally succeeded.

RUN WITH ME

On a morning in August, Charles couldn't decide whether to clean out the cedar closet upstairs or the shed out back. Cole offered to flip a coin. That settled that. While the boy readied himself to read to Rose—with Beast as his trusty backrest—Charles climbed upstairs to pull everything out of storage.

He was wrangling a set of wool blankets out of a back corner when Cole's voice reached him.

"Dad! Stranger!"

Charles hurried downstairs to find a courier requiring a signature.

"Who's it from?" Cole asked.

He took a deep breath and shook his head. It was from Ally's lawyers. "Just more papers."

"You need Mr. Hunter?"

"Yes." Shooting a pleading look at Beast, who was watching from the dining room, he said, "I'll have to give him a call."

The wolf padded toward the back of the house. And no doubt out the nearest window or door.

Charles tapped Cole's head. "You should finish reading to Rose."

Alone, he sank to the bottom step and waited for the soft rap on the front door. Drew let himself in. Charles budged over. His friend joined him on the step and held out a hand for whatever had arrived via registered mail. Feeling more than a little sick, Charles hid his face in his hands and waited for Drew's verdict.

"It's finished," he murmured. "It's final."

Charles simply nodded. He had nothing to add.

Daroo-fen knew how little experience he had being somebody's comfort. But as the days wore on, he began to suspect that he was only half the problem. Charles didn't seem to have much experience accepting comfort. He seemed bent on toughing it out. Alone.

He could hardly criticize. His own habits had been equally restrictive, and they'd helped him survive in less than ideal circumstances. But Charles' acceptance had given Daroo-fen the rare chance to recall himself. And he wanted to return the favor.

"Run with me."

"What?" Charles glanced down, then at the door, for Coop ranged freely at this hour.

Daroo sat on the floor, leaning against the lower cupboards, where Beast had lain a moment before. "Not everyone who runs with the packs is a wolf. Run with me."

"I can't." He went back to cleaning paintbrushes. "I couldn't keep up. And I can't leave the kids."

He wrapped his hand around Charles' ankle. "You set the pace. Trust the rest to me."

Wary, weary, he said, "I can't run away. This is the only home I have left."

Which was true, even though it was not. "I'll show you a moonlit pool."

"Do you mean … your den?"

"We won't leave your property." Daroo built his case. "Running together isn't running away."

Charles looked out the kitchen window, at the woods and mountain beyond. "What about the kids?"

"A pack runs together." Daroo-fen knew this could make a difference. "A walk in the woods. One night in the den. All of us."

"Okay, I guess." Charles managed a half-hearted smile. "I'd like that."

TRADE WITH ME

Charles tried to focus on the path, on his son, on the questions he was asking, but his thoughts kept scattering. Maybe this had been a bad idea.

Drew called a halt. "Let's reorganize. Trade with me."

And before he knew it, his friend had unwound the intricate swaddling from his own body and was twisting it around Charles' torso.

"Can I have a turn, too?" asked Cole.

"I don't see why not. Perhaps this evening. When the air cools, you can share your warmth with your sister."

Charles smiled at his son's obvious excitement over the prospect even as he welcomed Rose, who was only too happy to be tucked up against his bare chest. She'd grown a lot since his return to Pine Hall. Six months old in another week and beginning to navigate. Emptying so much of the house had effectively baby-proofed it. An unexpected perk. And Beast more than earned his keep by sprawling across doorways like an enormous baby gate.

"Take your time," murmured Drew. "We're in no hurry."

Charles checked the angle of the sun. The afternoon was getting on. "Won't we need to set up camp?"

"Everything is ready."

Drew bent to kiss the top of Rose's head, which brought him very near. Charles caught a whisper of anticipation and a hint of yearning. Although fleeting, it was enough for him to understand that this was important to Daroo. And that was becoming important to Charles.

With long, sure strides Mr. Hunter, lawyer and friend, caught up to Cole and swung the boy onto his shoulders.

Cole waved in a way that clearly said, *Look at me!*

Charles returned the gesture and trailed after them. Was he ready for this? Nope. But he hadn't been ready for most of the things that had come his way. Except maybe Rose.

Caressing her hair, returning her smile, Charles told her the truth and made it a promise. "I love you."

They were miles from the house—but still on Cooper land— when Drew waited for Charles to catch up and took his hand to steady him over a fallen log beside the trail. Moss and decay and mushrooms didn't account for the brief tingle that put Charles' hair on end.

Something had changed.

Up until that point, Charles had known where they were. Yes, it had been a while, but he and his dad had walked these paths together many times. Past the log was a forest that grew stranger with every step. The trees gained height and girth, and things kept flitting and fluttering in his periphery. Gone the moment he turned to look.

They were following the creek again as they wended their way uphill, toward what looked like a wall of stone half hidden behind a semicircle of ancient holly trees. Beneath them lay a pool of water, smooth and clear and deep. Charles watched as it silently, steadily overflowed, its waters welling up and spilling out in the direction of home.

"This is where it begins?" he asked in a hushed voice.

"Yes." Drew's gaze was thoughtful. "It's a good place for beginnings."

Charles had to look away, so he asked Cole, "Okay up there?"

His son was unusually quiet. Perhaps it was the setting. This part of the woods was as awe-inspiring as a sanctuary. It demanded hush. Drew lifted him down and moved toward the rockface. Skirting a stand of ferns, he showed Cole the way in. A moment later, the boy was scrambling upward. Charles followed.

The stone stairs couldn't have been entirely natural, yet they looked as if they'd been an integral part of the topography for hundreds of years.

Cole's voice carried down. "What's in this cave?"

"A den."

"What kind of den?"

Charles caught up as Drew answered. "A good one."

Cole asked, "Is it safe?"

"Very safe."

"How do you know?"

"It's mine," said Drew.

Which was more than Charles expected him to say. Then again, it wasn't like Cole to ask questions first. He usually leapt in without a thought for the consequences. Had something spooked the boy?

Cole asked, "You live in a den?"

"Sometimes."

"I thought you lived in town," the boy challenged.

"I do. Sometimes."

Cole folded his arms over his bare chest. "So you're like Dad?"

"Me?" asked Charles.

His son rolled his eyes. "You both have rooms in the woods. Yours is a library. Mr. Hunter's is a den."

Drew inclined his head, then swept a hand toward the entrance. "All the comforts of home."

Charles sat on the ledge outside the den's entrance, feet dangling over the edge as he waited for the moon to rise high enough over the forest for its light to reach the pool below. The season for fireflies was past, but there were other things winking and weaving in amongst the trees. It was kind of frustrating. Nothing held still long enough for him to get a good look.

Beast trotted out of the den, and Charles gave one of his ears a casual tug.

Daroo-fen had been swapping forms all evening. *Drew* had lit a fire in the hearth just inside the door as well as several lanterns, each safely out of reach thanks to a hook or high niche. They lit a series of linked rooms, some with short passages that led into more private spaces. In a way, the den was as empty as Charles' house. There was plenty of room for twenty people, yet Daroo-fen was alone.

Cole was all set to be a cave dweller.

Beast had put in his appearance soon after the tour. He dogged the boy's steps while he explored the vicinity. Sure his son was safe, Charles had opted for a nap, burrowing down with Rose amidst the furs and blankets in one of the recesses.

Now it was night, and the air was soft, and Charles felt safe and calm. And wide awake.

Suddenly, one of those elusive creatures slipped into focus, but when he went to point it out to the wolf, the thing vanished. "Where'd it go?" he muttered.

His friend shifted, and *Daroo-fen* grabbed his hand. With contact came clarity.

"Most people don't notice them." Daroo watched his face with a little half-smile. "You're gaining."

Charles shook his head to express his confusion.

"My strength is becoming yours, just as yours is becoming mine." Daroo nodded to the rim of pale light cresting the treetops. "That's one reason I brought you here. I want to tell the moon your name."

MOONLIGHT ON WATER

"You're going to introduce us?" He couldn't decide what this meant, let alone what might happen. "Like, 'Hey, this is Charles.' And the moon will be all, 'I've heard so much about you!'"

Daroo-fen huffed. But he didn't deny it.

Charles's gaze jumped to the moon's swelling curve, his thoughts racing. He'd heard a few story songs, the old ones Daroo would tell him, his voice a deep thrum that was its own kind of music. From those, Charles had figured out some of what Daroo's people cared about.

Home and family were so important, they were practically

sacred. And they owed an enormous loyalty to the Moon, who was actually a person, not an orbiting satellite. She wasn't so much a goddess or Queen of the Wolves or anything. She had her own people, so it was more of an alliance. The closest thing he could compare it to was that thing when two far-off places became sister cities. Daroo's people and the Moon's people were on friendly terms, and that sometimes led to visits, and those visits came with favors.

If last night's ballad had any truth to it, wolves sometimes intermarried with members of the moon clan. Dozens of verses were dedicated to the various tactics that eager young wolves might use to lure a moon maiden—the embodiment of a moonbeam—into reach. In this particular song, most of these strategies failed in funny ways. Because you couldn't trick them. They only lingered in the presence of a fortunate few. Good guys. Noble types. And even then, capture was far from assured. Only if a wolf could coax an elusive moonbeam into a shadow—ideally his own, which was all kinds of euphemistic—would he be able to bring her into his den for keeps.

Charles cleared his throat. "You're not trying to set me up with a moon maiden, are you?"

Daroo-fen huffed again. Giving Charles' hand a small squeeze, he said, "Run with me."

"The kids," he protested.

"Asleep."

"I can't leave them alone."

"I warded the passage. They're safe." Daroo leaned into him and all but begged, "Run with me."

Charles knew this was why they'd come. It wasn't the time for roadblocks. "How?"

"I'll carry you."

He balked. "Like a child?"

"Like a *rider*."

Without any further explanation, Daroo-fen transformed into a wolf who was easily twice Beast's size, nearly crowding Charles off the ledge as he crouched. But this didn't need explaining. Grabbing handfuls of fur, he pulled himself aboard.

"Kind of terrified right now," he admitted.

Beast stood and shifted his weight, forcing Charles to adjust his position.

The wolf gave a small hop, and the message was clear—*get a grip*.

So Charles did, laying low and clinging tightly, just in time for a leap that stole all the breath he needed to scream. Except the fall never came.

From the ledge, Beast sailed higher, bounding from one invisible point to the next. He wasn't going particularly fast, and there was a lightheartedness to his springing gait. Or maybe Charles was picking up on Daroo's elation. They were certainly close enough.

Daroo was joyous. Charles hoped it'd prove contagious.

"This is new." After one downward glance, Charles decided to keep his gaze fixed on the stars. "Flying."

Daroo slowed to a walk, strolling eastward toward the rising moon.

Charles straightened in his seat, windswept and breathless and exhilarated. From here, it was easy to believe that magic was real and anything was possible. But some things were impossible to forget. "The kids?"

Everything shifted beneath him, and he was left sitting astride Daroo's shoulders in much the same way Cole had earlier.

"Charles, I must be in this form ...."

" ... if I want to talk. Yeah. I remember." Charles wasn't sure where to put his hands. The stranglehold he was leaning toward probably wouldn't be polite. "The kids?" he repeated breathlessly.

"Safe." Daroo gripped his ankles. "Would you feel more secure ...?"

He swore and muttered, "Not a fan of this position."

"I have you."

Charles really hadn't expected Daroo to simply sit in midair. Leaps and bounds had fit in the framework of flying. But sitting was ... bizarrely casual. Still, he *did* feel much safer, cradled by strong arms with a lap for support. Daroo didn't remark or tease, which killed most of the awkward. But still.

"Are the songs you told me real?"

"As testimony, I doubt they would hold up in court." Daroo gazed placidly at the rising moon. "Much may be figurative, but there *is* truth to the old stories. Things that must not be forgotten."

"I want to believe in them," admitted Charles. Something inside him desperately needed the kind of loyalty wolves sang about.

A promise that would never break.

A vow worth keeping because it was shared.

Something he would have a say in.

Something that would save both of them.

"How does this work?" he asked, his gaze locked on the rising moon.

"This?" Daroo softly echoed.

"Well, I mean ...." Charles hesitated, because maybe he was

way off base. "Am I here because you have something to say to the Moon about me? Or am I here because we have something to say that the Moon needs to hear?"

Daroo's breath caught.

"Because I liked that ballad. The one about the wandering wolf who dragged his best friend along on an adventure, chasing the Moon across the whole world, making all kinds of promises if she'd only grant his wish. A moonbeam to call his own." Charles stole a look into wide eyes. "He thought she was giving him the cold shoulder, but he was kind of dense. You can't be given something you already have."

"His friend," Daroo-fen murmured.

"He was so busy looking for moonbeams, he somehow missed the obvious. His friend was a star. Or the embodiment of starlight. Or something equally shiny." Charles had liked that part. Because it was all how you looked at things. Even if nothing changed, you could understand stuff differently. "That whole time, his friend was granting his wish, just by sticking close."

Daroo took a slow, deep breath, like he was trying to calm himself down. Charles was about to apologize when his friend huffed. All things considered, it seemed a good sign.

"Am I to be the wolf or the star in your story?"

Charles said, "I'm pretty sure I'm the dense one."

"And having come to your senses, you want to reenact the final stanza." Daroo-fen's eyebrows lifted questioningly. "You and I will become pactmates."

"Is that even a thing?" Charles was afraid he was being childish and said as much.

Rather than answer, Daroo-fen's attention strayed. Down.

Charles risked a peek. They weren't all that high, and despite their romping around, they hadn't gone all that far. In fact, he could see the pool outside Daroo-fen's den, gleaming on the forest floor as it reflected the moon.

When the smooth surface shattered with a sudden splash, Daroo muttered, "This kid."

And Charles was falling.

SING MY NAME

It was over in a twinkling, but not the pretty, starry sort. This was more of a screeching, shattering near-collision, prefaced by a perilous drop and ending in a sloshing capture. Daroo-fen had somehow stopped their plunge mere inches above the water, thrust in a hand, and hauled Cole out by the back of his shirt.

Charles reeled him in. "Are you hurt?"

His son coughed and nodded, then shook his head.

"Rose?" he asked.

"Safe." Daroo skipped the stairs in a stomach-dropping leap and plunked them both down before the hearth, stirred up the embers, then stalked away, tail switching.

Cole stared after him. "Dad?"

"Yeah?"

"That was Mr. Hunter, right?"

"Yes."

His son was no fool. "*And* Beast?"

Charles sighed. "Yes."

Crowding closer, he leaned up to whisper, "Can we keep him?"

"Crazy not to, yeah?"

They shared a grin of agreement.

Coop wasn't afraid. Daroo-fen had braced for seven-score questions, the answers to which shared a den with the secrets he'd sworn to keep. Perhaps Charles had warned him not to ask. Or maybe this kid—this confoundingly irrepressible kid—was going to take him at face value. As if it didn't matter where Daroo had come from, so long as he was here.

Once Charles had toweled the boy off and had him put on an over-large T-shirt, Daroo scooped him up and carried him toward their quarters. "Save any further exploration for morning," he advised.

"I wasn't *exploring*," said Coop. "I was spying."

He'd known that the boy suspected. He'd even encouraged the idea in small ways. And more pointed ones, like allowing Coop to ride on his shoulders ... and find handholds in hair that felt very different than it looked.

"Quite successfully."

Coop reached up to touch his hair, his ear, and finally his cheek. "Do I still have to call you *mister*?"

"Have you lost all respect for me?"

"No. But *mister* is good manners for company and strangers. You're part of our family."

Daroo-fen said, "That *was* the promise you made the day you captured me."

Coop narrowed his eyes. "You *let* me."

"I did." He lowered the boy onto the mound of furs in the hushed inner room.

"Good thing, huh?" Coop whispered.

Inclining his head, Daroo murmured, "Leave room for us."

The boy caught his arm and solemnly asked, "How about ... Uncle Beast?"

This kid. Daroo-fen huffed and firmly answered, "*No.*"

Charles appreciated the faint light offered by the night lantern's shuttered flame. He could see for himself that the children were here and safe and his. They were all nested together, with Cole curled up to his sister and Charles at his back. Like they fit. Like they were part of a set.

Or maybe they were part of a pack. Because it was hard to ignore the way Daroo-fen curved his greater bulk around Charles. It was a good fit.

"Charles?"

He turned his head slightly to show he was listening. But Daroo eased backward and encouraged him to roll over.

When they were face to face, he said, "We were interrupted."

Charles hummed a sheepish affirmative. "You can forget it if it was stupid."

"No." Daroo asked, "Do you want a pact?"

"Would it be allowed?" You never could tell when some

restrictions might apply.

"Any promises we make and keep help to define a pack and its purpose."

Charles took his time figuring out what that might mean, and he couldn't see a downside. "*Are* we a pack?" he asked.

"Semantics," Daroo said, all lawyer despite the wildness of their locale. "Whether we use human terms or wolvish ones, the ties that bind us cannot be denied. Only explored and ... further defined."

"And a pact?"

"An exchange of promises."

Charles shrank a little inside. "Like exchanging vows."

Daroo-fen gently said, "I am willing. I am also willing to wait."

"Thanks." Charles wasn't unsure. More like uninformed. "How does it work though? Just make a promise while the moon's shining?"

"The simplest way to formalize a promise is to exchange names."

"Right. But you already know my name, and I know yours."

Daroo lazily waved a hand. "I'd give you a new name, and you'd give me one."

"Are we talking a legit name change? Or a new family name? Or ... pet names?"

"I suppose we *could* resort to endearments, but a nickname would suffice. That is the usual way of things for friends."

Charles chuckled. "Okay. I can live with that."

Daroo-fen mussed up his hair and left his hand resting there, not quite pulling him in, but keeping him close. "When you're ready, I will sing your new name at moonrise."

"You'll give me a wolf name?" That was kind of cool. Flattering, even. "By any chance, did you have a name all picked out?"

"Yes."

"Will you tell me?"

He crooned a soft series of notes that climbed right up Charles' spine.

"Again?" he whispered.

Daroo-fen repeated the cadence.

Charles asked, "What does it mean?"

"The ideas don't carry over exactly. A literal translation would be 'founder and filler of the lone den,' which incorporates a play on words. I am a lone wolf, yet I sing for another. The intonation also implies the idea of 'one and only,' that ours is the best of dens thanks to the one who made it."

Which was a lot of words.

All smugly delivered.

And suggesting a punchline.

Charles poked Daroo's chest. "How would you say my name in plain English?"

"In layman's terms?" With a secretive air, he murmured a word into Charles' ear. Like it was a compliment. Maybe even an endearment.

The kicker was, he *meant* it. Charles could tell how much. His friend fairly radiated approval.

So Charles decided he liked his wolvish name. Because it was all about how you looked at things. Nothing had changed, except how he was understood. And appreciated.

FIVE YEARS LATER

"Dad! DAD!"

Charles hurried to the front room. "I'm here. What's wrong?"

"Look, look, look!" Coop's voice broke with adolescent urgency as he pointed at the television screen. "They cut in a few seconds ago. Across all channels."

He flipped through to demonstrate. Every station was emblazoned with banners that screamed, **BREAKING NEWS!**

"What's happened?" asked Charles, because the words scrolling across the bottom of the screen were more confusing than anything.

Non-human.

Coexistence.

Treaties.

Reavers.

Shock.

Worldwide.

"Is this for real?" asked Charles.

Coop got right up next to the screen, which showed a row of five people on a stage. Some kind of government building, by the look of things. The camera zoomed in and panned back and forth, offering a closer view of calm smiles and pointed ears.

"Back, back, back, already," Coop grumbled. And when the cameras finally obeyed, he jabbed his finger at one of them. "The taller lady. Dad, she has a *tail*."

It took that long for Charles to realize what must be going on. He sank to a seat on the edge of their couch. "Those people.

They're just like ...."

"Where is he?"

"In that winter survival burrow thingie you built. Listening to Rose read."

"It's a *snow den*." Coop hurried from the room. A moment later, Charles heard him holler from the back. "Dad wants you! There's something about *reavers* on TV!"

Not two seconds later, Daroo-fen strode into the room—tail puffed, jaw teetering on the edge of a drop. With one glance at the screen, he sank to the floor, murmuring apologies to Rose for the rush and helping her out of her pink snowsuit.

Coop took over and coaxed his sister onto the couch with him. The boy was nearly as good as Charles at knowing what their wolf wanted, but for entirely different reasons. Charles suspected that they'd worked out a secret system of signals. Ones that often worked to Daroo-fen's advantage.

The moment Charles was in reach, Daroo pulled him down onto his lap. Hardly normal, but hardly surprising. This was major. An event requiring both confidence and comfort.

Charles asked, "Did you know about this?"

"No." His arms tightened. "I'm isolated here."

"Those are your people?" asked Coop.

"Yes."

With every passing minute, more secrets that Daroo had kept from them were made public. But it was big, impersonal stuff. Facts that didn't matter as much as five years of being family.

Charles finally had a word. "You're Amaranthine."

"I am."

"And you come in peace?" teased Coop.

Daroo-fen huffed.

Finally the guy in the middle stepped forward to speak into a bristle of microphones. His voice carried, as did his calm, and he took the time to introduce his companions. Dog. Wolf. Fox. Dragon. They were dignitaries or something. Representing different races.

With a pleasant smile their leader gazed upon those gathered. He seemed to look into every face, every camera, while his audience grew … and grew still. Into the hush that encompassed a startled world, he offered greetings in a dozen languages, then continued in measured English. "My name is Hisoka Twineshaft, and I speak for the Amaranthine clans."

THE END

"Ours is the best of dens thanks to the one who made it."

homemaker

GOVERNED BY WHIMSY

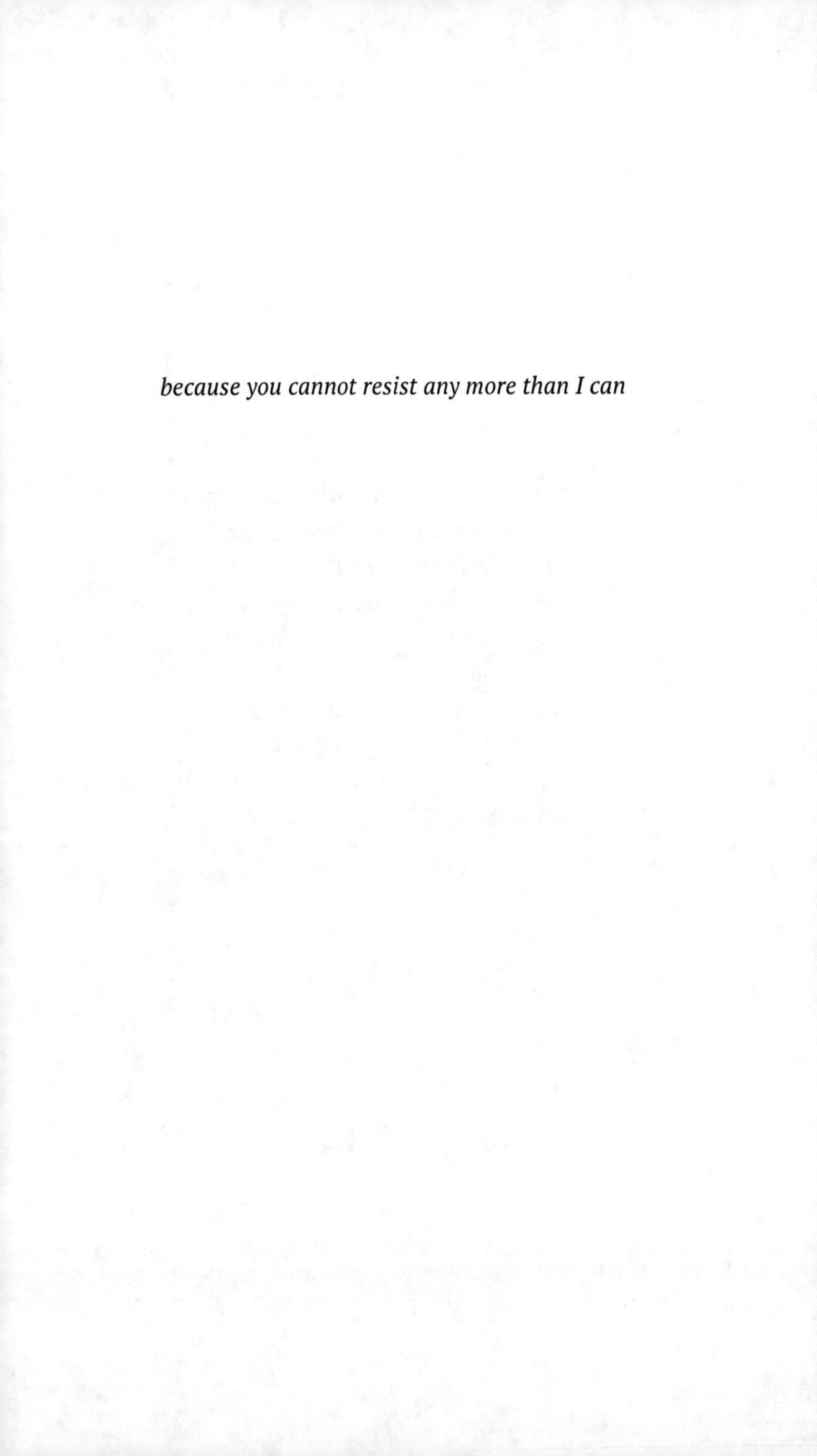

because you cannot resist any more than I can

"In the oldest of avian traditions, parents would keep a piece of the eggshell from which their child hatched. These keepsakes were made into ornaments, to be used as tokens for courtship. All avian clans recognize the significance of a gift that includes an eggshell."

TAMIKO AND THE TWO JANITORS

PUTTING OFF THE INEVITABLE

O h, my darling, we are *very* late."

"Are we?" Greta patted the topmost parcel in her accumulation. "They'll forgive it once I show them this lace."

A smile warmed Lulu's cautionary reminder. "We will not be among moths, my darling. Who can say if her ladyship's boys will have a care for lacy confections?"

Impossible. "Felines like their finery."

"Be that as it may, duty calls." Lulu adjusted her grip on half a dozen bundles and bags as she directed, "Disembark at the next corner."

Spying a promising lineup of shops, Greta happily stepped off the trolley, full skirts swishing. Even after frittering most of the day in a series of boutiques and bakeries, she wasn't entirely over the novelty of paved walkways or the satisfying *click* her kid heels made against them. A constant reminder that they were a long way from the rustic heaths and wide hearths of Evernhold.

This human city's style reminded Greta of Dimityblest or even Sylvansleek architecture. Tantalizing in its variety. Begging to be explored. Perplexing in its variance from the world Greta knew.

To fit in among the unendowed populace, she'd adopted the current fashion. Her outermost skirt was a modest blue, unremarkable at a glance, which is all anyone spared her. So long as she didn't call attention to herself by exclaiming too loudly, walking too quickly, or lapsing too deeply into the customs of the feline court.

Assuming the females were in charge had raised eyebrows. Silly males.

Showing her delight with her best imitation of a purr had earned a few odd looks. No matter.

Kissing the porter had admittedly been a mistake. Force of habit. So much to remember!

"Slow down, my darling." A hand at Greta's elbow checked her stride yet again.

"I thought you were in a hurry."

Lulu glanced at the sky, her lips pressing into a firm line. It was intriguing that an Amaranthine like Lulu had so much more experience with humans who weren't a part of the In-between. She'd been an immeasurable help when it came to preparations for this journey ... as well as with smoothing things over along the way.

Even in human guise, Lulu looked every inch a lady of the moth clans, with soft browns and creams in the subtle plaid of her skirts and the graceful drape of her short cape. She said, "We are off course."

"We're lost?" Greta indicated a shop window with a tempting display of ribbons. "Let's step inside and ask for directions!"

"You have already spent your entire allowance. And lightened my own purse." Lulu steered her away from the trove of satin and grosgrain. "More to the point, we are *not* lost."

They took a turning onto another busy thoroughfare, and Lulu kept them striding purposefully. Greta cast longing looks into shops, but she could tell that her mentor was done indulging her.

"How do you know the way?" asked Greta.

"I studied maps." Lulu spared her a glance and softened her voice. "I wish I could do more, but at least I can see you safely to your new appointment. Canarian and Catalan are good boys. They'll do what's necessary without asking too many questions."

Greta chose to ignore the potentially ominous undercurrent those words carried. Her lady mistress might be changeable, but she'd parted with a whisker. "Are you sure? Cats are curious."

"Quite sure." Lulu tucked her arm through Greta's. "They don't like questions themselves."

"How are they connected to Lady Evernhold?"

"I told you."

Greta shook her head. She'd never been very good at digesting information. Once the words started piling up, she tended to tune them out. As if hiding from the preponderance of facts. Since she wouldn't remember the details anyhow, why listen in the first place?

Lulu patiently went over it again. "Canarian is Lady Himeko's son, and Catalan belongs to Rand. They are the same age and close as brothers. Closer, even."

That was confusing. "Why would Lady Evernhold permit a strange kitten in her clowder?"

"For Rand's sake." They turned onto a street where the buildings soared taller. "Or have you not noticed how thoroughly she dotes on her First Consort?"

Greta knew the depths of that affection better than anyone. "But why are their sons *here*?"

Lulu sighed. "They are only passing through, my darling. Your new hearth is more of a berth. These boys, they gallivant."

Surely this had been mentioned before. Greta knew there had been many words. Too many to hear. She'd found greater comfort in the wordless purring of Lady Evernhold's consorts. Rand, Petros, Mnemba, Rhaymus, Chiilu—did they miss her?

"Where have you gone to, my darling?"

Greta whispered, "I want to go home."

Lulu's expression saddened. All she could give was a repeat of assurances. "Canarian and Catalan are good boys."

"What if they don't approve?"

"Of a touch of drama? They are no stranger to scandal." Her mentor hustled her along. "Trust me, Greta, they are the right scoundrels for this situation. The very sort you need."

MADEMOISELLES DIMITYBLEST AND DEMERARA

Carriages clogged the theater district's wide avenue, and Greta could have stayed for hours, gazing at the finery of alighting passengers. She memorized the cut and color of every coat and cape, thrilled over the clustering of flowers and the curling of feathers.

Gemstones arrayed rings and broaches, but Greta found those

disappointing. Empty sparkles.

She touched her own ear, where blue and violet stones dangled. The crystals chimed sweetly, eager as ever to sing for her. Quirky little remnants. A surprisingly apt gift from the father she rarely saw and barely knew.

He was a ward, and she had his affinity. Though not his classification.

Greta's mother had been a cosset of some renown, and in the feline tradition, Greta had taken her surname. *And* her place in Lady Evernhold's cortege. Even though the academy had granted Greta a pinion's classification. Even after her little hobbies had drawn the attention—and patronage—of Lulu Dimityblest.

"My darling, we are *exceedingly* late."

Greta whispered, "Did you see the lining of that cape?"

"The hour is half gone, Greta." Lulu tugged at her arm. "This is not the best way to begin."

"Painted silk!" she exclaimed in reverent undertones.

"Where?"

"And *that* one. How many yards of tulle do you think she employed?"

Heads together, they twittered softly over the extravagances and shook their heads over examples of poor taste or shoddy workmanship. Greta had no idea how many minutes had gone before a voice cut in.

"Do I have the pleasure of addressing Mademoiselles Dimityblest and Demerara?"

They whirled guiltily.

Tailored gray suit. Chartreuse vest. Velvet shoes. Peridot cuff links. Fanning feathers in the band of the hat in his hands. The gentleman's tone was cautious, and Greta could guess why. He looked her up and down through glasses with lavender-tinted lenses, shaggy eyebrows on the rise.

Greta rearranged her many parcels, using them as a shield.

"Who might you be?" Lulu's posture slowly shifted. "Canarian?"

"None other."

He lowered his glasses, revealing eyes of the same deep orange as his mother's. Mahogany hair swept away from his brow in waxed waves. "I'm widely known as Monsieur Canarian Leclerc, founding member of the acclaimed Leclerc Company. How may I be of service, ladies?"

His smile was pure Petros, and Greta moved without hesitation, flinging herself at that fragment of familiarity. The first glimmer of home in many lonesome miles.

Canarian caught and spun her around, graceful as a dancer. "Here now, love," he gruffly chided. "You'll have the world wondering how we're acquainted."

But instead of pushing Greta away, he whisked her into the relative privacy of an alley, escorting her toward a staff entrance. Lulu bustled along behind, but without protest. So it seemed safe to assume that they'd reached the entrance into exile.

"I'm sorry," Greta mumbled. "I'm not used to humans and all their rules of propriety."

"Don't apologize for courtesies I'll welcome here and now." So saying, he bent and brushed his lips to her brow. "If I'm not mistaken, you're in want of my embrace."

Greta leaned into Canarian, who enfolded her gently. When

he added light touches and a hint of a purr, teardrops formed. He and Lulu traded hasty words in an unfamiliar language, but Greta couldn't bring herself to care. She was tired of explaining. Let them sort it out.

"... cannot refuse. Not if I want to keep certain freedoms," Canarian was saying. "However, I have to wonder why Mother would send us a sweetmeat she obviously cherishes."

"Trust," said Lulu.

Canarian grumbled under his breath. "Time is short, but your answers are shorter. Work with me, Lulu. What's going on?"

"You requested a reaver escort. Greta is a pinion."

His sigh was almost a hiss. "Do pardon the indelicacy, but I beg you to consider *my* position. Your pinion is pregnant."

MISSING GOES BOTH WAYS

"Must we have this conversation *here*?" Lulu waved a hand at the darkening alley.

"A thousand pardons. I've been inconsiderate." Canarian set Greta at arm's length and suggested, "We'll save all the fussy details for later, when Cat can hear. He has a part in tonight's performance, and I've arranged for a private box ... if you'd care to join me?"

"What would be the point?" Lulu demanded crisply.

"The point?" Canarian opened the door and bowed. "Equal parts indulgence and pleasure. The Leclerc Company is here to entertain. Come one, come all!"

Lulu stood her ground. "It would be better if I were to accompany my apprentice to her accommodations."

"The box is private, and I can promise deep chairs and a cushioned footstool, hot tea and cold sandwiches." He addressed himself to Greta. "And you can get a look at our Ambrose. He shines brightest on the stage."

Greta drew a blank. "Who?"

"We're an able bunch as actors go, but Ambrose is a true master. He's our star." When Greta shook her head, Canarian's face fell. "Ambrose P. Merriman, unrivaled in this or any generation. He's gained fame and earned acclaim on three continents."

Into the awkward silence, Lulu asked, "What of him?"

Canarian stroked one shaggy sideburn. "He's the reason we requested a pinion. Mostly a formality, but it's required, you see. Contractual obligations and proper oversight. Since we mingle so freely with humans."

"Your star performer is Amaranthine?" asked Lulu.

"Not something we *advertise*, but yes."

"And he requires a pinion?" pressed the moth.

"Ambrose has many requirements." Canarian got them moving by the simple expedient of scooping up Greta and carrying her along an ill-lit hallway. "And frankly, we cannot travel without a reaver."

Lulu had followed, though she didn't sound happy about it. "Greta isn't here to pamper your prima donna."

"You misunderstand. He isn't begging for companionship. Far from it. Ah! Here we are!" They'd reached a faded door at the end of a dingy hall. Carefully setting Greta on her feet, Canarian murmured, "Give him a chance?"

Why did that sound like a plea for mercy?

He opened the door onto a different world—regal with red plush and frosted by gold. In this part of the theater, stairways curved, and light glittered through crystals. The very air seemed to hum with grandeur and anticipation. Pulling aside a drape, Canarian revealed a carved door that he opened with the brass key hanging from his watch fob.

The private box was hushed and cozy. Once they took seats, Canarian served them from the table waiting in the corner. Putting her feet up, Greta finally allowed herself to slow. Beyond the heavy velvet drapes, the swell of voices grew hazy, and she sat up a little straighter in her chair, afraid she might drift off and sleep through her first play. If only she had some needlework to occupy her hands.

"How is mother?" Catalan inquired, coming to kneel beside her chair.

"She is well," Greta promised warmly. "Strong, beautiful, soon to deliver, and pleased by the prospect."

Lulu added, "This will be her tenth."

A small smile played at the corners of Canarian's mouth. "Is she hoping for a daughter?"

Greta giggled. "After nine sons, you have to ask?"

"How long have you been with her?"

"All my life. I was born into her hands. Just as my children were."

Canarian's concern showed in response to her wistfulness.

"There's no cause for worry." She reached out to touch his cheek, marveling over his strong resemblance to his mother. "They're *also* well and strong and beautiful. They're at academy."

"You miss them."

"More than I could have imagined."

He winced.

She tweaked his nose. "You looked like your father just then."

"Which one?" he joked.

Feline culture existed in matriarchies, and it wasn't uncommon for the lady mistress of a clan to attract multiple consorts. Himeko Evernhold enjoyed the companionship of five consorts; three of them had fathered one or more of her sons.

"Petros may be the kindest soul I know," murmured Greta. "He must miss you."

"Missing goes both ways. As you and your children no doubt know." Canarian's fingers lightly touched her abdomen. "At least you'll have *this* one for a while."

Greta really wished he was right.

HE TREADS THE BOARDS

The curtain rose with a whisper of heavy cloth, and Canarian moved Greta's chair closer to the railing so that she could see the full panorama.

Theatricals weren't something Greta associated with feline custom, let alone Amaranthine culture. She'd listened to storytellers in the song circles. And to bards and their ballads. Many clans used dance to recount great events in their history. But cats were sensualists with a passion for grooming. If pressed, Greta would have pinpointed *massage* as their highest art form.

Yet counter to his culture, Canarian Evernhold was a playwright.

Greta feared she'd disappoint him, that the words would be too many for her to follow, and she'd lose their meaning. But a man hurried onto the stage, caught up in his own troubles. And she was caught as well.

When the curtain swung low, hiding the players as thoroughly as if sigilcraft were involved, Greta was honestly dismayed.

"An intermission," Canarian explained.

She would rather have returned immediately to the story, but Greta was glad enough for such luxuries as water closets and a second pot of tea.

"What did you make of our Ambrose?"

"Was there an Ambrose?" Surely not. She'd have remembered a name like that.

"The tall fellow in the red doublet," supplied Canarian. "He plays the king."

Greta laughed at herself. She'd forgotten that she was meant to be watching for him.

Lulu asked, "How many Amaranthine are in the company?"

"All of us." With a nod to Greta, he added, "Excepting yourself."

"All males?" the moth inquired.

"You might consider it a founding principle." Canarian frowned. "Will you remain with your apprentice, Mistress Moth?"

Lulu's eyes flashed challengingly. "At least until a mare can be arranged."

"If you'll accept it, we've a herdless colt acting as our healer." With a small shrug, he added, "We attract ramblers and vagabonds alike."

"I will need to see for myself." Lulu's lips thinned anew. "I will not neglect my responsibility."

"Nor we ours," Canarian assured.

Greta settled back into her chair, hands restlessly empty as she awaited the play's continuation. The story was a tangle of near misses and conundrums, and she wanted so much for each person to find some piece of happiness. Especially the innkeeper's daughter, whose kindness to the cursed prince had not gone unnoticed.

Oh, my.

"*All* males?" she asked.

With a broad wink, Canarian said, "You may compliment Cat on his gown later."

The house lights finally dimmed, and Greta moved to the edge of her seat. Now that she knew what to look for, she had no trouble picking out the Amaranthine in need of a pinion.

Ambrose P. Merriman was all long lines and sharp angles, yet he managed a flowing gait. She couldn't help wondering if he was naturally regal or if he'd adopted a royal bearing because he'd been cast in the role of a king.

His hair was dark and straight, draping around his shoulders in a somber veil. From a distance, she couldn't make out his eyes. Or tell if the arch of his brows was natural or part of his stage makeup. She decided that he was not so much beautiful as striking. But one thing was clarion clear. Mister Merriman had a voice that held his audience captive and convinced them of his truth.

Greta had long enough to wonder if Canarian had cast him perfectly or written the entire play for his star before the tale reclaimed its hold.

She cared what happened to the people on this stage.

Their story was as real as she was.

And for the moment, nothing else mattered.

STRIDE INTO THE LIMELIGHT

Ambrose noticed the difference immediately. A reaver in the audience. Were they being *observed* again? Tiresome. He refused to allow the quibbling of petty bureaucrats and the worries of cagy recluses to keep him from his rightful place. Let alone distract him from his final performance in this city.

What cheek.

He banished the nuisance to the far reaches of his periphery. He had far better things to accomplish this night!

Only ... Ambrose noticed a *different* difference.

From those fringes of his attention, little ripples of emotion kept working their way forward, begging for attention.

He thundered, and they trembled.

He whispered, and they crept closer.

He hinted at his inner struggle, and they keened.

He promised, and they believed in him.

The small voice—if that was the right term—might have been distracting if each response wasn't the very one he *wanted* to evoke. This reaver, whomever they were, was wholly taken in. He commanded them with every nuance of his performance.

By the end of the first act, he was playing to an audience of one. A soul held captive.

What power.

Before his entrance in the second act, he peered out from the wings, scanning the balconies and boxes, seeking that singular soul. But it was as if they'd been warded against him. Or simply gone. Had they abandoned the play without seeing it through?

But no. When he seized his moment and swept into the unfolding scene, he was welcomed by a quaver of anticipation. Not only was the reaver still here, they'd been waiting for him. And that knowledge drove him to heights that threatened to steal the show. Not that any in the company couldn't rally. Tonight would be a *worthy* finale.

What splendor.

Only ... a fresh difference presented itself.

The small voice—though it was really more of a song—tuned itself to the play's scenario. Opening a way. Warbling a willing air. Was the reaver acting consciously? Surely not. For this was a terrible breach of etiquette. Yet threads of power reached out, offering support where none was needed. Absurd as it sounded, the reaver was trying to lend aid to the persona he'd assumed. To the fictional hero who had yet to see his way through the play's myriad plot twists.

Ambrose nearly laughed.

He was the master of this stage, the king of this story. Gently brushing aside the unnecessary offer, he carried on. *Watch us, reaver. Trust us to the finish.*

Once more, as ever before, he would faithfully lead them all to a good ending.

Ambrose vaulted up the back stairs, in a more celebratory mood than usual. Final performances often left him wistful. True, the company offered the occasional reprise, but those opportunities came rarely. In the morning, they'd dismantle this world and stow it away. And he would miss the home it had become for him.

For tonight, though, he wanted to boast to his friends and bid them toast his triumph. Better than swelling ovations or flung flowers, he'd ensnared a soul, ruling over it and reveling in one faceless reaver's captivation. A fine display. An even finer compliment.

One he could share.

Finding the drape parted and the door partially open, Ambrose strode into his friends' private box. But his thoughts scattered like startled birds at the sight of the people he cared about most fawning over two females.

Females.

Here?

Ambrose drew himself up, eyeing the intruders narrowly. This was unheard of. Untenable. An unabideable breach of conduct. Nay, this was *sacrilege*. With traces of his kingly role coloring his tone, he leapt to their defense. "*What* is the meaning of this?"

WHATEVER MY LADY WISHES

"Excellent! Here is our Ambrose!" Canary scratched sheepishly, though carefully enough that he didn't muss his coiffure. Because there were *ladies* present. In a place that was meant to be safe.

Ambrose's attention jumped to Cat, whose attitude was a better guide to Canary's state of mind. Their director was equally fresh from the stage and also still in costume—full lips stained red and green eyes generously enhanced by kohl.

"My king," Cat crooned, using the voice of the innkeeper's daughter. "We have been graced by gifts from the illustrious House of Evernhold. Will you permit an introduction?"

Cat and Canary were consummate actors, convincing even offstage. They knew how to bury feelings, but Ambrose understood them better than anyone. He knew how much they chaffed under their inherent weakness. Whether by custom or by some quirk of instinct, males of the feline clans bowed to the whims of their female counterparts.

An odd pecking order, to Ambrose's way of thinking. Chivalry was all well and good, but compulsion could be inconvenient.

In situations like this, Ambrose usually provided Cat and Canary with the out they sometimes needed. It was their pact. A solemn vow that had become the cat clansmen's safeguard. No social obligation was more important than Ambrose's expectations. No delicate question required their answer if he silenced them. No lady could bid them stay if Ambrose wished to go.

Did Cat mean to invoke their pact? Ambrose tipped his head to one side, silently asking how he was supposed to respond.

"Banish your reservations, my liege. We are neither beset nor besieged." With a deep curtsy, Cat continued in his own light baritone. "For once, the Mother's gift doesn't beggar us."

Ambrose cautiously inclined his head.

And so Canary introduced the interlopers.

The Dimityblest female was much like every other person from the moth clans he'd met, if a trifle brusque. She clearly didn't have any designs on Cat or Canary. But that didn't explain the imposition.

Despite his pique, Ambrose didn't stray from the expected script. However, rather than the meeting of palms, he bowed over Lulu's hand in the manner of nobility. "To what do we owe the pleasure?"

Her mouth compressed. "That is no concern of yours."

"Untrue, dear lady," quietly countered Canary, whose arm slipped around the shoulders of the human woman. "He *will* be concerned."

"Though not excessively. Our Ambrose has a history of *un*concern, which some have found … disconcerting." Fondness shone in Cat's eyes, and his hands traced a form that begged with Ambrose to show a king's grace.

To a woman? It was the sort of thing almost any feline would ask and expect. But not Cat and Canary. Not without good reason.

He spared her a second glance. Shortish. Plumpish. Pleasantish. Thoroughly underdressed for the theater, but not dowdy. And sizing him up just as critically. Ambrose drew his royal robe more closely around his body, and her gaze lifted to his—brown and bright and brimming with understandable admiration.

Pivoting subtly, he rebuffed her interest. Only to catch an answering shift out of the corner of his eye. She'd taken the standard receptive posture. A reaver, then. Ambrose noted the wardstones sparkling among the loose tendrils of dark hair framing her face. Either they masked her presence, or she had none.

"This is Reaver Demerara," announced Canary. "Recently of …."

Just then, a light tap sounded. The felines exchanged a look, and Canary held up a hand to forestall any further interchange. He opened the door to Fairlee Longbrawn, one of their porters.

"Sorry to interrupt, sirs." The young bovine clansman kept his gaze firmly on the toes of his boots. "Problem at the station, sirs. Seems it's about the baggage. Dekel's in a right fit."

A conference of undertones continued. Some discrepancy between the number of trunks and the space available.

Fairlee murmured, "It's not fitting. No way, no how."

Canary sighed. "Can't be helped. I'll find the space they'll need."

"Not much to spare."

"Don't underestimate my creativity," countered Canary. "Warn Dekel. Set change. Three days should do it. Reserve the siding."

The porter hesitated. "He won't like it."

Canary laughed. "I'll appease him somehow. Give us an hour, there's a good lad."

The moment the door closed on Fairlee's retreat, Ambrose grimly repeated his earlier query. "What is the meaning of this?"

Cat dropped all pretense and wearily stated, "Our company has company. These ladies will be traveling with us."

What drivel. What a disaster. Ambrose struggled to control his tone. "What for?"

"For you," said Canary, returning to the woman and pulling her against his side. "Greta is your new pinion."

ARE WE ALMOST HOME?

Greta barely recognized Catalan when he returned a short while later in a natty suit that banished any trace of feminine allure.

Without all the paint and powder of the stage, his complexion proved to be several shades darker, which lent his eyes even greater brilliance. She studied him closely, intrigued by the transformation.

"Looking for someone?" he asked lightly.

Encouraged by his smile, Greta admitted, "Your father."

Catalan toyed with the handle of his walking stick. "I am the image of my mother. Jaguar clan."

Traditionally, feline matriarchs looked to the future of their house, bearing children to carry on its name, each according to their kind. Indeed, a lady mistress's first and second consorts—like Rand and Petros—were selected with an eye toward breeding. But after that, anything was possible.

Fickle tastes. Changing fashions. Temporary dalliances. Tangled bloodlines.

Housecats—more rightly *hearth*cats—spoke for the feline clans. They were prolific and powerful, having long cooperated with reavers. Outnumbering their wilder cousins—lion and panther, cheetah and tiger—hearthcats were the elite. And therefore desirable.

Himeko Evernhold had exotic tastes and an adventurous streak, so Greta had grown up with the comings and goings of her lady mistress's passing fancies. But a lady's chambers were one thing; her *hearth* was another matter, closely guarded by her consorts. Greta had trouble imagining Lady Evernhold ever letting Rand go to another.

Then again, she remembered hearing something about Petros having seniority, even though he wasn't Himeko's favorite. So perhaps Rand had been wooed away from a previous mistress? Far from uncommon, given feline proclivities. But still hard to imagine, given Evernhold's current stability.

In the privacy of her home, Himeko showed her consorts every consideration. They loved her for it, each in their own way. And they cherished one another. Evernhold was strong because its protectors nurtured the bonds that kept conflict at bay.

Rand, their lady's best-beloved, with his infectious smile and attentive manner.

Petros, brimming with confidence and competence, who ordered their household.

Mnemba, a musician whose heavy leonine gaze invariably intimidated outsiders.

Rhaymus, a sultry panther clansman procured for his technique with massage.

Chiilu, a cloud leopard who employed sigilcraft and seduction with equal facility.

The five consorts had always been part of Greta's home, although not in a familial or fatherly capacity. Because she was tasked with their tending, they teasingly called her their *other* lady mistress. To them, she was someone trusted, someone lovely, someone dear. And Greta knew that they loved her, each in their own way. Just as she loved them.

"No, no, no, dear lady." Catalan kissed a tear from her cheek and searched her gaze. "I shall be better to you than all my fathers before me. Canary's heart is set on the matter, so you may depend upon my devotion."

"That's cute." Greta managed a small laugh at his obvious confusion.

"Your nicknames. You call him Canary, and he calls you Cat."

His shoulders tensed, then sagged. "I'm being quite serious."

And in his attentiveness, she saw a little of Rand, which intensified her longing for Evernhold. But also her acceptance of Catalan as someone to trust. Greta quietly asked, "Are we almost home?"

"Nearly." Lips quirking, he added, "We'll have you aboard and abed soon."

"Aboard?" she echoed, glancing guiltily at Lulu. This had probably been covered earlier.

"Our travels on this continent are accomplished by train." Cat's smile widened. "The Leclerc Company makes its home aboard the *Cat's Canary*."

DESTINY LEADS TO DUTY

Ambrose refused to have anything to do with the pinion who'd been foisted on the company by Evernhold's matriarch, including the mad scramble to find space for two females. To avoid the whole fiasco, he kept to his private carriage, forcing Canary and his crew to rearrange the train around him.

On the third morning, Canary knocked lightly. "Are you awake?"

Ambrose flicked open the latch and stalked away.

Letting himself in, Canary jauntily proffered a tray. "Have a good sleep? You must be ravenous."

"I have not slept," he replied stiffly.

"But we thought ...." His friend's smile floundered. "Naturally, we *assumed* ... after the final performance, most of the cast needs the respite."

Ambrose dropped into the room's only chair and crossed his legs. "So you *did* spare me a thought?"

Canary carefully countered, "One or two. I apologize for not checking on you sooner. We've all been ... ah ... preoccupied."

"By the females."

With a gusty sigh, Canary set aside his tray and came to kneel before Ambrose. "I should have come sooner. Please, forgive my lapse."

He sniffed.

"Now, Ambrose." Canary studied him over the top of his spectacles. "Don't sulk."

"I do *not* sulk."

But before he could complain in full, the affectionate buffoon had him thoroughly enfolded, as if he could make up for rude absence with an excess of kneading and purring. Sly fingers found their way into his hair, and Ambrose's resolve weakened. He never could resist a preening. Feline though he may be, Canary was as good as a nestmate to him, considerate of his avian quirks and requirements.

"You've been avoiding us." Canary managed to make it sound as if *he* were the injured party.

Ambrose sighed. "Not *you*."

"Colt will have my whiskers if he sees you like this. Why haven't you slept?"

"Clearly, I've been too busy *sulking*," he grumbled.

"This won't do, birdie mine." Canary favored him with an exasperated smile. "Don't punish us by punishing yourself. It's doubly cruel."

He lowered his gaze. "I couldn't get comfortable, knowing you must be ... preoccupied."

"Jealous?"

Ambrose shrugged. "Concerned."

Canary caught his hands and kissed them. "Just as I'm concerned for you. We should tuck you in with Greta. Boost your vim and double your vigor!"

"You cannot mean ...!" Ambrose wavered. "You *sleep* with her?"

"Well, no. But she slept in our bed while we reorganized. We had to put her *somewhere* during the shuffle."

Granted, felines had different notions about closeness and companionship, but after all those two had done to extricate themselves from the obligations of cat and clan ... what nonsense. "Send her away."

"I cannot." Holding up a hand, Canary added, "I wouldn't, even if I could. Mother always did have excellent taste."

Ambrose grumbled peevishly. Feline tastes rarely kept to any discernable standard.

"Greta is descended from cossets." Canary was clearly giddy with the news. "She is exquisite."

"You are *indulging*? Are you mad?"

Her control is excellent. As—may I remind you—is mine." All gossip, he continued, "A ward for a father, hence the rise to pinion status. As savvy as she is sweet. Most of the crew is already smitten."

Meaning Ambrose's opinion mattered less than lint.

"Once we're away from the station, I'll see Cat to sleep." A gentle tug. A pleading tone. "Join us. Take what you need."

"Will *she* be there?"

"Naturally." His unconcern never wavered. "Eventually. While I don't like to criticize a lady, it's becoming increasingly clear that she lacks a certain something. In a word: punctuality. Truth be told, my next duty is to find her and fetch her home."

Ambrose narrowed his eyes. "I'm a duty, then?"

"Nay, a destiny," countered Canary. "Come, birdie mine. I've been lonesome for your company, and we have future triumphs to discuss."

Which *was* true. Planning a new production was a distinct pleasure. But Ambrose wasn't entirely ready to end his boycott. He slumped deeper into his chair. "You say *come*, but where are you going?"

"Into the city. Our tardy passengers will be in the shopping district." With a canny gleam in his eye, he asked, "Didn't you want to visit that haberdashers once more before we move along? I could escort you there first."

Ambrose sighed. "In what role?"

Canary pretended to consider. As if he didn't always know how best to cast his star. Ambrose awaited direction with a curious sort of resignation. Their playwright was full of surprises. Ones that kept audiences flocking to every performance. But even when Canary was playing at plays, his roles were demanding.

"Let's cast you as ... disapproving manservant. Polite, because you know your place, but with a superior sort of dignity that'll put the mistress in hers."

Relieved to be a side character in the grand scheme of things—and a contrary one at that—Ambrose murmured, "*Please* tell me you're not stepping into the role of romantic hero."

"Muscle, I should think. A groom or footman. Unless we bring Fairlee. Which may not be a bad idea, given the accumulation of parcels the ladies jumbled home yesternoon." With a small shake of his head, he said, "I'd rather not have to unload the oxcart."

Ambrose gave in. "The sooner they're found, the sooner Cat can sleep."

"Very true." Canary radiated weary gratitude. "And you?"

"I shall disapprove." Extricating himself from his friend, he searched his closet for a suit with an appropriate degree of restrained dignity.

"Even if she can offer superlative tending?"

But Ambrose was already immersed in his role. And what use did a disapproving manservant have for a reaver's tending?

WASN'T HIS HAIR BLACK?

Greta poked through jumbled trays—mismatched buttons, cast-off lockets, gaudy hatpins. In a place like this, patience could lead to discovery, minutes turned into hours, and a thousand pretty daydreams fueled plans she hadn't realized she'd be making.

"Has Catalan talked to the costumer yet?"

Lulu bent over an array of half-spent spools. "Monsieur Leclerc has been exceptionally busy. I am certain he will come to your request in due course."

Crossing to a battered bureau, Greta eased open the topmost drawer and gasped over the quantity of costume jewelry inside. She picked through the higgledy-piggledy tangle with an eye toward usable stones. "Have you seen our room?"

"The compartment will be adequate, if a bit crowded." In a tone that meant Lulu was probably repeating something she'd mentioned earlier, she added, "That young Longbrawn promised to have your trunks moved in yet this morning."

A cuckoo clock on the wall bonged and wheezed.

Lulu sharply addressed the shop owner. "Is that the correct time?"

Reaching into a display case filled with pocket watches, the old man ruminated over one or two, then nodded. "Near 'nough, miss. You fancy a timepiece?"

Suddenly, Lulu was at Greta's side. "Oh, my darling. I fear we are late. Again."

She hummed and nodded, even as she pulled out the bottommost drawer in the shopkeeper's bureau. And heard the whisper of crystals. Sinking to her knees on the dusty floor, she tuned out all but the hints of a remnant song.

In what seemed like no time at all, a hand was at her elbow, a voice in her ear. "What a state you are in. Come, young mistress, do not grovel in the dust and dirty your hands. It is unbecoming a lady."

Greta glanced up in utter confusion. A stranger bent over her, radiating disapproval. "I'm sorry?" she managed.

"And well you should be. Now, if you will permit."

She couldn't ignore the hand at her elbow, nor the strength that steadied her to her feet. But neither could she fathom why this person was keeping her from the drawer and its treasures.

He was quite tall, and his somber suit was neatly tailored to his frame. Ash blond hair had been combed away from lean features, and silver-rimmed spectacles partially obscured eyes of such a pale gray, they were nearly white.

With a small shake of his head, he took a handkerchief from an inside pocket and wiped his palms, as if touching her had somehow soiled them.

"I'm sorry," she repeated, aghast.

Only when he turned his shoulder to her, offering a solidly Amaranthine rebuff—and a glimpse of his nose in profile—did she make any kind of connection. "Mister ... Merriman?" she whispered.

"If you are quite finished ...?" he inquired, making it very clear that he expected an answer in the affirmative. "I know you would not want to cause any *further* delay."

Greta cast a longing look at the bureau drawer.

He followed her gaze, then turned to the proprietor. "How much for the lot?"

The old man, whose bafflement matched Greta's own, was equally apologetic. "I sell the odds and bobs, sir, not the furnishin'."

With exaggerated patience, Ambrose asked, "How much do you want for the contents of that drawer?"

"W-well," hedged the man. "What'd you be willing to give?"

Canary, who'd apparently been lounging—and laughing—beside the entrance this whole time, named a price that caused the old fellow to brighten considerably.

"Have you a bag?" asked Ambrose.

After a hasty rummage, Canary came up with a musty carpetbag. And without any care or ceremony, Ambrose jerked free the drawer and upended it over the raggedy sack.

"Satisfied?" he asked in an aggrieved tone.

Greta nodded and held out her hands to take the trove.

Holding it away from her, Ambrose purred, "Do you think me so inconsiderate? Leave your things to me."

"Are you sure?" She gestured apologetically to the small mountain of bags and bundles heaped in front of the counter. "This was our … last stop."

With a withering smile, he addressed himself to Canary. "Perhaps we *should* have brought the oxcart after all."

"I'll get these." Canarian gave a wink and cheerfully urged, "Be a gentleman and lend her your arm, Ambrose. Then we'll be on our way."

To Greta's great astonishment, Ambrose changed both his posture and his attitude. The thin veil of servility dropped with the pocketing of spectacles, and exuding the regal bearing she'd seen on stage, Ambrose adopted a more chivalrous air and bowed over her hand.

Had his previous rudeness been an act? Was he taking direction from Canarian? Maybe the two were playing some game known only to actors.

Used to the mercurial moods of the feline courts, Greta gave the matter no more thought. Better to accept what was given with gratitude. And to ponder something even more baffling. Hadn't Mister Merriman's hair been black?

THE OBJECTIFICATION OF MALES

Ambrose offered his arm like the gentleman Canary expected him to be, but the woman didn't even notice the jut of his elbow.

Half a step ahead of him, she'd raised her palm to the level of her shoulder, her posture expectant.

He shot a look at Canary, who rolled his eyes and mouthed something indistinct.

With a small shake of his head, Ambrose begged for further direction.

In an undertone that carried well enough for Amaranthine ears, Canary said, "Think like a cat. *She* does."

What absurdity.

Lulu naturally overheard, and she did try to help, tucking her arm through Canary's in the manner of human society. Unfortunately, Greta failed to notice. She was too busy scrutinizing an array of tarnished junk in a glass-fronted case that she must have overlooked.

As much to get the woman outside before he was forced to part with any more pocket money, Ambrose grudgingly tailored his response to her expectation.

Coming up close behind and a little to one side, he placed his hand atop hers, then settled his other at her waist. This was a game Cat sometimes played with Canary, for theirs was a toying kind of affection. Otherwise, Ambrose mightn't have known the proper form, which was brazenly possessive by avian standards.

Think like a cat, Canary had said. So Ambrose did. But he found he didn't care for the implications of this role. Because this position was both submissive and ... ornamental. Ladies of the feline clans treated their males like accessories, changing them out to suit their mood, the occasion, or a moment's whim.

Him, a consort?

The thespian in him could appreciate the challenge. The avian in him couldn't work out any sensible approach. The only cats who'd ever made any sense to Ambrose were his two friends, who'd run from the vagaries of the feline courts.

Improvisation then. And a necessary compromise.

Pressed close, Ambrose treated this like a dance. With firm pressure and subtle dominance, he controlled Greta's heading and pace. She might be in front of him, but he was in control. To his relief, she didn't mince, so they more-or-less kept up with Canary's long strides. But they were also earning their share of odd looks.

This was not the sort of place humans expected to encounter a promenade. He cleared his throat. "I have never considered myself decorative, and by local custom, this is not decorous."

Greta came to a full stop. "You aren't a cat."

"Nor do I usually play the part."

"I'm so sorry, Mister Merriman. What would you prefer?"

He released her and stepped back. "An immediate return to the *Cat's Canary*."

She glanced around. "Are we close? Oh, look at the trim on that shawl!"

And she was gone. Along with her attention. Without any apparent care for his preferences. "Canary," he called.

His friend was gracious enough to pause, though he was already half a block further along.

"What am I to do with her?"

"Get her safely aboard."

Ambrose frowned. "In what capacity?"

"Be yourself."

"That rarely goes well," he protested.

With a small shake of his head, Canary wearily said, "I doubt she'll notice."

And he walked on with Lulu, leaving Ambrose to his own devices.

SOMETHING FOR YOUR TROUBLE

"Ms. Pinion," began Ambrose.

"Call me *Greta*," she replied, not looking away from a clothier's window display. What was so interesting about tassels?

"I doubt that will be necessary."

"A name isn't necessary?"

He had her attention now, even though he didn't want it. "Calling," he corrected. "I cannot foresee any need to call on you."

Her mouth formed a little 'o,' and then she shook her head. "You're wrong, you know."

Ambrose didn't like this woman. Not one bit.

"About being decorative." Her gaze swept over him with the same intensity she'd been giving trinkets and turbans and taffeta. "Someone with your bearing could carry off *anything*. And in grand style. The costumers must adore you."

To his astonishment, she stepped right into his personal space and ran a hand over his lapel, exploring the fabric and stitching. Highly irregular.

She hummed in a disappointed way. "This is good, if a bit plain."

Should he insist she unhand him? It seemed a line more suited to innkeeper's daughters and damsels in distress.

His chagrin doubled when she slipped the button holding his

coat closed and lifted it away from his body. This particular suit was lined in the traditional colors of the Scatterlight clan.

Greta clearly approved of her discovery. "I take it back. You're full of surprises, Mister Merriman."

They were drawing attention again. And he couldn't get away. Because now she'd taken his hand in both of hers. "Ms. Pinion," he warned.

"May I beg a favor?" She addressed him with such urgency. "I wouldn't ask if it weren't important."

What ...? He couldn't even find a word.

Falling back on the gentleman schtick, Ambrose managed a calm response. "Canary would undoubtedly urge my cooperation."

"May I look inside?"

To his way of thinking, he had already endured a more intimate inspection than someone of his convictions should have to face. But then he realized she was pointing. At the musty bag of drawer-clutter.

"There are at least two remnants in here. Small and lonely." Her eyes were soft with sympathy. "I was hoping to rescue them when you came along. Very gallantly, too. Thank you for securing them for me."

"Crystals," he said, not entirely clear how he'd been cast as a savior of pebbles.

"In the bag. Yes." Her smile was confident. A woman used to getting her way. "May I?"

"On one condition."

Her brows drew together, as if confused by his rebuttal. "Yes?"

"We cannot continue blocking the walkway." Waving a hand at

a nearby café with outdoor tables, he said, "That would be *slightly* more discreet."

Ambrose saw her seated and placed the bag in her lap. "Do you drink coffee or tea?" he inquired.

But she ignored him.

He stepped indoors to order refreshments. When he returned, Greta had already disgorged half the contents of the bag. The oddments were fanned across the café table, mostly arranged by color. And she was humming. With intent. In the manner of certain reavers, she was calling to the crystals, as if reassuring them that help was on the way.

Taking the chair opposite hers, Ambrose tried to remember if any of the reaver escorts assigned to him had ever been wards. Most had worn the colors of the assorted diplomatic divisions— liaisons, translators, secretaries. Nondescript entities with a knack for fading into the background. Too polite to interrupt or intrude. Cat insisted they were essential, but Ambrose had always found them extraneous. Dull. Dismissable.

Not the sort to upend a drawer for a couple of pebbles.

Ambrose sipped his tea and watched closely as Greta sifted through her haul. Although she had stated her aim, she wasn't treating any of the other pieces as obstacles. He couldn't imagine what she saw in the tangled chains and mismatched buttons.

A quarter of an hour passed, and her beverage cooled before she finally unearthed her remnants. "Oooh, you dears," she murmured.

Before she could make a further spectacle of herself, he reached across the table and set his hand over hers, obstructing her view of her found treasures. Inadvertently intercepting the overflow of delight intended for two chips of green no larger than lentils.

Recognition was instantaneous. *This* was the reaver who'd been in the theater during his triumphant final performance. What a perverse little plot twist.

"Aren't they lovely?" she asked.

"Passing fair. But this must stop if we're to reach the station today. You are making me late." And since it might have more of an influence on her actions, he added, "You're making Canary wait."

She glanced around in confusion. "He's gone?"

"Long gone."

"Do you know the way back?"

Ambrose sighed and stood. Propping the carpetbag under the table's edge, he swept her piles haphazardly back inside.

"Wait, wait!" she gasped. "One thing!"

He didn't see which curiosity she plucked up and folded into her handkerchief, and he didn't much care. His patience was at an end. Taking her by the arm, he steered her along the streets, ignoring her exclamations over passing window displays.

Ambrose threatened to blindfold her. Twice.

Finally, he bustled her past the station platform to the siding where Drexel and his crew were loafing about with nothing to do. Marching Greta straight into Canary's hands, Ambrose stalked off in the direction of his private refuge.

"Wait! Mister Merriman, please wait!"

Gritting his teeth, he turned and offered a thin smile. "*Now* what?"

"You're wonderful. Please accept this token of my earnest regard."

Reaching for his hand, she set the item she'd secured earlier on his palm. A stick pin with a tiny egg mounted on its finial. It had somehow survived the mish-mash of both drawer and carpetbag. He twirled it between his fingers, admiring its delicacy, confirming its authenticity. A hummingbird egg, carefully preserved, neatly mounted, artistically flecked with gold leaf. Quite refined. A statement piece he would have coveted if he'd encountered it in any shop.

By the time it occurred to Ambrose that he very much needed to refuse this gift, Greta was gone.

TRADITIONS ARE FOR KEEPING

Ambrose showed the pin to Canary, who studied it closely before offering it back. "A wonderful find. I think it's genuine."

"Yes, it's gold," agreed Ambrose.

"I mean that the artisan was probably Amaranthine." He radiated approval. "Greta has a good eye. It's perfect for you."

He was missing the point. "I can't possibly accept."

"No?" Canary slouched more deeply into his armchair. "Help me understand why."

This was a conversation they'd had often over the past decades. One or the other would run up against some little taboo that was unique to their clan. And Canary found these variances fascinating. He liked to explore the structures and strictures. And to rebel against them.

"The giving and receiving of items containing eggshell have significance for the avian clans." Ambrose held out the pin. "She's given me a courting gift."

Canary shook his head. "She probably didn't know."

"*I* know."

"If you don't want it, simply give it back to her."

Ambrose hesitated.

Understanding dawned, and Canary burst out laughing. "You *like* that little bauble."

Face heating, he murmured, "I cannot deny its attractive qualities."

"Oh, birdie mine. So you keep it. That would mean ... what? That you're under some obligation to pursue her?"

Ambrose slowly shook his head. "According to the dictates of tradition, she would be courting me."

"But she *isn't*."

He wished he could explain away the gift as easily. But Greta's words had been so close to those traditionally offered. And he knew that by not-refusing, he was accepting her advances. He'd also be interpreting any future gestures as preludes to greater intimacies.

Canary stood and took Ambrose by the shoulders, every trace of humor gone. "This really bothers you."

He nodded once.

"Then we'll have it all out. Come to our compartment this evening. Bring Greta's gift and allow her to establish her intentions and your attendant obligations. Say it plainly. And if you're polite about it, she'll probably even let you keep your prize."

He nodded again.

"And I insist again that you join me and Cat. We all need a long rest."

"Thank you."

Canary bussed his cheek. "You're being silly, but I like your nobility. Maybe this would make a good plot for a play."

"I thought our next thing was decided. Didn't you want to do a story inspired by Bethiel's lore?"

"Maybe I can do both." His friend took the position for a dance, and he led Ambrose through the opening steps. Eyes sparkling, Canary accused, "You're always giving me the best ideas."

I'LL TAKE THE SETTEE

The *Cat's Canary* was in motion, and the familiar clatter and sway provided a backdrop to Ambrose's solitary meal. The appointed hour had come and gone, and he was still closeted in his private carriage. Dithering over his decision. Wallowing in his solitude.

On stage, he was as bold as Canary asked him to be. It was so much more difficult without a script. How should he proceed? Could he keep both his pride and his preferences? Which consequences would he face? What choice did he have?

In the end, all he really wanted was his nestmate, even though Canary's companionship now came with a condition. Ambrose needed to make peace with the reaver.

Slipping the woman's gift into his vest pocket, he let himself out his back door. Twilight had deepened into a starlit darkness that carried the scent of smoke and seawater. But there was light enough to see that his needs had been given priority. During the grand shuffle, his friends had placed their carriage directly behind his.

Closer than ever.

Kind as always.

Gathering his resolve, Ambrose knocked.

Three dull heartbeats later, the door opened, and he was

gawking at Greta, who'd abandoned anything resembling proper women's attire. A colorful kimono clung to her curves. Below, she wore a reaver's breeches, although the sturdy cloth had been bleached to a soft gold and embroidered with an extravagance of coral flowers and twining vines. Beaded slippers gleamed in the soft pink light of Cat's favorite lantern.

"Ms. Pinion," he managed, unsure where to look.

She hushed him with a finger to his lips. "They started without you."

"I'll just …." Ambrose edged backward, ready with excuses, but her hand at his wrist waylaid him.

"Inside. You can still join." With tugging and tutting, prising and pushing, she had him through the door, which she warded behind him. "Trains are surprisingly drafty," she murmured. "Please, make yourself comfortable."

He wasn't sure what he'd expected to find. Probably something more compromising. But both of his friends had retreated behind the folding screen that hid their bed. And the woman had clearly been seated in the green velvet chair nearest the stove. Padding across the thick tapestry rug, she returned to her post, propped her feet on a cushioned stool, and scooped up a length of cloth caught in an embroidery hoop. Evidence that she wore her own workmanship.

"Here you are." Canary came out from behind the painted screen, tying the sash of a robe that was probably modest by feline standards. "Welcome. Cat's keeping the bed warm for us."

Ambrose's attention jumped to the woman, who seemed comfortable despite her host's dishabille.

"You're late." Canary's voice held a subtle roughness, and his eyes were heavy-lidded. "Lovely, yes?"

He could only offer a bewildered shrug.

"If you mean *me*," interjected Greta, "I have him on the wrong side of a couple of wards. Mister Merriman isn't privy to your tending experience."

Canary's smile showed actual fondness. For this female. He murmured, "Very considerate. What do you say, Ambrose? Her tending will relax you, or Cat and I could groom you."

Ambrose blushed. "I only intended to speak with her."

"Ah, so you did. Very good. Have at it, and have it done." Canary kissed his forehead and whispered, "Your usual spot awaits, birdie mine."

"Perhaps," he murmured, even as he shook his head. "For now, I'll take the settee."

GIVE HIM HIS DUE

Greta watched out of the corner of her eye while Canarian shook out blankets and built a nest for an auburn-haired Ambrose. The company's star actor seemed to accept this treatment as his due. He folded his lean frame into the available space and leaned into the little touches his friend lavished.

Although she knew almost nothing about avian behavior, Greta could tell that Canarian's fussing was different than the interaction between feline consorts. Which likely meant that he was catering to his friend's preferences.

This was the real cat and canary. A smile curved Greta's

lips. She had no idea if there was a canary clan somewhere in the world, but it would be more than appropriate if they were Ambrose's people.

Their camaraderie stirred her curiosity.

She wondered how they'd met. She wanted to ask how long they'd been friends. But her training held true. Greta could not intrude upon this moment, even as she encouraged others to linger in it. A good cosset offered ease and elation, sweetness and strength. Her greatest asset was her presence, yet it was considered bad etiquette to call attention to it.

Await—that was the first rule. Let the Amaranthine initiate.

Greta knew why she was exceptional. She had good breeding, excellent patronage, and the kind of confidence that comes from the constant application of one's skills. Daughter to a diva. Raised among consorts. Ever since her mother's passing, Greta had been her lady mistress's treasure. Which had led to one indulgence after another.

School, even though textbooks couldn't add luster to a soul.

Tutelage, since Greta found so much happiness in her little hobby.

Allowance, which never seemed to be enough, despite Lady Himeko's generosity.

Mentoring, because the consorts had unanimously supported her apprenticeship to Lulu.

Contracts, for Greta was from a long line of cossets, and lines needed continuing.

Forgiveness.

"Greta?"

She looked up from her sewing and smiled for Canarian.

He said, "I'd like your professional opinion. Does our Ambrose need tending?"

"For shame," she gently chided. "Only he can say for certain what he needs, and those needs are not open for discussion."

"You would do him so much good," he insisted.

She could, but not unless Mister Merriman wanted the heartening. Greta knew the look and feel of trust, and she didn't have his. "Thank you, Canarian. Go to Catalan."

He hesitated, clearly torn.

Ambrose touched his shoulder and echoed her order. "Go to Cat. And leave room for me."

Canarian brightened and touched their foreheads together. Greta couldn't hear what he whispered, but she didn't need words to understand people. Already attuned to Canarian and Catalan, she had no trouble picking up on their feelings. They loved *their* *Ambrose* with typical feline ferocity.

It made her miss home. In a sense, it made her love Ambrose a little bit, too. Which *actually* meant that she loved Canarian and Catalan. Their trust was becoming hers. Could it work the other way?

Pausing beside the screen, Canarian said, "Please, Greta love. Just like before would be perfect."

"My pleasure," she assured.

"Ours entirely," he returned with a grateful gesture.

Greta liked this part of tending, when she reigned over a space, filling it with peace and pleasure. Everything settled until the only sounds were the silken rasp of thread through cloth, the muted crackle of the fire within the enamel stove, and the low murmur of Canarian's voice as he coaxed his partner through the stages for a long sleep.

These Amaranthine were far too accustomed to getting by with little naps here and there, forcing their bodies into a semblance of humanity. Even though their needs were so different. They were meant for deep rest. To give themselves over to oblivion in a haven made safe by friend or by kin.

Tonight, Greta was their safety. And she knew many a way to ensure their sleep was sweet.

Soft rustles and sighs gave way to a deep purr, and Greta shared Canarian's satisfaction. All was as it should be, and he'd soon follow his bedmate into slumber. She gave a little more, letting power sway over them in time to the rhythm of the rails that were their road.

A soft gasp recalled her to the state of her wards.

In the soft glow of the lamp with its rose-colored glass, Ambrose Merriman's eyes were wide and dark ... and willing.

OH, YOU CAN TELL

Greta blurted, "Are you ready, Mister Merriman?"

It was only a tiny breach of etiquette. *He* should have been the first to speak, but she wouldn't make him ask. Otherwise, he wouldn't take the strength he needed. Not because he was disinclined. At least, that's the impression he gave. She might understand better if he let her in.

He was resisting her, though. Like a child fighting sleep. So silly.

Setting aside her embroidery, she asked, "May I approach?"

He didn't answer, but he didn't deny her request.

Picking up her footstool, she set it beside the settee, sat, and presented her hands. "May I touch, Mister Merriman?"

"Is that necessary?" he muttered.

"No. But it would allow me to sense your responses more quickly. Then I can tune my tending to your wishes without any need for words."

He didn't hesitate for long. Few did. Few *could*. So Greta was in familiar territory, and when Ambrose Merriman placed his hands in hers, she was ready to guide him.

"Too much?" she asked softly.

For a moment, his mouth opened, but no sound came. He shook his head.

"More, then?"

"Is that wise?" he asked in a voice gone husky.

"I think it would be best." She sought his gaze and nodded once. "You can trust me, Mister Merriman. This is what I do. It's part of my birthright as a reaver."

He looked away. "Your duty and delight?"

"This isn't *duty*, Mister Merriman." She let another ward slip, and he sucked in a startled breath. "This is trust."

How long had it been? Several years, now. Ambrose hadn't gone in for tending since leaving Europe. With the necessity of taking on reaver escorts, there had always been access. He was aware that Canary partook, as did Cat. But up until now, the reavers assigned to them had been bland things. They never stayed long, and none of them had inspired interest. Let alone trust.

Up until now.

It was mortifying to be so thoroughly drawn in. What had Canary said of the crew? *Smitten.* Ambrose could see why. It had nothing to do with Ms. Pinion being female. In his experience, a soul was a soul was a soul, regardless of the gender of the body in which it resided. The attraction wasn't physical, yet the desire to be closer took hold with surprising strength.

He forced his eyes open, needing to assure himself that he hadn't reached out. "Wait," he whispered.

Greta's presence immediately dwindled. She was retreating, and he hadn't meant for *that.*

"Wait," he begged again, feeling foolish and awkward and … yes, still mortified.

"What is it, Mister Merriman?"

"Let me do it." He needed to control the pace, rather than be swept into hers. "I want to do this my own way."

"My pleasure."

And her trust was entirely his. She left herself wide open, a pool of patience, utterly passive. He tested the fringes of her reservoir, a cautious mingling of souls. She welcomed him, warmed him. Impressed him.

Slowly, carefully, he let her surround him. And it was exquisite.

A shared intimacy that whispered secrets. His to her. Hers to him.

"You are with child?"

Her eyes opened—too quickly, too wide. "Oh, you can tell? Yes, I am. These are early days, so it's not obvious yet. Unless I'm tending. Canarian could tell right away, though. Scent."

She was flustered. He could feel her discomfiture.

"Are you bothered?" she asked. "I may be able to use a ward ...."

"No," he interrupted. "Not *bothered*. But I feel like an intruder in another's nest. Surely your mate wouldn't approve."

"I am bondless, Mister Merriman."

How sad. He'd overheard remarks. Enough to know that this was the reaver way. It wasn't as if he disapproved. Their way was as different as his was from Canary's. But the reaver way had always sounded so ... lonely.

Was she lonely? He shouldn't infringe upon her simply to satisfy his curiosity. But there was a strain of sadness in her soul's song, and it called to him.

Ambrose didn't remember moving. But when Ms. Pinion's hands gently covered his, he was touching silk. Perched on the edge of the settee, his long legs on either side of her, he'd pressed his hands to her midriff.

"Are you curious about my child, Mister Merriman?"

He tried to pull away, but she didn't let him.

"It's all right. I'm glad." Even her smile was sad. "*Every* life is precious ... right?"

Ambrose tried to fathom this nestling's future. "The other parent," he ventured. "You did not love him?"

She laughed softly, and a tear slipped down her cheek. "I'm sure I love him very much."

MY SHOES ARE MISSING

Ambrose woke slowly, drenched in a pleasant sense of satiation and safety. The train had stopped, but a steady vibration remained. Purring. Fingers stroked through his hair, and he angled his head appreciatively. His friends were always stealing his wigs and hairpins, and Ambrose secretly hoped they'd never stop.

With a low trill, he stirred.

Cat's calm gaze and soft kiss welcomed him home.

"I fell asleep," Ambrose croaked.

"You slept for days."

He glanced around, still muzzy. Canary's favorite lamp cast the whole room in its usual rosy glow, and with drapes pulled, he couldn't guess at time.

"It's just us." Cat's smile was completely relaxed. "We needed the respite, you more than anyone. You outslept the entire company."

"How long was I deep?"

"Five days." Anticipating his next question, Canary said, "We've arrived, and we'll stay put for at least a week. In part because some of us have kin in the area. But also because this city has an Amaranthine market, and the costume department is pleading for high-quality fabrics."

Ambrose wouldn't complain if their tailor brought in Dimityblest wares. The more bolts, the better. Nothing compared.

"Any requests?"

"A blue suit. Not navy, but not cobalt. Pacific, I think." He rolled onto his back, folding his hands across his stomach. "Mmm …

and scarves trimmed in tassels. Or beads. Canary will have me in turbans for the next role."

Cat propped himself up on one arm and grinned down at him. "I meant breakfast. What are you hungry for?"

Ambrose thrust aside his disappointment with a sigh and admitted, "Everything."

"Here or there?"

He stretched languorously before deciding. "Have the trays brought to my compartment."

Ambrose poked his head out of the cats' compartment when he heard a familiar footfall. Balancing two laden trays, Canary mounted the stairs to the platform between their train cars.

"You changed your mind?" asked Canary. "Where do you want breakfast?"

"I wish to return home."

Bemused, he said, "You've long legs. It's what … three strides?"

Opening the door further and waving a hand at his feet, Ambrose explained, "My shoes are missing."

Canary clearly didn't see the problem. "Afraid to sully your stockings? No one will notice if you skim across. Get the door for me?"

Ambrose hastened to comply, and he *did* keep the soles of his feet a fingerbreadth above weathered boards. "I'm *not* being fussy."

"You embody fussy." Canary's tone was entirely fond. "It's an endearing quality, birdie mine."

"But my shoes …!"

"They'll turn up. And if they don't, we have a few days. Buy more."

"My proportions require specialty craftsmanship. And fittings." Which was as close as Ambrose would come to admitting he had big feet.

"Aren't those yours?" Canary asked, nodding toward the narrow bed.

Ambrose's missing shoes rested upon the coverlet. Alongside a second pair of footwear. He stole cautiously closer, unsettled by the idea that someone had invaded his nest. But a bright trill slipped from his throat as he picked up one of the new shoes.

Soft soles, supple sides. He strongly suspected they'd been shaped from calfskin. However, it was the extravagant embellishments that stole his heart. Row upon row of ribbon and beads created lustrous patterns in pale greens, delicate yellows, and soft blues. The very kind of extravagance that he both craved and could not have. Yet here they were—long, narrow, and tapering to elegant points.

"Ah! Hearth slippers." Canary nodded approvingly. "How do they fit?"

Ambrose pulled one on and quickly added its mate. They molded to his feet, a perfect fit. What bliss.

"Gifts truly are the way to an avian's heart. She'll win you over, yet."

"What?"

"Those are hearth slippers. We wear them at home." Canary stole an orange slice from the nearest tray. "Cats do. Surely you've realized those are from Greta."

Ambrose could only weakly repeat, "What?"

"Speaking of Greta ... after you finish all this, I'd appreciate your help." He patted the back of Ambrose's chair. "Sit. Eat."

"Why do you need my help?"

"Where to start?" Pacing slowly, his hands clasped behind his back, Canary said, "As it happens, Greta is a Dimityblest apprentice."

"I thought she was a pinion."

Canary brushed that aside with a lazy wave. "Complexities are part of her charm. When it came out that she has a way with a needle, Clemmorn immediately recruited her. I shared some of my plans for the next production, and Greta's sketches were perfect. So when she offered to find sufficient fabrics, we didn't hesitate."

Ambrose looked up from his meal. "However ...?"

With a wry smile, Canary said, "She's spent the last two days and our entire annual costume budget in the Dimityblest warehouses."

He blinked. That was a considerable sum.

"I'd planned to put a stop to further excesses, but with this and that." Canary shrugged. "She somehow managed to get an early start."

Ambrose stretched his legs in order to steal a peek at his new slippers. "What do you expect *me* to do?"

"Sate yourself, first. Then we'll end her spree." Pushing forward a selection of pastries, he murmured, "Do what I can't, birdie mine. Refuse her."

THERE SHE GOES AGAIN

Ambrose was passingly familiar with the bayside city and the Amaranthine market that counted as one of America's best-established urban enclaves. The Leclerc Company had occasionally performed in their public sector's theaters, but Ambrose wasn't one to wander about and explore. And social obligations left him moody.

"No performances?"

"Not unless we revive something for the Song Circle." Canary wandered past a tanner's stall, nose twitching. "Do you want to?"

"They'd welcome us?"

Canary frowned. "We're not outcasts. More like … novelties."

It was Ambrose's opinion that mingling with ordinary humans was simpler, despite the risks. Their audiences admired them for their dedication to their craft, and their efforts met with both acceptance and applause. But any return to the Kindred meant being called into question for their unusual choices.

"We'll be back on this coast in autumn. Bookings for the new play."

"Which you're still writing."

Canary's eyes sparkled. "Not to worry. Your grand romance is coming together nicely."

Ambrose rebuked him with a low trill.

"Lord Beckonthrall's then," amended his friend, though his smirk remained.

Time to change the subject. "Are you tracking her?"

"Trying." Canary tapped his nose. "It would be easier if she hadn't visited every single shop on the square. Some more than once."

Ambrose considered the assortment of fancywork on display. It was easy to imagine such dainties appealing to Ms. Pinion. Dimityblest clothiers were superior to all others. "Didn't you mention a warehouse?"

Canary hummed. "These shops offer ready-mades. The warehouses sell raw materials."

A niggling knowledge took Ambrose by surprise. Catching his friend's arm, he pointed. "She's there."

Immediately changing course, Canary asked, "Did you spot her?"

"A different sense." Ambrose quietly admitted, "Echoes, I think."

"From tending?" Canary's eyebrows jumped. "I get nothing. Then again, she wards herself."

Ambrose didn't want to try to explain, so he simply walked on. But the tug at his soul reminded him of the evening when a then-faceless reaver had reached for him. Tumbled impressions hinted at her mood, which was good. Happiness. Anticipation. Longing. It was almost as if she were pining for him, which left Ambrose uncomfortably aware of his lapse.

He'd somehow failed to broach the subject of gifts. He blamed her tending.

The hummingbird egg pin was still in his possession. Though not on his person.

And he couldn't imagine giving up those beaded slippers. Had he been wooed?

Ambrose quailed inwardly. What if these echoes were symptomatic of a nascent bond?

"I see Fairlee and Lulu." Canary's stride checked. "Ah. She's done it again."

Fairlee stood beside a heaped handcart and greeted them with a hesitant wave. The first words out of his mouth were, "Sorry, sir."

Canary cuffed his shoulder. "Is all of this yours?"

"No, sir. Not me." He cast a pleading look at Lulu.

She had no apologies to offer. With crisp dignity, she said, "No one can deny the quality of Dimityblest cloth."

"Truer words were never spoken." Canary cleared his throat. "I'm sure we can find room ... somewhere. Shall we, Fairlee?"

Canary began gathering up loose parcels, while Fairlee gripped the cart handles.

Lulu rushed to steady the tippy load. "I will need to show you which things go where."

"By all means," Canary murmured. "We'll leave the rest to you, Ambrose."

"Me?" he protested.

"Please."

Which was hardly fair. Because while it was true that Canary couldn't refuse a lady, it was equally true that Ambrose couldn't refuse him.

KEEPING TO A BUDGET

Ambrose's steps slowed as he wound his way through the Dimityblest warehouse, where cloth spilled from bins in decadent waves. What splendor. While he *would* back up Canary, Ambrose wouldn't mind if the costumers brought in such choice cloth.

Winding through the labyrinth of shelves, he spied jewel-toned thread, neat packets of needles, and all sorts of closures. More interesting were the trimmings, which would undoubtedly inspire eye-catching fashion. Feigning indifference, he sailed on.

She wasn't even surprised to see him.

"Which of these?" she asked, holding up two cards of buttons.

Refusing to be distracted, he said, "It's time to return to your berth."

Greta's gaze turned speculative. "If you were a dragon, what color would you be?"

"I'm *not* a dragon."

"Neither am I, but that's never stopped me from imagining it." She stepped closer and fussed with his tie. "My lady mistress fostered ties with a nearby harem. Lord Yonkeep was generosity itself both to us and to his ladies."

What that had to do with anything was a mystery.

She went right on. "Red would be striking, but gold is more traditional for the dragon lord in Bethiel's story."

"These are for me?" Ambrose reconsidered both the buttons and his wording. "For my costume?"

Holding first one card, then the other up to his chest, she studied the effect. "Blue would be a departure, but you'd be stunning in the right shade. And your eyes! Well!"

Ambrose rather wished she'd go on.

Instead, she reached up to touch his dark brown braid. "Have I ever seen your true colors?"

"That is a very personal question."

Greta's brows arched. "Is it?"

"Intensely." He looked away but answered, "Glimpses, perhaps. Since my soul has been laid bare before you."

She actually pouted. "That's not the same as running my fingers through your hair and matching a hatband to its hue."

He could feel color creeping into his cheeks. Returning to her earlier question, he stiffly said, "Silver, gold, or white are traditional, perhaps because the winds are differentiated by the colors of the seasons they represent."

Her eyes widened, and she dove toward one of the displays.

Glass buttons that rivaled the wares of Murano glittered temptingly. Nothing he owned would have made sense with such vibrant colors. Yet they appealed.

Greta rushed back to him, triumph putting a gleam in her eyes. "You will shine like a star!"

She'd gathered buttons and beads, sequins and stones, all intended to catch and scatter light. "So many?"

"And more," she assured. "You'll catch every eye and command every scene, win every heart and woo the very winds to your side."

"Not me," he whispered. "That isn't me."

"But it *is*." Greta spoke with such conviction. "These become you, and you'll become him, and it will be … rapturous!"

He wanted to see the vision she saw.

He wanted to drape himself in starlight.

But he didn't want to disappoint Canary.

Clearing his throat, he said, "Allow me to pay for these."

She seemed confused. "There's an expense account or something …?"

Which she'd no doubt decimated. Ambrose couldn't allow her to add to the Leclerc Company's deficit, but neither could he let go of the vision she'd cast. And by spending his own coin, he wouldn't be accepting another gift from her. "I must insist."

"As you like, Mister Merriman." She crooked a finger and whispered, "Have you any leggings? Or better yet, silk stockings?"

Ambrose hesitated. "Why?"

She patted at her hips and found a pocket, from which she withdrew a fold of paper and the stub of a pencil. In a free corner, she scribbled as she spoke. "Tucked here. Flowing from here. And with spangling, so whenever you lengthen your stride or pivot ... glitter everywhere. You know?"

Her drawing was no larger than a coin, yet it captured a mood that would undoubtedly shape his portrayal of Lord Beckonthrall. Touching the paper, he cautiously murmured, "Silk ... stockings?"

Moments later, his hands were filled with whisper-light fabric, while she draped this scarf and that scarf over his shoulder. Some even had fringes.

One of the Dimityblest clerks came over, and after a quick conference, fresh bolts of fabric arrived in an endless procession. Ambrose feared he was enjoying himself.

When they asked him to stand, he struck a pose.

When they asked him to walk, he strutted.

Greta was detailed with her compliments, although he tried not to let them get to him. But when she looked him in the eye and crooned, "You *beauty*," he didn't toss off his customary rebuff.

He was too busy wondering if she was seeing him or seeing stars.

WONDERFUL WITH A NEEDLE

Greta hummed as she anchored another crystal to the silken length of Ambrose's new stockings. It had been ages since she needed to start a pair from scratch, but with legs as long as his, finding a ready fit had been impossible. Seams could be troublesome, but she knew a few tricks to minimize their presence.

Under her needle, whimsical sigils fanned. The beads from her private stash sang back, learning the tune she was teaching, echoing her hopes as she strengthened their voices.

Spring to his step.

Safety to his footing.

Flourish to his turnout.

Finesse to his lines.

A soft knock interrupted her contemplations, and Greta smiled. "Enter, Canarian."

He let himself in, eyes widening at the state of her compartment. "What's all this?"

"I had some ideas." Greta supposed there was more clutter than usual, between the unpacking and her new purchases. "For the play."

Canarian stepped with care, moving to the center table, which was strewn with sheet after sheet of foolscap. He picked up one and another in quick succession, and his smile widened as he went. "Inspired!"

"Thank you," she murmured.

He peered at her over his glasses. "These are all Ambrose."

"Such graceful lines. He's an ideal model!"

"I agree. He *is* magnificent, but he cannot play every part." Canarian held up the designs she'd created for the four winds.

Greta was crestfallen, but Canarian was right.

"Ah, I'm sorry to disappoint you." He came to crouch at her side. "I may not have finished the final scenes, but the cast is decided. Would you like a list, so you can modify your designs?"

She sighed over her loss, laughed over her own foolishness, and kissed Canarian's cheek. "You must think me silly."

"You amaze me," he promised.

Only then did she realize that Canarian had dressed with unusual flamboyance. "What are you wearing?"

"My costume." He smoothed a hand across cobalt velvet. "Our company is performing in the Song Circle tonight. You won't want to miss it. Our Ambrose steals this show, despite playing the villain."

Greta asked, "How long do I have?"

"The enclave will gather at twilight."

"Then I can finish this first. Wait a moment, please."

Canarian's glance jumped between her and her handiwork. "Does Ambrose know you're adding frippery to his underthings?"

"He'll like it."

"He will." His tone took a serious turn. "He won't be able to refuse something like this."

"Why would he?" Greta asked. "This is meant for him."

With a soft smile, Canarian asked, "Will you come to see him?"

"Yes." Tying off a final knot, she proffered the stockings. "If you'll give him these."

DO NOT LOOK AWAY

Ambrose knew he was being foolish. Ms. Pinion had been *assigned* to him. If long, searching looks had been directed his way, they were inspired by her duties as a reaver. She was his escort, little more than an usher. In a pinch, she'd protect him, but not for personal reasons. True, tending was deeply personal, but she was cosseting every member of the company.

Her compliments were situational, even incidental.

Her gifts were offhand, incurring no obligation.

Her designs would clothe the whole cast.

He wasn't being singled out.

Canary sauntered in and shook a finger at him. "You haven't told her."

"I have no idea what you're ..."

"Greta," he interrupted sharply. "Why doesn't she know that her gifts carry significance for you?"

Having just rehearsed all the reasons her attentions *didn't* matter, Ambrose was ready to spin them out. But something in Canary's hand sparkled enticingly, and he found himself reaching. "Is that ... for me?"

"She's determined to spoil you." Canary yielded the prize. "Usually by this time, you've tallied up nearly as many grievances against your pinion as they have against you. But she has no complaints. Only compliments."

Ambrose warbled softly as he unfolded her gift, which glittered with crystals he'd never seen, let alone purchased. What's more, when he drew these on, her sigils would touch his skin. What intimacy.

"Are you blushing?"

"Did she say anything?"

Canary touched his face. "Am I to be your go-between, now?"

Ambrose fidgeted. "Did she say anything?"

"Yes, birdie mine. She said she'll be watching tonight."

Despite early concerns over the Amaranthine reception of a tale intended for a human audience, from the moment Ambrose took the stage, he ignored Kith and Kindred alike. Once again, he played to an audience of one. Pleasantly aware of his pinion's watchful suspense, he strove to give her every reason to keep watching.

In a peripheral way, he was aware that the play was going well. More intriguing was Ms. Pinion's complex reactions to his nefarious deeds.

She thrilled at his threats.

His charisma became her quandary.

She shivered over her fascination for him.

Only when his scheming imperiled Canary's character did she retreat from him as if stung. As was only right. For in every story produced by the Leclerc Company, good did prevail.

Applause greeted their finish, a familiar thunder.

But in keeping with Amaranthine tradition, Catalan stepped to the fore in order to introduce the entire cast, since the learning of names was the first mark of respect.

After this prolonged curtain call, Ambrose stood with Canary, foreheads touching as they let their on-stage conflict fall away. "You were frightening, birdie mine."

"Only because you asked me to be, playwright."

"Methinks your misdeeds unnerved your pinion." With a nudge, Canary urged, "Gently."

They turned to see Catalan bringing Greta forward.

Ambrose may have enjoyed quavering her soul from the stage, but her awed approach didn't set well. She was still under the sway of a villain who'd returned to their script's pages.

Sweeping forward, he fluttered blackened claws, then presented his palms. "Ms. Pinion," he chided. "The tale has ended."

Her fingertips were cool. Her eyes too wide.

Ambrose sighed and firmly said, "There is only me. I am here."

At the sound of his usual, unaffected voice, a flicker of relief washed between them. Followed by gladness. Chased by a wordless whisper that tickled his consciousness, downy soft and different.

But undeniably there.

And somehow aware.

Of him.

Ambrose lived with a trainload of bachelors, so it wasn't as if he knew much about the carrying of young. But it seemed clear that all this time, he'd actually been playing to an audience of *two*.

THEY KNOW MY VOICE

Ambrose closed himself up in his compartment until the *Cat's Canary* left the station. Only when the night was deep enough to guarantee that the lone human aboard would be abed did he steal out. Moving swiftly along swaying passages, he was briefly disoriented because of the reorganization of cars. But Colt's compartment was still centrally located. He was their healer, after all.

With a courtesy tap, Ambrose eased the door open.

Colt's quarters were larger than most, since they did double duty. He and Hallow bunked here, but two additional beds and a large table crowded the space. Sickness and injuries weren't common, but Colt presided over naps and kept them dosed with an assortment of teas and tonics.

"Pardon the intrusion," Ambrose managed. His voice barely quavered.

Colt looked up from the communique he was reading, gaze clear, smile easy. "This is a pleasant surprise. Join us, Ambrose."

His bunkmate lay with his back to the room, blankets pulled up over his shoulders, but Fairlee was there, too, and greeted him with a shy smile.

Ambrose hesitated on the threshold. These three served Leclerc Company as part of the stage crew, not as actors, so he rarely interacted with them. He couldn't think how to begin, but where else could he turn for answers? "May I have a word?"

Colt immediately rose and crossed to him. A big, warm hand cupped Ambrose's cheek as the horse clansman searched his eyes. "You're too pale," he said gently. "But not ill, I think?"

"No."

"Ill at ease?"

Ambrose closed his eyes and muttered, "Somewhat."

Pulling him into his shoulder, Colt turned slightly. "Fairlee, will you give us some time."

The younger male set aside the rope he was braiding. As he passed by, he touched Ambrose's elbow in a silent offer of support.

When the door clicked shut, Colt asked, "What can I do for you?"

"Do you know anything about … young?"

"Children? Our lifestyle here doesn't allow for much interaction." He rubbed circles into Ambrose's back. "But yes, I know many things. Most things, I should think."

"So you'd know if something was perfectly normal?"

"Yes."

Ambrose plunged straight in. "Why can I sense the pinion's child?"

"Greta's baby?"

"Yes. Why would her young be responding to *me*?"

Colt hummed. "Have you been in close contact with Greta?"

"Tending. Once."

He hummed again. "When you say *sense* …?"

"I suspect the child is responsible for the echoes I've been experiencing since that one session." Ambrose guessed he may as well have it all out. "I know where she is. Catch impressions of her emotional state. And … I would swear the child knows my voice."

"Well. I may know many and most, but I clearly don't know everything." Colt admitted, "I've never heard of a human baby forging a prenatal bond. However, Greta *is* a reaver, and it's possible that her child has an unusually strong presence."

From the bed in the corner, Hallow's voice came. "*Or* that her child isn't entirely human."

A WEAKNESS FOR FINERY

Await. Await. Await. But waiting for the person standing outside her door to get around to knocking was becoming increasingly distracting. So Greta called, "Could you give me your opinion on these sketches? And I want you to approve the trimmings for your cape."

Ambrose Merriman made his entrance.

He was back to a silvery blond, though he hadn't bothered with the glasses this time. Those intriguingly pale eyes of his flew wide, and he teetered on the threshold. Greta glanced around, uncertain what had rendered him speechless.

"Good evening, Mister Merriman," she said. "Please, be welcome."

"What ...?" His arms swept dramatically wide. "What *is* this?"

"My room." She supposed it was a little messy. "Or did you mean those?"

She and Lulu had anchored five dressmaking forms at intervals along one wall, and four of them were swathed in lengths of fabric that evoked the unique qualities of the four winds from Amaranthine lore. The fifth held a glory of silver and gold, the ingredients for *his* costume.

Remaining so close to the door Greta suspected he was clinging to its handle, Ambrose asked, "Where is your chaperone?"

She pointed up. "Out."

"On the roof?" he asked, sounding shocked.

Greta smiled. "She sometimes gets the urge to soar. Especially on moonlit nights."

His gaze jumped from trunk to tabletop to shelf. "How many cartloads did Fairlee have to pull for you?"

"Most of this is mine." Greta set aside her embroidery and folded her hands in her lap. "I brought everything with me, since ... I don't think I'll ever be able to go back."

Ambrose studied her for a moment but sidestepped the invitation to ask more. "Why would a pinion have all this?"

She gestured to the armchair across from hers, but he turned away to study the sketches littering the table. Not exactly a rebuff, but not exactly friendly.

"Most of my work involves nothing but existing. I needed more occupation." Tracing an embroidered sigil, she added, "I like to sew."

"Understatement," he blandly accused.

Greta smiled.

Ambrose loitered about, poking his nose into anything she'd left in the open, but never touching closed books or drawers. While he had nothing to say, she had the distinct impression he was working his way up to speaking. *Await. Await. Await.*

"Is … is this for me?" His fingertips grazed the standing collar of a short cape she'd draped over the back of a chair.

"Put it on, Mister Merriman." And when he shot her a questioning glance, she nodded. "We'll check the fit, then consider the trim."

He swung it around his shoulders in front of a full-length mirror borrowed from the costume room. Its tiers flared just the way they were meant to. Ambrose pivoted, paced before his reflection, then slowly flushed pink.

"You're pleased?" she guessed.

"I will accept it." Rounding on her, he gravely asked, "Why would you do this for me?"

Greta dared to ask, "You love nice things, don't you?"

"I do."

"That's why." She moved to the table and shifted several sketches. "For trim, we could go with simple piping, silver cord, glass beads. I may even have enough pearls, which would pick up the luster of your eyes."

His lashes fluttered, and he sank to one of the stools beside the table.

She ventured, "Were you going to ask for tending this evening?"

Ambrose looked genuinely confused. "Isn't it too soon?"

"Not at all."

He lowered his gaze and murmured, "Thank you all the same, but … do you have these beads in this same blue?"

As she rummaged through her trunks, Greta tried to remember the last time an Amaranthine had come to her for anything besides cosseting.

This was shaping up to be a rare evening.

YOU CARRY THE DAY

Traveling by train suited the Leclerc Company's unique needs, but it did require patience on everyone's part. In order to share the rails, they had to run at odd hours, and whole days could be spent on special sidings that were managed by members of the In-between. Their eventual goal was far to the east, but the journey was being accomplished in carefully timed fits and starts.

During a lazy afternoon on an especially picturesque siding, Ambrose allowed himself to be drawn in by Canary, only to discover that his proposed sun-basking session would have a cosset in attendance.

"Do us all some good," Canary assured.

Ambrose needn't have worried. More than half the company turned out to laze along the nearby riverbank. Long, sweet grasses proved temptation enough for Fairlee to revert to truest form. The big ox was soon joined by Colt and two goats with majestically curving horns, who all grazed contentedly.

Joining his friends on one of the many picnic blankets anchored by wardstones, Ambrose tried not to think too much about the idyllic atmosphere, knowing Ms. Pinion was at least partially responsible.

Their menagerie grew to include a goose and an otter, who were naturally attracted to the water. Gallorin, a frog clansman, waded through the shallows, mumbling to himself as he studied a script.

"Give us your opening monologue," called Canary.

Flashing a smile, Gallorin launched into Bethiel's opening address. Of course, Canary had modified the original tale for his play, but the Amaranthine references were recognizable to any Betweener. Gallorin was both angel and narrator for the unfolding story, and when his Bethiel reached a dramatic pause, all eyes turned to Ambrose.

This was the dragon lord's entrance. Although, in Canary's adaptation, he'd present himself as a lonely sultan who longed to fill his palace with color and beauty and song, if only he could find a wife. Having already committed the part to memory, Ambrose took his cue, and their dialogue rang across the water.

The sultan's plight and prayer drew smiles from all who knew how much trouble he'd invited.

While many stories and songs warned of a dragon's wiles, this tale took the other side, reminding dragons to be careful with their words, for wishes came with consequences.

At the scene's end, Canary laughed aloud and pulled Ambrose into a playful embrace. "You're wonderful at everything, aren't you?"

"If you say so."

"Oh, I do!" His friend quirked a brow at Cat, and Ambrose was soon sandwiched between them.

Cat said, "Villain or noble, you carry the day." Raising his voice, he asked, "Isn't that right, Gallorin?"

The frog clansman offered a cheerful response, but Ambrose missed much of what they said. Because that soft certainty had returned the moment he'd pitched his voice to be heard.

"Are you even listening?" asked Cat.

Ambrose blinked. "Were you saying something?"

"Nothing of import." After a considering look, he murmured, "What's wrong?"

"Did you hear that?"

Cat quietly asked, "What should I be listening for?"

Was it a sound? Not really. Ambrose lamely asked, "Did you *feel* that?"

They'd captured Canary's attention. "What are you talking about, birdie mine? Are you catching resonance?"

Ambrose shook his head, then nodded. He let the subject drop. Because asking Canary and Cat might amount to a breach of Ms. Pinion's privacy.

He would need to go directly to her.

YOU CAN TELL ME

Greta hadn't expected company that evening, but Ambrose came grumbling to her door and insisted on watching her work. Which was so like him. He was as reluctant a friend as he was an ardent one. But not in the usual way. She was accustomed to attracting Amaranthine, yet Ambrose seemed more enamored of her collection of frills and furbelows.

"How are you with stitchery, Mister Merriman?" she asked.

"Not my expertise." He fluttered his fingers. "Though I'm not unwilling to assist."

She set him to work threading needles and sorting beads, a task he accepted readily enough, perhaps because he'd realized that her current project was intended for him. A second pair of beaded hearth slippers. She feared his first pair would soon wear out, he wore them so often.

"Are these for me?"

"They are yours." Greta smiled at his obvious pleasure. "Will you wear them?"

He lowered his gaze. "I will wear them," he promised.

Greta wondered at his tone. They were very nice slippers—ultramarine and violet upon velvety black—but not something worthy of vows.

Ambrose toyed with a spool of thread. "I love them."

"I hoped you would." Something was definitely on his mind. Again. *Await. Await. Await.*

"I would not presume to understand the ways of feline mistresses or reaver women, but in the customs of my clan, gifts such as these are a form of courtship." He was still struggling with eye contact. "Your gifts are exceedingly fine, and I want them all. Even though acceptance invites … more."

That had been a lot of words, but Greta heard every one of them. "Have I imposed upon you?"

Ambrose heaved a shuddering sigh and melted from his chair, coming to kneel at her side. "No. I understand that you're not pursuing me. And I cannot possibly establish a nest on such a transitory branch."

Was he apologizing? She wasn't entirely sure.

"Only reciprocation would bring about certain … instinctual obligations. However, I cannot deny that some form of bond exists. Perhaps you are unaware? It has taken days for me to understand what I am feeling."

He'd lost her. Too many fiddly, roundabout words. But Greta was good at expressions, and his was filled with concern. She asked, "Is something wrong?"

Edging even closer, he whispered, "May I touch?"

"You may."

He took her hand between his. "Why is your child different?"

"Oh." Greta tried for a smile, but she wasn't any kind of actress. "You can tell?"

"A little. During performances. And tending."

His bewilderment didn't seem put-on. Then again, he was a splendid actor.

"When you tend, this one receives and is glad. Their love for you resonates through the connection." Ambrose tipped his head to one side. "And for me."

That surprised her. "They love you?"

"Perhaps not. Perhaps it is merely my voice." The gaze he lifted held apology. "I fear I may offend, yet I cannot deny my curiosity. Is your child not entirely ... commonplace?"

"Y-you can tell?"

Ambrose nodded.

"Yes." It was almost a relief for Greta to confess the truth. "This one's father is Amaranthine."

IF NOT FOR THEM

"I knew it was *possible*."

He did? Greta hadn't known until it was too late for anything but apologies.

Ambrose quietly pried, "What of the father?"

"How much do you know about feline customs?"

"A little." He frowned and added, "Not enough."

Greta ran her finger over patterns of beads as she searched for words. "I have a son and two daughters—twins who were recently taken to academy. It was harder than expected to let my girls go, and my lady mistress decided I needed cheering up. She entrusted the matter to her consorts."

"One of them is the father?"

She nodded.

Ambrose fidgeted and whispered, "You are not certain which one?"

Greta said, "Foreign delicacies were brought in to tempt my appetite. We tasted all sorts of exotic dishes, and I'm pretty sure the sweets were laced with pollen. Star wine may have contributed to a certain ... vulnerability. Because he's kind and gentle and *feline*. If I asked for anything, he wouldn't have refused. In the end, I'm at fault."

"Did none of them step forward?"

She felt the first tear slip from under her lashes.

"They *all* did." She tried to blink away her tears. "Even Lady Himeko's brother pleaded my case. He was the one who suggested sending me here. Before matters could worsen."

Ambrose trilled softly and daubed at her cheeks with a frilled handkerchief. "They banished you?"

"They *protected* me!" She took hold of his lapel, giving it a small shake. "The cat clans don't look kindly on misfits or halfbreeds. Rand and Petros and Mnemba and Rhaymus and Chiilu—they were *frightened* for me. Other women in my position have been … put down. This was their only alternative."

"Sanctuary with Lady Evernhold's rebel sons?"

Greta sniffled. "Canarian and Catalan will hide me and harbor my child, should they survive. I'm told *my* chances are slim."

"How slim?"

"Nobody knew for sure." With a small shrug, she reminded, "The cat clans don't normally allow pregnancies like mine to progress."

Ambrose shook his head, then shook it again. "Why are you not outraged?"

How could she be? "They're my oldest friends. I've known them my whole life."

"Is that not worse?" He clearly didn't understand. "To be mishandled by one's own family."

"This child's father is … *was* my peer. A trusted friend. A *cherished* friend." Greta knew it was different in other clans, especially avian ones. "We could mingle as equals because of the connections we shared with Lady Himeko."

Ambrose's eyebrows slowly lifted. "You *do* know. You are certain of the father."

"Yes." Greta's actual memories were hazy, but she knew Himeko's consorts with the intimacy that came from years of trust and tending. "I think my lady mistress knew, too. That's why she agreed to send me to Canarian."

"Does *he* know your child's unique nature?"

"I don't think so. No." Fresh tears washed down her cheeks. "But when the time comes, I want my baby born into his hands.

They will need their brother."

She broke down, and Ambrose gathered her up, crooning and shushing by turns. And when Lulu bustled in, looking windblown and flustered and furious, he wouldn't give way. Only cut the moth off with dramatic flair. "Do you want to know *why* I'm less shocked than I may have been?"

Lulu was in no mood for theatrics. "*Your* state of mind was the last thing on mine."

"Tell us, Mister Merriman." Greta didn't think he was the sort to offer hope if it was false. "Why have I failed to shock you?"

He still held her, still held *them*. "Because, Ms. Pinion. Another member of our company also boasts a dual heritage."

HALF AMARANTHINE, HALF HUMAN

Ambrose stormed down the passage, determined to get the help his pinion needed. Their healer clearly didn't have all the information he needed to make the weighty decisions that lay ahead. What negligence. What nonsense. What ninnies.

He barged into Colt's and Hallow's compartment. After much flailing of arms and flinging of insults, he got both males moving in the right direction. Colt with considerably more speed than Hallow exerted, but that wasn't so unusual. The reclusive backstage crewman preferred to lurk well outside the limelight.

Back in Ms. Pinion's compartment, Colt hurried forward and dropped to one knee. Hands already probing, he alternated between asking Greta questions and looking to Lulu for confirmation.

"Are you in pain?"

"Have you been resting?"

"How far along?"

"What small complaints have begun?"

He had a soothing voice, an open expression, and a calming effect. Ambrose had never before wondered why someone of Colt's abilities would choose to live herdless. Then again, everyone in the Leclerc Company had their reasons.

Colt went right on checking Greta's hands, her ankles, her pulse, her personal wards. "Now, then," he murmured. "Tell me what I need to know, Miss Greta."

Her teary gaze pleaded with Ambrose.

Did she really expect him to speak for her?

Sweet skies, she *did*.

So he slipped the jaunty capelet from around his shoulders and draped it around hers, taking his place—or at least the role into which he was being cast—behind Greta's chair.

Colt's eyes widened.

Ambrose wished he wasn't blushing. At least he had the healer's full attention as he laid the matter succinctly before him.

"So that's how it is." Rather than being scandalized, Colt's smile turned achingly sweet. Patting Greta's hands, he murmured, "You're one of the lucky ones."

She burst into tears.

Probably from relief.

Under Ambrose's watchful eye, Colt offered his arms and calmed her with low hums and soft reassurances. That she was safe. That they were here. That there was hope.

Ambrose sacrificed a second handkerchief and fought back the sudden urge to touch her hair.

"You need to meet my friend. Hallow and I share a compartment. We've been friends since he was just a little guy." Turning expectantly toward the door, Colt said, "Come along, Hallow. She's warded."

After a moment's hesitation, Hallow stepped into the open. He was slim and pale, a youth with sharp features and a stiff manner. Straight black hair hung loose around his shoulders, and he glanced around the room with deep red eyes.

"Come along, Hallow," Colt repeated. "Don't be such a grump."

Flashing a look of injury, Hallow flowed across the room with a swooping gait that caused the leathery folds that webbed under his arms to billow slightly. He presented himself to Greta with a silent bow.

"Use your words," teased Colt.

Sinking to one knee at his bunkmate's side, Hallow offered clawed hands in a standard greeting. His regional accent was a match for Colt's, lending credence to their long association. "How do you do? My name is Hallow Brunwinger. I apologize for withholding myself from association. Especially if my presence can bring some comfort."

"You're ... half?"

"Yes." He lifted an arm, giving her a clearer look at a misfit wing. "Bat clan."

Greta asked, "Your mother?"

"She is well enough. My father was human." Hallow's gaze turned apologetic. "I'm not sure what any of you expect from me. It's not as if I was much use during my own birthing."

Colt slung his arm around Hallow's shoulders. "You're *here*. Isn't that enough?"

"I'm not the one she needs," grumbled the youth. "Leave her to Ambrose."

A valid suggestion, given the bold declaration he'd made by wrapping her in his cape. But he'd been playing a part.

Mostly.

ONLY IF YOU INSIST

Greta gave up on the swirl of words surrounding her. Conscious of Ambrose's nearness, she automatically lifted her hand above her shoulder, signaling for his attendance. But, wait. He hadn't liked being treated like a consort.

However, before she could withdraw her hand, his palm met hers. "Will you go to Canary now?" he asked.

"Come with me?"

Ambrose inclined his head, helped her to rise, and firmly tucked her arm through his. Signaling his intention to take the lead, which still struck her as different and daring.

Colt and Lulu and maybe even Hallow looked ready to follow, to add their voices to her story. But she shook her head. It reminded her too keenly of the crowding of consorts who'd begged for Lady Evernhold's understanding, for secrecy, for mercy.

Himeko's brother had calmed that storm of dismay. If not for him, Greta wouldn't be here now, relying on another compelling voice to carry the day.

"Mister Merriman?"

He paused in the passage. "Ms. Pinion?"

"Will you tell him?"

"Only if you insist." Ambrose searched her face. "He's the sort of person who will try to understand."

She thought so, too. But she was more confident in Ambrose's ability to command the room, to influence his friends. "I don't know how to explain."

"Tell him what you told me."

"But …!" she protested.

He faced her, so close she could count every stitch in his seams. Standing between her and the way forward, as if protecting her from the future.

Greta whispered, "How will they ever trust me again if they think I entrapped his father?"

Ambrose answered just as softly. "You have their trust."

"They'll find out I don't deserve it."

He raised a finger along with a brow. "In Canary's plays, there always comes a point when all seems lost. Not because it *is*, but because it seems so. Yet there will be a chance meeting, a small change, a difficult choice, *something*. And the way forward becomes miraculously clear."

"This isn't one of Canarian's plays." Greta could barely speak past the tightness in her throat. "This is *real*, Mister Merriman. All is lost. *I* am lost."

"No," Ambrose countered. So gently, so sure. "This is the part where you discover that you have been the hero all along."

Greta gaped at him.

With a superior smile, he whirled her into a cramped variation on the waltz that carried her further along the passage. Toward her fears.

"I'm disgraced." How could he pretend otherwise? "Sent away."

"Sent *here*. To us."

"To die."

"To live." Ambrose stopped short and scooped her up, quickly skimming across the lone gap that remained between them and the Evernhold carriage. "And to bring life."

Back on her feet, Greta said, "If you're so sure, you speak. Maybe we'll *all* believe you."

He shook his head. "Nothing I say or do will change what's always been true." Very carefully, almost reverently, he touched her hair. "Did you know that in all of Canary's plays, the happy ending comes as a surprise, even though all the necessary elements have been there the entire time?"

Greta had only seen two of Canarian's plays. Each had harrowed her heart, yet fulfilled every hope. And then some. "You put a lot of faith in his stories."

"I do."

He was acting like someone who already knew her story's end, and Greta found his smugness oddly uplifting. "Why are you so happy?"

"Oh. You can tell?" So he *could* tease. "Perhaps because you have brought so much to my friends. May I touch?"

Which was the silliest question ever. His hands hadn't left off holding her from the moment he'd returned with help. "You may."

"Canary and Cat have abandoned their home hearth, and they have no wish to become consorts. Their choices have given them what they wanted most. But this freedom has excluded them from one of our people's greatest joys." His fingertips settled over her midriff. "They have no mistress who will entrust them with a child. Yet here you are, carrying a precious secret that will bring a kitten to their hearth."

Suddenly, the compartment door opened, and Canarian leaned out, face full of questions. "What's this about *kittens*?"

ALL WILL BE WELL

Ambrose was spared answering, for Canary immediately leapt to a second, more urgent question. "Greta love, have you been crying?"

He touched her cheek and moved to gather her up, but stopped with a startled huff. He'd noticed the cloak.

"Do you have time for us?" Ambrose asked.

Canary touched his cheek as well. "All you ever need."

And he stepped back with arms widespread, leaving Ambrose to usher in Greta.

The compartment showed evidence of the felines' occupation. Ledgers and receipts cluttered the table. They'd probably been sorting out the damage done by Ms. Pinion's spending spree. More interesting to Ambrose were the playbills from past productions that Cat had arranged. Would they be drumming up something extra?

Curious as he was, Ambrose's current role took precedence.

But Canary was more interested in defining that role. "Why is Greta wearing your cape, birdie mine?"

"Don't leap to conclusions," he sighed.

"How can I not?" His friend quietly pointed out, "You would never do such a thing without good reason."

"Ms. Pinion asked me to speak for her." Ambrose tilted his chin challengingly. "She is under my protection."

"Is *that* the shape your favor takes?" Canary smirked. "She's winning you over—body, soul, and wardrobe."

Cat spoke up then, brows knit. "Why does our reaver have need of a spokesman?"

Ambrose guided Greta to a chair, then drew himself up beside it. "She is carrying your child."

Canary froze, then shot a look at Cat, who raised his hands and shook his head. The former cleared his throat and said, "Not so, friend. Ms. Demerara came to us in this condition."

"She *is* carrying your child," Ambrose insisted. "For the babe will be delivered into your hands. A half-sibling born in exile. A halfer in need of the haven we represent."

The resulting silence broke when Canary's breath hitched. Cat stole up behind his best friend, wrapping him in his arms and asking, "Which of our fathers …?"

With a roll of his wrist, Ambrose silently indicated Canary, whose eyes began to water. Dragging Cat with him, he knelt before Greta and whispered, "Truly?"

She nodded shakily.

Ambrose grumbled, "Have you any of the reprisals she fears?"

Canary's eyes rounded, and Ambrose went so far as to nudge him with the pointed toe of his hearth slipper. That worked to loosen the cat's tongue. And then he was babbling apologies and endearments and compliments and vows.

"W-with your permission, Ambrose," Cat stammered belatedly, for Canary was trying to kiss away each of Greta's tears.

Ambrose merely rolled his eyes and waved them on. *Felines*.

All would be well. Probably.

If the Maker was kind, Greta would deliver a son. Heaven only knew what drama lay in store if Canary and Cat were called upon to raise a baby sister.

ANSWER FOR YOUR DEEDS

Ambrose wasn't entirely sure what traditions were in play when Canary insisted that Greta spend the night in their bed, but she accepted with such a wistful smile, it must have been a kindness. From behind the screen, Canary's voice carried in a softly-sung lullaby.

Meanwhile, Cat lured Ambrose onto the settee, where a little overlapping soon led to outright entanglement ... and inquisition.

"Why was Greta wearing your cape?"

"I told you," Ambrose muttered. "You needn't read into it."

"You shouldn't read *out* of it," Cat countered. "You've taken a fancy. Have you taken it farther?"

Ambrose summoned up a glare. "Don't be ridiculous."

"Don't be obtuse. If all you did was surrender your cape, why is her scent clinging to you?"

He'd forgotten, really. It was only the impulse of a moment. "I suppose there was some dancing."

Cat's incredulity doubled, then melted into amusement. "*Ambrose*! That's avian courting behavior, pure and simple."

"Coincidental." Yet he couldn't deny he'd enjoyed his role … while it lasted. "She needed cheering. It was a distraction."

His friend pulled him closer and kissed him lightly. "Your kindnesses may be the sparkle on the surface, Lord Scatterlight, but down deep, you may have to concede that she's wooed and won you."

Ambrose considered those depths. And found that still, small voice waiting.

"Her child knows me. I think." Shoulders hunching against the delight that brought him, he lamely added, "Somehow."

"By jaguar clan traditions, a child is born knowing their mother's voice and listening for their father's." Cat's fingers set to kneading the tightness from Ambrose's frame. "That's why if there's any uncertainty, cubs and kittens whose coloring offers no useful clues to paternity are given to the consort whose voice they adore."

"Her child is feline. A fosterling for you and Canary."

"Oh, we'll raise the child together. All of us." His gesture included the entire trainload, their unofficial enclave. "But especially *us*."

"You're including me?"

"As if we'd exclude you," Cat scoffed. "I suspect, friend of my heart and this hearth, that when the days are full, Greta's wee kitten will be born into a nest."

LETTERS BROUGHT BY HERALDS

"How's your Shakespeare?" asked Canary.

"Undiminished," assured Ambrose. "Although I prefer *your*

scripts. Too many tragedies can weary a soul."

A few days had passed, as had the miles, and with them, the mess on Canary's table multiplied. Fanned playbills now shared space with the contents of a correspondence packet brought by a Dimityblest courier during the night.

"Our clerk in the next city has alerted us to a sudden opening." Cat waved the missive. "Ruffin Theater's been struggling with sore throats and sniffles. Too many actors under the weather, and now their leading lady has laryngitis. I've written back, offering to fill in. *If* they'll give us a two-week run."

"Frankly, the timing couldn't be better." Canary's smile turned wry. "The slot would help to defray certain…unforeseen expenses."

Ambrose hated to ask. "Greta?"

He was quick to defend. "We could consider the costs she incurred as an investment."

"Toward our next *three* productions," cut in Cat.

Elbowing Canary, Ambrose said, "You'll have to write plays to match the color scheme of the bolts in our stores."

The playwright's eyes took on a shine. "That *would* be an interesting challenge."

"All that aside, I believe there's a Shakespearean production in our near future. One of the comedies." Cat tapped the stack of playbills. "And a short run of an old favorite. You may choose, Ambrose."

They were in the midst of narrowing the possibilities when a knock came at the door.

Fairlee shuffled inside, a small, square envelope in his hand. "This was missed, sir. Mixed in with the others."

Canary took it and turned it, checking the seal. "Ah."

As soon as the young bovine excused himself, Cat quietly asked, "Has the Mother put a paw in?"

He shook his head, unfolding heavy paper. The note must have been brief, for he spared it barely a glance. Sidestepping Cat's question, Canary announced, "Two things worry me."

Ambrose gestured for him to continue.

"Our courier needed a word with Lulu, and neither requested privacy. I overheard their conversation." He shared a troubled glance with Cat. "She was recalled."

"By her clan?" asked Ambrose.

Canary scratched behind an ear. "Apparently, she only stayed on when she found out Greta would be the solitary female in our company. We've allayed any fears. And eliminated any reason for further delay."

"When will she separate from us?" asked Ambrose.

"It's done," said Cat. "She's gone."

What haste. Ambrose frowned. "Has she so little regard for her apprentice?"

Canary said, "Lulu Dimityblest has *every* regard for her *former* apprentice. Before leaving, she demanded that Clemmorn, Cat, and I bear witness. Mistress Moth bestowed highest honors. Greta attained her mastery."

Ambrose felt sure the woman deserved the elevation. But to be left alone? Surely this would redouble her home-sickness.

Cat asked, "What has become your *second* concern?"

Lifting the note, Canary said, "My uncle. He requests a meeting."

BACK BY POPULAR DEMAND

Greta was still reeling from her attainment when Clemmorn broke the news that he had little more than two days to pull all the costumes for two productions out of storage. And he wanted her help.

As he pulled one trunk after another, Greta grew increasingly frantic with delight over the treasures they held. She even dared to hope that he'd let her amend some of the costumes before the first performance. Especially Ambrose's.

By the end of the first day, she was utterly wrung. Canarian scolded and Colt dosed, and Catalan curled up with her so she wouldn't have to sleep alone.

She spent much of the next day with Clemmorn in the theater, attending to final fittings. The atmosphere was surprisingly calm. The whole company was familiar with these plays and slipped easily into their roles. So it was fun, but Greta kept turning to say something to Lulu. Only to remember that she wasn't there.

And wouldn't be. Because she couldn't be.

By day's end, Greta was more heartworn than worn out. She was grateful when Canarian came to claim her, and doubly so when they didn't return to the train, where she'd have felt Lulu's absence even more keenly.

Catalan had secured rooms in a hotel along the same street as the Ruffin. For her comfort. Ambrose joined them. And that, too, was a comfort.

"Have we forgotten anything?" asked Canarian.

Ambrose drawled, "Surely not."

Four trunks rested against the far wall, which seemed a bit

excessive, even if they did have a fortnight's stay ahead. In the first, she found clothes and personal items, and in the second, a generous sampling of her sewing things. However, the last two trunks baffled her. They were empty.

Finding it difficult to get comfortable in a featureless room, Greta pulled several things from the box of supplies. Soon, the desk and tabletops took on the brightness of cloth, ribbon, and trim. But how to put them to use?

Canarian said, "You should sleep."

"Soon," she murmured, fingering a skein of foggy blue embroidery floss.

Ambrose came to her side. "Will you sew?"

"I want to. Do you have something I can embellish?"

He extracted a clean handkerchief from an inner pocket. "Will this suffice?"

Snatching at it as she might a lifeline, Greta made her selections and retreated to the chair closest to a lamp. Soon, the only sound in the room was the rhythmic tug of her needle. Her whole being calmed, and the atmosphere warmed toward sweetness. Not quite tending, but close enough to tease.

Canarian came to sit on the arm of her chair and watched the curling feather patterns emerge under her needle. Blue and gray and green and gold. With speckled eggs to anchor each corner.

He smiled and said, "You spoil Ambrose."

"He lets me." She arched a brow. "Will you surrender a trifle for me to trim?"

"If you asked me to." Canarian searched her face. "But you never have."

Greta shook her head. "The last thing you want is orders. Besides, you have your style, and he has his. You wouldn't enjoy my little elaborations."

"Our Ambrose has grown increasingly splendiferous under your attentions."

From across the room, Mister Merriman grumbled a low protest. But Greta found that she agreed. With every passing day, he gained new luster. And not only onstage. Ambrose cut a compelling figure. Ruled every room. Drew every eye. Or hers, anyhow.

Despite the conjecture and criticism of many Amaranthine, he was doing what he loved, just as she was doing what she loved. That their passions were so complementary was either the kindest of serendipities ... or the keenness of foresight, for Himeko's brother was reputed to work in mysterious ways.

Speaking of mysteries. Greta's meandering thoughts circled back to the trunks. "Why are those empty?"

"Ah," said Canarian, looking rather sheepish. "It was Cat's idea."

Shouldering the blame with grace, Catalan said, "This is one of the largest cities in this part of the country. They may not have an Amaranthine market, but there are many shops. And you've shown a certain fondness for visiting them."

Canarian gazed at her over his glasses. "There will be leisure hours. Any of us would gladly escort you."

Greta nodded cautiously. "Which costumes did you need me to change."

"Oh, this isn't for the company." Canarian slipped his hand under hers. "This is for *you*."

Cat added, "All we ask is that—if *at all* possible—you limit yourself to the space available. Two trunks. No more."

She grasped that this was meant as a gift, and she knew she should be grateful for their generosity. But she still wasn't clear what they expected her to fill the trunks *with*.

Her glance in Ambrose's direction brought him to her other side. With an earnest air and heightening color in his cheeks, he offered two words of elucidation. "Baby things."

WHERE IS THE BALANCE?

Greta quickly learned that she did indeed have leisure hours— whole mornings and afternoons during which her presence was not required. And evenings, as well, since she was extraneous to the Leclerc Company's long-established routines.

During most performances, Greta kept to the hotel suite, which became increasingly cluttered and colorful, thanks to her daily forays into the shops. This evening, she had Colt and Fairlee for company.

Colt coaxed for stories about her other children, so she reminisced and bragged and felt better for it. His interest was genuine, and his whickering laugh raised her spirits. Fairlee surrendered his overshirt and looked on with bashful delight as she embellished the yoke and collar with a profusion of spring flowers.

"You're the first to ask," she said, hoping Fairlee would start a trend.

"Except Ambrose," countered Colt. "He's always peacocking around, putting your work on display."

Greta's needle paused midway through broadcloth. "Mister Merriman never actually asks."

"No?" Colt's tone remained neutral. "Why have you singled him out?"

Is that what she was doing? Greta added a few more flowers before admitting, "He wants more than he asks for. And I find myself wanting to please him."

Fairlee quietly said, "You please him."

Colt shook his head. "I'm sure Ambrose enjoys your gifts, but what of balance?"

"Oh, he *can't* reciprocate." She laughed softly. "If he were to give me presents, that would count as courting."

Both males gawked at her.

She began adding a cluster of rosebuds around a buttonhole.

"So you *did* know," murmured Colt. "He talked to you?"

Greta appreciated their concern. "I trust him, and he's beginning to trust me. We'll find our balance eventually."

Colt seemed dissatisfied, but Fairlee was smiling. "You *are* balanced."

"We are?" asked Greta.

"He pleases you."

And she pleased him. At least, that was Fairlee's assessment.

Was it as simple as a matter of matching preference? Greta's whole life had been ordered by others, not that she had any cause to complain. Because the one time she'd shown a preference— for sewing—her lady mistress had accommodated her. Neither of them realizing that Greta's skill would attract Mister Merriman's favorable opinion. And make her life easier now.

His panache pleased her. Her presents pleased him. But did it stop there?

No. At least, not for her.

His blissful expression when he handled fine silk. The concentration with which he sorted beads. Every trill that slipped out when she presented him with a garment. The commanding way he'd drawn her into a waltz. His stubborn need to dominate their connection. All the yearning he couldn't quite hide when he spoke of her child.

Oh, yes. Mister Merriman pleased her. But as things stood, that would have to be enough.

REVEALING HIS TRUE COLORS

By the second week of the Leclerc Company's engagement at the Ruffin, Greta had realized that *she* wasn't the true reason Catalan had booked rooms at the hotel. No, no. It was the decadence offered by the suite's adjoining bathroom.

Every morning, she woke to the familiar sounds of an extended grooming session. The scent of bath salts. The swish and patter of water. The murmur of low voices. Usually, by the time Canarian and Catalan emerged, one or another of the crew would be tapping at the door, carrying communiques or questions. Or pushing a cartload of breakfast.

This morning was a little different.

They'd wrangled some company.

Ambrose emerged from the ensuite with flushed cheeks and towel-wrapped hair. His pants billowed loosely in the manner of many clans' traditional attire, the cloth an uninterrupted pale coral that begged to be embroidered. The shirt was similarly uneventful.

Perhaps a touch of ribbon in that same sunrise hue?

"Methinks the lady has chosen her next project," Canarian said cheerfully.

Catalan chuckled. "May as well surrender the key to your wardrobe now, Ambrose. She won't be satisfied until she's added a flourish or two to all you own."

Ambrose merely inclined his head. "Good morning, Ms. Pinion."

"And to you, Mister Merriman."

"So formal," sighed Catalan. "Too formal by far."

Canarian pushed Ambrose to a seat on an ottoman and worked at the towel. "My fault entirely. It's our usual way, using his pseudonym. We're overdue for a proper introduction. Don't you think, birdie mine?"

Greta was picking up on enough undercurrents to guess that their whole exchange was scripted. Were they bullying Ambrose into confiding more? Or creating the opening he needed?

But then Canarian stepped back, the towel in his hands.

Ambrose's shoulders hunched, but then he cast a shy look her way. Through a curtain of still-damp hair—fine, straight, and startling in its hue.

Fussing with the shoulder-length locks, Canarian said, "Come and be introduced, Greta love."

She slipped from the bed and Catalan held a robe for her. Once she'd knotted it, he escorted her into position before Ambrose, who lifted his palms. But she bypassed them to touch his hair.

"Oh, my," she breathed. Then with more feeling, "You ... you *beauty*."

Canarian gripped the avian's shoulders and announced, "Lord Ambrose Scatterlight hails from one of the smaller bird clans."

Catalan nudged her with an elbow. "Care to guess which one?"

She *could* have, but that was hardly the most important matter at hand. Greta quickly covered Ambrose's palms, then slid her hands into a supportive position. Leaning in to study the play of morning light and highlights through his hair, she excitedly shared, "I have several excellent crystals that would complement you *perfectly*. And a whole bolt of painted silk."

His lashes fluttered. "Painted silk?"

Canarian snorted with laughter and whispered, "Told you so."

Catalan blandly muttered, "It's *flamingo*, by the way."

Which would have been her third guess, if she'd bothered to try. But Greta was more interested in the show of trust ... and the implications that came with the offering of Ambrose's true name.

She'd resigned herself to less, yet here he was, giving more.

MUCH TO MY SURPRISE

Colt and Fairlee escorted Greta to the company's final performance at the Ruffin, which left her giddy and taught her the meaning of ovation. In the aftermath, she helped Clemmorn with the gathering, cleaning, and storing of every costume. That part left her wistful, since it felt like another kind of goodbye.

Before returning to the train, she fulfilled her duty as Ambrose's pinion by tagging along to an appointment with the local newspaper. She felt bad about the whole thing. Why had no one warned her? When nervous, he came off *so* haughty. Mercifully, Canarian was there and did most of the talking. Even *she* said more than Ambrose. Although in parting, the reporter complimented the illustrious

Mister Merriman's hatband. And earned a genuine smile.

A day and a night were needed to move everything back onto the *Cat's Canary*, but they had to wait for an opening in the railway schedule before they could move along. And into this lull came a restless sort of doubting.

What awaited her at that final station?

She didn't want their journey to end.

More than anything, she dreaded another goodbye. And sticking to reaver etiquette was far from comforting. Maybe it was more polite to await, await, await. But she was fairly certain that Ambrose was like his friend Canarian. *He's the sort of person who will try to understand.*

So she spoke first.

"We get along, don't we, Mister Merriman?"

"Much to my surprise."

"Will you hear me out?"

Ambrose stopped poking through a pile of mismatched buttons. "As you like, Ms. Pinion."

"I've been through this twice before, but never alone."

He studied his claws. "You're not alone."

"Not entirely," she conceded. "But something is lacking. I lack something I think I need."

"I can understand instinct."

"Maybe that's it." Greta shook her head. "I don't really know."

Ambrose said, "Canary and Cat will devote themselves to you."

Greta wished that was the case, but she knew better. "They're devoted to each other. And I won't impose on them. They don't want the kind of obligation that I represent."

She winced at her own words. He had to realize by now that she hoped to impose on him.

Yet he sat quietly, studied closely. At least he was willing to listen.

"I don't think I can ...." Greta's voice wavered. "I don't want to be alone during the months that may be the last in my life."

"You're not alone." Then more quietly, so carefully, Ambrose said, "You are my pinion."

"I'm not a pinion any more than you're a king or a scoundrel or a dragon lord." Greta needed him to understand what she needed most. "That's what I do, not who I am."

"Understood." Ambrose tipped his head to one side. Then the other. "That part of our tale has ended. There is only me, and I am willing. What do you need?"

"Somewhere to go at the end of the line. Something to do." She found the courage to ask, "Please, Mister Merriman, let me be your seamstress."

He touched the back of her clenched fist with a single finger. "Face this fully. I am no more Mister Merriman than you are Ms. Pinion. Ambrose will do."

Greta managed a nod.

"And I think perhaps you have more concerns than facts. These rails have their limits, but *their* end doesn't necessitate ours. *Cat's Canary* is Leclerc Company's home. All of us are here because we have no other place to be." Ambrose hesitated, then firmly spoke four simple words. "We will continue together."

"Aren't we going somewhere?"

"Usually." Ambrose shook his head. "But bookings are temporary."

She wondered why she'd been so certain there was a destination.

"We make stops at stations to bring in supplies and to lend credence to our identity within human society. We stop, but we never stay for long." His gestures were tight, succinct, utterly confident. "I have it on good authority that you are universally adored by the members of the Leclerc Company. And Canary and Cat would fight to keep you."

"The company's cosset."

He countered, "The mother of their child."

Greta giggled miserably. Either way, she was only valued for containing something desirable. A soul. A baby.

"An uncle was mentioned," Ambrose added. "Would he really have been sent to do you harm?"

"Uncle?" She thought for sure she'd missed something. "You've heard from Canarian's uncle? No, no. *He* wouldn't. He *couldn't*!"

"Cat has gone hissy and wants to jump rails. Or reverse course. Canary hasn't asked you about warding the train against strangers?"

"No?" At least, she didn't think so.

"All that aside." Ambrose lay a second and third finger on the back of her hand, then slowly covered it with his own. "I wonder if it's the *wisest* course, taking on a seamstress."

"But ... you love the things I make."

"With increasing regard." His hand tightened around hers. "But do you truly want employment? Ply my instincts even a little further, and we shall neither of us lack for any good thing."

Greta got a little stranded in his wording, which was too roundabout by far. She asked, "You want more presents?"

"I would not refuse them. However, I will begin looking for ways to match your generosity." Scanning the stuff before him, he plucked up a trifle and held it out. "Here. A token of my affection."

This was a strange game. "It's a button."

"It's a *gift*." His smile was small and smug.

Greta's heart began to beat faster. "I thought gifts incurred certain obligations."

"They do."

"What kind of commitment does one little pink button signify?"

Ambrose joined her in contemplating its delicate perfection. "The only kind I know how to give."

NO ROOM FOR DOUBT

"I am quite serious," Ambrose said awkwardly.

Greta slowly adjusted her posture into something nearing receptivity, but he was getting enough mixed messages to muddy the waters. Afraid to hope. Resigned to end. Willing to doubt.

So he circled the table and dropped to one knee. Raising a hand in a command for attention he said, "Did you know that in all of Canary's plays, the happy ending comes as a surprise, even though all the necessary elements have been there the entire time?"

Her surprise melted into amusement. "You told me before. Is this the part where you discover that *you* have been the hero all along?"

Ambrose inclined his head. "Much to my surprise."

"I'm not sure what I'm supposed to do."

"Very little can proceed if you are not amenable to my proposal." He tentatively admitted, "I could have put more thought into a gift."

Greta quickly closed her fingers over the button and held it to her heart. "I like it."

"And me?"

The nod was hardly more than a twitch. "But I might not live. And … I'm going to die."

Which was *not* a rebuff. Token protests at best.

"I am aware," he assured. "I am willing."

"Ambrose, I don't want you to be sad."

Her concerns were for him? "Then make me happy."

The notion seemed to intrigue her. "Could I?" she asked, meaning it.

What simplicity.

So he took her hands and promised to hold them. He kissed her fingertips and begged for future finery. He touched her hair and confessed his fascination. He told her the color of his blaze and guided her fingers to its place

And when she gazed at him with eyes that were wide and dark and willing, he made the vows that granted this human woman the shelter of his wings and the splendors of his nest. Her sweetness made him tremble. Her trust was his elation. Her only question broke his heart.

"What if it ends poorly?"

Ambrose, whose faith in every story was many centuries stronger, countered, "What if it never ends?"

TENDING IS ALWAYS HONEST

Greta already had Ambrose's pledge before he began his courtship. Perhaps that's why his behavior didn't change all that much. Or maybe it meant that she'd missed the signs, and he'd been displaying for her since the beginning.

He still showed up to thread needles and sort beads. But there was more in the way of dancing, and when she was ready for bed each night, he pulled a chair close and held her hand while spinning out tales of the avian clans.

Ambrose asked for nothing more. Not even tending.

So she led the way, drawing him into her presence.

He seemed to understand. "Tending is always honest. Take my measure. Trust what you find, even if it comes as a surprise."

And each time, Greta *was* surprised. By his candor. By his attachment. By his gratitude. By the person he became when she was the only one who could see. Vast and strong and dazzlingly confident. Then again, he was like this on the stage, leading the way, ruling the moment, pulling you in so that he was more sun than star.

"You *beauty*," she whispered.

Ambrose quirked a brow and matched her regard. "*My* beauty."

Flustered, she slipped into a receptive stance.

Amused, he mimicked her posture, reminding her of the balance he'd requested. If she wanted to make him happy, he would devote himself to her happiness. If she decided to please him, her pleasure would become his privilege. Trust for trust. Kindness for kindness. Love for love.

Greta couldn't outdo him, couldn't resist him.

"Do you think this is love?" she asked.

"Do you mean this shade of blue, or the harmony you've achieved between sigil and stone?" Ambrose trilled softly even as he twirled before the mirror. Preening in more ways than one. "*Or … are you becoming infatuated with me?*"

"Would you mind?"

For an answer, Ambrose finally got around to kissing her.

Ambrose's many attentions so captured Greta's that she hardly noticed their arrival at the big and bustling train station in the easternmost city on the line. But she no longer feared this destination. It wasn't final.

And there were bound to be shops.

Before anyone could disembark, Catalan announced that the necessary arrangements had been made. The Leclerc Company had rented an entire floor in a building managed by one of the city's urban enclaves. Because midsummer was nearly upon them.

"Dichotomy Day?" Greta hadn't looked at a calendar in weeks.

Canarian explained, "We've arranged for the full course of days. The company is a mixed bag, but we've been together long enough to create our own traditions."

"Join our circle." Touching her shoulder, Catalan said, "For once, hospitality to a reaver will be our delight."

Greta asked, "Don't you always have a reaver with you?"

With a faint grimace, Canarian admitted, "This is where most of them parted ways."

Catalan blithely added, "Thanks to our Ambrose."

"But *our* Greta will be staying on." Canarian took her hand and slyly said, "Thanks to our Ambrose?"

She didn't mind his teasing smile, not when his whole manner radiated approval.

The enclave sent transportation, and all the way there, Greta pointed out likely looking boutiques and bakeries. Ambrose feigned indifference but noted street names. Colt pointed out that fresh air and long walks were good for her health, and Fairlee volunteered his cart.

Everyone's mood was high and bright when they rolled through a set of gates that gleamed with complex sigilcraft. Greta picked up enough identifying markers to know that spiders were at work.

As they disembarked in a peaceful courtyard, Canarian pointed the way, and Catalan fell in step beside Greta. "Will you ward the rooms for us?" he asked. "It's mostly a formality, but it would be a homey touch."

"My pleasure."

But when they reached their place, it was already too late.

A MOST AUSPICIOUS DAY

Catalan was in front in a twinkling, a hissing barrier of black fur. Greta wanted to hurry forward almost as much as she wanted to run away. Ambrose spared her from deciding by taking a position behind her ... and easing the excess of his new cape around her.

"Stay by me," he urged in an undertone. "Let the cats sort out their differences in their own way."

Feline spats could be noisy. And violent. Greta turned and quickly traced her finger over Ambrose's vest, adjusting her personal wards to include him.

He swayed and grabbed her shoulders. "Are you trying to protect me or seduce me?"

Belatedly, she realized that in her haste, she'd removed every barrier between them. Unfastening one of her earrings, she whispered to it and pressed it into his palm. A temporary measure, but sufficient to the needs of the moment. "Stay by me," she demanded.

His eyes widened.

With careful deliberation, he removed the hummingbird egg stickpin from his cravat and placed it in her hand. "I will stay," he promised.

While she didn't grasp the full significance, Greta knew the exchange meant something to him. And that she'd pleased him.

A warning yowl tapered off to a growl, and Canarian hurried forward, placing himself between the coiled jaguar and the … well, he was hardly an intruder.

"Uncle," he greeted. "To what do we owe the pleasure?"

"Peace, nephews. Did you not receive my letter?" Hands spread in a respectful greeting, Lady Himeko's brother offered a small smile. "You should have received ample notice of my plans, but I do apologize for startling you. Quite humbly."

Canarian grimly said, "You're a long way from your usual haunts."

"I come and go as I please. Much as you do."

Catalan returned to speaking form and snapped, "Why are you here, Uncle?"

"Dichotomy Day is a time for reunions. Families should be together, don't you think?" And then his gaze sought hers. "May I approach?"

She welcomed him gladly enough, which may have been the only reason his nephews permitted it. Her trust became theirs. And she *did* trust this person. "Are you here to see me, Uncle? Did

Lady Evernhold send you?"

"I am here at the bidding of no other than myself." He offered his palms. "Peace, Reaver Demerara. Or…should I say Lady Scatterlight?"

She glanced up in time to see Ambrose's dignified nod.

"You should," he said.

The cat took this news entirely in stride. "An auspicious day for unions. I am pleased to be counted among the witnesses of your bonding. May I add to their number?"

Touching a finger to his lips, he slipped three crystals from an inner pocket and offered them. One pink and two blue. Fine specimens that were clearly tuned as anchors. What had he warded? No, wait … these were keyed to illusions.

At her touch, something vanished with a faint pop. Catalan and Canarian hissed oaths, astonishment plain on their faces, for they were picking up the traces now. The scent of secrets. The giggles of girls.

Out from under his cloak—which was lined with some of the most beautiful painted silk Greta had ever seen—peeped Ava and Ada. And then Neven crawled into the open, too, eyes dancing with merriment.

"Mother." He jumped to his feet and dusted his knees. "Did we surprise you?"

All Greta could do was open her arms. Her children ran into them.

There was a confusion of introductions, during which Colt quickly laid claim to four-year-old Ava, calling her a clever filly and giving her flowers from who-knows-where. Canarian cuddled Ada, who liked being called kitten almost as much as the nonsensical ballad he dedicated to her arrival. Nine-year-old Neven was making the rounds of the room with Ambrose, who kept his arm around the boy's shoulders as he made certain Neven met everyone in the company.

"Why do this for me?" Greta asked.

"I heard a song among the stars," he murmured. Shaking his head, he answered more clearly. "Dichotomy Day has long been a time of reunion. Didn't I say? I'm sure I did."

"Can they stay?"

"These children belong with their mother. Even my sister was forced to concede the point." He smiled serenely. "During academy breaks, I will escort them to your hearth."

"It's really more of a berth."

"An intriguing one." His gaze swept the room. "I have rarely seen representatives from so many clans come together for a singular purpose."

"Maybe it's because they have so much faith in Canarian's storytelling." She indicated his nephew. "He always knows just what to do, and he always leads us to a happy ending."

Slowly, flared eyebrows lifted.

Greta laughed and leaned closer. "Pay attention, Uncle Hisoka. This could be the part where *you* discover that you've been the hero all along."

THE END

Abundant thanks to all who lend their support by reading, rating, and reviewing my stories, wherever they may be found. ::twinkle::

ALSO BY FORTHRIGHT

AMARANTHINE SAGA

Tsumiko and the Enslaved Fox
Kimiko and the Accidental Proposal
Tamiko and the Two Janitors
Mikoto and the Reaver Village

SONGS OF THE AMARANTHINE

Marked by Stars
Followed by Thunder
Dragged through Hedgerows
Governed by Whimsy
Hemmed in Silver

AMARANTHINE INTERLUDES

Lord Mettlebright's Man

PATREON EXCLUSIVES

Bard & Barbarian

When I reach 400 patrons, I'll begin publishing a new subscription-based storyline on Patreon. Loosely based on the old Amaranthine tale, "The Wolf and the Moon Maiden," this serial will involve three sisters, twelve pledges, and the long-awaited stirring of a sleeping landmark. Become a patron at https://www.patreon.com/forthrightly

never more than
FORTHRIGHT

a teller of tales who began as a fandom ficcer. (Which basically means that no one in RL knows about her anime habit, her manga collection, or her penchant for serial storytelling.) Kinda sorta almost famous for gently-paced, WAFFy adventures that might inadvertently overturn your OTP, forthy will forever adore drabble challenges, surprise fanart, and twinkles (which are rumored to keep well in jars). As always... be nice, play fair, have fun! ::twinkle::

FORTHWRITES.COM